SHE HAD NO ONE ELSE TO ASK

"I'm out of the business," Chase said firmly. "I'm not going back to Hong Kong."

"The guy we were supposed to follow turned up dead in Macau," AnnMarie said. "It was Tommy Fong."

Chase ground his teeth together, tempering his rage. "What happened to him?"

"Autopsy said he was attacked by some kind of large animal. I know he was a friend of yours." She pulled out a manila envelope and handed it to him. "This was taken a few days before his body was found."

Chase pulled out a photo. It showed an Asian couple stepping off a sampan. Fong wore an expensive three-piece business suit. "Who's the girl?" he asked.

"Don't know."

Chase turned the envelope over and a small jade pendant slid into his hand. "What's this?"

"The coroner found it in his stomach."

"I'll go to Hong Kong, but only to find out who killed my friend. I don't care about looking for your double agent. Understand?"

WILLIAM H. LOVEJOY
YOUR TICKET TO A WORLD OF POLITICAL INTRIGUE AND NONSTOP THRILLS. . . .

CHINA DOME   (0-7860-0111-9, $5.99/$6.99)

DELTA BLUE   (0-8217-3540-3, $4.50/$5.50)

RED RAIN   (0-7860-0230-1, $5.99/$6.99)

ULTRA DEEP   (0-8217-3694-9, $4.50/$5.50)

WHITE NIGHT   (0-8217-4587-5, $4.50/$5.50)

THE HONG KONG KONG SANCTION

Mitchell Sam Rossi

Pinnacle Books
Kensington Publishing Corp.

http://www.pinnaclebooks.com

PINNACLE BOOKS are published by

Kensington Publishing Corp.
850 Third Avenue
New York, NY 10022

First Printing: June, 1997
10 9 8 7 6 5 4 3 2 1

Printed in the United States of America

For Judy
with all my love

Chapter One

Catalina Island, California

The sky was still black and speckled with stars as it tried to hold on to the night. But the eastern edge of the morning was quickly dissolving from dark violet to blue. The wind was low and out of the west, and in the distance the long stretch of the mainland was appearing behind a copper haze of civilization.

The white-hulled ketch *Aiko* rested quietly in the clear waters of Avalon Harbor. The old double-masted sailboat, constructed with teak decks and mahogany-sided cabins, rose and dipped with each rolling swell. The harbor mooring lines, one off the bow and one off the stern, strained as the waves passed beneath her.

Although the influx of summer sailors had yet to voyage the twenty-odd miles from their harbors to populate the small anchorage, the wide beam and deep full keel of the forty-six-foot *Aiko* forced her to moor at the outer crest of the bay's breakwater. The night was still and the sea calm save for the occasional long roller that rumbled by.

Lindsay had known the Harbor Master would assign him to the farthest moorings. It didn't matter. He was determined to keep his routine. Every morning and every evening, he would swim from his boat to the beach and back again, and if his leg felt good, he would swim at noon, too.

It was his therapy now that the doctors had released him. "Use it or lose it, Mr. Chase," the middle-aged doctor with the trimmed beard and polished smile had said. "You're in fairly decent shape; if you keep up a vigorous program I suspect you could possibly get sixty percent use of your leg back. Maybe more. It was a nasty accident."

Yeah, real nasty, Lindsay thought to himself as he arched a cupped hand over his shoulder and reached out into the water ahead of him. He pulled another stroke through.

The "hunting accident", as he had characterized it to the therapist, was no accident at all. Lindsay's right femur had been shattered by a .25 caliber Teflon-coated bullet from either a Fabrique Nationale 30–11 or Hecker & Koch PSG-1 sniper rifle. The small, specialized round had been placed there precisely by a marksman from a hundred and fifty meters away and on the third level of the track bleachers.

Or maybe it wasn't that precise. Had Lindsay been on the other side of that rifle and pulled that trigger, he would have put the bullet through the target's head or heart, or at least lowered his aim three centimeters and taken out the whole knee. Then there would have been no chance of a recovery and no need of therapy.

But Lindsay was recovering. Kicking hard and fast, he glided through the water and out into the harbor. It was painful and tiresome and each time he dove into the water, he wondered why he bothered. But the sea was crisp and cool and it washed over him, healing him, rebuilding the muscles that had been severed and the ligaments that were sheared from splintered bone.

The effort wasn't healing the memory. The images and the sounds and smells and tastes of that afternoon outside the Happy Valley horse track, when he was standing with a crowd of reporters and keeping to his cover while at the same time trying to do a job.

The British were suicidal, Lindsay determined that day. The Duke and Duchess of Ashbury, the fourth cousin to the heir, had dropped into Hong Kong with no security.

Just a quick deviation from their travel plans. The Duke's wife had never been in the colony and wanted to visit before the communists took over. Lindsay had been instructed by his station chief to be at the racetrack when they arrived. There were rumored threats of assassination of any royalty that ventured to Hong Kong. No one took the threats seriously, but frustration was growing with the government's callous handling of its loyal subjects and no one wanted to take chances.

MI5 didn't ask for him. The British secret service never would. The last thing they'd do would be to request Yank help. Of course, Lindsay would have been there anyway. He was, after all, posing as a reporter for the *International Herald Tribune.*

The Rolls-Royce limousines arrived on the grassy back-stretch and the Duke and Duchess emerged into an unse-cured crowd. They were greeted by the Governor and the track's director and a throng of reporters shouting questions about the Queen Mother and Charles's latest romance. Then mayhem reared its ugly head and coughed with gun-fire. It came from everywhere and yet from nowhere. The crowd scrambled in a massive wave of panic.

In the Duke's face, Lindsay saw uncertainty and confu-sion. Although he knew the man had seen warfare, it had not been for many years. The British secret service instantly pulled him back into the car. The Duchess, however, was jostled out of reach and pushed against the Rolls' front fender. In her porcelain eyes, Lindsay saw raw terror. That deep, horrifying fear of inevitable death. In two quick strides, he rushed to her, grabbed the back of her delicate neck, and shoved her to the ground.

The sniper riddled the impregnable doors of the armored limousine. Still pressing the Duchess to the muddy turf, Lindsay drew his automatic and frantically looked for telltale signs of the assassin. Lindsay never fired a shot. He never saw them. The sniper's bullet ripped into Lindsay's leg as though an invisible man with an invisible hammer had taken a full swing and cracked it across his knee. The pain came with such violent convulsions that his body seized his brain and closed it down.

Four days later Lindsay opened his eyes in an intensive care unit on the Yokota Air Base outside Tokyo. The doctors had just decided the leg could be saved but were still worried about a concussion Lindsay had suffered when he fell against the car.

The doctors and nurses knew nothing about the Duke and his wife. Lindsay remained in the hospital for twenty days and four surgeries. When the fear of concussion dissolved, he was transferred to another wing.

There, he was finally debriefed. The Duke and Duchess had escaped injury. The Hong Kong police and British Secret Service concluded there was only one gunman. Rifle casings were found in a section of the track's bleachers that were under new construction. Beyond that, they knew nothing. Political unrest and anger over British emigration laws were the official explanations.

Lindsay's mind came back to Avalon. He switched from the front crawl to the breaststroke. As his head popped up above the water's surface and he took a breath, he realigned himself with the *Aiko's* stern.

For the past twelve months, Lindsay Chase had only thought about that day, about the fear he had seen in the Duchess' face. And how, after seven years, his termination had come so quickly.

The morning sun was now above the horizon, alighting the sky and turning the dome completely blue.

He grabbed the swim ladder and hoisted himself to the first rung. High on the cliffs, the gentle chimes of the old adobe bell tower echoed across sleepy Avalon. Lindsay looked at his watch. Six-thirty A.M.—0630, as his mind automatically converted it to the military equivalent.

When he stepped to the next rung, he noticed the stainless chain that hung across the opening in the stern rail was unlatched and dangled loosely against the wood. Lindsay stared at it, sure that he had latched the chain earlier. Slowly, he slipped quietly back into the water.

With a deep breath, he dipped beneath the surface and swam under the hull to the bow. Using the algae-encrusted mooring line, he silently pulled himself aboard. So as not to rock the *Aiko*, Lindsay carefully crept along her center-line. His bare feet felt the sun-warmed teak deck as he moved to the round glass and steel hatch above the forward cabin. Like a clam in repose, it was set ajar for ventilation. Lindsay loosened the locking screw and opened it completely. Swinging his legs in, he dropped into the ketch.

Twin V bunks filled the bow cabin; the upper one was used for the storage of extra sails and lines. He had removed the mattress in the lower one and converted it to a shelf for cardboard boxes of canned food, soft drinks, and Cup-A-Soup containers.

Lindsay dug out the small Smith & Wesson revolver he kept hidden in the fishing locker. He moved to the cabin door and pressed his ear against the thin teak wood. Not a sound. He wondered if he had forgotten to hook the chain himself.

He twisted the brass doorknob and stepped cautiously into the galley. No one. Yet something was wrong, something out of place. The coffeepot. It was not on the stove but in the sink. He had definitely left it on the stove.

A delicate hand filled with a menacing black Beretta 92 automatic snaked from behind the door. The cold barrel touched him in the earlobe.

Lindsay froze. The woman's other hand reached out and pushed a piece of chocolate donut into his mouth.

"There are enough calories in these to kill you," she said with a seductive voice.

"Goddamn you," Lindsay mumbled as he swallowed the donut.

"You've lost it, Linds." She laughed as she stepped from the closet-sized bathroom next to the bow cabin. AnnMarie Gandel was a tall, strong woman with bold features, deep green eyes, and short sienna-brown hair. One of those unfortunate women whose genetics gave her the thick body frame of a man in a world that promoted soft and fragile features.

"What the hell are you doing here?"

"Hoping you swam in the nude," AnnMarie said, sliding the Beretta into her leather purse.

Lindsay proceeded through the cabin and out into the

cockpit. He grabbed the towel that hung over the pilot's wheel and began to dry himself off.

AnnMarie knew Lindsay well. She had been his COS, his Chief Of Station, in San Francisco and then again in Hong Kong when the CIA decided it was time to put their shadow agency in place. The Agency knew that the U.S. Consulate, their once busy intelligence-gathering center, would become obsolete when the British withdrew at the end of June and the communists marched in. The Far East, they feared, was going to become an information blind spot. Thus, they moved in R-50.

AnnMarie remembered his file. An average childhood, as average as one can have as the son of an army lifer. As was probably expected, he skipped college and enlisted in the military. Surprisingly, it wasn't into his father's Army but into the Navy and its Special Warfare Group.

By the time he was twenty-five, Lindsay had acquired enough recommendations to make any professional soldier envious. He had perfected recon in the Middle East during the Iran-Iraq war. And there was the incident in which he saved the lives of several naval officers during the "hot" protests in the Philippines.

It wasn't heroism, he had told her, as much as being ordered into the wrong place at the wrong time. In the Manila operation, he simply ditched an enraged mob of locals by driving his Jeep and its occupants into the river. It was no big deal. He knew the officers could swim.

It was true. He was always in the heat of things just as they exploded. Perhaps that's why the CIA brass liked him. He was a quick thinker who needed no direction from outside and that's exactly what they were searching for in the late 1980s when the Bush administration had secretly allotted the Agency the funds to develop an elite division.

Designated R-50, the shadow agency was soon nicknamed "the Rogue" by its internal staff. "The w*RO*ng *Gu*ys to *U*nder*E*stimate" was the office mantra because self-reliance was the focus of their operation. R-50's obscurity was so complete that its very existence was known by only a few high-ranking government officials. Unlike the head office, which operated within the strict controls of the National

Security Council, the CIA's shadow agency had been created to combat an era of terrorism and fanaticism. Its agents, its Prowlers, were unhindered by fragile technologies or stringent chains of command.

That was the lethal beauty of it. It was an octopus with far-reaching tentacles and no rigid form. Few people knew what the Prowlers of the Rogue were capable of.

Placed in major regions throughout the world, Prowlers worked real jobs and lived normal lives. Normal until a situation had either become too politically unstable or simply too hot for the CIA's field agents to handle.

Under those conditions, the Rogue's COS would sanction the Prowlers, take off the leads, and let them run like unleashed dogs who had just gotten the smell of fresh blood in their noses. That's what they were trained for. That's why they were chosen—for their sharp judgment, creativity under stress, and ability to focus on a single pretext: *A mission was to be fulfilled by any means possible, any means at all.*

With the blessings of the administration, the CIA had pooled its resources to find the best they could. The Agency's staff had sifted through thousands of files looking for candidates. Not surprisingly, Lindsay's record had caught their attention. Without warning, he was snatched from his station at Coronado, California, and, along with ninety-nine other surprised soldiers, was reassigned to Fort Bragg for special training.

AnnMarie also remembered he had once been married. It was a bad marriage that had lasted only three months and had ended messy. It had not produced any children, but his ex-wife still contacted him from time to time with requests for financial help.

Beyond that, she knew there were only a few other women in his life. She especially liked that about Lindsay. She leaned against the cool wood interior of his sailboat, her body tingling as she watched him. Virgin territory, she mused.

His six-foot body was lean and taut, powerful-looking in its simplest movements. His brownish blond hair had gotten lighter and longer in the months since she had seen him last. Her eyes traveled down his back, over his tight swim trunks to the pink scar on the back of his right leg. She could see where the surgeons had opened him up, cleaned out what was left of the femur and knee, and rebuilt it with steel and nylon.

She wondered what it would be like to make love to him. To feel his body against hers, to run her hands along those legs, that back. To smell his body in passion. With six years over his thirty-five, such thoughts came to her often about many men. Although she could not have picked a better place, it would not be today. The timing, like always, was bad.

Lindsay turned to her. His strong, clean-shaven jaw was clenched tight, his hazel-blue eyes sharp. "You're going to get us in trouble."

"Jesus, when did you catch paranoia?"

"When CIC mentioned federal prison."

"Screw counterintelligence," she said casually. She pointed to his knee. "The knee's looking good," she said, changing the subject.

He reattached the stern railing chain. "Miracle of modern medicine," he said, stepping back into the dark cabin. "Coffee?" He squeezed past her and fired up the LPG stove. A circle of tiny blue tongues of flame leaped forth.

"I was just about to make some," she said, sliding into the bench seat of the galley table.

Lindsay filled the kettle with fresh water and set it on the burner. "Good, then you can watch it."

He stepped into the forward cabin and closed the door. A moment later, Lindsay returned wearing a pair of khaki shorts and an oil-stained sweatshirt.

The pot whistled as he fished two porcelain mugs from an overhead cupboard. He spooned in a scoop of dark crystals and added the boiling water. "Let's see, you don't like sugar or cream, and"—he handed her the cup—"I don't like bullshit."

AnnMarie raised an eyebrow.

"Come on, AM," he said using his nickname for her. "What do you want?"

"I've gotta have a reason to stop by?"

"Last I remember, you were moving the station to Seoul.

But on a whim, you drop into L.A., charter a small plane to the island airport, catch a delivery truck into Avalon, and then managed to bribe one of the shoreboat skippers to bring you out to my boat. All before six A.M. on a Tuesday morning just to say hi." Lindsay smirked. "I'm flattered."

AnnMarie took a sip of her coffee. "It was a helicopter," she said innocently. "And we landed at the steamer's pier."

Lindsay grabbed a donut from the bin and headed outside. "Wonderful," he said over his shoulder.

She followed him.

Lindsay waved to one of the pink and powder-blue shoreboats as it gurgled past. The skipper tipped his hat. He was on his first loop of the harbor picking up the visiting captains and guests willing to pay his two-dollar fare for a ride to the Pleasure Pier.

Except for the huge, round, and red-tile-roofed casino perched on the eastern side of the harbor, the green pier dominated the small island city. With its small fish market, dive shop, and greasy hamburger stand, the Pleasure Pier was Avalon's town center, its hub of activity every day and every night.

Here both visitors and locals gathered to catch the rides on the flying fish or glass-bottom boats, to see the latest albacore or sailfish brought in from one of the fishing charters. Some came just to sit on the wooden railing and scan the beach for tanned college girls in French-cut bikinis.

Lindsay felt the wind on his skin. It was still only a lightly scented breeze and would probably remain as such. Avalon was waking to a beautiful day. The morning dew still clung to the cockpit seat pads. He flipped them over, sat down, and propped his feet on the pilot's wheel.

"Come on, spit it out," he said, taking a sip of his coffee.

She leaned against the frame of the cabin door. "You were the number one Prowler, Linds. I knew it and so did Sampson." AnnMarie eased herself into the opposite seat.

Lindsay sipped his coffee. "If you wanted to hand out compliments, you should've faxed them."

"I know the rules."

Lindsay lifted his hands in surrender. "It's your ass when Sampson finds out. And you know he will."

"I'll make a mental note of it."

"Good," Lindsay said. "Now, what do you want?"

"I had an operation go bad. Big-time."

"Forget it."

"I'm outside Hong Kong, Linds. All our assets have been turned over to the Brits. I have no one I can ask," she pleaded.

"It's been a year."

"Please . . ."

Lindsay sighed. "So ask," he said, taking another bite of his donut.

"You remember Morrison Shaddock?"

"Head of MI5."

"Former. A month ago he asked us to keep tabs on a local man. He was afraid all his agents were tagged and labeled by the Red Chinese. Out of professional courtesy, I sent in a team for preliminary surveillance. A man and a woman. Their cover was a young American executive and his new wife on their honeymoon. They flew into Kowloon from Tokyo. When they were driving through the Cross Harbor tunnel to their hotel on Hong Kong Island . . ."

AnnMarie looked up and found Lindsay's eyes were on her. With a deep breath she continued. "Inside the tunnel the car went out of control and hit the wall. They were both killed."

Lindsay didn't say anything.

"The car was checked," AnnMarie said. "It hadn't been tampered with. The medical examinations revealed cardiac arrest before impact. That happens a lot in car accidents."

"Was the car from MI5 or rented?"

"Rented."

"What was the weather like?"

"What?"

"The weather?" Lindsay asked almost casually. "You know, cold, hot, rainy, sunny, overcast. What?"

"It's springtime, I guess it's warm," she said.

"This time of year it's usually over eighty and humid," Lindsay remembered.

AnnMarie shrugged, "Okay."

"Did the car have air-conditioning?"

"I think so."

"Check the vents. They probably used prussic acid. It'll have discolored the plastic. Half a gram in each vent would do the trick. Close the windows, flip on the air, and instant heart attack."

"Jesus." She rubbed her palms on her slacks. "We figured it was poison, just not how it was delivered."

"Red Chinese are getting serious about staking their claim."

"It gets worse," she said. "Three days later, Shaddock is suddenly transferred back to London for a much-needed vacation. Somewhere, of course, where he can't be reached. The M bureau puts Babbitt into his place."

"Orson Babbitt?" Lindsay mused. He remembered the puffy-faced Brit. "He's a good agent. Not real smart, but a good company man."

"That's your opinion," she said. "The only thing I've gotten out of the asshole is how sorry he is about my agents and that his people are conducting a full investigation."

"They're hiding something."

"Yeah, and I know what it is. A double agent."

"Can't be. . . ."

"MI5 and the CIA have suspected a mole in the colony for the last eighteen months."

Lindsay sat up. "Why wasn't I told?"

"Had they located him, who do you think would've gotten the sanction?"

For the extermination, Lindsay thought.

"Hong Kong is too sensitive an area to have a mole operating freely."

Lindsay sat back against the cool wood of the *Aiko*. For some reason he was getting a sick feeling in his stomach. He could tell where this was going.

"Babbitt has slammed the door in my face and I don't like it. I was even told by the high-and-mighty to leave it alone."

"Sampson?"

She nodded. "In all fairness, I think he got pressured."

"From who?"

AnnMarie lifted her shoulders.

Lindsay was quiet for a minute. "Why you telling me all this?"

"I thought maybe you could—"

"No way!" Lindsay jumped to his feet. "No fucking way. I'm out of the business," he said firmly. A shiver ran across his neck. "Plus, I'm not going back to Hong Kong."

AnnMarie stared at the harbor. "The guy," she said solemnly, "the one we were to tag and follow. He turned up in Macau, dead."

"It happens."

"It was Tommy Fong."

Lindsay's legs weakened. He looked at her in hopeful disbelief. "From the *Post?*"

"Yeah."

"Oh, son of a bitch!" he screamed across the harbor. He cocked his arm to throw down his coffee cup, but knew he couldn't. He ground his teeth together, tempering his rage. "What happened to him?"

"Somebody returned him to his hotel room mutilated. Autopsy said he was attacked by some kind of large animal. They didn't know what."

Lindsay felt like vomiting. He sat back down.

"I know he was a friend of yours."

"He used to tip me when the *Tribune* was going to get scooped," Lindsay remembered. "He hated his editor." He laughed. "I never had anything good enough to give him."

AnnMarie disappeared into the cabin and returned with a thin leather briefcase Lindsay had not noticed. She pulled out a manila envelope and handed it to him. "The photo was taken a few days before he was found in Macau."

As Lindsay turned the envelope over, a small jade pendant slid into his hand. "What's this?"

"The coroner found it in his stomach."

Lindsay stared at her, then slowly looked at the Chinese jewelry. Not much bigger than a quarter, the ring of green jade was inset with a flat of gold set in the center and held by five uneven gold bands. Dropping it back into the envelope, Lindsay pulled out the color eight-by-ten photograph and a single piece of paper. The paper gave a further description of the pendant and its markings.

Lindsay looked at the photograph. It was perfect in quality. A snapshot taken from a moving car with high-speed film and a sensitive lens. It caught an Asian couple stepping off a sampan and onto the dirty cement wharf Lindsay knew could only be in Aberdeen, a township on the south side of Hong Kong Island. He recognized Tommy.

"You've got a lot of balls trying to use me."

"I'm up against a very cold wall, Lindsay."

He looked at the photo. Dressed in a fine three-piece business suit, Fong's pudgy face and neck topped a silk shirt and tie. It was out of character for his friend. But in Tommy's smooth round face and the gold tooth in his broad smile there was no mistake. "Who's the girl?" he asked.

"Don't know. MI5 is looking. Hong Kong isn't all that big, but it's populated."

"When did you get this?"

"Twelve hours ago."

"No one else has seen this?"

"I'll have to pass it along at some point."

"You're asking me to do something I can't."

"Did you ever see your CIC report? The final one?"

"What are you talking about?"

"Sampson never told you? What the counterintelligence center determined?" AnnMarie asked. "There was the possibility the Ashbury incident was a setup."

"You're grabbing for threads."

"Think about it. They hit you and no one else. There had to have been a leak to target you. One from deep inside. And you were just the first casualty, Lindsay. My agents were the latest. I'm betting it has something to do with MI5's cover-up and everything to do with Tommy's death."

Lindsay squeezed the stainless-steel rail and looked across the green sea.

"Go back to Hong Kong, Linds. Find out who put you into retirement."

Lindsay glanced at the photo on the seat cushion. "I'm going to find out who killed my friend. I don't care about the rest of it. Understand?"

"Yeah."

"And don't contact me. If there's a leak, you've already been tagged."

AnnMarie nodded. "As far as I'm concerned," she said flatly, "I haven't seen you since they rolled you out of the hospital in a wheelchair."

Chapter Two

"Sure, no problem, Mr. Chase. I'll watch her," Mike said as he untwisted the mainsheet purchase blocks of the thirty-foot Newport sloop he was cleaning. Mike was young, probably not much over nineteen, and muscular, with strong shoulders that one would think might limit his mobility. But aboard a boat, Mike moved with the grace and balance of an orangutan in a Borneo rain forest. He had a soft baby face and blond hair that had already begun its retreat to the back of his head.

Mike had developed a monopoly in this section of Marina del Rey harbor caring for thirty-odd boats during midweek while their owners were back at their suit and tie careers. Wash it, refit running gear, clean the bilge, varnish or paint, he could do any bit of minor maintenance asked of him and have it masterfully completed by the weekend. But it was never cheap and always in cash.

"Anything need fixin'?" he asked.

Lindsay thought a moment. "The traveler's coming up on the port edge. May just need bigger screws."

"Better to pull the whole thing, epoxy the holes, and

redrill,'' Mike said, finishing with the line and hanging it from a cleat.

No wonder the kid was driving a new BMW. Lindsay could already see the length of his bill. ''Probably. Do whatever it takes.''

''How long you going to be gone?''

''A couple of days, maybe a week. I'm visiting a buddy who's got a place in the mountains,'' Lindsay said, amazed at how easy it was for him to lie. It wasn't a lie, Lindsay rationalized. It was insurance.

''Why would anyone want to live in the mountains?'' Mike asked, disappearing below into the cabin.

Like always the old 1940 Ford pickup truck started. Of course, it took the usual splash of gasoline down the single-throated carburetor and a jump from Mike's Bimmer to give the battery life. ''This baby's a classic,'' Lindsay said as he slammed the eagle-beaked hood closed. He ran his hands along the primer-gray paint. ''Wait until I fix her up.''

Mike shook his head. ''You need a new car, Mr. Chase. At least one that'll start.''

''Sometimes old is better than new,'' Lindsay yelled as the kid popped the sports car's clutch and chirped the tires in a flash of speed.

''Hell with him,'' Lindsay said under his breath. He looked at his truck, its dull-gray finish, the pimples of spreading rust, and the cracked side window. He smiled. It was just like the one his dad had owned and it ran about the same.

Climbing in behind the wheel, Lindsay headed out of the parking lot, down Admiralty Way, and to the freeway. It was just after five-thirty, and twilight was hanging over Los Angeles.

Lindsay prayed the evening commute would be thinning. No such luck. On the climb through the Sepulveda Pass, just before the Mulholland off-ramp, all forward motion stopped. Lindsay hung his arm out the window and watched the flathead's temperature gauge creep up.

* * *

That morning, after AnnMarie had left the *Aiko* to catch her waiting helicopter, Lindsay took the sailboat's rubber Zodiac to the pier. He bought a four-pack of Guinness's Pub Draught and a large bag of onion-flavored potato chips at the grocery store and paid his mooring fees at the Harbor Master's office.

Then, with a light wind across the aft quarter, he began his eight-hour journey back to the mainland. It was a lot of time to think about Hong Kong and Tommy.

"Being a paepaman is best job," Tommy said, his single gold-capped tooth glittering in his smile. He spoke in a heavily accented English that was almost impossible to decipher. "What do Amelican's call it? The sixth blanch of the govelnment?" he asked as he leaned closer to Lindsay over a wobbling table in a tea shop.

They were in Shau Kei, a small northern town on the coast of Hong Kong Island and it was six-forty A.M.

"Something like that." Lindsay yawned. He rubbed his hand over his face and felt the harsh stubble on his chin. Tommy had called at five forty-five in the morning urging him to take the first ferry from Kowloon. The ferry left at six A.M. and it was a twenty-minute walk from Lindsay's apartment. He had barely made it.

As he stepped into the tea shop, he half looked for Tommy and half hoped he wouldn't be there so he could return to bed.

"What's this about, Tommy?"

Tommy watched out the window next to their table and checked the docks. "You wlote stoly last week about paepaflower made in Kwu Tung without license. That was vely good, vely important," Tommy said, pointing his thick finger.

A round-faced old woman with no expression and a too-bright orange apron deposited cups of tea in front of them and left before Lindsay could ask for coffee.

"No one else thought so," Lindsay said as he sipped from the steaming cup.

"You good wlita, Lindsay. You need big stoly to show you

boss," Tommy said, glancing at the brown garbage scow that was edging itself into position along the dock. "My editor doesn't care about big stolies. Wants me to cover dog show. No fun." He turned his attention to the filthy tug as its crew worked to secure the mooring lines. "So," he said, pointing, "I find you stoly."

Lindsay turned sheepishly and looked through the window. From the far ends of three quiet streets that converged onto the sleepy docks came an army of dark blue Hong Kong police trucks. Skidding and screeching to a halt, the officers positioned their vehicles in a wall of calculated disorder.

The rear doors flew open as a platoon of armed police stormed the scow. The dock handlers and crew of the floating junkyard had no time to react and nowhere to run. In a matter of seconds, they were surrounded.

Lindsay looked at Tommy. "Smugglels," the Chinese man said with a smile. "Wlite good stoly, Lindsay. You know I can't cover it."

It was too bad. Neither could Lindsay. It would have been a good story, too, front-page stuff, just like Tommy suspected. The smugglers had filled old car tires with their shipment of *sabu*, the latest methamphetamine import from the Philippines. But it was the kind of piece that brought notoriety to a reporter, and after all, Lindsay Chase was only posing as a reporter. The last thing the Rogue wanted was for him to do well in his alleged position.

The freeway traffic finally began to break free and the flow increased as the Ford topped the hill and dove into the valley. Lindsay checked his watch. If he was lucky, he figured he'd make Bardsdale by sunset. Although he thought about calling ahead, it was better to arrive unannounced. He was sure of that. Better for all concerned.

By the time Lindsay arrived, Bardsdale was cooling down from the hot spring day. It was late afternoon, midweek, and the few visitors in town had rumbled through in giant semi trucks and trailers and in rented U-Hauls. They were here for only two reasons: a meal at the Denny's or to edge into the gas station to top off their tanks. Soon they'd be back on Highway 126 heading for Ventura or to catch Interstate 5 to L.A. or Sacramento or someplace beyond.

Lindsay had made better time than he'd planned. He had found a clear road to push the Ford to sixty miles per hour. He might have chanced seventy if he had trusted the flathead. Without a radio or cassette player to bring Billie Holiday along for the ride, Lindsay's northbound trip was accompanied only by the rush of wind and a squeaking truck bed.

He pointed the Ford at the transition for Highway 23 and dropped off at Bardsdale's sole exit. A left turn off the ramp and a quick right put him on the main street and headed him toward a line of cream-colored stucco buildings that formed city central.

He tucked the old truck against the curb in front of a combination drug store and market, slid out, and slammed the door without bothering to lock it. With his pine cane in hand, he strolled to the antique store half a block up the street.

Mr. Ed's Second-Hand Clocks and Such had a huge storefront window stuffed with fake antiquities. Tall cabinets of burled wood and marble-topped dressers that filled the window were also used to display the costlier novelties. Candlesticks and beaded purses. Columns of fountain pens. Silver serving trays that had once been handled by white-gloved butlers were now decorated with cobwebs. Gold pocket watches and not-so-precious jewelry were flaunted across a dusty black velvet cushion of a 1930 méridienne.

Lindsay stared into the window and wondered which of these forgotten trinkets had been a mother's birthday gift or a beloved heirloom passed from one generation to the next until its last custodian needed cash more than sentiment.

As he entered, three tiny bells attached to the front door announced Lindsay's arrival. He was greeted by a wall of grandfather clocks standing guard like muscular sentinels. Lindsay edged his way inside the dark interior. Mr. Ed's was a mixture of one part antique and nine parts junk. The good stuff filled the window, the jetsam filled the rest of the store from floor to ceiling, teetering on the constant verge of collapse.

Then there were the clocks. Wall clocks, kitchen clocks, electrical clocks, clocks shaped like cats with swinging tails, clocks in frying pans and old hubcaps. There were clocks from ships, clocks from planes, and school clocks with thick minute hands that had been the focus of children anticipating recess. And, of course, all of Mr. Ed's clocks clicked and clacked out of sync.

It all reminded Lindsay of his aunt's garage, that mysterious cavern of treasures and obscure oddities. It was also amusing how authentic it all seemed—so much so, he had heard the fabricated little establishment occasionally turned a profit.

Lindsay made his way to the back and saw the proprietor, Truby, standing behind a long glass cabinet. The old man's face, lined with age and worry, was set in its usual scowl. His high forehead crushed into his heavy gray brows. A middle-aged woman with long dangling earrings stood in front of him fingering a colorful silk scarf and squabbling over the price.

At the far end of the shop, a young couple inspected a dilapidated Firestone floor radio that had broadcast *The Shadow* and *The Jack Benny Show*. The girl with long brown hair clasped her hands together and smiled at the boy. She was in love with it. The boy shook his head unconvinced and moved toward the door.

As they exited, the girl promised Truby they'd be back. The boy, however, was still shaking his head. Lindsay heard Truby agree on a price for the scarf and the middle-aged woman left with her purchase.

Truby turned to Lindsay and his scowl subsided. "I picked that up for fifty cents." He grinned. "She's thrilled to talk me down to four bucks. It's the same thing every week with her."

"You've found your calling."

"Finally." Truby slipped the woman's money into the cash box. "How've you been?" He stretched out his hand.

Lindsay met it. "Just wonderful."

Truby leaned over the counter and looked at Lindsay's

leg. He saw the scars under the cuff of Lindsay's khaki shorts. "Rotten business, all that. I'd heard they reattached everything from the hip down."

"Never believe rumors."

"Then you're not living on a boat?"

"That one's true."

"Jesus, Linds, you get shot in the leg or the head?"

"It's peaceful," Lindsay said, staring at the pocket watches in the case.

"I had my fill of boats in '43," Truby said lightly, then his tone changed. "You here for a pocket watch?"

Lindsay looked at him, weighed his former teacher for a heartbeat, and then said, "I need a favor."

The old man did his own weighing. He remembered the first time they had met. Fort Bragg in late '88. Truby had given up fieldwork and taken an assignment as an instructor and adviser for the CIA's latest subagency.

The Agency was scrambling to create a new machine, a new weapon for an uncharted arena. For the first time in history, the topography of world politics was changing with the power and speed of an earthquake.

Suddenly the overlords of Langley found themselves facing a new era, a post–Cold War era where the comfort of knowing your enemies and your allies was being replaced by a world where friend and foe swapped places in the nanosecond it took to transfer data from Cairo to P'yongyang.

For the handpicked recruits, each of them already a highly skilled and seasoned soldier, training was merciless. Far worse than anything Truby had to endure in his career with the Agency.

But the CIA had set unusual parameters in order to weed out the simply strong soldiers from the choice ones. Physical strength was not an advantage here. The men and women who thought brute force and muscle would advance them were quickly humiliated by a few weeks of agonizing maneuvers in North Carolina's Green Swamp and the hundred-mile jaunt around California's China Lake Weapons Center in the Mojave Desert.

Those who graduated from these excursions were treated to the next phase, the psychological torment. The ninety-hour drills without sleep followed by unending questions that had no answers. And a roster of hateful, almost medieval tortures designed not to inflict pain but to cause mental breakdown.

It was at the drum that Truby saw what they were searching for in Lindsay's eyes. The recruit had just finished his time sealed in a steel fifty-five gallon drum that had been filled with water to within two inches of its pouring spout. Once encased, the spout was the only opening for light and air. The soldier within could do little else but take small bits of air and wait for his release. It could be two hours or two days. The recruits never knew.

Lindsay had survived nineteen hours when the instructors cut open the drum with an acetylene torch. As they moved to help him out, he refused. He climbed from the watery gauntlet on his own and only then did they realize the torch had badly burned Lindsay's shoulder. He declined medical treatment until the others in his training group had finished their time in the drum.

As Truby watched Lindsay pull himself from the water, he saw the resolve in his face and he knew this recruit had set his mind on accomplishing whatever was before him, regardless. At that moment, Truby knew he was staring at the man who would be the Rogue's finest agent. And Lindsay was, for a time. A time that ended with the events in Hong Kong.

"Just a small favor," Lindsay added.

"Whatever I can do, Linds," Truby heard himself say, and realized he trusted Lindsay without question.

"This is between us."

Truby nodded. "Understood."

Lindsay leaned on his cane. "I need a handgun, one I can take on a civilian airline without being tagged."

"I may have what you need," he said, stepping around

the counter. He locked the front door and flipped the OPEN sign to its OUT-TO-LUNCH side. Beckoning Lindsay to follow, he slipped through the curtain-covered hallway that led to the store's rear storage room and office.

Halfway down the hall Truby stopped in front of a large cherrywood armoire. He drew a skeleton key from his breast pocket and unlocked it. "Made a few changes since you were here last." Inside the antique clothing cabinet was a narrow staircase that twisted left and rose steeply toward the attic. "Put it in myself." Truby smiled as he switched on the interior light.

The tight stairwell was low, forcing Lindsay to negotiate it bent at the waist. As he emerged into the secret room above the store, he flexed his leg painfully.

Truby's lair was not what he expected. There were no crates of machine guns or ammunition boxes stacked along the walls. No surface-to-air missiles, radar-jamming units, or surveillance computers. The armory he assumed would be there wasn't.

Instead the converted attic was an elegantly decorated study with a rolltop desk, red leather chairs, and bookshelves. A small louvered vent allowed in a fresh breeze from the street. Paintings of English fox hunts hung from one wall, and on the other a wide-screen television and video and laser disc equipment were set into the paneling. A large oriental rug covered most of the polished hardwood floor.

"Very nice," Lindsay said.

"I may run a backwater distribution center, but I do so with class," Truby said with pride. "The world has gotten to be very unpleasant. Bosnia, Tibet, East Africa. Who can keep up with it? I've got six warehouses out here and three in Florida."

Lindsay inspected the stereo equipment. "Playing soldier is the second oldest profession."

Truby pressed his hand against the paneled wall where Lindsay stood. It swung open, revealing another room. "I do keep a few things on hand," he said. "For special occasions."

The second room was much smaller, and instead of bookshelves and paintings, the walls were decorated with rows of automatic rifles and handguns on wooden pegs.

"Try this," Truby said, taking an awkward-looking black automatic pistol from its hook. "Not pretty, but it holds fourteen rounds in the magazine and one down the throat."

"Caliber?" Lindsay asked as he leaned his cane against the wall and took the gun.

"Nine millimeter."

"I'd prefer a .45," Lindsay said as he weighed the gun in his right hand, then shifted it to his left. The diamond cut in the handle gripped at the flesh of his palm. Even in a heavy rain, Lindsay knew the gun would not slip.

"If you don't kill whatever you hit, bring it back and I'll give you a full refund."

Lindsay laughed. "Okay. What about airport security?"

Truby took the gun from Lindsay. Pulled back the slide, pushed the release, and dismantled the weapon. "It's all ceramic. Not a piece of metal in it, not the barrel, not even the springs. It even takes special aluminum-cased ammo." Truby slapped it back together. "That's what they call state-of-the-art."

"I knew you'd come through," he said.

The phony clock-store owner picked up Lindsay's cane. "You taking this?"

"Unfortunately, we're rarely apart."

Truby moved to the other end of the room. Leaning against the corner was another cane finished in black lacquer. On the end was a small polished brass tip. "You know what a bang stick is?" he asked.

"Sure, it's for killing sharks. Uses a shotgun load or a gas bottle. You hit the bastard in the side and it blows his guts out, which usually attracts more sharks."

Truby unscrewed the brass tip. "Same principle. It uses a single twelve-gauge cartridge. Here's the safety," he said, showing Lindsay the tiny indentation under the hook. "You release it with your fingernail, turn it hook up, and jam the thing into whoever you want to blow in half."

"What if I drop it?"

Truby tapped it on the floor. "If you don't hit the safety, nothing. If you do, you're going to make a hell of a mess. The drawback is you've only got one shot."

Lindsay ran the cane though his fingers. He twirled it back and forth like a drum major as he switched from his left hand to his right. With a snap, he brought it down to his side.

"There's also a four-inch throwing knife hidden in the shaft." Truby showed Lindsay how to retrieve the blade quickly.

"Pretty damn clever."

"I'd like to take credit, but it's not my design. A Bavarian count in the nineteenth century had one made using black powder and glass fragments. He was worried about thieves on his way home from his mistress's house," Truby said.

"And people say times change."

Before stepping back to the other room, Truby handed him two boxes of ammunition for the automatic.

"The accounting boys aren't going to miss these, right?"

"They allow me a little slack. Not much, but a little," Truby said as he shut the door. "So where are you headed?" He'd have never asked if Lindsay was on an assignment or had he not given his word of silence. But when he saw the look in Lindsay's eyes, he knew his mistake.

Lindsay immediately saw his friend's reaction and realized what he had done. "Sorry, Trub, I didn't mean—"

Truby raised his hand slightly. "Forget it."

"Old habit," Lindsay confessed.

"Yeah, I know."

The senses that had been dormant for so many months were rushing to the surface. Lindsay's internal defenses were coming on-line again, his body gearing up, his nerves tightening. Once more, he was trusting no one. "It's scary how quickly it comes back," he admitted. He saw the pain in his former mentor's face. "Far East," he said simply. "I'm going to the Far East."

Truby nodded. My God, he thought, Hong Kong. Lindsay was going back to Hong Kong. "Here." Truby pulled a leather shoulder harness from the bottom drawer of the desk. "Feels like you never left."

"Maybe not to you," Lindsay said slipping the 9mm into the holster.

"At least you're not stuck in a backwater town watching inventory pass through the door."

"Thanks for the toys."

"Anytime."

Lindsay turned and, with the help of the new cane, headed down the stairs.

Truby moved to the attic vent and peered out the slanted louvers and watched Lindsay walk toward the old truck. Bad judgment, Truby thought. The Rogue let one hell of an agent go.

Then, unconsciously, the old agent began to smile. In his gut, Truby knew Lindsay Chase was on his way back.

Someone else watched Lindsay climb into his truck, but with only one eye. An electronic, high-resolution digital eye of the intelligence-gathering satellite, SHARP-View, positioned twenty-four thousand nautical miles overhead.

Truby didn't know about it, but the $2.3 billion watchdog with its array of silver-foil antennas and laser-tracking cameras recorded everyone that entered and exited his store. It relayed its photos to the government's active repeater INTERSTATE 5 satellite every twelve minutes. From there, the data was transmitted in precisely timed pulses to the broad-dished receivers posted inside Andrews Air Force Base.

Once captured, the data was transferred to the National Imagery Agency in Washington. The NIA then redigitized the data to enlarged color images and passed them along to the counterintelligence center for analysis. CIC shouldered all the responsibility for the security of personnel, facilities, and information within the CIA.

But there was one problem in letting satellites do surveillance. They were indiscriminate. The images of the woman leaving Mr. Ed's with her new scarf were no more important to SHARP-View's circuitry than those of Lindsay entering. That, along with budgetary cuts in personnel and computer time, meant Lindsay's trek across Bardsdale's main street would go unnoticed for several hours.

And that gave Lindsay a head start.

Chapter Three

Peking, 1898

China. The Middle Kingdom. The belligerent empire that looked upon the rest of the world with hateful, suspicious eyes. For a thousand ages its people survived dynasties and conquests, conquerors and an unbroken lineage of a stone-willed theocracy.

But from this seemingly eternal tyranny arose at its center a city more magnificent than any other in history. Not in the Egypt of the Pharaohs, nor the Rome of the Romans, not even under the Emperors of the Japans. This city was the greatest monument man had ever created. Or would ever again. This was the heart of the great Chinese, the first gate on the path to heaven, the place of the Dragon Throne. This was Peking.

And like a mysterious siren drawing sailors to unseen rocks, this mightiest of cities lured men from beyond the Four Seas. Chinese peasants and foreigners, scholarly and barbarian, they all came to see its beauty and experience its grandeur.

Surrounded by high, monstrous walls and wide, yawning gates, Peking was thick with marble temples and gold-tiled palaces. Slow-flowing moats scented with lilies crisscrossed the landscape and filled its vast sanctuaries.

By the sixteenth century when the powerful Bannermen warriors of the Manchus marched down from the north to crush the Ming Dynasty and take China for their own, Peking was already three thousand years old—a continuous succession of cities, each more beautiful than the one previous.

The Manchus were no different, and when the newest elite of Chinese society took their Peking residence within the sprawling walls of the Tartar City, they created the glorious Imperial City, and within that, the Forbidden City, the celestial home of the Emperor.

Dominated by huge palaces with bright yellow roofs that seemed ablaze under the noontime sun, the Forbidden City was, in and of itself, nirvana. With giant lakes and terraces and sweet-scented gardens edged by white marble pathways, this was China's holiest of holy places.

At this moment, with his mind on earthly troubles, Chief Eunuch Li walked hurriedly without seeing the beauty around him. He was a thin man with protruding lips and small, shrewd eyes. He kept his scalp shaved clean except for a traditional queue of black hair that fell like a thick rope down the center of his back. His wrinkled skin was dark and parched like that of his ancestors, who had come from the north fleeing the first Mongols.

Close behind Li trailed a figure dressed in the drab clothes of a eunuch servant. But this man was no servant of the palace. He was the bringer of death, Li determined. A demon in human form, and he had come to destroy his mistress, the Dowager Empress Tzu Hsi.

For three days the demon had kept a vigil outside the northern gate, demanding audience with the Empress. Li had sent the head guardsman to threaten the man if he didn't go away. But the warrior had returned with a small package and a message for the Empress.

The words the head guardsman whispered cut into Li like a cold spike forced into the back of his brain. The contents of the package reaffirmed his fears. Li went immediately to the Empress, finding her on the morning terrace.

"Empress?" Li announced himself.

"Is that you, Lein-ying?" her voice came from somewhere behind the billowing drape of fine silk.

"Yes, Venerable Buddha," Li said, using a nickname he had given her and which she had happily accepted. "I am sorry to interrupt." Li stepped onto the stone terrace.

Though the Dowager Empress was formally in a state of retirement and her nephew was now Emperor, everyone knew she was the center of Manchurian power. A quick-witted as well as quick-tempered woman, Tzu Hsi had reigned over the empire for thirty years, during which the world about them had changed many times over.

In her younger days, Tzu Hsi was known as much for her Manchu beauty as for her wisdom and courage. But now, at sixty-two, the Empress was looking her years. For most of her life, she had carried the burdens of state for a quarter of the world's population.

Dressed in a white and blue robe embroidered with a golden dragon, Tzu Hsi sat in a huge red-lacquered chair. Her hair, dyed daily by her servants, was as black as coal, and in it, she wore a delicate tiara of violets and silver. Heavy white powder covered her forehead and her narrow Manchu nose, and on her cheeks she insisted on the palest of rouges. Her wide almond-shaped eyes were as bright as her mind was sharp.

Li moved to the foot of the chair and bowed his head to the floor.

"What troubles you, Lein-ying?"

"The man at the northern gate. . . ."

"He persists?"

Li nodded.

"Why do you aggravate me with this? Tell the guards to send him away. If he doesn't go, arrest him. Then the guards can do what they wish," she said flatly, tossing the remains of a fig back onto the plate.

Li looked up. "He says he is from Shantung and claims heritage of the Manchus," Li shuddered. "He claims his father was the doctor Yao Pao-sheng and that he is your child."

The Empress squeezed her hand into a fist. "A lie."

Slowly Li pulled the small leather pouch from inside his long sleeve and offered it.

The Dowager Empress took it from Li's shaking hands. Slipping a long fingernail under the knot, she untied the drawstring. The contents rolled into her palm.

Li studied her face. The pouch contained a *pang-tze*, an archer's ring worn on the thumb, and made of red jade. Carved along the edge was the emblem of T'ai Tsung, an emperor who had climbed the Dragon for the Long Journey over nine hundred years ago. Li was not sure if it was genuine or if the Empress had ever seen it before.

Tzu Hsi clutched the ring. "I told him to sell it and use the money," she said gently.

The old eunuch felt his stomach churn. "Pao-sheng swore he would say nothing," Li said, remembering how he had threatened the young doctor as he was smuggled out of the Western Palace with a child that could not be.

"I must see him," she said, her voice a whisper.

"It is too dangerous," Li warned. "The Censors' eyes are everywhere. The Emperor will find out. Please, Venerable Buddha, do not tempt fate."

"Bring him," she said, staring at the ring.

So now, trailing behind Li through the vast gardens and along the huge green lakes of the Imperial Palace was the young man who claimed to be the illegitimate son of the Dowager Empress.

It had been Li who had introduced Yao Pao-sheng to the Empress. After the death of her Emperor, Tzu Hsi had become increasingly restless and unhappy. Knowing the Empress better than anyone, Li understood the reason for her discontent. Tzu Hsi was, after all, a young woman and had enjoyed the worldly pleasures with her Emperor.

His dangerous plan to aid his mistress's woes had worked all too well. She had an immediate interest in the young doctor and it was not long before she was pregnant.

Had the knowledge of the child leaked out, she would have been put to death, as would he. But they hid her growing stomach beneath layers of silken robes and when the child was delivered, Li smuggled Yao and the infant out of the city to save them all.

As the old eunuch and the young man moved through the sacred halls, Li didn't notice the package he carried so carefully under his coat.

Finally they reached the doors of the private chambers. Li motioned him to remain silent. The young man nodded. The eunuch tapped lightly on the door. He waited and tapped again. He slowly pushed the door open and motioned the young man to follow. "Kneel." Li pointed to a spot in the center of the dark room.

Taking a small bundle from under his coat, the young man laid it before him. Then he kowtowed with his forehead pressed to the cold stone floor.

From the far end of the room, the young man heard another door open. Quick footsteps followed. There was the screeching of a heavy chair as it was pushed across the floor and set in front of him. The smell of incense became strong, forcing him to choke back a cough.

The footsteps retreated and left a long silence.

"You claim to be the child of the doctor Yao Pao-sheng?" the voice was deep and coarse.

"I am his son, Yan, born within the walls of the Western Palace," he answered, his head still to the floor. "In the year 1876."

"And I am to believe you?"

"For four days I was kept within the White Cloud Temple and then smuggled out of the Forbidden City by my father and the sister of Chief Eunuch Li."

Tzu Hsi stared down at the young man who was dressed as a eunuch but spoke so assuredly of his Imperial birth. She turned and looked at her trusted Li. The old man stood motionless beside the high-legged throne on which she sat.

"You either stole the ring or cheated it from Yao," she accused, trying desperately to convince herself this man was not her son.

"No, Venerable One. You gave it to my father to sell during lean times. But"—Yan moved to lift his head then thought better of it—"although lean years came, he could never part with it."

"Why not?"

"I think, Empress, because it was a gift from his beloved."

Tzu Hsi took a deep breath. She had told no one, but forcing the handsome Yao to leave with their son had torn at her heart. But she knew there could have been no other way. Death would surely have come otherwise.

"Look at me," Tzu Hsi said finally.

Yan slowly looked into the cotton-white face of the Dowager Empress. Veiled in a mist of smoky incense and with long twisting fingernails and high coiffure, she looked like an exotic demon.

Li, too, lifted his eyes toward his mistress. He wanted to see her expression, to see if she saw the image of Pao-sheng in the young man.

Instantly she brought her hand to her mouth. Here was the face of her lover unchanged in twenty years. The only man, besides her Emperor husband, who had touched her heart. "What . . . what has become of Pao-sheng?"

"He died of pneumonia two years ago," Yan said, sorrow still in his voice.

"Why have you not come before now?" she asked suspiciously.

Suddenly, from the package on the floor before him, there was the faintest cry. Yan quickly touched the side of the silk cocoon and the sound stopped.

"What is that?" the Empress demanded.

Still on his knees, Yan gently lifted the package over his head. "A treasure, Venerable Ancestor. A treasure that has brought me to you."

The Empress slipped from her chair and moved to him. "Stand," she ordered.

Yan did but kept his chin to his chest. He peeled back the thin sheet of silk.

Bound comfortably inside was a small infant boy. He suckled a knot of gauze moistened with soybeans. The baby's sheepish eyes smiled as the Empress looked down upon him.

"He is your grandson," Yan said, his heart pressed against his throat as he waited for her reaction.

In the light of the burning lanterns that lined the room,

Tzu Hsi looked at the baby and suddenly, for the first time in her life, she was unsure of what to do. She glanced quickly to Li, but the old eunuch, too, was in shock. "How dare you bring this here?" the Empress said, returning to her chair.

"But nothing greater could I have brought to you," Yan said. He unwrapped his son and lifted the naked infant before her.

Tzu Hsi hesitated. Li tried to intervene. He pulled at Yan's shoulder, but the young man would not give way.

The smooth-skinned baby, with only wisps of dark black hair on its head, gurgled contently. Her eyes turned to Yan. "If you are my son, what is it you want from me?" she asked.

"For you to hold your grandchild."

"And then?"

"Nothing."

Tzu Hsi's curt laugh cut through the quiet palace. "You come to claim your heritage, yet you want no riches or position."

"Recognition is enough. I know now that I am truly the son of the Dowager Empress and cousin to the Son of Heaven. I will tell my son, who will tell his, and the secret of my family will be passed from generation to generation with pride and honor."

The Empress stared at him for a moment. Then, carefully, she took the infant into her arms. For the first time in many years, Li saw a warm smile on his mistress's lips.

"Lien-ying," she said, not taking her eyes from the child, "take the best cart from the workers' shed and fill it with provisions. And find the strongest donkey, a young one that will pull my son and grandchild for many years." She looked at Yan, then added, "And have two gold bars hidden within the cart."

"I—" Yan began to protest.

"I can do nothing about your position. The Emperor is my nephew, but there are many who would use your existence to strip me of my place and condemn me to death."

"You do more than I could have dreamed."

She handed him the child. "Take your family and return to Shantung. Speak to no one of this," she warned.

With his son in his arms, Yan dropped to the floor. "I shall never betray you, my mother."

"Go now," she said, folding her arms into the broad sleeve of her silk robe.

Li clapped his hands and from behind a small door two eunuchs appeared. "They will take you to the Hata Gate of the Tartar City," Li told him. "The cart will be there by dawn."

Yan bowed to the old eunuch. "Thank you," he said. "Thank you." He glanced one last time at his mother and then followed the two eunuchs from the chamber.

Li moved to his mistress and bowed low. "I did not know about the child," he said, fearing her wrath.

"It doesn't matter," she said, staring at the door through which Yan had gone. "His journey is long and dangerous."

Li was surprised by the dark tone of her voice. "Very long, Venerable One, and very dangerous."

"Your friends in the south province. The ones you constantly jabber about? Do they still wish to drive the *gweilo* from our country?"

"Yes," Li said, a grin forming on his face. "They want to chase out all the foreigners."

"If they succeed, they will gain influence with the Emperor."

"The Boxers of Shantung will be loyal to whomever supports their cause."

"Then see that the assassin you hire to rid us of this problem empowers us with them," Tzu Hsi commanded.

Li's smile widened further. "The British would be best, but they will ask a high price."

"Promise whatever they want. If the Emperor or the Censors learn of my son, you and I will both be mounting the Dragon for the Long Journey," she said. "And I do not plan on riding so soon." Tzu Hsi headed toward her chambers, leaving the Chief Eunuch to his conspiracy.

It was a private courtyard hidden behind a small shop surrounded by high walls and adjacent buildings. In the center was a black lifeless pond edged with stones. A huge sycamore grew in one corner and reached out across the yard with thick branches creating an impenetrable ceiling. Set in deep moss-covered alcoves were chairs and tables for young couples to sit and drink tea and look into each other's eyes. But this early in the morning the tables were empty and the yard was dark and cold.

Li entered the court uneasily. This, he thought, was a perfect haven for demons. "Mr. Brigham?" he called out as his eyes darted from corner to corner.

"Here, Chief Eunuch." Brigham's voice came from one of the corners. He moved gingerly across the moist floor to where Li could see him. He bowed low, taking his green plaid cap from his head. The Englishman was dressed in a fine ivory-colored cotton suit with a red bow tie, which to Li looked as though a hand-painted butterfly had landed on his throat.

Li had dealt with the diplomat in the past and despised him deeply. He was an evil man. His gentle appearance was almost feminine, with a smooth pale complexion and long slender fingers. He was soft-spoken and made a point of knowing and subscribing to China's elaborate customs and etiquette. Such men were the most dangerous, Li knew, for they were demons with the comforting grace of angels.

"I am honored to be taken into your trust, Chief Eunuch Li," Brigham said in perfect Mandarin. He remained bent at the waist for the proper duration.

"No, it is I who am honored, Mr. Brigham," Li said. "Thank you for coming on such short notice."

"Your message stated it was urgent," Brigham said with a smile.

Li stepped farther into the courtyard. He couldn't keep himself from looking around, expecting monsters to jump up from the pond. "These are odd times," he said.

"True, this has not been the best of years," the Englishman said as he moved to one of the unsteady tables. He waited for Li to sit, set his cap on the center, and seated himself.

Li sat stiff-backed while Brigham reclined more comfortably. He had been summoned by the eunuch and this gave him the position of authority during their meeting. Before they even began, Li was in Brigham's debt.

The Chief Eunuch leaned forward across the table. "I am in need of a favor in private matters."

Brigham studied the Chinaman. "You have no trust for foreigners."

Li shrugged. "But I have heard the English talk about their word of honor. It is a binding vow between gentlemen?"

"It is."

"That is why I come to you and not to the French or the Germans."

Drumming his fingers on the tabletop, Brigham tried to dissect Li's strategy. It was useless. He had been in China for seventeen years and still he could not tell what a Chinaman was thinking. "What private matters could be trusted to a foreign devil and not to those behind the sacred walls? Unless they regarded the Emperor."

"It does not," Li snapped. "At least"—his voice trailed off—"not directly."

"Very well, Mr. Li. You've baited your hook and I'll bite onto it."

"Do I have your word?"

The Englishman weighed the request. Brigham wondered if the Chinese was truly revealing some dark secret from within the Forbidden City or merely building some dramatic story in order to cajole a foolish request for the young Emperor.

"Yes," Brigham said sheepishly. "You have my word that nothing said between us will be repeated."

Li was pleased, though he had no real reason for trusting him. "There is a man traveling south to Shantung. He leaves the Chinese City this very moment by cart," Li said gravely. "He cannot be allowed to reach his destination."

Brigham leaned forward, placing both elbows on the edge of the table. "Who is he?"

"A messenger. There is unrest in Shantung."

"Is he a Boxer? A member of the I Ho Chuan?"

Li was taken aback by Brigham's knowledge of the secret society. The I Ho Chuan, or Society of Harmonious Fists, were calling for the removal of all *gweilo,* the foreign devils, from China. "Yes," Li said quickly. "It is a growing concern."

"It should be. If they grow too strong, Li, there is no telling what the Europeans will do. And if there is bloodshed, their first response will be to bring more troops."

"The Emperor is aware of that. But there are factions within the Imperial family who are not. That is why I've come to you."

Brigham stared at Li but still found nothing in his face. "This is quite a request."

"If it is too much . . ."

"No," Brigham said. "There is a man in Peking who can do what you ask. But"—Brigham looked questioningly at Li—"surely, Chief Eunuch, the Emperor has assassins loyal to him?"

"One can never know his true allies. Even if one is the Son of Heaven."

"Yes," Brigham agreed. "But then . . ." The Englishman stopped himself as he suddenly remembered Li's true alliances. "It's not the Emperor you kowtow to, it's the Dowager Empress." Brigham leaned smugly in his chair. "The man who travels to Shantung is no Boxer."

Li's eyes widened and his fleshy lips drooped over his slacking jaw. For the first time, Brigham could see fear on the Chinese face.

"He's a threat to the old witch, isn't he? A great threat, at that. Why else would you breach the sacred walls for help?"

Li regained himself. "By coming to you," he said, his voice now deep and harsh, "I give your government a chance to come under the good graces of the Empress. Do you not want that chance, Mr. Brigham?"

"Without question. Whenever our two governments work together, it can only benefit both. But"—Brigham grinned—"don't take me for a fool, Chief Eunuch. I know this favor will cost my man his life."

Li feigned a look of shock.

"If I have your so-called messenger killed," the Englishman went on, "your Boxers will descend upon my man with the knife still bloody in his hand. And they will parade his head though the streets as proof of the murderous foreigners."

Li stared at the Englishman.

"There will be accusations," Brigham continued as he casually adjusted his bow tie. "Some small uprising, a murder or two of a few missionaries, maybe even a diplomat. Could even be me." Brigham waved his hand. "More troops will be dispatched, but in a few weeks it will all die down and you will have accomplished what you needed."

Li was unsettled by how accurately the foreigner had guessed his plan. He rose from his chair.

"For such a service," Brigham said flatly, "you're going to have to make it worth the trouble."

The Chief Eunuch stared at Brigham. "You are willing to send your man?" Li was shocked.

"For a price. A very, very high price."

Li slowly sat back down. "What do you want?"

"Hong Kong's new territories and Weihaiwei."

"What?"

"The treaties are before the Emperor and his Censors. But the Dowager Empress has the power. Give England a deed of ownership, not just a lease, and I promise you, the man Tzu Hsi fears will not live out tomorrow."

"That is too much."

"The Empress is not worth a few thousand acres of land?"

Li looked at the black water of the pond and contemplated the price the Englishman was asking. Even with Li's limited knowledge in affairs of state, he knew Weihaiwei was out of the question. It was only two days' ride from Peking. Two days' ride meant a few days' march. No, that was too close to grant the foreigners a permanent foothold. Much too close. But Hong Kong?

Li had seen charts and maps of the distant archipelago and had heard the long-drawn-out arguments between the generals and princes in the Hall of Official Meetings. He knew the Emperor favored the ninety-nine-year lease England wanted for the islands and the peninsula. "The lands before Kowloon, yes. But not Weihaiwei," Li bartered.

"All of Hong Kong, then, including the new territories.

A deed of ownership negating both the Treaty of Nanking and the Treaty of Peking."

"But not Weihaiwei?"

"Then include the surrounding islands and the land extending to the Shum Chun River?" the Englishman pressed.

Li weighed everything to the best of his ability. "I will take it before the Empress, but I can make no promises."

"Remind her that the longer the delay, the further away from the Forbidden City the man will travel. And the more difficult he will be to find."

Li nodded as he stood. "I will send word to your house."

"No," Brigham said as he, too, stood from the table. "Send only the deed to Hong Kong. But be sure, Chief Eunuch Li, that it bears the Imperial Seals."

Li was not surprised that this Englishman knew of the most precious symbols in all of China and that the seals of the Imperial Court would make the deed unquestionable to the Censors and to the Chinese people themselves.

Li's lips turned to a wry smile. "You are a very learned man, Mr. Brigham. Very learned and very shrewd."

"Something I've gained from my Chinese hosts. It's kept my head on my shoulders."

"And may it remain there until our business is over," Li said as he bowed formally. The eunuch turned and disappeared down the stone path.

Brigham picked up his cap from the table, brushed off the brim, and set it squarely on his head. Leaving the courtyard, he headed north along Pewter Lane.

He was a very careful man, Brigham, and though he was heading back to his small house, he was sure not to return the same way he had come. The unrest in Shantung, Brigham knew, was already permeating the city walls.

After crisscrossing his way through the Tartar, Brigham reached his gateway. A stray calico cat had spread itself lazily across the threshold forcing the Englishman to take a long awkward step through. Once inside, he secured the heavy wooden barrier with a thick plank across its width.

"Well?" came a deep voice from the shadows.

Startled, Brigham's hand moved to the Weberly Mark 1

revolver hidden in the waist of his pants. The shriek of sharp steel leaving a scabbard cut the morning. He froze.

"It is only I, Brigham," the voice said, and the Englishman recognized it.

He sighed. "Don't do that again," Brigham said as he turned to the man.

The powerfully built Head Guardsman with the long thin mustache dripping from the edges of his face looked at the foreigner through dark eyes. Then slowly the Manchurian smirked. "Shadows scare the barbarians from across the Four Seas."

"And invisible demons make the great Bannermen of the Guard tremble," Brigham parried.

The Guardsman shrugged. "So tell me what you learned from the weasel."

"It's true. He's the She-devil's son."

"She has deceived us." The Guardsman groaned. "The Emperor must be told."

"Don't be a fool. Li knows you spoke with him. Do you think you'd have a chance getting near the Emperor now?"

"Neither of us have long to live," the warrior said.

"I've guaranteed myself a least a day," Brigham said. He was sure he was safe until his end of the bargain was complete. "But you, my old friend, I'm afraid you don't have much time to leave the city."

The member of the mighty Bannermen of the Guard, in his stiff woolen coat, stood motionless in thought. He turned to the Englishman he had befriended years before. "It is time for my watch," he said.

Realizing the proud warrior would never flee, Brigham put his hand on the Manchurian's shoulder. "May you guard the gates of Ping Yi's palace," he said referring to the Chinese God of Thunder.

"And you," the Head Guardsman said. He unlatched the gate and stepped into the street. With a nod, he was gone.

Brigham laid his plans quickly. He sent his two servants to the market, telling them he was inviting a dozen guests for dinner. This left him to an empty house and freedom from prying eyes.

On the export list from the embassy, he checked the

sailing date of the next British ship out of Weihaiwei. It was in two days. That gave him enough time to get there and secure passage.

He pulled out his traveling trunk and began to pack. From the armoire, he removed the thick whaler's coat he had worn as a much younger man coming to this alien country. He stuffed it inside. He packed extra clothes, his favorite books, a photograph of his mother, and several boxes of ammunition for the Weberly.

Then he sat down at his writing table and transcribed two letters. The first was to the Sergeant, the man at the embassy whom Brigham knew he could trust to fulfill his half of the deal.

Pity, Brigham thought as he dipped his pen into the inkwell and wrote. Too bad he had to send this man to his death. He had enjoyed the company of the Sergeant many times at the embassy's banquets and gatherings. He was a huge man with a quick sense of humor and a deep laugh, but more importantly, he was a military man of unbending loyalty.

In the letter, he told the Sergeant of the great importance of his mission and what it meant to England's position in China. At the bottom, he reiterated the details Li had given him, wished him luck, and signed it.

The second letter was to Queen Victoria herself. It explained exactly how he had secured the deal for the deed to Hong Kong and how he had dealt with Chief Eunuch Li of the Forbidden City for the assassination of the illegal son of the Dowager Empress Tzu Hsi. He also noted that the deed would supersede any lease, even those mandated by the Emperor.

Then, with a sudden and uncharacteristic wave of sentimentality, Brigham apologized for the barbaric act of murder he had agreed upon in the name of England.

Finally, Captain Alsworth Brigham III walked outside, sat down in the garden courtyard of his Manchu home, and awaited the messenger from the Forbidden City.

Chapter Four

Hong Kong Island

Lindsay decided on a direct flight on United Airlines. He would have liked to have gone through Tokyo, or perhaps some other route with several stops, but he knew Flight One would be packed with tourists and businessmen, and that was the objective. To blend in. Lindsay was a target. Not a hot target; a cold, passive target. No one would, or at least no one should be looking for him. But his face was known. After the assassination attempt on the Duke, Lindsay knew the faces in that crowd were now residing on several kilobytes in every counterterrorist database in the technocracies of the Western Hemisphere.

And as the date for reunification approached, he knew the Red Chinese were increasing their watch over the colony. Just as the British were. It was their last gallant effort at saber-rattling before their dubious withdrawal.

The 747–400 jetliner shuddered slightly, then the massive structure of metal and plastic settled back into its seemingly motionless journey. Lindsay sensed the pilot's adjustment in course and altitude through his thickly cushioned seat.

He could tell they were heading southwest by the angle of sunlight cascading into the cabin.

It was an old navigator's trick he'd learned at Miramar Air Force Base when the CIA decided the recruits for their shadow agency should be able to pilot anything with wings or whirling rotor blades. Not that they needed to be good pilots. The agency wasn't going to spend either the time or the money on that. No, the new wave of operatives only needed to know how to get an aircraft off the ground and fly it from point A to point B. The rationale being that if an agent had to escape a decaying locale and the only means was by aircraft, he damn well better know how to work the thing.

Lindsay had spent four weeks above a California desert training in seventeen different types of aircraft, from French civilian to the former Soviet Union's finest seek-and-destroy warplanes. For Lindsay, every moment had been a thrill.

While most of the other recruits wound up with their breakfast dripping from the instrument panel, Lindsay had had the time of his life.

He should have joined the Air Force instead of the Navy, Lindsay told his training officer after their first day in the air. "I have to fly these every day," the young flight instructor said with a thick Alabama drawl. "Don't get me wrong, sir. I love it. But human nature don't let you hold to the same thing for too long. Marry yourself a *Playboy* centerfold, it don't matter. Soon enough, you'll be flipping through *Penthouse*.

"You folks are luckiest," the instructor concluded, though he knew very little about Lindsay's small group. "I hear you get to do a little of everything."

The instructor was right. More right than he could have imagined. A little of everything, and in the U.S. arsenal, that was a lot.

Fort Bragg was weaponry, close assault, and hand-to-hand combat. San Diego was underwater infiltration and demolition, along with several days aboard a Los Angeles Class fast-attack submarine. The swamps near Fort Polk and the high mountains of Fairchild Air Force Base each offered their own hellish environments for an education in survival and training in the unconventional techniques of behind-the-lines warfare.

After ten months of physical strain, the lessons went into the white-walled classrooms of Langley. Military computer systems, counterattack electronics, and advanced surveillance equipment became as second nature as riding a bicycle, field-cleaning an M60 machine gun, or sabotaging a Soviet-made Silkworm missile.

Yet, beyond all the magic of high-tech weapons and the miracles of modern warfare, the Rogue was designed to rely on its basic component: its operatives. This was a new twist to the old game. While most of the world of spy-counterspy marched forward, the Rogue was conceived to move backward. Back to the days when field personnel relied upon themselves and not the frail infrastructure of computers, satellites, and electronic gadgetry.

It was a bold move for the CIA, but a necessary one. Since the time the Pharaohs battled the Hittites, the men who waged and practiced war knew nothing could tip the scales more than intelligence. And no nation on earth was more vulnerable to having its electronic eyes and ears crushed than the United States.

Thus, the justification for Lindsay and his associates. They were latent weapons deeply entrenched and all the Rogue wanted to do was make sure they were entirely self-reliant. And that, they discovered, was attained in individuals who could best tap into their primordial sense.

Man had evolved from his animalistic intuitions into a creature of logic and wisdom, one of contemplation and consideration. Shaped by his changing society and sophistication, he learned to suppress the inner savagery and brutal instincts that had once given him an edge over the natural world.

But the CIA's psychologists found that man's veil of civilization was thin and fragile. Strip away the translucent barriers and the truculent impulses were right there, just below the surface. Self-hypnosis was the quickest doorway to the primordial brain, a small fist of cells above the spine where the human animal continued to pace relentlessly. It was the armory that held the inner strength that a panic-stricken woman used to lift a two-ton car from her trapped child. It was also where the undying resolve rested in a sailor adrift in a four-foot raft in the middle of the Pacific Ocean who could stay alive for six months.

It didn't, however, bestow clairvoyance. That was something Lindsay knew firsthand as he sat in his airplane seat rubbing his knee. It didn't warn you what was going to happen the next day or the next second. Or from which direction the bullet would come.

Lindsay pulled down the plastic window screen to block off the bright sunlight reflecting off the jetliner's wing.

He tugged the envelope from his leather carry-on under his seat. It was the second time he had looked at the photograph during the flight. The first time was a few hours out of Los Angeles when he had taken only a quick glance. He wanted his subconscious to work the image and make his mind crave for added detail. Now he studied it and the particulars jumped at him. Gold cuff links on Fong's expensive white shirt, a well-tailored gray suit, and black eelskin belt. His friend had acquired a few more pounds since he had seen him last.

The girl was Asian, probably Chinese but maybe not. Something about her suggested she wasn't full-blooded. The camera had caught her slightly turned, the sun highlighting her firm jaw. Her face was fresh and clean, her makeup applied at a minimum. Almond eyes were half closed in midblink and her long black hair was twisted once and pulled across her right shoulder.

She was tall, lean, and stood at least three inches over Fong's own five-foot-four. She wore a conservative peach blouse and a white skirt that stopped just above the knees. Below the hemline were muscular calves clad in sheer nylons.

Lindsay couldn't decide if she was attractive. It wasn't a good photo. Definitely not flattering, but it was enough for him to recognize her.

The odd couple were holding hands as they stepped from the sampan. No. Lindsay looked closer. Fong had his hand around the girl's wrist. Tight or loose? Was he helping her or pulling her? The photo didn't tell.

Lindsay then noticed the delicate gold chain around her neck. It looped low into her blouse just above the ascent of her breasts. The chain hung straight as though weighted by something, something small and hidden beneath the silky fabric.

Tilting the envelope, Lindsay poured the pendant into his palm. Was this dangling at the end of that chain, he wondered. Why would it have found its way from the warmth of her skin to the pit of Tommy's stomach?

Lindsay fingered the piece of jewelry. He assumed it had a moderate value. Although the ring of green jade was dark and uniform, it was scuffed and scratched. The dot of gold inlaid in its center was stamped through with the Chinese character meaning "tenderhearted." The five tiny bands around the jade also bore characters. On four of them were the symbols for north, east, south, and west. But the fifth, the one between south and east, showed the Chinese character meaning "fire."

Lindsay looked at his watch. Five-thirty P.M. Hong Kong time. There would be another hour of flight, then they would drop into Kai Tak International. Early evening would be hectic inside the airport, and with luck he'd blend into the crowd as they tried to get their luggage from frail-looking porters who understood English but refused to use it.

Lindsay rubbed his face. He could feel a headache beginning just behind his eyes. Twelve months was a long time to be away. Who to see first? Tommy had many friends, but Lindsay knew only a few of them. There was one, Lindsay remembered, one he knew he could trust.

For a second, needles dug into the back of his skull as a wave of anxiety swept across him. He imagined a hidden rifle waiting for him to step off the plane. Waiting with a teflon-coated bullet.

Hong Kong was hot. Muggy hot, and the noise of the congested city was intensified with the bright windless day. It took an hour from when the wheels of the airliner touched the runway until Lindsay emptied his suitcases into the drawers and closet of his room on the seventh floor of the Harbor

View Hotel in the Wan Chai sector of Hong Kong Island. A businessman's hotel, it was sparse but accommodating. Cream-colored walls, brown carpet, brown bedspread on a sagging mattress. It would do.

Wan Chai, too, carried the age-old reputation as accommodating. This was Hong Kong's center for the exotic pleasures found in the late night. Here were the bars of *Suzy Wong* and her sisters, where soldiers once came on leave to drink and whore and escape the nightmares of Korea and Vietnam. This part of the colony never closed and never slept and was where curious eyes never lingered for too long.

Lindsay moved to the large window and stared out across Victoria Harbor. The darkening skyline of Kowloon seemed filled with a prickly sea of huge glittering stalagmites. This was hard evidence of how suffocating civilization could be and how much human beings could tolerate. In the year since he had last been in Hong Kong, the city had grown. But not like other cities—growth here was vertical. With land at a premium, sixty-floor buildings found their footing on barely half an acre of dirt.

The colony was forever doused with the acrid smell of the welder's torch and the musty odor of mason's powder. Except after the rain. For a few hours, until work commenced again, a tropical rainstorm would briefly cleanse the city, wash away the grit of the metropolis and bring forth the fragrances of its tiny porch gardens that hid within the steel and concrete landscape and kept the inhabitants sane.

Lindsay stood under an icy shower before changing into tan slacks and a cotton shirt. He ate a quick snack in the coffee shop on the second floor, then stepped outside and caught the white and red tram into the Central District.

Rolling steadily, the two-story tram inched its way through the afternoon traffic along Des Voeux Road. Finally, Lindsay clutched his cane and leaped awkwardly to the pavement. Pursued by a blare of horns, he cut through the cars and onto the crowded sidewalk. Cat Street was still two more blocks away, but Lindsay figured he'd better walk it. There would be no swimming in this harbor.

Officially the avenue was posted as Lascar Row and the continuous argument was whether the nickname of Cat Street came from a century of cat burglars selling their wares in its alleys or from the welcoming bordellos that once lined its curb.

Lindsay headed up the narrow sidewalk until he came to a street of familiar storefronts. He was relieved to see the small spice shop he was looking for was still in business. The merchants on each side, however, had changed. The fabric retailer on the left was now selling cellular phones and pagers from Japan and personal computers from Taiwan. The storefront on the other side was covered with plywood sheets and gave no clue as to its next life.

Lindsay entered Zhang's Spice Shop expecting a strong bouquet of musty herbs and biting spices. Instead, he was welcomed only by diluted scents. Gone were the open wooden barrels of ginseng, the ropes of shredded bamboo skin, dried gecko lizard for sexual potency, and the vast array of anise seeds and deng xim grass. The spices that once lined the wall now filled modern glass cabinets. The shelves stacked with uncut fang ji roots, salted seahorse, and other exotic animal pieces brought in from mainland China were now sealed in large glass jars with chrome lids.

At the rear counter, a young girl stood beside a new cash register with illuminated green numerals. She twisted her braided ponytail between her fingers as she watched Lindsay approach.

Lindsay smiled at the girl. "Is Mr. Zhang in?" he asked in flawless Cantonese.

The girl's mouth dropped slightly in surprise. She had expected the tourist to look around, take a picture or two, and then leave without a purchase. They all did that from time to time. She neither nodded nor shook her head, but simply disappeared through a doorway that Lindsay remembered led into the house behind the store.

A moment later, a young man with a round flat face and narrow eyes emerged. The girl remained half hidden near the doorway peering at the tall tourist.

The young man moved behind the counter to where Lindsay stood. Lindsay noted his black American-made

Levi's, short-sleeve designer shirt, and the cellular phone that hung like a six-shooter from his belt. He eyed Lindsay suspiciously but grinned with perfectly white teeth.

"May I help you?" he said in English.

"I'd like to see Mr. Zhang."

"I'm Mr. Zhang."

"No," Lindsay specified. "I'm looking for Zhang Jing."

"That's my father. I'm sorry, he no longer runs the store."

"Could you tell him Lindsay Chase stopped by?"

The young man's expression changed instantly. The tight lips and sharp eyes softened. "The reporter?"

"The same," Lindsay confirmed.

"Please," the young man said, motioning Lindsay toward the back door. "He will be very happy to see you." As they stepped past the girl, the young man whispered for her to bring tea.

Lindsay followed young Mr. Zhang through the back room and into a narrow hall that led into a tiny kitchen filled with the rich aromas. In the next room, two young boys sat transfixed in front of a new color television that was showing an American movie about a boobytrapped bus racing through Los Angeles. They didn't look up from the nonstop action as Lindsay passed.

Young Mr. Zhang led Lindsay out the back door and into an enclosed garden that was not more than ten feet by ten. It was a lush patch of Eden dissected by a clothesline draped with women's underthings. The hot air smelled of mulch and starch.

In the far corner of the yard, on his hands and knees, Zhang Jing worked the dark, freshly turned soil. In his late sixties, his sparse gray hair looked like the bristles of a cactus on the back of his leathery neck.

"Ba-ba," young Zhang called to his father. "There is someone here to see you."

"Who?" Jing barked as he struggled to his feet. The awkwardness of Jing's movements gave Lindsay a disheartening feeling.

With his right arm hanging useless at his side, the old man used the nearby fence post to lift himself. Young Zhang moved to aid his father.

"Who's here?" Jing asked as he turned. He smiled crookedly as he saw the American standing in his garden. He wiped his left hand on his trousers and extended it.

Lindsay shook it with his own left hand. He wanted to ask, but he could not find the words. Lindsay's expression, however, gave him away.

"A small stroke," Jing said passively. "Last June."

"I didn't know."

"Ah." Jing gave a dismissing wave with his good hand. "I have been dealt far worse in my life. I adjust."

Jing's son helped him to the wicker chair in front of the circular stone table. Lindsay took the opposite chair. The young man pulled up a third chair and sat between them. Jing put a hand on his shoulder. "You never met Mun?"

"He was in college, I think."

"NYU," Mun said proudly.

Jing's smile widened. "A man can do nothing better than have a son, Lindsay."

The girl stepped from the house with a steaming pot of tea and three white porcelain cups. "And a beautiful daughter, too," he said as he set the tray on the center of the table and poured the tea. "And you'll go to college like your brother, right, Anson?"

The girl smiled shyly and slipped back into the house. Men were to talk now and she knew not to listen.

Jing eyed Lindsay's leg. "We all went to the hospital that day, but the nurses said you had been transferred to a special facility in Tokyo. It was very strange. We have very good hospitals here with good Chinese doctors."

"I know."

"I thought maybe you'd been killed and the newspaper was covering it up."

"No such luck."

"So you are back at the *Tribune?*"

"No."

"Just as well. There's no free press here anymore. The communists intimidate the newspapers and the broadcasters."

"So I've heard."

"Beijing wants to censor all the news from the West. How

are the taipans supposed to run their business under such rules? They're chasing them out of Hong Kong.'' He shook his head in disgust. "I fought the Japanese when they invaded. Now my country is invading my home and there's nothing I can do.''

The crippled man across the table, Lindsay remembered, led the Chinese resistance in Hong Kong during World War II. He helped over seven hundred Chinese escape their bloody occupation. The Japanese executed his first wife and young family in retribution.

"You've come about Tommy Fong," Jing said as he noisily drank his tea.

Lindsay nodded as he sipped from a white porcelain cup. The tea was hot against his tongue but sweet and quenching.

"For a story?''

"No. No stories.''

"He died badly," Jing said softly.

"I know.''

"The cops had to use fingerprints to tell who he was," Mun added.

"Any idea what he was doing?''

"He hadn't been around for several weeks.''

"Anybody go to the *Post* and ask?''

"The police are investigating.''

"The *Wen Wei Po* reported he was smuggling for the Sun Yee Triads. And they chopped him up," Mun said.

"*Aiya,*" Jing spat. "Tommy had nothing to do with gangsters. That paper is a mouthpiece of Beijing. They print lies.''

"You haven't heard anything else?" Lindsay asked the older man.

"Someone said he was staying at the Conrad Hotel, in the Imperial Suite. But that was talk at the mah-jongg table.''

Lindsay folded his arms and leaned back into his wicker chair. "Ritzy place.''

"The most expensive in Hong Kong," Mun said.

"I don't believe it. If Tommy had such money," Jing said, "his friends would be after him for his debts.''

Lindsay held his cup as Mun poured him more tea.

"You poke about," Jing warned, "and his fate may turn into yours.

"That's why I'll need some help."

Jing grinned. *"Maijiang."*

"No. No *maijiang*, Jing. You don't owe me anything."

The old man's face turned serious. "When those punks came to my shop for protection money, there was no need for you to get involved. But you showed them I had no need for their services. Up and down the street they forced the store owners to pay, but me, they never bothered again.

"The money I would have had to pay put Mun through college. You know it is not easy for a Chinese to admit, Lindsay, but I will always be in your debt."

"Then here." Lindsay reached into his pocket and drew out the folded manila envelope. He slipped out the photograph and handed it to Jing. "Tell me who she is and we'll call it even."

"She is very beautiful. I wish I did know her."

"Did you know Tommy owned such an expensive suit?" Lindsay asked.

"Andy Lee and I saw him outside the Government House all dressed up like that. He acted as if he didn't know us," the old man said with a shrug. "Andy was mad as a cat, but Tommy was that way sometimes. Very secretive." He passed the photo to his son.

"This looks like Aberdeen," Mun said.

"Yeah, north docks," Lindsay confirmed. "How about this?" Lindsay dropped the pendant into Jing's hand.

"They sell this sort of thing on Kansu Street."

"Is it worth anything?"

"'Twenty-nine dollars and fifty cents in American money," Mun guessed. "If the gold is real."

"It looks older. Maybe it's worth something more." Jing handed it back. "Where did you get it?"

"A friend."

"Lindsay!" a cheerful voice came from the house. He turned to see Mrs. Zhang with her broad toothy smile. She rushed to him and wrapped her arms around his waist as he stood. *"Fun-ying,"* she said welcoming him.

"You look well," Lindsay said.

"You lie." She laughed. Mrs. Zhang saw the black cane leaning against the table. She looked down at Lindsay's legs. Her eyes darted back to his face, concerned. "Your leg?"

"It's the only place they got me," he said.

"When we didn't hear from you, we feared it was worse."

"Sorry, I didn't call but . . ."

"American newspapermen are impossible to kill," Jing goaded his friend.

Seeing her husband's teacup empty, Mrs. Zhang automatically moved to fill it. "Did you see what my son has done to the store? All modern. We have computers to keep records and a fax machine to order directly from our suppliers in Taiwan. Soon we will be able to send all our children to the American university."

"*Aiya* . . ." Jing raised his good hand in mock protest. "Our guest has not come to hear your boasting. Make us dinner."

"No, I can't stay," Lindsay pleaded, but Mrs. Zhang would hear none of his excuses and disappeared into the house to begin the preparation.

Dinner had been filling after the fourth dish, when three more were still coming out of the kitchen in the hands of Anson. There was roast chicken, hot flower soup, fish cakes, and deep-fried vegetables. It was a meal Mrs. Zhang had made, Lindsay knew, only because he was there. No matter how well the store was doing, such extravagant dining was only common in the households of business tycoons and taipans.

He left a little after nine P.M. and headed back down the hill toward the harbor. His knee felt good. Mrs. Zhang had given him a small plastic bag of black powdered herbs, some of which she had added to his tea. "Put it in anything hot you drink," she said, handing him the bag. "It will help." He hooked his cane over his arm and walked unaided all the way to Wing Lok Street.

From there, he walked to Connaught Road and caught

a city bus crammed with storekeepers, teenagers, and businessmen shouting into cellular phones while rushing home for late dinners and a few moments with their children.

At Queensway and Tamar Street, the bus squealed to a stop. Lindsay made his way to the door and was swept out with the wave of darkly clad teenagers heading for the sparkling Pacific Place shopping plaza.

This was the generation too young for the local pubs and topless bars, yet they needed to escape the constraints of home and parents. Thus the subculture of the shopping mall. It was the same here as it was in Liverpool or Rapid City. The climatically controlled environments of marble-lined halls and cavernous music stores and clothing boutiques had replaced the drive-in theaters and corner ice-cream parlors.

Lindsay didn't follow the rush inside but edged the mall entrance and headed up the hill above the plaza. There, perched over the huge shopping and entertainment complex, was the exclusive Conrad Hotel. At over fifty stories tall, the wedge-shaped blue and silver glass building overlooked Harcourt Road and provided a panoramic view of the harbor.

The young Zhang was right: This had to be the most luxurious hotel in the colony. Lindsay moved to a vacant bench across the street and sat down. In the span of thirty minutes, he noted four limousines, six Rolls-Royces, half a dozen big Mercedes Benzes, and a vintage Bentley come into the circular driveway to pick up or drop somebody off. Each time the vehicle was met by a valet in white uniform trimmed with gold.

Everyone walking through the sheet-glass doors was dressed in the most fashionable attire. Businessmen and their wives, businesswomen and their husbands, all going to dine at the Capriccio or the Pierrot or maybe to enjoy an evening at the Hong Kong Philharmonic.

Lindsay had stopped to check one thing at the Conrad and he was annoyed to see it so well implemented. Its security. At the main entrance it had so far been flawless. Not one person had entered or left without careful, though respectful scrutiny by two uniformed doormen. At the secondary entrance there was another doorman and a uniformed guard at the ticket booth for the underground carport the hotel shared with the shopping mall.

Lindsay realized if Tommy had a suite here, he was going to have a hell of a time getting into it.

Chapter Five

Hong Kong Island, 1898

The young boy under the white linen bedsheets looked up from the Bible perched on his chest as he heard the side door downstairs swing open and slam against the stone wall of the church. It had done that many times during the monsoon winds of June, but it was now October and the weather was mild.

The chimes of the grandfather clock in the outer hall near his parents' room had just struck the last bell of nine and was still echoing in his head.

Closing the heavy book, Nathan Harrington pushed a strand of his fine blond hair from his eyes and listened. The night was silent again, peaceful and content. Then he heard it: a sound as of someone pulling a sack of potatoes across the wooden floor of the vestry, one floor below his room. Nathan held his breath as the scraping continued. Then silence.

"There is nothing to fear here, Nathan," his father had said the first night they had moved into the drafty cathedral of creaking doors and dismal rooms. "This is the house of God. Where else could you be safer?" Then his father had blown out the candle and left Nathan to sleep in the darkness.

They had come to this small church on the north side of Hong Kong Island four years ago when Nathan was two. His father, Edmund, and his mother, Lona, were missionaries, which, Nathan surmised, made him and his sister, Elisa, missionaries, too. They had come from Cambridge. Well-to-dos who wanted to do more.

But China had existed for thousands of years without foreign religion and it was in no hurry to allow the Christian God and its righteous flock within her borders. So the Harringtons took residence in Hong Kong and waited. His father had traveled to Peking many times to press their cause, but the emigration papers never came. Finally Edmund had decided there were enough lost souls to save in Hong Kong, and that's where they'd remained.

The sound came again, the sack being pulled farther across the floor, and with it a moan. A deep, heavy moan of a man in agony.

Nathan crawled across his large quilted bed and slid off the side. He lifted the brass candlestick from the nightstand and stepped from his room. Cautiously, he descended the staircase to the main floor. He held the edge of his nightgown, more for comfort than for concern of dragging it. Each step along the stone floor chilled the bare bottoms of his small feet. Passing behind the altar, he crept toward the solid inner door of the vestry. In the flickering light, the giant iron hinges looked like black fingers stretched across its timbers.

The bolt squealed with alarm as Nathan pulled it back. With the candle ahead of him, he opened the door. The flame bowed to the moist breeze of Victoria Harbor as it whirled in through the outer door. Across the bay, Kowloon was in clear view, her lamp-lined streets ablaze like fireflies caught in a spider's web.

Nathan cupped his hand around the candle, allowing the flame to stand again. Suddenly, from the shadows, he felt a cold hand grab his naked ankle.

Nathan screamed. The candle dropped, dying as it hit the floor. He ran, but something held him at the threshold by his nightgown. Madly he pulled at the thin material until it ripped and he was sent toppling out the door and into the hall. He looked over his shoulder, expecting the ghastly creature to lunge at him from the darkness.

Instead, the hall began to brighten of its own accord. Nathan looked to see the huge, barrel-chested figure of his father rushing toward him carrying a large candelabrum.

"What in God's name are you doing, Nathan?" Edmund reached down and lifted his son by the arm. "Get off the floor."

"In . . . in there," Nathan said between quick breaths. He felt his father squeeze his shoulder with reassurance.

"Come on, let's see what it is," his father said, his green eyes glittering in the candles' flames. Edmund Harrington was a big, powerful man standing over six feet, with silver hair and beard and thick dark eyebrows, a descendant of masons who had built Cambridge University. A man with giant hands and a soft-spoken voice who followed the teachings of God. Extending his arm, Edmund let the circle of light lead them into the vestry. His nightgown billowed around him as he stepped into the room.

The crumbled, lifeless figure of a man lay stretched out on the floor. "Shut the door," Edmund said quickly as he knelt beside the man. Nathan wrestled to pull the outside door closed.

"The hall door, too," his father instructed as he set the candelabrum on a small bookshelf.

Nathan did what he was told and then returned to his father's side. The man was English. His clothes, although torn and stained, were of the finest quality. Clutched in one hand he held a thin leather pouch.

Edmund rolled him over and propped him up against the wall. There was a deep slash across his right cheek. Nathan had seen the man before, several times in the churchyard speaking with his father.

Pushing his eyelids up, Edmund searched for a response. The man jerked his head away. He moaned painfully and coughed.

"Shaftsbury, it's me," Edmund said as he held the man's head. "What happened to you, man?"

Shaftsbury opened his eyes slowly. "The pouch." Shaftsbury's voice was hoarse and low. "The pouch," he said as he began to look around in panic. "Where is it?"

"You shouldn't have come here," Edmund said sharply. His father's voice revealed an anger Nathan had never heard before.

"The pouch!"

"It's here," Edmund said, trying to calm him. He grabbed Shaftsbury by the shoulder and the man let out a cry that made Nathan wince.

Pulling off his coat, Edmund found a bullet hole through the left side of Shaftsbury's chest and another through his right forearm. "Nathan, in the drawer there's a knife. Get it."

"There's no time," Shaftsbury said weakly.

"You should've gone to headquarters."

"I tried." Shaftsbury rolled his head to the side and coughed blood onto the floor.

Nathan handed his father the knife and Edmund cut the sleeve from Shaftsbury's coat. "You're bleeding to death," he said as he used the cloth to make a tourniquet.

"Edmund." Shaftsbury grabbed him by the nightshirt. "You have to get this to the Governor." He waved the pouch weakly.

"It'll wait."

"No! My God, man, you don't realize," Shaftsbury said as he opened it with his good hand and pushed the letters at Edmund.

Nathan's father set the knife beside him and looked at the papers in the candlelight. Nathan moved closer and peered over his father's shoulder.

Nathan could see they were written in Chinese, with a column of English translation on the side. There looked to be a half dozen sheets of handmade pages, and as Edmund flipped through them, Nathan only picked out a few words. But at the end of the last sheet he saw an elaborate design of two dragons circling a flaming pearl. It had been imprinted there with a pasty yellow ink.

"Where did you get this?" Edmund said finally as he looked up.

"From the Dowager Empress herself," Shaftsbury said, his teeth clenched as he took a breath. "It's payment, Edmund, for a deal she made with Brigham."

"But the treaty's in place."

"It doesn't matter. Those are the Seals of the Imperial Court. The New Territories, Kowloon, all of Hong Kong is now British soil. It's all ours."

"That can't be." Edmund was stunned. He read Brigham's letter to the Queen. "Oh, Mother of God, what has he done?"

"Brigham never made it out of Peking. I met his ship and found this hidden in his sea trunk. I didn't know I was followed." Shaftsbury took another breath and Nathan could see he was getting weaker.

"What is going on here?" Nathan's mother pushed open the hall door. Her white nightgown was illuminated in the dancing candlelight as she stepped into the room, her chestnut hair, usually tied in a thick chignon, undone and falling in soft full waves over her shoulders. Her gentle green eyes widened as she saw Shaftsbury's blood-soaked clothes.

"Go back to bed," Edmund said, his voice carrying that strange anger again. "Go on, right now."

But Lona heard nothing of her husband's words, nor the urgency in his voice once she saw the blood. From the wooden cabinet against the wall, she drew the extra linens and began to tear them into strips. "Nathan, run for Dr. Welsh. Be quick."

"No!" Edmund grabbed his son's wrist before he could get to his feet.

"Mother?" Elisa, Nathan's little sister, was at the edge of the door rubbing her eyes with small fists. Under her arm she held a rag doll made by their grandmother in Hertford. Her nightgown was a size too big and dragged across the floor like a miniature wedding dress.

Edmund stood and turned to his wife. Both anger and plea filled his voice. "All of you to your rooms. Now!"

It was then Nathan heard the quick footsteps on the stone path outside. A wave of terror stole his breath as he realized that he had not secured the bolt across the latch. He turned to warn his father, but there was no time. The door burst open with a single kick.

God played an awful trick then, slowing the events and allowing young Nathan to watch them as if everything were taking place upon a stage. He first heard the scream of his sister as she backed away, and then that of his mother as the Chinese man came in from the outside darkness and started to shoot wildly with the ugly black gun, its long muzzle spitting flames and thunder.

But the man seemed to hit nothing. Nathan saw his father reach under his nightgown and, as if by magic, a revolver appeared in his hand.

Edmund Harrington didn't have to aim; the motion was smooth and well practiced. He fired twice, once to the heart, once to the head. Both bullets hit their targets and the man crumpled in the doorway.

"Oh, God!" Lona screamed.

Grabbing his wife, Edmund pushed her back toward the church door. "Go to the cellar!" he ordered, but she was too afraid to leave him.

Edmund knelt beside Shaftsbury. The Englishman was dead, his eyes frozen open. "Bastard," Nathan's father said as he pushed the papers and the letter back into the pouch.

More quick footsteps, and a shot from the distance penetrated the doorway, shattering the stone wall near Edmund's head. As he pushed Nathan to the floor, the next bullet caught the big man's shoulder. The following two found his chest and stomach.

"Edmund!" Lona dove toward her husband. She never reached him. The men shooting from outside took her life with a single bullet through the throat. She fell across Nathan.

"Nathan," his father hollered as he pulled his wife's body from his son. "Listen to me! Take your sister and go to the army headquarters. Run as fast as you can, son!"

But Nathan was frozen, his eyes wide with fear. He could not move as he stared at his mother and the thick red blood that poured from the gaping hole in her neck.

Edmund fired a shot out the door, then grabbed Nathan and pulled him close. He stared into his son's eyes, and in a deep, powerful voice he said, "Don't feel, Nathan, not now. You have to take Elisa. You have to protect her for me." And with one hand, Edmund shoved his son toward the hallway. "Now go!"

As Nathan scrambled across the floor, his hand landed on Shaftsbury's pouch. Unthinking, he clutched on to it, taking it with him as he raced for the door. Looking back, the last image Nathan saw was his father pulling his mother's body into his arms.

Nathan didn't see the rest. He had left the doorway before his father put his gun barrel to his lips. Damn the army, Edmund Harrington thought, damn the Crown and Queen Victoria herself. Then he pulled the trigger.

Elisa was behind the altar, huddled under the thick velvet drapes that surrounded it. Nathan knew she would be there even before he heard her crying. It was her secret hiding place that everyone knew about.

Nathan grabbed her thin wrist. "Come on," he whispered. After that last shot there had been no more, but inside the vestry, he heard men yelling, not in Cantonese but in Mandarin.

"Mother?" Elisa cried.

Nathan didn't answer her. Hunched over, they ran down along the pews, out the north entrance and into the street. The air outside was cool and the street was shiny black from a light rain that had dissolved into a clear night. Wan Chai Gap Road was winding, dark, and deserted, and by the time they reached the crossing where it split into three other avenues, they were tired and out of breath.

Leaning against an old fence, Nathan looked at his sister. Her shoulders shaking with fear, but there were no longer tears. There was no time for them. He pulled her closer to him under the shadows.

"Two ways to the headquarters from here," he whispered. "The way Father goes or the shortcut."

"We're not supposed to take the shortcut," she reminded him.

"It'll be okay this time," Nathan promised as he pushed away from the fence. He looked up the road toward the church but saw nothing. Taking Elisa's wrist, he began to run again.

The shortcut would go through the *wan*, one of the areas set aside for Chinese residence. Nathan's father had warned him never to go there at night, and during the day only when he was accompanied by someone from the church. But Nathan's worry now was getting to the British headquarters. Father would understand, he thought as they headed down one of the narrow alleys.

Elisa could barely keep up with her brother's pace. She fell once, tripping over a metal pan and sending it clanging against the cobblestones. A window opened and an old woman looked for the cause of such racket on a quiet night. She said something under her breath, but Nathan didn't bother to translate it in his head.

The *wan* seemed different at night. It was as though Nathan had never been through this part of the city before. His frustration built into anger as he feared they were lost. Finally, stepping from the alley, he could see the glow of Kowloon. It gave him bearings as he knew the garrison was near the waterfront. He turned to Elisa and smiled. "A few more blocks," he said.

The two children were almost out of the *wan* when the men bolted from an alleyway in front of them. Squeezing Elisa's hand, Nathan froze. At first the men looked in the wrong direction; then one turned and his eyes fell on them.

He yelled in Mandarin.

"Run!" Nathan screamed as he yanked her back toward the *wan*. But Elisa couldn't keep up and was further terrified by the new urgency in her brother's voice. Nathan desperately kept her running.

Out of the night came thunder. It pierced Nathan's ears as he felt Elisa tug away from him, her hand jerking from his grasp. At first he thought she had fallen. But when he looked at her crumpled body laying against the stone walk, she was as lifeless as the rag doll she still clutched.

Thunder again, and with it an explosion of pain ripped into his side. He stumbled backward but kept to his feet. He moved to his little sister. "I have to take you to the headquarters," he told her. "Father said."

The second bullet caught his left thigh, spun him about, and threw him to the ground.

From half-consciousness, the world turned gray and ghostly, yet the sounds around him were sharp and clear. He heard the men approach, one of them walking with an odd scraping step. Then someone was rolling him over and he could hear their heavy breathing as they knelt beside him.

As they pried Brigham's pouch from his hand, Nathan managed to open his eyes and see the harsh Chinese face hovering above him. It was lined hideously with thick red scars across the left cheek that ended at the nub of an ear. The man's olive-black eyes locked on to Nathan's. He snarled like some grotesque animal, grabbed Nathan by the throat, and lifted him. Nathan felt the warm ring of the pistol barrel press against his forehead.

From somewhere in the alley a creaking door opened and someone yelled. Another angry voice from somewhere else, then another from above. The gun was pulled away and his body released.

Nathan fell at the man's feet. Only inches away from his face, Nathan saw the strange black shoe of the man with the gun. It was cut off sharply at the instep, leaving no toe, just a flat of thick leather. A clubfoot, Nathan recognized. Once he had teased a clubfooted beggar and his father had scolded and lectured him on the hardships of others.

In the darkness of the *wan*, Nathan heard more voices, angered voices, coming closer. There was shouting, then Nathan heard the footsteps of the man with the clubfoot and his companion as they quickly ran away.

After a moment there were other hands on him, gentle hands. It was then the pain brought him sleep.

Chapter Six

Hong Kong Island

The animal panted deeply as it rested in the shade beneath the broad leaves of the banana tree. Stretching out its powerful forelegs, it flexed its muscles and lifted its head, welcoming the fresh breeze that came across the meadow.

The chattering of monkeys and the squawking of birds on high tree limbs filled the valley. It was a pleasant day, a lazy day. Still, the animal was careful to listen to the world around him. He was aware of everything. Every noise, every smell and taste that drifted on the wind. Not a shadow nor sparkle of light through the branches would go unnoticed.

He rolled onto his side in the thick grass. It was soft and cool. This was a comfortable place and he came here often. As he settled in for an afternoon nap, the animal sensed a subtle change. Something new was on the breeze. It was faint but distinct and it came from the lower valley, where the twin creeks met and where the black boulder had fallen last winter. He sat up.

It was a message. A lilac branch had been broken and, unlike the fragrant aroma of its purple flowers, its greenish sap carried a more pungent smell. It drifted fast and strong into the meadow.

But what had shattered the small branch? A brutish hog? A

clumsy fawn following its mother through uncertain terrain? Perhaps a . . . The crushing of the wet gravel along the creek suddenly filled the animal's perceptive ears. There was no question now. Whatever it was, it was moving toward him.

To the animal, things were simple. Anything coming here was either prey or a predator. There could be nothing else in his world because he knew of nothing else. Prey was always welcome into his realm. But if this was something else, a predator who came to kill, then that, too, would be welcome because that sparked a different kind of hunger. A hunger that was always within the animal.

If the maker of the sound crossed the far line of trees, then in his mind it would become prey. This was his domain, his territory.

The animal realized the sound had changed. The movement of the intruder had turned into a quicker pace. His ears perked up, his panting stopped, and he turned his head, trying to detect new sounds, new signals.

Nothing but prey, he told himself.

The sound changed again as the intruder's pace turned to a full run. Now there was no doubt; it had come to challenge, come to kill.

Nothing but prey.

Adrenaline surged into the animal's veins and the pumping of his heart turned into a deep pounding in his chest. His eyes sharpened and his nostrils flared. More air, fresh air. Feed the lungs, quench the blood, power the muscles.

Nothing but prey.

In an instant, the animal was ready for the assault that was coming. To his feet, he bound toward the far side of the meadow, charging the oncoming menace. Faster and faster he ran, his potent legs catapulting him toward the spot where he knew it would emerge.

Nothing but prey.

As the powerful animal reached the thicket, the branches parted and the intruder broke through. It was a shadowy figure of a man, a faceless man with a high-powered rifle. The animal lunged, his claws extended. . . .

Lindsay sprang up in bed, his chest heaving in surges. His hands clutched the edges of the bed, almost tearing through the bedsheets. Every muscle in his body was taut, drawn tight like the strings of a musical instrument.

He eased himself back into his pillows as he tried to

control his heart. The thin sheets, drenched with his sweat, clung to his skin.

After several minutes, he wandered into the bathroom. Splashing cold water on his face, he stared at the mirror with bloodshot eyes. It was beginning again. Whether he wanted it or not, his mind was wrestling with its dark secrets again. The shrink in the military hospital, with his gray Freudian beard, had warned him. "It's not going to take much to trigger it," he had said. "You have to separate yourself from everything you once were.

"The mind is very powerful, Mr. Chase. We don't know that much about it," he had said, looking over Lindsay's evaluations. "I can only guess what you boys were into, but you've tapped into parts of the brain I wouldn't even want to know were there."

The doctor had set his folder on top of the crisp white sheets of the hospital bed. "Don't handle a gun, Mr. Chase. Don't take out your old gear. Don't drive by your old office. None of that. It's like being an alcoholic. You're always an alcoholic. The difference being, most drink and some don't."

Well, Lindsay was drinking again. Drinking heavily. All the training the CIA had given him was flooding back. Lindsay wondered if he could still control it. That rush of power his mind generated over his body. Or, as he had been warned, would it control him?

The mirror told him he had slept for the last ten years. He stepped into the shower and let the water wake him.

The warm early morning greeted Lindsay as he stepped from the lobby of his hotel. Predawn Hong Kong was dark and wet and quiet. The tapping of his cane was soon lost in the growing noise of traffic and the shuffle of shopkeepers rushing to begin the day. They emerged from the trams and buses like single-minded fire ants attacking a hornet's nest.

That was the miracle of Hong Kong. Its business was business and its population pressed forth with transcendental determination. Let the communists come, they seemed to mutter under their breaths. Let them stand in the streets wearing their oversized caps and cadre uniforms clutching old copies of Marx and Mao and let them wonder how it all works. How this clod of dirt on the tip of the dragon's toe could be the third largest financial center in the world. Let them come. We will continue our business as usual.

By the time Lindsay reached the looping overpass that transferred traffic from Queensway onto Justice Drive, Mun was already there waiting behind the wheel of his father's green delivery van. It was one of those Japanese models built for impossibly narrow alleys and small drivers. With a wire-thin steering wheel, faulty speedometer, and no fuel gauge, it had witnessed much better days. Days before the bumper had fallen off and the crack in the windshield looked like a varicose vein. Wearing a pair of powder-blue overalls and a Detroit Tigers baseball cap turned backward on his head, young Mun fit his part perfectly.

"This is cool," Mun said as Lindsay climbed into the passenger seat. "My dad's always told me about his crawling a mile though the city sewer to get messages to the underground."

"He saved a lot of people during the war."

"I hope we don't have to."

"Save people?"

"Crawl through the sewer."

"Me neither," Lindsay said as he slipped into the overalls Mun had brought. It was the largest he could find on short notice. Mrs. Zhang had sewn the shop's logo onto the back. "Did you call?"

"Yeah. The Imperial Suite was booked and paid for through the end of the month," Mun said as he edged into the growing traffic and merged onto Queensway. "Don't you think the police would have searched it by now?"

"I'm hoping they didn't know about it."

The traffic thickened and they slowed to a walker's pace.

"We've talked about starting our own underground. My friends and me. When the soldiers get here, it's going to be the only way to survive."

Lindsay thought for a moment. He remembered the third of June in Tiananmen Square. The CNN broadcasts of young men like Mun running bloodied and scared. And he remembered seeing a photograph in his editor's office of a huge banner hanging from one of Hong Kong's business towers; BLOOD MUST BE PAID WITH BLOOD it had said. What could they do? A handful of Chinese yuppies against an entrenched dynasty of faceless emperors? Nothing. They could do nothing. "Don't, Mun," Lindsay said finally. "Work the shop and send your sister to college."

"That's easy for you to say." Mun grunted with disappointment.

"What did you bring?" Lindsay returned to immediate business.

"Birds' nests."

"Wonderful. . . ."

"I know guys who've bused the Golden Leaf. They serve only the best Cantonese. I doubled the price on the invoice to get you in. Too cheap and they'll know this is a scam."

"I hope you're right."

"You want me to wait?"

"Only until the guard gets busy with something else. Then take off when he's not looking. That way he'll think we left together."

"I could start a diversion or something?"

"No," Lindsay said, taking the baseball cap from the would-be subversive. He pulled it low over his face. "You just go back to work. I'll call you if I need anything."

Mun shrugged unhappily as he made a right turn into the looping driveway and darted into the delivery tunnel that led under the hotel. On Lindsay's instruction, he drove past the guard booth and into the shipping bay. The uniformed guard, with clipboard in hand, leaped from his tiny glass closet and chased after them.

Mun climbed from the truck armed with his own clipboard. He waved to the guard. Lindsay stepped to the rear of the panel truck. Sliding back the flimsy door, he hooked his cane on his forearm and lifted out the cardboard box of carefully packed birds' nests.

"Who you delivering for?" the guard asked sharply.

"Zhang's Spice Shop. First time we deliver here." Mun turned on the charm and broken English. "Lucky for us, other store all out of bird's nest. Golden Branch chef call us directly. Rush order."

"Golden Leaf," the guard corrected him. "Why they'd order birds' nest from a spice shop?"

"Because we have freshest in Hong Kong. Arrive from Shaoguan this morning. Chef lucky we have his order. Here." He shoved the clipboard into the guard's hand. "Sign, sign."

As the guard scribbled his initials at the bottom, Mun glanced toward the truck. Lindsay was gone.

The former agent moved down the sterile hall toward the kitchens. The clattering of pots and pans drew him toward a set of double swing doors. A dishwasher, an elderly man in his seventies, stepped out. He looked up at Lindsay, somewhat startled.

"Kitchen?"

"Kitchen?" the Chinese dishwasher realized Lindsay didn't know where to deliver his package. He looked at the writing on the box. *"Aiya . . . Qing ni ba-ta gei wo!"*

"Sorry, don't speak the lingo," Lindsay lied.

The man nodded understandingly and led Lindsay farther down the hall. Rounding two corners, he pointed Lindsay toward another set of white swinging doors. Through the small glass window, Lindsay saw the commotion of another kitchen.

"Golden Weef," the man said in the best English he could muster.

Lindsay thanked him and waited until the man retreated down the hall. He found a storage room and slipped inside. Hiding his delivery among boxes of cleaning fluid, Lindsay peeled off the overalls and crammed them and the cap under a fifty-pound sack of rice. Straightening his slacks and shirt, Lindsay stepped confidently into the hall.

He walked through the kitchen of the Golden Leaf, side-stepping the hustle of cooks and waiters. They were all too busy with dim sum orders to notice him.

Entering the restaurant, Lindsay weaved through the freshly set tables of white linens and ivory chopsticks. The tuxedoed maître d' looked questioningly at Lindsay as he gave him a nod of approval and exited the dining room.

As Lindsay knew, the entrance of the Golden Leaf Restaurant was one floor below the gamboge-colored lobby of the Conrad. He climbed the zigzag staircase, crossed the luxuriant marbled floor, and passed the sweeping, columned walls decorated with giant chrysanthemums and butterflies.

At the elevators, Lindsay stabbed the up button with the tip of his cane and waited. Sensing the concierge's curious eyes from across the lobby, he rocked carefree back and forth on his heels.

A chime from above, and a vacant elevator arrived. Lindsay stepped in and pressed the button for the top floor. With effort, he kept himself from making eye contact with anyone. The steel doors slid closed and the elevator whisked Lindsay upward.

The Imperial Suite was easy to find. Lindsay headed down the lavishly carpeted hall toward the side of the Conrad that faced Victoria Harbor. The most expensive suite would have the most extensive view. A brass plaque labeling the suite hung like an address marker on the thick mahogany door. People who stayed here liked that sort of thing. If they intended to spend thousands of dollars a night, then they wanted it announced.

Lindsay looked casually up and down the hallway. He was pleased to see no cameras or sensors. Security was at the perimeter of the Conrad. Inside, the most expensive hotel in the colony lavished its guests with nothing but the finest of Asian graces and traditions.

Laying his hand on the door, he pressed his ear to the jamb. Nothing. Dead silence. Lindsay evaluated the electronic key card lock above the brass doorknob. It was the newest gadget to give hotel guests a sense of comfort. And like the new gas station pumps and ATM machines, only a coded credit card key could open it. Or so hotel guests thought.

Lindsay reached into his pocket and withdrew the thin magnetic strip he had borrowed from Mrs. Zhang's refrigerator door. It was an odd request, but Mrs. Zhang reattached her Chinese calendar with a piece of tape and thought little more of it.

Slipping the strip into the key slot, Lindsay sawed it back and forth. A subtle click, and Lindsay opened the door.

The room was exactly as it was named. Imperial. An exquisite combination of strong, dark Chinese furnishings and Western style. The entry room was filled with lush green potted palms, its blackwood tables and chairs polished to a spotless shine. Thick, soft carpets drew Lindsay inward.

In the dining room on the left was a glass table surrounded by twelve leather chairs. A line of miniature statues of Chinese gods and goddesses stood at attention in a rosewood cabinet. To the right was a study dominated by a black lacquer wardrobe containing a wide-screen television and stereo equipment. An English writer's table was perched in front of floor-to-ceiling windows. Outside, across the harbor, Kowloon was bathing in the morning sun. Lindsay found himself enchanted by the view.

The slamming of a dresser drawer from deeper inside the Imperial pulled Lindsay instantly back to where he was and what he was doing. In quick, silent steps he was down the hall and at the edge of the master bedroom. Like the rest of the suite, the room was filled with fine furniture, cloisonné figures of armored elephants, and fanciful ivory Buddhas.

From the dressing room, someone huffed in frustration and hammered another drawer. Setting his cane against the wall, Lindsay edged the doorway of the spacious dressing room and peered inside.

With her back toward Lindsay, the woman rifled the vanity drawer. She wore a short black skirt and a silver satin blouse. Her hair, long and black, flowed over her slender shoulders to the center of her back. She was tall, with long toned legs on top of black dagger heels. Lindsay got a glimpse of her face as she stepped past the full-length mirror attached to the wall. It was her. The young woman in the photograph from Aberdeen. Stepping off the docks she seemed attractive, but here, in person, her beauty caught Lindsay by surprise. She had porcelain skin and sharp, nutmeg-brown eyes set in a fashion model's face with high cheekbones and a small nose.

"Son of a bitch!" she slammed the drawer closed. On the marble vanity, she eyed a small urn adorned with red hibiscus flowers.

"Lose something?" Lindsay asked calmly.

She turned and glared at him. Then she grabbed the crystal lamp beside the urn and launched it. Lindsay ducked as it exploded against the wall.

She darted for the door. Lindsay caught her by the wrists and pulled her back into the room. She swung wildly, her fingers like a cat's claw scratching at his face and taking a sliver of skin from behind his ear.

"Jesus." Lindsay pushed her away in time to avoid the next flinging fingernail. He spun her around and twisted her arm into her back. The girl screamed at the sharp bolt of pain, but still she struggled to get at him.

Lindsay torqued her arm further, cupped his hand over her mouth and nose and cut off her breath. He pulled her close and whispered into her ear, "Keep thrashing around and you're going to pass out."

The girl's chest heaved as she tried to free herself. Reaching back, she shoved her free hand between them and sought his most vulnerable possession. She found what she wanted.

"Shit!" Lindsay screamed from the immediate pressure. He slid his hand from her mouth to her throat. "Let go or I'll break your neck."

"And I'll rip you right out of your shorts."

Lindsay's fingers dug in around her thorax. He cared neither to kill this girl nor to receive the injury she was about to inflict. It was a standoff. "Truce?"

She hesitated. "Truce."

Lindsay eased his grip. She eased hers. His hand slipped away as he released her arm. She retracted her claws. They broke away from each other.

"Who the fuck are you?" she asked, rubbing her neck.

"A friend of Tommy Fong. And you?"

"His housekeeper."

Lindsay was about to grab her again and persuade a better answer when she suddenly looked past him. Her eyes widened with real fear.

He turned as the butt of a handgun slammed against his temple. His legs crumpled beneath him as he fell to the soft carpet.

Lindsay reeled from the pain. He felt a bony knee drop into the center of his back, pinning him to the floor. The cold steel of a gun barrel pressed against the back of his neck. Across the plain of carpet, Lindsay saw a pair of Nike running shoes under the cuff of tattered jeans. Another pair of shoes, cowboy boots of expensive alligator and ostrich leather, stepped into his view.

"The *gweilo* a cop?" Cowboy Boots asked.

Lindsay was rolled onto his back and the gun barrel shifted to his forehead. He kept his hands to his sides as the young Chinese sifted through his pockets. Crawling up the man's throat was the tattoo of a blue winged dragon.

"He's clean. No I.D.," he told Cowboy Boots.

Cowboy Boots was a thin wiry man, not much older than thirty, with a pockmarked face and cold eyes. His hair was slicked back Valentino-style. He drew a cigarette from the pocket of his Armani suit. "British?"

Dragon Throat shrugged.

"Say something, *gweilo,*" Cowboy Boots insisted.

Lindsay stared at him.

He kicked Lindsay in the ribs. "Say something."

"Ouch," Lindsay said dryly.

Cowboy Boots lifted an eyebrow. "An American." He looked at the girl. She had backed herself up against the wall. Her eyes darted from the door to Cowboy Boots and to his footmen. She'd never make the distance and she knew it.

"I'm getting very tired of this, Suzette," Cowboy Boots said as he stepped casually around Lindsay.

"I don't know him," she said.

Cowboy Boots moved close. He blew a lung of smoke out the corner of his mouth. "You don't?" As he glanced back at Lindsay, Suzette lashed violently at the Chinese thug. He had been expecting it. He parried her strike and retaliated with the back of his hand. The blow sent her to her knees and brought blood to the edge of her mouth.

Lindsay lurched upward, but the man with the gun had his knee in the center of his chest. "Danny," the tattooed man called Cowboy Boots, "we need this guy?"

"No. Float him," the thug said with a wave of his cigarette. He turned his attention back to the girl.

Lindsay knew the term. It was a clear reference to some-one floating in the harbor . . . dead.

The gun barrel remained on Lindsay's forehead as he was pulled to his feet. Lindsay got his first tally of the room. The Chinese in the jeans and Nikes stood just out of arm's reach with a chrome Colt .45 hanging in his left hand.

A third man, who stood at the door, was as thick and motionless as a bronze Buddha. His hairless domed head was perfectly spherical, marred only by two narrow slits for eyes, a narrow cut of a mouth, and a snub nose. Even his ears seemed to recede into his smooth skull.

Danny in the cowboy boots lifted Suzette by the hair. He pressed her to the wall. His cigarette dangled precariously near her face. She turned away, her eyes locking on Lind-say's. Her venom was gone, diluted by raw terror.

Danny followed her gaze and saw the man with the dragon on his neck move the gun to Lindsay's temple. *"Aiya!"*Danny snapped. "Not here. Take him to the parking lot. When you're done, meet us out front."

Dragon Throat nodded. He shoved Lindsay toward the door.

"Have a good swim," the one in the Nikes chuckled.

"Marty, go with him," Danny ordered the smiling Chinese with the .45.

As they stepped from the master bedroom, Lindsay heard Danny strike Suzette again. She screamed. "No more games," he threatened, and hit her again.

Lindsay's cane was still propped against the doorjamb and just out of reach. He was now sorry he had set it aside.

In the elevator, Lindsay was surprised to see Dragon Throat fish a key from his pocket and insert it into the control panel. The elevator descended nonstop to a private parking floor.

"Reserved parking? That must cost a premium," Lindsay said.

Dragon Throat stared stone-faced at Lindsay as he attached a cylindrical silencer to his weapon. Marty grinned.

The doors slid open onto a vacant parking floor. Dragon

Throat pushed Lindsay out. The two gunmen remained in the elevator.

"Wrong place, wrong time, huh?" Marty joked.

"Looks like it," Lindsay agreed as he watched Dragon Throat raise his silenced gun. "And all for a little piece of jade."

"What?" Marty asked.

"I was supposed to deliver a pendant," Lindsay said, slapping his pockets. "I was surprised you missed it."

Marty and Dragon Throat exchanged a glance as they stepped from the elevator. Marty moved close with anticipation.

"Yeah, here it is," Lindsay said as he reached into his pocket. But what he pulled out was not what the men had expected. It was pure primeval fury. Lindsay hit Marty with an upswinging elbow that lifted the Chinese off the floor.

Move! Lindsay's mind screamed. Pop, pop. Dragon Throat's silencer coughed, but its spits of lead found no target. Lindsay went low, his right leg sweeping the man's feet out from under him. He pancaked hard against the shiny cement floor, his head snapping back and sending him into oblivion.

Marty moaned as he tried to find his feet. Lindsay spun instantly about and, like a place kicker, punted the Chinese's face. The impact sent a tooth rattling across the garage. No doubt, when he woke, Marty would have less to smile about.

Lindsay snatched the silenced handgun and dove into the elevator. A twist of the key, and the elevator vaulted him back toward the Imperial Suite.

Lindsay entered the suite like one of Patton's tanks, its turret loaded and ready. He moved directly to the master bedroom. They were gone.

Meet us out front, was what Danny had said. Grabbing his cane, Lindsay rocketed out the door.

Holding Suzette tightly by the wrist, Danny reached for the rear door handle of the big blue Rolls-Royce Camargue as it slowed to a stop under the Conrad's rear facade. He looked over his shoulder at the Buddha.

"Zigao," he said impatiently. "Find them."

The big man nodded and disappeared into the hotel.

Danny's driver slid in behind the wheel as the valet held the door. There was no tip offered and the valet didn't expect one. He knew who these men were.

"Get in," Danny said as he pushed Suzette toward the car. He suddenly felt something hook his arm and pull him backward. It was a cane.

"She's with me," Lindsay said as he moved close to the harsh-faced Chinese. From under a throw-away newspaper he had grabbed in the lobby, Lindsay revealed the gun leveled at his gut. "Let her go."

"You don't know what you're doing," Danny said.

"Your friends in the garage weren't very nice. Don't piss me off any more."

Danny released Suzette's arm. She quickly stepped away.

"Now get in and go away."

Danny sneered. "I don't know you, *gweilo*. But I will."

"I'll look for your Christmas card in the mail," Lindsay said. He pushed the Chinese into the backseat of the Rolls and slammed the door.

Danny stared evilly at Lindsay through the side window, then motioned to the driver and the big car pulled away from the curb.

Lindsay turned to the girl, but she was gone. He frantically looked up and down the street. He caught a glimpse of her as she descended the stairway to the underground parking lot.

Lindsay ran after her. He heard the door of the first level close as he leaped down the stairs. He lost her in the dark oasis of parked automobiles. But from the back wall, he heard the grind of a starter motor and the pop of a small Japanese engine. A pair of headlights suddenly awakened and a silver Miata sports car leaped from between two sedans.

Lindsay darted through the cars to cut her off, though unsure how. He ran into the thoroughfare in front of the little two-seater. Its ear-piercing horn blared at him as Suzette aimed for the sunlight at the top of the exit ramp. At the last second, Lindsay realized she had no intention of stopping.

He dove from the oncoming car. As he hit the pavement, the silenced gun and newspaper flew from his hand. He rolled to his feet and chased after her.

The Miata accelerated up the ramp.

Lindsay's stride carried him even with the rear bumper for ten paces. "Wait!" he hollered.

It was no use. The car lunged from the lot, hit the street, fishtailed around a bus, and disappeared into the traffic.

Lindsay hobbled to one of the hotel's stone planters and leaned against it. His knee throbbed torturously. He looked back into the parking lot and saw a security guard standing over the handgun. The man was staring at him and talking excitedly into his two-way radio.

Lindsay cursed himself as he quickly headed up Justice Drive and into Hong Kong Park. Finding a shaded bench, he sat down and rubbed his stiffening knee. Well, he thought, at least she hadn't disappeared completely. He had a thread, a very thin thread on which to find her.

"It was green and about two inches square," Lindsay told Mun as he bit into the steamed dumpling. "With the letters T.M.A. across it in black."

Mun leaned forward on the table. "You think it was a parking sticker?"

"I'm hoping. It was right in the corner of the rear window."

"Then it shouldn't be too hard to find," the young man said in a loud voice.

The open-air restaurant in which they managed to find a table so late in the busy dim sum hour overlooked Kowloon Bay and was packed with Chinese gentlemen and their squawking birds.

The "walking" of a colorful pet songbird was an ancient hobby of Chinese gentlemen. And this tea house made a particular effort to draw these customers by suspending hooks over each table for the patrons to hang the elegant bamboo and mahogany cages of their tiny songsters.

Lindsay and Mun were forced to talk over the chattering

and continually sweep away the splatter of bird seed raining from the nearby tables.

A middle-aged woman in a yellow print dress and white apron pushed a wheeled cart to the edge of their table. Mun reached and pulled the lids from three steaming bamboo canisters.

"You still have chu yuen? Cool. I thought they'd be out of that by now." He snatched two canisters of the sliced pork liver and shrimp dumpling.

Lindsay took one and then a plate of lor mai gai and one of fun gwor. He loved dim sum. Loved the noise of the restaurant, the hustle of the waiters, the besiegment of the serving girls, and the grab-what-you-can atmosphere of it all.

"Who do you think the guys were?" Mun ventured.

"Triads," Lindsay said matter-of-factly. He pinched a dumpling with his ivory chopsticks.

"Maybe the pendant's some kind of crucifix to them."

"The Triads aren't cults of the repressed anymore, Mun. They're businessmen. The only thing they hold sacred is money," Lindsay said as he rose from his chair. He dealt fifty Hong Kong dollars onto the table to cover the bill.

"Where are you going now?"

"To take a hot bath," he said, lifting his cane from the back of his chair.

"I'll let you know about the sticker."

Lindsay waved over his shoulder as he limped toward the door.

Chapter Seven

Guangzhou, China

Captain Huang sat in the netted chair of the Soviet-made Mi-8 transport helicopter as it bucked against the afternoon wind. Gripping the steel seat frame, his knuckles were bleach white and he cursed whoever had sent for him. What could be so urgent that he couldn't have traveled to the army base by truck? What did they save? Two hours, maybe three?

He despised these contraptions. One flawed bolt, one fragmented piece of wire and they'd surely plummet to the ground in a blaze of flames. No, he preferred the comfort and stability of his patrol boat.

The pilot turned and waved four fingers at Huang. Four more minutes and they'd be on the ground. When Huang boarded the husky chopper, the pilot had seen his nervousness.

Many people hate to fly, the pilot had said. But not to worry. This particular chopper was a recent purchase from the Russians and she flew like a silk kite.

The transport banked right and swung low over the rows of green-roofed barracks of the People's Liberation Army. In the distance, Huang saw two more Soviet-made helicopters. The machines hovered over a lengthy black python slithering slowly along narrow-gauge tracks. Through the morning fog, the brutish locomotive bellowed steam in deep belches as it labored its way onto the military base.

Although covered with dark tarpaulins, Huang recognized the distinct silhouettes of its cargo. The unsettling hand of despair swept momentarily across him.

As the pilot had promised, he set the chopper down effortlessly. Huang unlaced himself from his safety harness and thanked the pilot with a sharp pat on his shoulder. Leaping to the packed soil, the gunboat captain hunched over and ran toward an awaiting canvas-topped Jeep.

"Captain Huang . . ." A young cadre standing next to the vehicle saluted.

Huang acknowledged the salute and climbed into the passenger seat. "Take me to whoever wants me," he said impatiently.

The driver swung the Jeep around and raced down the tarmac. As they proceeded to the headquarters building, Huang noticed the nearby storage huts being filled with fresh stocks of military supplies and ammunition. The anxiety he felt aboard the helicopter took on a deeper sense of dread.

The driver stopped in front of a drab, slat-sided, two-story building. Huang slid from the vehicle, brushed down his olive uniform, whipped the toes of his boots on the back of his trousers, and marched through the front door.

A middle-aged woman behind a simple desk and wearing the same olive uniform looked up from the phone. She put her palm over the receiver.

"Good afternoon, Captain. Commander Woo and Colonel Xi are waiting." She pointed him down the hall. Huang saw two armed soldiers framing a single door.

He nodded and barreled his chest with a deep breath. He knocked lightly, heard the welcome, and walked in.

Huang stepped to the center of the sparse office, where a brown folding chair was set in front of a lone steel desk.

"Please, Captain." the Commander said, motioning to the chair.

A young female soldier, perhaps nineteen-years-old,

entered the office from a side door. She circled Woo's desk
and set the simple tea tray with a brass pot and four porcelain
cups between the seated Commander and Colonel Xi.
"Tea?" Commander Woo offered.

"Thank you, no."

Huang knew Colonel Xi. He was a quiet, thoughtful man
with slight shoulders, crooked teeth, and thick black-framed
glasses that steamed each time he took a sip of his tea. He
had commanded Huang's gunboat unit for seven years.

Huang had never met the Commander of the southern
province army base, but he knew Woo was part of the old
guard and had participated in the legendary Long March.
He had close-shaven hair and canyon-size lines across his
face.

Except for a heavy, blockish phone, the only thing on
the desk was a large red folder. Woo placed his hand on it
and stared at Huang for a moment.

"You must be wondering why we sent for you."

Huang looked at Xi but found no assurances in his eyes. The
Captain nodded to Woo. "The man from Hong Kong . . ."

"You suspected he was sent by subversives?"

Huang shifted in his chair. "From my questioning of the
villagers and the evidence found on the man, yes."

"The villagers were forthcoming with information?"

"Of course."

"Some worry that the villagers near our economic experi-
ment in Zhuhai can be confused by their proximity to foreign influences."

"I've found no such confusion," Huang said firmly. "The
local administrator was very clear with his charges. The man
was passing though the village at night to meet with two
young dissidents. He wanted to distribute Western propaganda to poison our brothers and sisters."

"He was carrying this newspaper?" The Commander withdrew the front page of the *Asian Wall Street Journal* from the
folder.

"Yes."

The Commander looked squarely at Xi. "One newspaper.
Not even the whole newspaper."

Xi leaned back in his chair and crossed his arms over his

chest. "How many words of subversion does it take to twist the minds of simple villagers? The Captain believed this man's intentions were against the people's government. I find no fault with his success in stopping him."

"May I ask, Commander, is there a question about my report?"

"There are certain details we are unclear on," the Commander said, holding his heavy gaze on Huang. "His escape . . . it was unassisted?"

Huang looked surprised. "My interrogation was complete. He was unconscious when my second officer and I left him."

"You placed no guard?" Xi asked.

"One."

"Outside the door."

Woo poured himself more tea and offered to refill Xi's cup. "But not with him?" the Commander asked.

"He was being held in the forward locker. It's a machinist's storage room for motor oils and solvents. The vapors make staying there nearly impossible. I saw no need to subject my crew to that."

"You do not consider the cadres of the PLA sturdy enough for such posting."

"The Captain"—Xi came to Huang's defense—"has always been partial to his crew."

"Favoritism, Captain Huang? The teachings of Mao show—"

"I am concerned for my crew as a whole, Commander. As our Great Leader was concerned for his people," Huang cut short Woo's pending sermon.

Xi cleared his throat and continued. "You judged he was from Hong Kong and not Macau?"

"He carried Hong Kong currency," Huang said, pointing to the open folder. "It should have arrived with my report."

The subtle accusation was not wasted as Xi glanced at the folder. The Commander casually closed it. "It has been secured for the people."

"Of course," Xi said.

The Commander scratched his ear. "Your report says he

slipped his bindings and escaped through a ventilation shaft. A feat for a fifty-year-old man.''

"He managed to free himself from the cuffs supplied to us by the people's army, Commander. And as for responsibility of his escape, I have already offered to resign from my post.''

Huang heard the side door creek as it opened. He expected the reemergence of the girl in corner of his eye. Instead, a hefty man with three stars on his red collar patch stepped into view.

Huang leaped from his seat as he recognized the uniform. Xi and Woo rose to attention.

"Your resignation is unnecessary, Captain.'' The slow gravelly voice filled the room, took it over, commanded it.

General Ji Xinguo dominated the office with broad, thick shoulders. His soft neck rolled over the edge of his collar, and his fleshy face, forever darkened from his days working the deep mines of Baotou as a youngster, held intense olive eyes. At fifty-four, only wisps of white hair covered his bulbus head.

"Sit.'' The General pointed Huang back into the chair. "Everyone . . . this is not a trial.''

Xi and the Commander glanced nervously at each other as they returned to their chairs.

"Do you know me, Captain?''

"I know of you, Comrade General,'' Huang said in the best monotone he could muster. Even the most patriotic cadre found it difficult to look into the face of General Ji. He had been the Commanding Officer of the infamous 27th Army Division from Inner Mongolia that had so brutally squelched the students' counterrevolution in Tiananmen Square.

Unlike Beijing's resident army brigade, who could not bring themselves to fire upon students and civilians, Ji's soldiers did the unthinkable—they flooded the once-sacred square with the blood of their own people.

"Good,'' Ji said as he circled the table and sat down beside the Colonel. He laced his fingers together and rested his chin on his thumbs. "I am concerned with only one point of your report.''

Huang sat motionless, his eye fixed straight ahead.

"You found reason to return this man's body to the Hotel Lisboa? Why?"

"I . . ." Huang struggled for the right words. "I wanted to relay a message."

Ji looked down at the tabletop and smiled behind his hands. Then he cleared his grin and looked calmly at the gunboat captain. "You have the instincts of a great Maoist, Captain. You may go."

Surprised by his sudden dismissal, Huang hesitated. Finally he stood, snapped a precise salute, swirled about, and marched from the room.

Ji looked at the astonished expressions of the Commander and Colonel Xi and laughed. "Our young officer has fired our first salvo, Comrades. Now we prepare for the battle."

"But Comrade General, only one man crossed the border and with only an English newspaper in his pocket," Xi stated in confusion. "This is why you are asking Beijing for troops?"

"My request to bolster the 38th Division, Colonel, has already been granted," Ji said flatly. He saw the uncertainty in his officers but felt no reason to offer an explanation. "Before you go, will you please pour tea?" the General asked Xi.

The Colonel hesitated. He filled the cup to its very lip before rising from the desk.

Woo also moved to his feet. "With your permission, Comrade General. There is much to prepare."

Ji looked at them both as he reached for his teacup. He nodded his dismissal and the officers retreated from the room together.

Even if Ji had been inclined to explain, Beijing had already impressed upon him the importance of secrecy. In the last few months, the British Governor in Hong Kong had been taking aggressive steps to strengthen the colony's civilian government with widespread democratic reforms, including a fully elected legislature.

Through formal and informal channels, Beijing had protested every change and promised to dismantle the legislature after the reunification. But within the bowels of the communist government, deeper concerns were percolating. What if the British had no intention of leaving Hong Kong? What if they were building a Hong Kong constituency that would not let them leave?

It was known that China viewed the nineteenth century treaties involving Hong Kong as unequal and invalid. Did the British then consider midnight of June 30, 1997, a meaningless condition in a meaningless agreement? Would they, as it now seemed, extend their authority beyond the deadline?

It was an unacceptable possibility. Even the slightest delay in reclaiming the southern peninsula would be a monumental embarrassment to the people's government. After reviewing the local topography, the colony's political history, and current intelligence reports from their agents, Ji had determined the precise number of troops and mechanized contingency required to take Hong Kong by force. Then he had doubled that number and sent his request to Beijing.

Within two days, trains burdened with massive weapons of war and leagues of stern-faced soldiers of the People's Liberation Army had begun to roll southward to augment the standing forces of the Nanjing Military Region.

Looking out the dirty window, Ji watched as the tarpaulin was removed from the first camouflaged T80 main battle tank.

"They will name streets after you," his wife had said as she walked him to his awaiting car. "Everywhere there is a British name today, there will be a Chinese name tomorrow."

Yes, there would, he mused as he sipped his tea in the empty office and watched his soldiers at work. But there was more at stake than just Hong Kong. Taiwan was watching. If Beijing faltered or showed the slightest leniency here, it would send a message of weakness across the straits and into the minds of the Taiwanese leadership. The renegade province wanted independence, but that could never be. The island was an inalienable part of the motherland.

First Hong Kong, then Taiwan. That was the plan. Reunification of all of China. Only then would the pride and prestige and the very soul be restored to the great Middle Kingdom.

Chapter Eight

Hong Kong Island, 1898

"Enough, Inspector. I will not have you badgering the child again," the doctor said, the temples under his thin white hair throbbing in rage. "My God, man, what is the matter with you?" This was the second time the nurses had called him to the hospital in the last twelve hours to talk to Forbath. They couldn't control the staunch Englishman.

J. T. Forbath, the Chief Inspector of Her Majesty's Royal Police Department, shifted his weight from one foot to the other as he stood before the doctor's desk listening. Or at least somewhat so. The tall, lanky Inspector, with bushy yellow sideburns running all the way to his chin, was in charge of Victoria City and a very impatient man. He needed to move constantly about, forever pacing like a caged animal yearning for his freedom. He ran his fingers several times through his yellow-blond hair as the doctor spoke.

"We've hardly stopped the bleeding. Don't you understand?" the doctor continued, his voice now pleading. "He's under heavy sedation because he needs the sleep. He has to gain strength before I can remove the bullet."

Forbath raised his fist and slammed it hard onto the

desktop, splattering the doctor's ink well. He stared down at the physician. "No, it is *you* who doesn't understand, Doctor. I have a dead Englishmen from the Governor's office, two missionaries and their youngest murdered, and their son barely holding on to life. And I've just been informed the missionary may, in fact, have been in the clandestine service of our dear Queen. I need that boy to talk, Doctor. I need for him to tell me what in God's name happened."

The doctor snapped to his feet. "He'll do you no good dead."

"That's why we are so pressed for time," the Inspector said. He turned to his assistant, Bradley Dean, a young man with freckles across his nose, who was standing silently by the door. "Mr. Dean, get the nurse in here."

Without hesitating, Bradley stepped from the room.

Forbath looked hard at the doctor. "Tell her to stop the sedatives."

"What?"

"You're going to wake him."

"I'll do nothing of the kind," the doctor said, dropping back into his chair.

"Yes, you are," the Inspector said.

"He's too weak, Forbath."

"Then tell me you're certain he's going to live."

The doctor stared helplessly at the policeman. "I can't."

The door of the office opened and the nurse, a heavy German woman with the loose hanging cheeks of a bulldog, pushed in. Bradley entered behind her.

"You vanted me, Doctaur?" she asked thickly.

The doctor looked from the nurse to Forbath, then back again. He sighed. "No more sedatives for the boy, and bring me a flask of ammonium. Don't dilute it."

Her eyes questioned him. "Yes, Doctaur," she said, her cold stare moving to Forbath.

"And nurse," the doctor called. "Make the operating room ready. We'll take him into surgery as soon as the Chief Inspector is finished."

The nurse nodded, her gaze falling again on Forbath. She left the room.

"Two minutes. No more," the doctor said.

Forbath didn't argue. He needed to ask the boy only a few questions. There were many to be answered, but on these balanced all the rest. Forbath thought of it as a cross-word puzzle. Once the first word was laid in, you could play off its letters to find the others. But so far, the puzzle was empty.

The doctor, Forbath, and Bradley walked in silence down the narrow hall of the small hospital. The building had once been an opium storehouse, but the owners, who swore that their shipping operations were now strictly legitimate, gave the two-story structure to Victoria City as a gesture of good-will.

In truth, the main smuggling routes were now over the hill across from the peninsula and the old storehouse was of little use. They also hoped the gift would keep the local constabulary from looking too deeply into the holds of their vessels.

As the three men walked, Bradley lagged a step behind. He was a well-bred Englishman of high morals and strong character, but he was also only twenty-one years old and had only been in the colony for thirty-six days. Exactly thirty-six, and he was counting them one by one.

On loan from Scotland Yard, Bradley was assigned to Forbath as his assistant. The Yard wanted to know how the Chief Inspector could command so much authority over a people who were far more deceiving than decent. A horrid people who lived in tin huts, stole whatever they could not purchase, and thought nothing of trading their children to pay off debts.

If the British Empire was going to make its way into the great land of the Emperors, they were going to need more men like Forbath. And Bradley had been sent to learn from him. But this, Bradley thought as they entered the boy's room, this was exceeding his power.

The Harrington boy, after all, was English and not Chinese. The young assistant's gut turned as he wrestled with the idea of stopping Forbath and the doctor.

The head nurse sat on the edge of the boy's bed holding his small hand. He was still unconscious, his head resting on a soft pillow, his mouth open and his breath light. He seemed so slight under the crisp white sheets that covered him only from the waist down.

Bradley could see the wide bands of gauze crossing his stomach. On his lower left side, the dark spot was still moist and red in the center. The boy's left leg was raised slightly, as it had been this morning. The bullet had grazed the outside of the thigh. It was of little concern, but the doctor was watching for infection.

On the wooden table near the open window, a greenish flask filled with about an inch of liquid rested on a steel tray. A square piece of stiff paper sat on top.

"He's finally asleep," the nurse said softly as she stood.

"Get her out," the Inspector snapped as he moved to the side of the bed and looked down at the child.

The doctor motioned her to leave. "The bleeding hasn't stopped," he told Forbath. "The bullet must have torn into the stomach."

"How bad is that?" Bradley asked.

"Very," he said as he put his hand on the boy's forehead.

"Then the sooner I talk to him, the sooner you can operate."

The doctor stared at Forbath, then gave in. "Would you hand me that flask, Mr. Dean?"

As Bradley lifted the glass, the choking taste of ammonia leaped into his throat. He turned his head and held the container at arm's length. The doctor took the flask carefully. With one hand, he brought the mouth of the jar within an inch of Nathan's face. He removed the paper and waved the open flask back and forth under the child's nose.

At first there was no reaction. He must be dead, Bradley thought. Then the boy moved slightly as the doctor used the paper to fan more ammonia fumes toward him.

The boy jerked back, his body stiffening as he tried to retreat from the pungent odor. His eyes opened wide and Bradley saw they were bloodshot red. The boy let out a sharp piercing cry. Immediately the head nurse burst into the room, followed by two others.

"Out!" Forbath screamed.

The doctor pushed them from the hospital room.

The boy's cry tapered off to a whimper as he turned his head into his pillow.

"Nathan," Forbath said in a gentle voice Bradley thought him incapable of. "Nathan, can you hear me?"

Nathan buried his face deeper. He was trembling in pain and gasping in short breaths.

"Nathan, I'm a friend of your father's. You remember me, son." Forbath reached down and turned the boy's face slowly toward him.

With half-opened, tearful eyes, Nathan looked at him.

"What happened at the church? Who shot you?" he asked gently.

"He's too weak to answer you," the doctor said.

Forbath ignored him. "What did Shaftsbury bring to your father?"

Nathan's eyes began to retreat into his skull. Though he was fighting it, unconsciousness pulled him away.

"Where's the ammonia?"

"Enough, Forbath," the doctor snapped.

"No!" the Inspector said, taking Nathan roughly by the shoulders and shaking him. "Why did he go to the church?"

Bradley grabbed the Chief Inspector's arm and yanked him away. The doctor rushed to the boy. He put two fingers to Nathan's throat. He looked up at Forbath. "The Governor will hear of this," the doctor hissed.

"You'll only find, Doctor, that he was the one who sent me."

"Is he dead?" Bradley asked. The knot in his stomach was tightening.

"Not yet," the doctor said spitefully. He called for the nurses. In a choreographed rush, the women moved in and surrounded the boy's bed. A gurney was wheeled in and Nathan carefully transferred to it. Without a word, the doctor followed his patient down the hall.

"Well." Forbath straightened himself and brushed down his sleeve where Bradley had grabbed him. "We'll have to dig elsewhere," he said in a pleasant, businesslike tone as though nothing had happened.

The two men stepped from the shadowy halls of the hospital and into the overcast Hong Kong day. As they walked toward their horse-drawn carriage, Bradley saw a Chinese man perched in the rear seat wearing a vanilla-white suit and a white wide-brimmed hat. He sat straight and proper and held a walking stick that was as thick as a horse's leg between his knees.

"Ah, Mr. Chong," Forbath said, climbing into the carriage and shaking the man's hand. He sat down beside him. "So glad you could meet us."

Mr. Chong smiled broadly. "No trouble at all, Chief Inspector."

"This is Bradley Dean, my new assistant," Forbath said as he took the rear facing seat. "Mr. Chong is a friend of many years."

They shook hands.

Chong got to business. "Did the boy tell you anything?"

"No," Forbath said as he waved at the carriage driver to head on. With the snap of his whip, the driver set the dark-haired hackney into a trot.

"What do you know?" Chong asked.

Forbath looked at Bradley. "Mr. Dean?"

Bradley was unsure what the Inspector wanted him to say in the Chinaman's presence.

"Go on. Tell him."

Taking a clothbound writing pad from his coat pocket, Bradley cleared his throat. "Dead, Carter Shaftsbury. He was the associate liaison to the Governor. Also dead, Edmund and Lona Harrington, missionaries in the colony for three years. Nathan Harrington, their seven-year-old son, was found in the central *wan* with his sister, Elisa. She was dead, shot in the back. Nathan was shot twice, remains in a guarded state, but has little chance of pulling through." Bradley closed his book. "We know Harrington often traveled into China with the British envoy."

"Powerful acquaintances for a missionary," Chong noted with a glance at Forbath.

The carriage rocked gently as it continued along the rutted dirt road toward the wharf and the business center of Victoria City. The driver tightened the reins on the old hackney and it shook its muscular neck against him. They rounded the high bend where the steep hill gave way to a clear view of the harbor. The wide deep channel between Hong Kong Island and the Kowloon peninsula was filled with tall masted clippers and agile schooners. The distinct batwinged sails of the Chinese junks could be seen on the horizon.

"Continue," Forbath told Bradley.

"We went to Shaftsbury's home this morning and found a sea trunk belonging to a Mr. Alsworth Brigham. The attached papers showed it had been shipped from Weihaiwei aboard the schooner *Swan Girl*. She came in last night and is still docked at the Queen's Pier."

"Her skipper said Shaftsbury was waiting at the dock when they tied up," Forbath added.

"This Brigham was not aboard?" Chong asked.

"His name was on the register, but the skipper said he never arrived. The trunk was delivered to the ship just before her departure," Bradley said.

"Mr. Dean has sent a message to the embassy in Peking to try to find out exactly who this Brigham fellow is."

The Chinese man took out a handkerchief and wiped his forehead. "What time did the schooner arrive in Victoria?" Chong asked.

"About a half past seven," Bradley said.

"We've already figured that gave Shaftsbury just enough time to go directly home, open the trunk, take out whatever was inside, and meet Harrington at the church," Forbath said. "Our guess is that whoever did the killings was also at the pier waiting for the schooner."

"The mystery is what was in the trunk," Chong said. He turned to Forbath and ventured, "Any more?"

Forbath nodded. Bradley flipped past another few pages of his writing pad. "An old woman in the *wan* where Nathan was found saw two men standing over the boy. She did not see their faces but said one walked with a bad limp. And . . ." Bradley looked at Forbath, hesitating to give out too much information. Forbath gave no signal for him to stop. "The woman said she heard them speak Mandarin."

Chong shrugged. "That is not much of a lead, Mr. Dean. You will find many people in Hong Kong speak Mandarin."

"She also told us they made reference to Tzu Hsi," Forbath said without turning. He continued to watch the road ahead of them as the carriage closed in on the city.

Bradley, however, saw Chong's face lose all its muscular activity. The young associate had heard of the evil Empress and of her far-reaching power, but Bradley never thought he would see it as he did in Chong's eyes.

"An old woman could be wrong."

"True," Forbath agreed.

The Chinese man in the English suit looked nervously at the side of the Inspector's head. He spoke in a hushed tone. "If the She-devil has sent her agents here, Inspector, I suggest you bury your dead and pray the Manchurians leave quickly."

"How can you say that?" Bradley was astonished. "British subjects have been murdered."

Chong looked directly at him. "British subjects . . . Chinese coolies . . . there is no difference in death, young man. Do not comfort yourself with false delusions of superiority. With a simple wave of her hand, the Dowager Empress could send a hundred thousand warriors to tear Hong Kong apart and send it into the harbor, stone by stone."

"You forget, my friend," Forbath said harshly, "this is British soil."

"Borrowed soil, Inspector."

The Inspector leaned forward in the carriage, held on to one of the side rails, and tapped the driver on the shoulder. "To the ferry pier," he told him.

He sat back down and turned to Chong. "I'm going to test a theory. Suppose this Captain Brigham stole something from Peking and sent it to Shaftsbury. Whether Brigham planned to travel with it is irrelevant. Shaftsbury was at the pier for the trunk."

"As were the Manchurians," Bradley added the next piece to the puzzle. "But why go to Harrington?"

"Safety with missionaries? Or he already knows Edmund Harrington is more than just a dispenser of gospels."

"Why kill the children?" Bradley asked.

Forbath looked to Chong.

The Chinese shrugged. "What is the child of your enemy but another enemy about to come of age?"

After thirty-six days, this was Bradley's first glimpse into the Chinese mind.

"The Manchurians have what they came for," Chong stressed. "Leave it at that."

Forbath shook his head. "Shaftsbury and Harrington might have gotten what they deserved, but these Manchurians killed an Englishwoman and her child. That's an atrocity I won't overlook no matter the consequences. Can you?"

Bradley watched the Chinese man stare at the carriage floor. Chong was thinking, debating what Forbath was asking him, and weighing the risks.

"Two, maybe three trails from the colony to China. Best would be at Shatoujiao, then through Canton," Chong said, deciding to help the Inspector.

"But if you absolutely had to succeed in your return to Peking?" Forbath pressed.

"I'd buy passage aboard a smuggler's ship. The chances are a hundred to one of being caught. It's common knowledge the Royal Navy has not secured the waterways as much as they boast."

"True," Forbath agreed.

The carriage suddenly came to a jolting stop as the driver reined in the hackney and applied the brake lever. Bradley had not realized how far into Victoria they had gotten. Taken up totally by the conversation, he hadn't noticed that the driver had already weaved his way down to the wharf.

Suddenly they were amid a sea of men. Hundreds of Chinese coolies and European porters swarmed around the carriage, many with massive loads on their backs as they transferred incoming cargo from ships' holds to Hong Kong warehouses. They moved, shoulder to sweaty shoulder, in an unorchestrated union.

"I want you and Mr. Dean to spread the word that we are looking for these men. Two hundred pounds Sterling and a week's worth of unhindered passage to any Captain, of any nationality, that turns them over," the Inspector said as he stepped from the carriage and onto the muddy street.

"An enticing offer, Chief Inspector. And for me?" Chong asked.

"Four hundred Sterling. No one sends murderers into my

city. Empress or otherwise," Forbath said flatly. He turned to Bradley. "A full report on your progress by tea tomorrow, Mr. Dean."

"Yes, sir," Bradley said.

The Chief Inspector nodded to Chong, then stepped into the throng of workers. His yellow-blond hair illuminated him among grimy copper-toned backs and silky skullcaps. Then he disappeared.

Chong sat back in the carriage. "How long have you been here, Mr. Dean?" he asked the assistant.

"Just over a month. I'm here to learn about the Chinese."

Chong laughed out loud. "To learn about the Chinese? Well, I am sorry you wasted so much time. Because from this point on, your education begins." He winked at Bradley. Then he tapped the driver on the shoulder with the heavy walking stick and motioned the carriage on.

Chapter Nine

Hong Kong Island

With the insole of his foot, Lindsay spun the faucet lever that opened the bathtub drain. The water was starting to chill and he was too impatient to soak his knee any longer. As the tub emptied, he massaged the scar tissue, gently testing for tender spots. His jog behind the woman's car had taken its toll. Moving gingerly to his feet, Lindsay turned on the overhead nozzle and took a quick shower.

Wrapping the hotel towel around his waist, he walked into the main room and pulled the thick drapes aside to let in the late afternoon sun. On the night table beside the bed, he noticed the phone's red message light blinking.

He dialed the lobby. "I have a message?" Lindsay asked the Chinese girl at the switchboard.

"A letter was delivered to the front desk for you, sir," she said in a pleasant but hurried voice. She had other calls waiting.

"Would you have someone bring it up?" Lindsay asked.

The girl at the switchboard barely acknowledged his request before pulling the line and going on to her next call.

Lindsay was dressed when the bellhop finally brought the small envelope to the door. Lindsay tipped him accordingly, then locked the door with the deadbolt and chain.

Only his room number was printed on the outside of the plain white envelope, and that had been written with a felt-tip pen. It didn't take a lot of pressure to write with such pens, Lindsay thought.

Returning to the bathroom, Lindsay closed the door and turned off the lights. A sliver of sunlight seeped through the bottom edge. He threw his wet towel across the crack and sealed the small room in complete darkness.

Slowly, Lindsay ran the envelope through his fingers. It seemed harmless enough, one piece of paper, maybe two. But he remembered the two agents AnnMarie had sent here and how efficiently they had been dealt with. Those chemicals were state of the art and Lindsay intended to treat this delivery with a large amount of respect.

It didn't take a genius to lay a thin coat of photosensitive explosives inside such an envelope. It was somewhat amateurish but always effective in taking off a hand.

Lindsay carefully tore open the side edge. With his index finger, he felt inside the envelope and found nothing. Most pliable explosives, even when dry, would feel somewhat oily. He slipped the single sheet of paper out. It, too, seemed harmless.

Lindsay kicked the towel away and opened the door. He smiled. He had underestimated his friend's son. The piece of paper was a note from Mun.

> T.M.A. Tsui Museum of Art, 11th floor, Bank of China. The girl's name is Suzette Lauhu. She's a researcher.

Not bad, not bad at all, Lindsay thought. He looked at his watch. And in just three hours, too. Lindsay made a quick call to the museum. He was in luck. It was open for another thirty minutes. No, Ms. Lauhu had taken the week off, but yes, the curator was there until they closed and probably for a few hours after.

Lindsay wasted no time. Outside the hotel, he flagged a

red cab and pushed a hundred Hong Kong dollars over the bench seat. "Bank of China, quickly," he instructed the Indian driver.

"Oh, you do business with the Dragon? Careful," the driver said, tapping his dark-skinned cheek. "The cameras inside take pictures for after."

After. After midnight on the thirtieth of June. That's when the boogie man came out of the shadows and walked defiantly in the daylight. When the prosperity would stop and Hong Kong would begin its slow decline into a ghost town. That was the fear and a large number of Hongkongers weren't waiting to see if it was true. They were leaving the colony at alarming rates. The brain drain, they called it. Upper-and middle-management workers running to Canada and Australia and the States and to anywhere else that would take them before the demons arrived.

The Bank of China, the diamond-cut gleaming monolith of shimmering glass and zigzagging beams, rose twelve hundred feet above Des Voeux Road. It was the communists' glaring stake at the threshold of democracy. An impressive building designed to be the tallest in the colony in 1997. But that coveted position had been taken by the newer Central Plaza skyscraper in Wan Chai, which had been specifically designed for one-upmanship by having one more number on its elevator panel.

There were cameras outside the bank building as well. High-resolution cameras tucked into the steel corners. They watched the boulevards and sidewalks leading to the bank. Not so much for robbers as for demonstrators. The government of the People's Republic of China was acutely aware that their zenith of economic cooperation was also a blatant target. After all, the Americans saw their World Trade Center and a government building in Kansas bombed. If it could happen there, it could surely happen here.

The taxi dropped Lindsay at the front portal. Lindsay entered the huge cavernous lobby and stepped up to the two uniformed guards seated inside the circular marble workstation. He caught a quick glimpse of the late edition of the *Wen Wei Po*, a Hong Kong–based communist newspaper, resting on the counter. A small, insignificant headline reported the Chinese army's ongoing military exercises in Guangzhou.

"The museum?" Lindsay asked.

"Museum?" the guard eyed him suspiciously.

"The Tsui Museum of Art?"

"No, no," the second guard waved his hand impatiently. "Down the street. Bank of China building. This is the Bank of China tower."

"Oh," Lindsay said

"But it's closed," he said sternly.

"I thought it closed at six."

The guard glanced at his watch. It was 5:46 P.M. "It's on the eleventh floor," he said. "Side entrance."

"Thank you." Lindsay retreated from the imposing monolith and hurried down Queen's Road. He found the side entrance opposite the Hong Kong & Shanghai Bank building.

Lindsay rode the elevator to the eleventh floor with his back to the small camera poking its electronic eye from the plastic grading in the ceiling. Finally the doors slid back and Lindsay found himself on a small flight leading to the entrance of the privately owned museum.

Stepping into the anteroom, he was met by several pieces of Chinese history sealed in airtight cases. Atop a square pedestal rested a carved head of Buddha from the Yuan Dynasty, its dead eyes baiting tourists to enter and explore the museum.

There was an unsettling stillness here. Perhaps it was the lateness of the day or the way the few remaining patrons whispered in hushed tones as they always did in museums, libraries, and churches. Lindsay had never been able to figure out why. Maybe it was the wooden floors. Museums always had wooden floors despite their intrinsically amplifying the slightest noise tenfold.

Lindsay realized the floor was doing it to him, exaggerating the rhythmic tapping of his cane as he moved toward the information counter. He hooked it over his left arm and tried to walk quieter.

"*Dui-bu-qi,*" he said pleasantly to the middle-aged woman on the opposite side of the high counter.

Looking up from her work, she peered around the stacks of brochures and pamphlets describing the museum and its collections. They were in a dozen languages.

She smiled at him. *"Ni hao."*

"The curator's office?" Lindsay continued in Mandarin.

"I'm afraid Mr. Mow was called away," she informed him. "His assistant Matthew is in."

"That'll be fine," Lindsay said, hoping for a chance to rifle Suzette's desk.

"Let me find him." She picked up the museum's intercom phone and dialed.

Lindsay picked up one of the museum's tourist maps from the counter. He pretended to look through it as he listened to the woman's quick conversation. Then she hung up.

"I'm sorry. He's busy with the new exhibit. If it is important I can have someone get him for you."

"No." Lindsay changed his plan. "I'll just wait for Mr. Mow. Will he be in tomorrow?"

"Yes. He's always here by nine A.M.," she said, as if proud of the fact. "Would you like me to set up an appointment?"

"I'm not sure of my schedule. I'll just stop by when I can," he said. "Do I have time to look around?"

She glanced at the clock. "A few minutes."

"Thank you." Lindsay drifted to one of the glass cases and pretended to study the carved mask inside. It was a ghostly white face with fanged teeth and dragon's claws for hair. The Chinese infatuation with the underworld and its spirits always made Lindsay uneasy. Jing and Tommy took them for granted, as if they were simply bothersome alley cats to scare away or bribe with a morsel of food. If there were such things as demons lurking around, Lindsay had told his friends, he didn't want to know about them.

Inside the pamphlet, Lindsay saw the rear display was shaded to note the coming exhibition. He glanced over his shoulder. The information woman was putting her brochures away. It was closing time. Lindsay proceeded into the museum.

The new display looked as if a hurricane had recently passed. Everywhere there were opened wooden crates and shreds of packing paper tossed about. Of the dozens of unwrapped artifacts, only a few looked to be in their proper places, while others waited in various stages of preparation.

At the far end of the room, a young man in a baggy silk suit, and with blond hair cut oddly close around his left ear but dangling long over his right, positioned a reddish bowl on top of a stone pedestal.

Lindsay approached him from behind, watched him set the bowl in one position, eye it, then turn it a fraction to the left. The man leaned back and eyed it again. He rotated it to the right and inspected his work once more.

"Looks good," Lindsay said.

The young man jumped. "Shit! You trying to kill me?"

"Sorry."

The young man, not much over twenty, looked Lindsay up and down. Then he smiled that charming smile of feminine men when they knew they were confronting a heterosexual and had decided to flaunt their ways. "The museum's closed."

"Are you Matthew?"

"No, I'm just Matt."

"I'm looking for Suzette Lauhu."

"Isn't everyone?" Matt's blue eyes showed his disappointment.

"I don't know, are they?"

"Well, I am. She took the week off when I need her the most. Look at this place. Do you think I'm going to be ready? No fuck'n way."

"She give a reason?"

"Who are you, her broker?"

"A friend."

Matt laughed. "I've seen her friends. You don't dress well enough."

Lindsay looked at himself. "I didn't know researchers had a dress code."

"Researcher? That's a laugh."

"She's not?"

"She is. It's just that no one can figure out why. The girl hangs in fancy circles."

"You lost me."

Matt tilted his head. "It took me four years to earn my degree in Chinese art history. Two more working the warehouse before they let me curate a three-piece exhibit. She walked in off the street and they want to make her the assistant to the director."

"There must be something the curator sees in her."

Matt rotated the bowl ninety degrees. "I'd say the bitch was sleeping with someone if I didn't know her family donated most of these pieces." He shifted the red bowl again, then threw up his hands. "Ah, fuck it." He looked at Lindsay. "No, I don't know where she is," he said, and stormed off.

Lindsay exited the lobby of the Bank of China building wondering if his face had set off any alarms or if the Rogue had truly mastered the art of secrecy. He knew they hadn't. No one could, not fully, not completely.

If the communist agents scouring the security tapes didn't notice a former American agent within their midst, it was because they were complacent and poorly trained. After all, it had only been twelve months since Lindsay was a headline.

Stepping into the cool evening, Lindsay was surprised at what was waiting for him across the narrow street. A silver Miata, with its top down, was edged against the curb. Poised on its left front fender was Suzette Lauhu. In fitted blue jeans with a white cotton blouse and her long black hair dancing in the harbor breeze, she stood with her long legs crossed at the ankles, watching his approach with rich, nutmeg eyes.

Lindsay walked up casually as if they were old friends meeting at an appointed time. He looked at the front of the little sports car. "Glad I didn't scratch it."

"Someone ransacked my apartment. Was it you?"

"This is as far as I've gotten."

"Why are you looking for Tommy?"

Lindsay glanced at the bank building leaning over them like a nosy in-law. "I don't like to have my picture taken. How about you?"

She tossed him the car keys. "You drive."

"Okay." Lindsay stabbed his cane behind the seats and climbed awkwardly into the car.

"You okay with a stick shift?" she asked, slipping into the passenger seat.

"I'll manage." He fired up the four-cylinder, glanced in the mirror for a hole in traffic, and popped the clutch. The car leaped forward. "Have you eaten?"

"No."

"Good." The Miata responded with surprising agility as Lindsay cut and poked through the picket fence of buses and taxis. They sped along Queensway, over to Gloucester, and into the Harbour tunnel that connected the island with Kowloon peninsula.

Leaving the tunnel, Lindsay accelerated onto Hong Chong Road and continued north toward Beacon Hill. The road began to clear, its evening traffic finding their destination.

As he shifted into fourth, his hand brushed Suzette's arm. From the corner of his eye, he noticed her watching him. She ran her fingernails back through her hair, tossing it to the wind. It whipped around her face like a mist about a temptress. "I didn't get your name."

"Oh, yeah. We didn't have the chance at the Conrad."

"No."

"It's Lindsay. Lindsay Chase."

"Suzette Lauhu. But I guess you know that."

"Yeah, but it's always nicer to have a proper introduction." He put out his hand. She shook it firmly.

"So why are you looking for Tommy?" she asked.

"He's a friend and I'm in town."

"I don't really know him that well."

"But well enough to have his hotel key?"

"Don't get the wrong idea, Mr. Chase. I'm doing work for him."

"Lindsay."

"Well, Lindsay, that's all I'm doing."

"What sort of work?"

Suzette looked at the reservoir below as they weaved along Tai Po Road and drove deeper into the New Territories. "Research. You know, looking up things. He's on a story."

Lindsay sent the Miata into a tight right-hand corner, down-shifted and let the rear end drift slightly. The yellowish beams of the car's oversized headlights prodded the dark twisting road as it unraveled before them. "And your friends at the hotel? They doing research, too?"

"Listen, Mr. Chase—"

"Lindsay."

"Right. I don't know what Tommy's into or where he's at. He owes me for twenty hours of work and my rent's due. And now someone's torn up my place and they're going to pay for it."

Lindsay eyed her. They both knew she was lying. He was just expected to figure out her reason.

"Thai okay?"

"What?"

"For dinner?"

"Yeah, that's ... that's fine," she said, her voice remaining defensive.

"Perfect. I know a restaurant in Ha Hang."

The wind sweeping through the little car chilled as they motored along the inner coast road of Tolo Harbor. Traveling through the New Territories at night and beyond the growing metropolis of Sha Tin was perhaps the only way to glimpse the old Hong Kong.

Away from illuminated skyscrapers and flashy neon advertisements, the Land Between, as the territory was called, shrugged its urgency of modern development and yawned back to the slow pace of traditional China. Here, commercialism was held at bay by hand-planted rice paddies and plows pulled by water buffaloes.

Lindsay parked in front of the restaurant. It had changed hands and was now serving Indonesian. "I should have figured," Lindsay said as they looked at the sign over the door.

"No one's planting deep roots," Suzette said as she stepped from the car. "The communists are going to tear it all down anyway."

Lindsay studied her for a moment. Such ugly thoughts from such beauty.

"Come on," she said, moving to the door. "I like Indonesian."

The small eatery was empty except for the family owners.

Two young children played a game on a small computer at a rear table while the cook's frumpy wife rushed to greet the day's first patrons. She seated Lindsay and Suzette at the window table. Rushing to the kitchen, she reemerged with a pot of tea.

"Ready?" the wife-waitress asked.

Suzette looked over her menu at Lindsay. "Care if I order?"

"You've been leading so far."

"We'll split a plate of satay with steamed rice and vegetables."

The waitress jotted it down. "Drink?"

"Tea's fine," Suzette decided.

"Do you have rum?" Lindsay asked.

The woman looked worried. "I'll see." The waitress disappeared into the kitchen again.

"You a hard drinker?"

"In the right situation," Lindsay said as he watched Suzette unfold her paper napkin and lay it gracefully across her lap.

She steepled her fingers and rested her chin on them. "Before you ask, I haven't seen Tommy in a week."

Every nerve in his body told him not to trust her, but in this, at least, he knew she was telling the truth.

"I know you don't believe me," she continued.

"Oh, I do."

"Good," she said as she reached for her tea.

"Because he's dead."

Suzette's body jerked with a sharp spasm. She dropped the porcelain cup onto the table, splashing hot tea across it.

Lindsay grabbed the cup and righted it. "You okay?"

Her eyes were wide with bewilderment. "What do you mean, he's dead?"

The wife-waitress appeared with a towel and a new teacup. Lindsay waited until she was gone.

"I thought maybe you knew."

Suzette shook her head. "How?"

"I don't know," he lied. "He was found in Macau."

She studied Lindsay's face. "Is that why you're here?"

The spicy satay and steaming white rice came before he could answer her. Pressing her palms together solemnly, the wife-waitress apologized for not having rum. She brought Lindsay a terrible bottle of Chinese wine instead. He drank half of it as they ate in silence. Suzette stared out the restaurant window.

"It's going to rain," she said finally.

Lindsay placed his hand on her arm. "He was a good friend of mine. I came to find out what happened to him."

She felt the pressure of his fingers on her forearm. Strong and gentle at the same time. But her mind repeated the warnings she had been told over and over. Trust no one, no one at all.

"What was he having you look for?" Lindsay asked.

"I gathered files on the colony and the old treaties. He was interested in the transition. Just like everyone else, I think he was scared."

Lindsay knew she was lying again. He pressed her. "The men at the hotel. They were after something. A jade pendant?"

Suzette's composure disappeared for an instant. Her eyes darted across Lindsay's face. "Do you have it?"

"You know what it is?"

"Tommy said it was important."

"I'm sure he did," Lindsay agreed, deciding not to tell her where it had been found.

"Then you do have it?"

"Yeah."

"Tommy was a good guy. If there's anything I can do . . ."

"The files you found for him—where are they now?"

She shrugged. "Most I sent to his office over the Internet. The rest I dropped off at the hotel. They weren't there when I looked."

Lindsay crumpled his napkin and laid it beside his plate. "We should go before the rain starts." He paid the bill and thanked the wife-waitress and her husband-cook. The restaurateurs stood at the door watching Lindsay as he muscled the Miata's rag-top closed. Suzette took a maroon blazer from the trunk, draped it over her arm, and climbed into the car.

This late at night, the twisting road was clear of traffic and Lindsay pushed the car to its limits. As they crossed the hills and descended into Kowloon, the rain began to fall on the colony.

By the time they emerged from the tunnel, the evening storm had turned into a downpour. Lindsay drove into the underground garage of his hotel, found an empty parking space, and pulled in.

"I wouldn't go home if I were you."

Suzette grinned. "That's a new one."

"It's not meant to be a line."

"You're not asking me in?"

"Don't think it didn't occur to me, several times," Lindsay admitted. "But I don't want to drag you into this."

She leaned toward him temptingly. Her eyes traced his face, her lips open ever so slightly. "If you're not going to ask . . ." she whispered heavily.

He let himself fall into her eyes, fall to her persuasion. He leaned toward her pursed mouth.

"Then I'm going to have to insist," she said softly as he was about to taste her lips.

Lindsay's eyes fell on the small, blue-steel Walther .380 automatic that peeked so rudely from under her folded blazer.

Chapter Ten

Hong Kong Island

Lindsay slipped his key into the deadbolt latch of his hotel room. "Is this necessary?"

"Unfortunately," Suzette said, the small automatic still cloaked by her coat.

"Your rent must be murder," Lindsay said as he pushed open the door and flipped on the light switch. When the lights didn't come on, he knew he was in trouble.

Two barbed probes hit Lindsay square in the chest, penetrating his shirt. The sharp electric jolt overrode his nervous system and threw his body into hideous convulsions. He fell, or, more accurately, leaped against the door, his cane flying across the room as he collapsed to the floor in spasms.

In the midst of chaos, a heavy hand grabbed Suzette by the throat and yanked her into the room. She dropped the gun and blazer as she was slammed against the wall. A huge body pressed her into place.

Lindsay could hear nothing, his ears filled with a piercing hiss. His eyes were watering and his chest heaved as he gulped for air. When the lights came on, he realized he was laying in the fetal position.

"Amazing," Orson Babbitt said, looking at Lindsay. He was a squat, pugnacious Englishman with a pinkish, clean-shaven face. He marveled at the odd weapon that was still connected to Lindsay by thin copper filaments. "How'd it feel, Linds? Did it hurt?"

Another man stood beside Babbitt, a large Scot with thick arms and a dense red beard. He watched Lindsay with mild curiosity. The man holding Suzette was muscular to the point of stretching the stitching of his suit. He had her pinned flat against the wall.

Lindsay rolled onto his back and tried to stretch out. His body ached as if someone had pierced his flesh with a needle and was scraping it across his bones. "Fuck you, Babbitt."

Babbitt pressed the red button on the weapon.

Lindsay's body leaped off the floor in a grotesque seizure. His head flung from side to side as he began to vomit.

"Ah, Christ," the Scot said, stepping back.

When the pain subsided, Lindsay found himself again with his knees curled to his chest like a helpless newborn.

"Put him in the chair," Babbitt ordered.

Mr. Muscle kept his vise grip on Suzette as he used his free hand to help the Scot move Lindsay to the chair.

Lindsay tried to focus on the men standing in front of him, but his vision was blurred by his tears of pain. He could just make out the thin copper threads leading from his shirt to the Brit and the Air Taser weapon in his hand.

"You're quite a piece of work, Linds. But stupid. Very stupid."

Lindsay could say nothing. He was praying the pain would leave soon.

"What about this?" Mr. Muscle held Suzette out like a rubber chicken. She pulled at his fingers, but it was useless.

"Who's the girl, Linds?"

Lindsay turned slightly. Mr. Muscle had pushed her back against the wall again.

"A whore."

The Scot laughed. "You've got to be kidding."

Lindsay drew a breath. "I couldn't touch it before."

Babbitt eyed Lindsay cautiously. He handed the Taser to

the Scot. He stared along Mr. Muscle forearm's and into Suzette's face. Beads of sweat rolled down her brow.

"Is that what you are, sweetness? A whore?"

She couldn't answer until Mr. Muscle loosened his grip. When he did, she gasped. "*Aiya*, I no whore. Just working girl."

"A working girl?"

"From the Red Lion. He promise me dinner." She was breaking her English the best she knew how.

Babbitt cupped her right breast in his thick hand. He squeezed her, feeling the lace of her bra and her softness through the blouse. Suzette froze, unsure what to do.

"You still have taste, Linds. You must be getting quite a pension to afford this," Babbitt said over his shoulder.

"What do you want from me?"

Babbitt moved to the former agent and, grabbing him by the hair, lifted his head.

"I want to thank you. I only got one shot last time. Now I get a second." The pinkish man chuckled. He made a gun out of his finger and thumb, pointed at Lindsay's forehead, and dropped the hammer. "I always figured you were the mole."

"You bastards shot me? You fat son of a bitch . . ."

"Don't thank me. I wanted a full sanction. It was your boss who only let us sideline you. The softhearted moron wasn't convinced you were the double. I was. Or at least close enough."

"You're dead, Babbitt."

"Don't take it personally. It was an assignment." The British agent waved his hand dismissively.

"I wasn't it."

"Really? I wish I believed you," Babbitt said as he reached into his coat pocket and withdrew a short, stiff leather strap filled with buckshot at one end. "I don't like this electric stuff," Babbitt said. He shrugged his shoulders and tried to express himself with animated hands. "There's no feedback. No feel. I like this much better."

With a snap of his wrist, he hit Lindsay across his right knee with the leather blackjack. The pain sent stars across Lindsay's eyelids as he screamed at the top of his lungs. He fell to the floor clutching his knee. "Admit it, Linds. You were the mole, weren't you?"

"Fuck you," Lindsay screamed.

Suzette struggled to free herself. She kicked at the muscular British agent. He turned his hips, protecting his groin and offering his ham-sized leg.

An electronic buzz suddenly filled the room. The Scot drew his cellular flip-phone from his pocket.

"Yeah?" He listened. His eyes leveled on Babbitt. "You sure? He's not going to be happy about this." He collapsed the phone and returned it to his pocket.

"What?" Babbitt asked impatiently.

"They want us to put him on a plane."

"No fuck'n way!"

"That was the Foreign Office. They want him out of Hong Kong."

"I'll get him out!"

"In one piece. On the first plane to the States."

"Shit," Babbitt screamed. "Goddammit! Shit!" He looked down at Lindsay. He kicked him in the stomach. "Not until I'm finished with him." He kicked him again and again.

Suzette lashed out at Mr. Muscles again. "Hey, hey," he yelled her.

Babbitt circled Lindsay like a vulture. With the heel of his shoe, he stomped on his bad leg. Lindsay curled and rolled, trying to protect himself. Instinct and fury told him to leap up and kill Babbitt, but he was still connected to the Taser.

"Babbitt . . ." Mr. Muscles was becoming angry.

"Take her back to her bar."

Mr. Muscles released her. "One word out of you, bitch, and you're dead. Understand?"

"Understand," Suzette said, rubbing her throat.

He pushed Suzette toward the door. She glanced sadly at Lindsay as she picked up her blazer and what lay beneath it. "See you later, mister."

Lindsay was too weak to look at her. He continued to cover his knee with his hands.

Babbitt glared at Lindsay in disgust. "Damn it to hell," he yelled, throwing his blackjack across the room.

The Scot pulled a handkerchief from his pocket and wiped the blood from under Lindsay's nose. "Come on, you get to fly business class."

"He's not going alone," Babbitt snapped. "We're taking him ourselves."

"What are you talking about? He's not getting away."

"You don't know him."

With the copper filaments still piercing Lindsay's skin through his shirt, the MI5 agents lifted him to his feet. He stumbled weakly.

"Grab his cane," Babbitt instructed the Scot, and shouldered Lindsay himself. "For your own sake, you better be able to walk onto that plane," he told the American.

The agents dumped Lindsay into the back of a royal blue van and raced toward Kai Tak International. The earliest plane to the states stopped in Hawaii and was leaving just after midnight. Babbitt phoned the Foreign Office and informed them that he and the Scot were personally escorting Lindsay across the Pacific.

The junior supervisor pulling the late night duty tried to dissuade Babbitt from boarding the flight. There was no need, he insisted. The proper authorities would greet Mr. Chase in Honolulu. Aggravated by the supervisor's stupidity, Babbitt yelled at him to secure three airline tickets and to inform the CIA of their flight schedule. Then he hung up on him.

At the airport, the Scot helped Lindsay through the terminal. They draped Babbitt's raincoat over his shoulders, hiding the copper filaments that trailed into the Scot's pocket.

Babbitt took Lindsay's cane as they boarded the 747. The young brunette cabin attendant noticed the pain in Lindsay's face. "Kidney stone," Babbitt explained when he saw her concern. "He's going to have it removed."

"Can I get him something? Tea? Warm milk?" she asked.

"You want anything, buddy?" Babbitt asked.

Lindsay's bloodshot eyes stared at the Englishman. "No, I'm just wonderful."

"Isn't he amazing?" Babbitt grinned at her as he ushered Lindsay deeper into the plane.

The Scot slid into the window seat, then Lindsay, then Babbitt on the aisle. "Here." Babbitt handed him his cane. "Now just sit tight and enjoy, and be thankful your people want you."

Lindsay's head throbbed like a rumbling volcano. He looked slowly around the airplane and was not surprised that it was filled to capacity. More brain drain, he thought.

The ground crew pushed the massive aircraft away from the boarding ramp with a powerful diesel tractor. The wingtips cleared the terminal building and the operator maneuvered the nose of the jet in line with the taxiway. His co-operator disconnected the tow bar, its safety strap, and his communications link to the cockpit. With a wave, he turned command of the plane over to its captain.

Lindsay felt the rumble of the jet engines as they ignited and the aircraft began to taxi toward the runway. Overhead, the no smoking and seat belt signs lit up.

"Buckle up, Linds. I wouldn't want anything to happen to you." Babbitt smirked.

Lindsay heard the two distinct clicks of Babbitt's and the Scot's seat belts and, though he made the motion to buckle his own, he left it unlatched.

The captain's voice came over the intercom describing their flight time and weather. The cabin attendants hurried along the aisles double-checking the overhead storage bins and checking that everyone's seat backs were in the full upright position.

Lindsay looked past the Scot's beard, out the oval window and across Kowloon Bay. As always, the lights of Hong Kong Island were glowing with an unstoppable brilliance.

The captain released the brakes and smoothly pushed the throttles forward. The 747 lumbered forward quickly, picking up speed as it fought to break the invisible forces that held it to the earth.

As Lindsay sensed the nose lift, he slipped the thin knife from the shaft of his cane. Then, with all his might, he jammed it into the top of the Scot's left thigh. The man screamed. Lindsay yanked the electric barbs from his chest and shoved them into Babbitt's putty face. Babbitt grabbed at Lindsay, but the Scot was recoiling and pressed the Taser button. With the electric blast, Babbitt's body jerked and stiffened. His eyeballs flashed red as the charge popped their blood vessels.

The Scot realized what he had done and struggled to unfasten his seat belt. With the back of his elbow, Lindsay pulverized the man's nose. Blood splattered everywhere. Lunging over the seats in front of him, Lindsay grabbed the red lever of the emergency door and pulled it.

The hatch swung open automatically, inflating the emergency chute out the side. Alarms blasted the cockpit. Warning lights flared. The captain immediately stood on the brakes as his first officer shut down the engines. At 180 miles an hour, the eighty-ton aircraft squirreled down the long stretch of black pavement.

The interior lights flickered as the fuselage twisted and torqued. Along the entire cabin, the overhead luggage compartments popped open like jack-in-the-boxes and suitcases flew toward first class. The plane reverberated with the screams of terror.

The captain began to tame the tyrannical jetliner as it skidded toward the end of the runway and the ocean channel beyond. The right landing gear slipped into the soft gravel apron. The plane pivoted abruptly and stopped.

Grabbing his cane, Lindsay dove out the hatch and down the escape chute. He could hear the sirens of the emergency vehicles as he dashed across the tarmac and slithered down to the jagged boulders that edged the breakwater lining the runway. Staying low, he crept along the water for the quarter mile back toward the terminal. He followed a small access road to a chain-link fence, breached it, and headed for the highway.

As he reached the thoroughfare that led from the airport, the silver Miata pulled up to the curb. Suzette rolled down the side window. "Decide not to leave?"

"I didn't like the movie selection," Lindsay said as he

opened the passenger door and slid painfully into the car. "And where's your companion?"

"Gweilo find surprise in my dress."

"You kill him?"

Suzette reeled from the question. "No, I only wounded him. I don't kill people."

"Glad to hear it."

"Did you?"

He glanced back at the runway where the distant emergency lights reflected red off the black waters of the bay. "Not this time," he said darkly.

"Where to?" she asked.

"Back to my hotel."

"You're kidding."

"I wish I was, but that's where the pendant is," he said as he slammed the car door.

Chapter Eleven

Aberdeen, Hong Kong 1898

Mr. Chong brought his finger to his lips and made sure Bradley saw him in the darkness. Then he led the Englishman through the maze of boxes and crates along the narrow wooden pier.

The overcast of the early day, pushed by a cold stiff wind from the South China Sea, had turned to rain. Now, as twilight gave way to night, there came an eerie silence. The silence when the earth took time to soak up the moisture on it, and with that dampness, the sounds of the evening.

Earlier, before the clouds thickened and turned black, Bradley's carriage driver thoughtfully pulled to the side of the road and erected the carriage's cloth top.

"The road will get dangerous if the rain is heavy," the driver explained.

Holding his hat on his head, Mr. Chong leaned out and looked at the sky. "It will pass quickly," he said. "But your driver's right. It could get very slippery going into town. It's best to wait." He motioned to the driver. "The road widens a little further down. You can stop under the trees there."

The man returned to his seat and directed the horse onward.

"How is it one so young becomes an assistant to a Chief Inspector?" Mr. Chong asked Bradley.

Bradley straightened in his seat. "I did well in my law studies and didn't want to stay in London. I had asked for Morocco."

"So you have a traveler's heart."

Bradley nodded.

"Morocco." Mr. Chong waved his hand as if brushing the African country aside. "A clump of sand on the edge of a larger clump. Hong Kong . . ." He leaned forward as if about to reveal an age old secret. "This is the gateway to the Middle Kingdom. I know you have heard stories, but China is greater than any told, larger than human comprehension." He sat back. "Your luck, Mr. Dean, your Chinese joss, is very good. You have come at a good time."

The driver found the trees Mr. Chong spoke of at the edge of a large rolling meadow that overlooked Lamma Channel. He settled the hackney and carriage beneath them. As the rain fell, the driver built a small fire in a sunken hollow between the tree roots. Soon he served steaming tea to Bradley and Mr. Chong.

"The Inspector is an interesting man," Bradley said. "Do you know much about him?"

"What he allows to be known," Mr. Chong said, carefully sipping his tea. Just off the fire, its temperature was near boiling.

"There've been several parties at the Governor's house, yet he never attends."

"He's not a social man," Mr. Chong agreed. "But he understands Hongkongers and our hardships. In the *wans* he has many friends."

"You being one of them?"

"A minor one."

"You seem to be in good confidence with him?"

The Chinese in the Western-styled suit set his cup down and looked out at the rain-swept meadow. "Several years ago, the Inspector arrested an Englishman for beating a Chinese whore to death," Mr. Chong said in a low tone.

"The man's father was a taipan, a very important business owner. The Governor wanted the matter resolved quickly and quietly. He sent word to the magistrate to fine the man and set him free.

"Forbath wouldn't have it. He knew the girl. Some people say he knew her intimately." Chong grinned. "He swore the man would stand trial for her murder. The making of so much commotion for a Chinese, a whore at that, cost the Inspector most of his British friends and almost his position. But he held his ground," Mr. Chong said as he reached out and lifted his cup again.

"What happened?" Bradley asked.

"The man was fined and set free," Mr. Chong said. "The next day he was found with his throat slit open."

"Forbath?" Bradley was shocked.

Mr. Chong shrugged and drank his tea.

"Even if that were true, why would it draw your alliance?"

"The prostitute was my sister," Mr. Chong said calmly.

An hour later the rain became a drizzle, then stopped completely. By the time the driver put out the fire and stored his cookery, the setting sun had slipped beneath the evening clouds and was reaching across the bay with long fingers of gold.

"I have a friend who lives outside the village," Mr. Chong said as they continued along the road to Aberdeen. "He is the best rat-catcher in Hong Kong. Quite well-to-do. We'll stop there and have something to eat."

Bradley felt his stomach turn momentarily.

"When it's nightfall, we'll leave the carriage and walk the rest of the way into town."

"You don't want to be seen?" Bradley asked.

"We are going to call on Yak-san Kung. He and I have an agreement. He is one of the few smugglers that neither the British nor the Chinese have ever caught. He is known as Lingsyou, "the Leader," to other smugglers. So he has a reputation to uphold. To be seen with me would tarnish it."

"You have quite an assortment of friends, Mr. Chong," Bradley joked.

Chong let out a laugh. "The Lingsyou is no friend. He'd

as soon kill me if he thought it was to his advantage. It is not, nor is it to mine to see him dead or arrested.''

"Smugglers aren't the most trustworthy sources.''

"Yak-san is very smart and very shrewd. We will tell him Forbath's offer. If he decides to help, we will certainly find the Manchurians. If he doesn't, at least the offer will be passed on."

Mr. Chong and Bradley found the house of the rat-catcher. It was a large, well-kept structure nestled into the lush green hillside overlooking the natural Aberdeen harbor. The small fishing village below spread out from the slopes, down to the shore, then to the pier and junks and sampans lashed together taking its populace out onto the water. This was an ancient township, one of the first on the island and made up mostly of fishermen, boat builders, and smugglers.

Although Mr. Chong's friend and his wife watched Bradley with suspicious eyes, they were pleased by his compliments that the dinner they served, which was comprised mostly of vegetable dishes, was the best he had ever eaten. As soon as the dinner was done and the dishes cleared, the rat-catcher supplied them with thick dark coats and wide straw coolie hats to allow them unnoticed travel through the streets.

Now, from behind a stack of crates, the two men viewed the Lingsyou's huge junk at the end of the pier. Mr. Chong saw no one guarding the pier or the low-slung sailing ship. It would be better if someone was there, Chong thought.

"See anyone?" Bradley whispered.

"It appears deserted," the Chinese said. In the darkness, he was a black silhouette, his features lost in the veiled night.

"Go that way." Chong pointed toward the gangplank with his thick walking stick. "I'll look over here."

Bradley nodded, then he hunched over and moved toward the bow of the ship. Walking on the balls of his feet, he was acutely aware of the blood pumping through the arteries of his neck.

Slipping between two large bamboo baskets, Bradley pulled off his hat. Below him, oily waves slapped against the pylons, then gurgled down through fists of black mussels clinging to the wood.

Bradley nervously peered around the baskets. No one. The forty-foot stretch between the bow and the amidships rail was silent and empty. Chong had warned that the boat would be heavily guarded, but there wasn't a sign of life aboard.

High above the deck, atop the mainmast, a red swallowtail flag with the image of a cat's black paw print in its center fluttered in the wind. It was the flag of the Lingsyou, the insignia of the pirate and his crew.

Beyond the vessel, Bradley could see a scattering of fishing boats on the dark horizon, their large lanterns hoisted out over the waves to attract fish.

Easing himself back, he looked down the row of crates and baskets, trying to see where Chong had gone. It was too dark; the night and the shadows blended together into a black curtain.

On his face, Bradley felt a raindrop, then another on the back of his hand. As he looked skyward, a cold steel blade came quickly and silently to his throat.

Wearing a bright orange robe, Yak-san Kung sat alone at the circular table in the center of the main cabin. With a cup of warm Japanese sake in front of him, he read from a thick leatherbound book.

He was a man of fifty years, with dark skin weathered from sun and sea and from his hard profession. His eyes were hazelnut brown and set far apart on a round face. His long dark hair was braided and laid flat along his backbone. An educated man, he was well versed in the British laws of the colony, especially the ones concerning smuggling.

Three light taps came at the cabin door and then a louder one.

"Mun hoi joi," Yak-san said without looking up.

"Lingsyou," a stubby crewman announced as he opened the door and pushed his captive into the captain's quarters. "I found him on the pier."

Although Bradley's hands were bound tightly behind him,

the stubby crewman kept the knife at his throat. A swift kick to the back of his legs dropped Bradley to the floor. The crewman slipped his knife into its sheath.

Yak-san closed his book, peered down his flat nose and over the edge of the table. "What was he doing?" he asked as he looked at the Englishman. He could see the fine clothes beneath the coolie's coat.

"Spying," the crewman said.

"I'm the assistant to—" Bradley tried to say, but the crewman's heavy boot found his ribs. Bradley fell face first to the wooden floor, gasping for breath.

Yak-san pushed himself away from the table. He knelt down beside Bradley and looked at his face. "You are the assistant to the Chief Inspector of Victoria," Yak-san said in English. "Mr. Dean, isn't it? Bradley Dean."

Bradley's breath was returning. "How do you know that?" he choked.

"How do I know?" Yak-san looked surprised. He stood up. "What do you think I am, an illiterate coolie? It is my business to know."

Bradley struggled to his knees. The twine around his wrist was biting deep into his flesh.

Yak-san lifted the heavy book from the tabletop and held it for the Englishman to see. "Have you ever read this man's work?"

Bradley recognized the first edition of Melville's *Moby-Dick*. He shook his head.

"Huh," Yak-san grunted. "It's very difficult. Too much about whaling. But I like the captain." He tapped the cover with his finger.

Suddenly the cabin door burst open. The stubby crewman reached for his knife, but all he saw was the blunt end of Chong's walking stick. He crumpled to the floor next to Bradley, his nose broken and gushing.

Chong stepped in and locked the door behind him. He retrieved the knife and cut Bradley free.

Yak-san looked up from his book. "Have you ever read this, Ching-yi?" he asked Chong.

Chong glanced at the pirate as he helped Bradley to his feet. "We are not here to discuss literature," he said.

Bradley looked from Chong to Yak-san, then back to Chong. "I was a decoy," Bradley realized as he rubbed his wrists.

"And a very good one," Yak-san said.

"Plus we have all saved face," Chong said. "That's something you must remember. Now let's get to business." Chong took off his thick coat and tossed it aside.

Yak-san set the book on the table. "Why have you come to pester me, Ching-yi?"

"We are searching for two men who may be looking for passage into the mainland."

"They murdered a British family," Bradley added.

"Many ways into China. The river is not the only one."

"No," Bradley said. "But it's the surest."

There was a hurried knock at the door. Chong and the Lingsyou looked at each other and Bradley could see the alarm in their faces.

"Do not bother me," Yak-san hollered in Cantonese.

"Tang is not at his place," a crewman said from the other side of the door.

Bradley heard the dismay in the man's voice. He knew the man he spoke of was unconscious and bleeding at his feet.

"Then look for him, you stupid turtle," Yak-san said angrily.

"Yes, Lingsyou." Quick footsteps retreated down the companionway.

Yak-san turned to the Englishman. "Why should I help the police?"

Bradley placed his hands on the table and leaned in. "For the capture of these men, we are willing to pay two hundred pounds Sterling and a week's worth of unrestricted passage."

Yak-san rubbed his chin. He looked at Chong. "Tell me, my old friend, who did these men murder that would compel Forbath to offer such a reward?"

"Missionaries and a government man," Chong said truthfully.

"Missionaries? There's a crime in this?"

Chong grinned, but cleared his smile when Bradley glared

at him. "The Inspector believes they were sent by the Dowager Empress."

Yak-san leaned back in his chair, his orange robe billowing over the armrest. "Monsters of the She-devil are dangerous cargo to carry."

"Very," the Chinese in the white suit agreed.

"If I hear of these men, I will send word," Yak-san promised. "If the reward is good."

"It is," Chong promised. As he turned toward the door, he looked back at the Lingsyou. "Even though he is a foreign devil, Forbath will stand by his word."

"Leave by the stern. No one is there," Yak-san told him. Chong let Bradley out the door first, then followed.

Yak-san sat motionless, thinking. Finally, he moved to where his crewman still lay unconscious. With the side of his foot, he kicked the man. "Get up," he screamed. "Get up, you disgusting dog!"

The man rolled to his side. Feeling the first waves of pain, he touched his damaged nose and cried out.

"You let them get away, you fool," Yak-san roared.

The stubby man scrambled to his feet. "I'm sorry, Lingsyou."

"Go to the galley and let the cook have a look at your ugly face," Yak-san told him.

The stubby crewman, with the blood pouring from his nose and running through his fingers, left the cabin quickly. The cook was a butcher when it came to doctoring, but he had plenty of foreign whiskey for the pain.

A few moments later, Fu-laing, Yak-san's second in command, walked into the cabin. He was a bitter man whom the Lingsyou trusted like a brother.

For all his life, Fu-laing had been hated and scorned for who he was, the offspring of a Chinese mother and a Manchurian father. The two races were considered as different as the robin and the crow and their children were thought of worse than demons.

Fu-laing was completely bald, his head hairless except for the thin mustache that drooped below the edges of his chin by several inches. He wore a dark *shamfu*, the thick coat's sleeves rolled up to his elbows. "I saw Chong and the Englishman leave," he said directly.

"They came earlier than I had expected."

"Were you correct?"

Yak-san smiled as he moved to the cupboard and took out the sake and a second cup. "They were looking for those very men." Yak-san moved back to the table and poured the rice wine. "They're wanted for murder and they carry a heavy price on their heads."

"Murder?"

"Of missionaries."

"Aiya." Fu-laing smiled.

"No. It is not good. Forbath fears they were sent by the Empress."

Fu-laing eyes widened. "Bannermen? Here? To kill missionaries?"

"It does sound foolish."

"We should ask them. If they are Bannermen of the Guard, we may be endangering ourselves taking them upriver."

"They are still in the forward cabin?"

"Waiting for our departure."

"Bring them," the Lingsyou instructed.

The two men who had come to Yak-san seeking safe passage to Canton and promising him payment of twenty pounds Sterling upon arrival were awakened and brought roughly to the captain's quarters by Fu-laing and two other of his crewmen.

Pushed into the center of the cabin, they stood side by side. The older Manchurian, the clubfooted one with the badly scarred face, let his younger companion do the talking.

"What is this?" the young Manchurian demanded, pulling himself loose from the crewman. He was a young warrior, broad-chested and strong. "Why are we treated like this?" He directed his question to Fu-laing, for he knew the half-breed spoke both tongues.

"The Lingsyou has questions to ask," Fu-laing said.

"Tell them there is a price on their heads, a substantial price, and I want to know why," Yak-san said from where he sat at the table. Fu-laing translated.

The young warrior replied, his voice deep and threatening.

"He says they will double any price offered by the authorities, but their reasons for coming here are their own."

It was then Yak-san noticed the clubfooted Manchurian was holding his traveling pouch tightly across his chest.

"They were asleep?" Yak-san asked Fu-laing.

"Yes, both."

The clubfooted warrior watched the smuggler captain with sharp, unwavering eyes as he circled the table and moved to him.

"Yet this one brings his bag," Yak-san said. "And the other doesn't." Yak-san's eyes met that of his crewman's.

Before the Manchurian could react, the crewman yanked the bag from his hands.

The young warrior reached into his coat, but froze as the point of Fu-laing's knife pressed his chest.

The clubfooted man, too, refrained from moving as he felt a dagger at the base of his spine.

The crewman handed his captain the bag. Unraveling the twine drawstring, Yak-san emptied its contents on the table.

As the leather pouch dropped onto a pile of old clothes, the clubfooted man inched forward. This brought more pressure from the dagger and he stopped.

Yak-san unwrapped the pouch and slid out the yellow-colored papers. With it came the handwritten note.

As Yak-san opened it, Fu-laing recognized the stamp of the Imperial Seals. Though similar to Chinese, the Manchurian writing was distinct enough so Yak-san could not read it. But he understood the English words beside it and as his eyes took in what was written, he lowered himself slowly into his chair.

In disbelief, he looked from the papers to the Manchurians. "Ask them if these are authentic."

"What is it?" Fu-laing asked.

"Ask them!" Yak-san demanded, and he studied their faces.

Neither Manchurian spoke, but their eyes showed such a hatred for the men around them, Yak-san knew what he held was real.

"It is a deed to Hong Kong," Yak-san told Fu-laing.

"What?" Fu-laing wasn't sure he had heard correctly.

"It grants the territories to the British for all time." A devilish grin crossed his lips. "What do you think their Empress would pay for such documents?"

"The sun and the moon," Fu-laing said in awe.

Rerolling the papers and slipping them back into the pouch, Yak-san noticed the handwritten note that had fallen on the table. He opened it and read Brigham's letter to the Queen of England.

Yak-san couldn't help himself as he began to roar with laughter. "The gods have spread fortune upon us, Fu-laing. Like never before. Not only is the Dowager Empress at our whim, but so are the foreign devils themselves."

"Bu-shi!" the clubfooted Manchurian screamed. He reached into his coat. Without drawing it, he fired his revolver through his trousers and into the groin of the crewman behind him.

The younger warrior whipped around and hit Fu-laing in the throat with the edge of his hand, sending him into the bulkhead.

The other crewman in the cabin already had his gun free and leveled at the clubfooted man, but he pulled the trigger a second too late. The clubfoot's bullet entered the crewman's right eye and exited along with two-thirds of his skull.

The young Manchurian leaped at Yak-san. He hit the smuggler with his forearm and tore the pouch and letter from his fingers. The warrior thrust them into the hands of his companion. Without hesitation, the clubfooted one clutched the pouch and documents under his arm, threw open the cabin door, and ran out.

Yak-san drew his gun and fired wildly.

As the warrior scrambled for the exit, he felt Yak-san's first bullet shatter his right shoulder blade. The second ripped into his lung. With his remaining strength, the young Manchurian lunged at the open door, his outstretched hands grabbing the frame. As the third and fourth bullets tore into him, the Bannerman of the Guard dug his fingernails into the wood. When he died, his grip locked his body in the doorway, ensuring his companion's escape.

Chapter Twelve

Hong Kong Island

Suzette relinquished her small automatic to Lindsay as they pulled into the vacant parking lot off Fenwick Street.

"I'll meet you at Jaffe and O'Brien in fifteen minutes," he told her.

"You'll be there, right?"

"You think I'd leave you after what we've shared?" he smiled.

Suzette watched Lindsay rely heavily on his cane as he limped across the street. When he rounded the facade of the Performing Arts Center, she backed out of the parking lot and headed east.

Lindsay entered the hotel lobby, waved to the lone clerk at the desk, and rode the silent elevator to his floor. His room was empty and undisturbed. Babbitt was undoubtedly explaining to the authorities who he was and what had happened on the jetliner. He was in a jam, Lindsay thought, smiling to himself. This was a real embarrassment for MI5 and it would be a while before they could send a search team to comb the place.

Cramming his clothes into his black leather carry-on,

Lindsay pushed Truby's automatic into its holster and slipped the holster into his waistband. He removed the pendant from the envelope with the Aberdeen photo. Where to hide it? He suddenly knew the perfect place.

Exactly fifteen minutes after he had left her, Lindsay stepped onto the curb at Jaffe Road. A few seconds later, the Miata pulled up. He dropped into the passenger seat. With no place else to put them, he held his suitcase and cane across his lap.

"Where to?"

"Back through the tunnel."

Suzette piloted the little car by Lindsay's directions. As they entered the Kowloon Tong area, Suzette became suspicious as to where they were headed.

"It's not that bad," Lindsay said, standing outside the car.

Suzette folded her arms and shook her head.

"There's no place else to go."

"What about my apartment?"

"It was ransacked."

"So maybe they won't go back," she said.

"Don't count on it."

"They'll find us here."

"Not for a few hours."

"Oh, that's reassuring," Suzette said, looking at the small, one-level motel illuminated by a handful of dim lights. It was one of a dozen blue motels located throughout the seedy district. Charging hourly rates, the managers were known for their discretion and would, upon request, even place signboards over their guests' car license plates.

"I'm tired and my leg is killing me. I'm getting a room with a bathtub and a firm bed. You can sleep in the car if you want." He slung his case over his shoulder and headed for the front office.

Suzette sighed. She wanted to go home, wanted to go anywhere but here. Yet she couldn't let Lindsay out of her sight. Not now. Disheartened, she slammed the car door closed and followed him.

Lindsay moved to the linoleum counter and tapped the tarnished bell. The manager, a frail man in cotton boxers and a stained sleeveless shirt, entered from a back room. On his shoulder he carried a fifty-pound bag of rice. *"Ni hao,"* he said, greeting them. "Sorry. Very sorry. Too busy. No rooms," he said as he flipped the bag onto a stack of four others against the corner.

"Your parking lot's empty."

"No matter." He disappeared into the back room.

"Oh, well." Suzette shrugged happily. "Maybe there's a vacancy at the Regency."

Lindsay looked behind the counter and saw a line of five-gallon water bottles and several cans of gasoline. The man returned with another bag of rice. He dropped it on the stack.

"What exactly are you preparing for?" he asked.

"The soldiers. They are going to storm the border tomorrow," he said nervously.

"They're holding military exercises."

"You believe the communists?"

Lindsay held up his hands. It was reasoning he couldn't argue with. "Here." he reached into his wallet. "You must have something available?"

Seeing the bills, the manager's mood changed. "Okay," he said, brushing off his hands. He eyed Suzette but did not recognize her as one of the regular girls.

"Yi-jian dai yu-shi-de fang-jian," Lindsay said asking for a room with a bath.

The manager's smile faded as he realized he wouldn't be able to overcharge a *gweilo* who spoke the language so fluently.

"How long?" the man asked, handing Lindsay a single key.

"To about noon," he told him.

"Two hundred dollars."

"Clean?"

"Yes, clean," the manager said, looking somewhat insulted.

Lindsay took an extra fifty Hong Kong dollars from his wallet and held the money up. "Very clean?"

The man's eyes focused on the money. He reached back under the counter and took out another key. He switched it with the one in Lindsay's hand. "Room six special," he said. "Very, very clean. All clean. Bath, sheets, blankets, room all very clean."

"We'll take it." Lindsay paid him. "You see," he said, holding the door for Suzette, "you get what you pay for."

One's definition of cleanliness, Lindsay decided as they stepped into the room, was based on a variety of disjointed events throughout a person's lifetime. But what he couldn't figure out was what horrendous incident could possibly have occurred in the manager's life to make him consider number six as special.

The tiny chamber was dominated by a double bed that sagged in the center from heavy use. A rickety nightstand held a simple lamp with a naked bulb. Thick red drapes were pulled from the curtain rod in two places and the wallpaper, a blue print with large white English roses, was torn and patched unevenly. The carpet accented the room with a stain that looked like blood.

"Lovely," Suzette commented.

"It'll do," Lindsay said, closing the door and locking it with two latches. He wedged his cane under the doorknob. Lindsay grabbed Suzette, spun her around, and pushed her onto the bed. "I don't like having a gun shoved into my gut. Even a little one."

"I don't know who the hell you are. You said Tommy was dead. As far as I know, you could have killed him."

"You're right, I could have. Now, what was he after?"

She hesitated. "I'm not sure."

"Try to guess."

"He was looking for the deed to Hong Kong."

"What do you mean, the deed?"

"What do you mean, what do I mean? A deed," she snapped. "A document that proves Hong Kong and the territories were given to Britain in 1898. It shows the treaties are invalid and China has no claim to the colony."

"That's ridiculous." Lindsay smirked.

"Oh, really? I didn't know spies were such experts in Chinese history," she parried.

"There can't be a deed. Somebody would have it."

"Somebody does, and that's who Tommy was trying to find."

Lindsay sat down on the edge of the bed. "You're serious?"

Suzette moved next to him. "Can you imagine what it'd be worth?"

"Yeah. Absolutely nothing," he said, standing.

"What are you talking about?"

"Beijing and that little group they call an army. They want Hong Kong. You think a piece of paper is going to stop them from taking it?" Lindsay asked as he disappeared into the bathroom. The wall pipes moaned as he started to fill the tub.

"You're wrong . . ." she followed him in. "The international community would . . ." The rancid smell of the bathroom hit her square in the face. "Oh, my God," she choked as she backed out of the room. "That's disgusting."

"I thought it might be." Lindsay opened his carry-on and withdrew a small plastic bottle of bubble bath. "Lavender. Compliments of the Harbor View."

"Use all of it, please," she said.

Lindsay stripped off his shirt and delicately peeled away the Band-Aids he had used to patch the twin cuts from the Taser barbs. He cringed as the tape took strips of hair with it.

"Ouch." Suzette wrinkled her nose as she watched.

"All in a day's work," he said, and smiled with his hazel-blue eyes.

They caught her for a moment, held her for longer than she felt comfortable with. She turned away. "Pressure from the international community will keep them out of Hong Kong."

"Don't count on it," he said reentering the bathroom.

As the tub continued to fill, Lindsay lowered himself into the steaming water. The bubble bath had created a thick carpet of white foam. This was the second-best remedy. The first being two days in bed with his leg perched atop soft pillows. Tomorrow would be the true test of his personal therapy. If he had worked hard enough, the leg would recover quickly. If not, he would be stumbling like a three-legged horse.

Suzette stared at the cheap painting on the wall and wondered how she had gotten herself into this. It suddenly did sound far-fetched that a hundred-year-old piece of paper would stop the communists. What about Tommy? Was it worth it? She had been warned about the men at the Conrad, but she didn't think they'd find her so quickly. Maybe, she thought, as cold fingers ran down her back, they should let fate play itself out.

She noticed Lindsay's bag on the floor. "How's the leg?" she called out as she carefully opened it. She ran her hand slowly through his clothes.

"It isn't there," Lindsay called from the tub.

She recoiled.

Lindsay tightened his jaw as he leaned against the cold porcelain tub. Every muscle was protesting his slightest move. Suddenly the bathroom door burst open. Lindsay grabbed Truby's automatic from where he had set it on the edge of the tile.

"You're wrong about the deed." Suzette stopped as she saw the cyclops eye of the gun staring at her.

"If you say so." Lindsay returned Truby's automatic to the chipped porcelain ledge. He was thankful the soap suds were allowing him some modesty.

"You're a spy, aren't you?"

Lindsay rubbed his knee under the thick bubbles. "That's a dated term. I gathered information," he lied.

"For which side?"

Lindsay's eyes narrowed.

"That's what the British guy said. That you were a mole."

"He was wrong."

"Then why'd he shoot you?"

"Because those were his orders."

"Well, that explains it. Who'd you spy on? I mean, besides the Red Chinese. The British? Other Americans? Hong Kong's important to the U.S., isn't it?"

Lindsay leaned back and closed his eyes. "I wouldn't know."

"I do. I learned a lot looking for files for Tommy. Do you know how many American businesses are here?"

"Nope."

"Over a thousand. Hong Kong buys forty-five billion dollars worth of goods from your country. We're America's twelfth-largest market. Interesting, huh?"

"I'm at the edge of my tub."

"Some people find it fascinating. While the British retreat, Americans invest. The Brits are concerned about saving face, but you Americans only want to turn a profit."

"I'm not here for the politics. I came to find who murdered my friend."

Suzette looked down her long legs and at the floor. "Isn't that enough to make you believe there's a deed?"

"And your friends at the hotel?"

"They're Sun Yee Triads. Tommy warned me about them. That's why he gave me his gun. The ugly guy was Danny Wei. He's pretty high up. He's got his own connections with banks and the Legislative Council. But he wants to use the deed to make a name for himself. All the gangs know they're going to be out of business when the communists come. Danny isn't the kind to waste his time if he didn't think the deed existed."

"What about Tommy? Why'd he want it?"

"To stop the communists," she said matter-of-factly.

"And you?"

"Is there a better reason?"

"This Danny Wei thinks you have Tommy's leads."

"But I don't."

"Good luck convincing him," Lindsay said as he leaned back and stared at the ceiling. "Babbitt doesn't care why I'm here, just that I am. He hasn't tied me to Tommy's death. Not yet."

"Then how did they find you?"

"My fingerprints. They were on the gun I dropped in the parking lot. Remember? When you tried to run me over."

"Oh, yeah . . ." Suzette bit her lower lip.

"The local police would've had to run the prints through the Interpol database. MI5 would have had the match," Lindsay said. Now everyone knew he was there. He thought

about his former boss and the hurricane that would soon
be landing in the main office of the Rogue.

"He wanted to kill you."

"It seemed that way, didn't it?" Lindsay said.

"I don't think I like your kind of business," she said,
clutching herself.

Lindsay understood. He thought like Babbitt thought.
What they did was simply a profession, like being a police
officer or a surgeon. It helped justify it, kept it sterile and
gave their work a palatable quality.

"Now what?"

"Now," Lindsay said as he pulled his towel from the rack,
"I'm going to get out of the tub and take a nap."

"You can sleep?"

"I learned a long time ago to sleep when it was safe,
because it was rarely safe."

"Am I safe with you?" she asked.

"Probably not."

"I guess I'll have to take my chances then," she said as
her eyes swept from his face to his broad shoulders, across
his arms, and to where his muscles flared along his ribs.
Catching herself, she smiled shyly and left the bathroom.

Lindsay stepped into the room with a towel around his
waist. He pulled a pair of khaki walking shorts from his
carry-on and returned to the bathroom.

"What about me?" Suzette asked. "I could use some clean
clothes." She had taken a seat in the flimsy chair near the
window but left the heavy dark drapes closed.

"We'll find something tomorrow." He set Truby's automatic on the nightstand. Throwing back the bedspread, he
slid underneath the thin yellow sheets, crunched a lifeless
pillow under his head, and closed his eyes.

"You're really going to sleep?"

"Only if you stop talking," he said, rolling away from
her.

Suzette pursed her lips together. She stared at him, at
the stranger who had come out of nowhere and saved her
life. He actually had, she thought. Whether Danny had killed
Tommy or not, he was capable of it. Tommy knew it, too.
He had told her to be careful. Why hadn't he?

Looking at Lindsay, Suzette realized from his slow breathing that he had already dozed off. She resolved herself to the fact that staying with him was probably the best place for her and if anyone was going to find out where Tommy had gone, it would be this American.

Unbuckling her belt, she yanked the tails of her blouse from her slacks and moved to the bed. She sat gently on the opposite side and slid off her shoes. Reaching over him, she flipped off the light bulb and then eased herself into the bed. As her head hit the pillow, Suzette felt the tension her body had been harboring for the past twenty-four hours release.

For a moment, she listened to Lindsay's breathing and felt it through the mattress. She turned slightly toward him and looked at the silhouette of his shoulders. At the edge of sleep, she imagined him as a long sloping mountain range, dark and forbidding under a midnight sky. Then the mountains faded and the room faded and sleep consumed her.

Chapter Thirteen

Marshall, Virginia

Gravel flew like shotgun fire from the tread of the Pirellis as the left side of the silver Porsche Carrera slipped off the narrow road and kissed the dirt shoulder. Accelerating, the driver brought the sleek car back in line.

He aimed the right corner of the sloping hood at the center of the bending highway. The road straightened and he leaned into the right pedal. The opposed boxer engine opened its throat, gulped a larger dose of fuel and air from its injectors, and converted it to power at all four wheels.

The driver held on, his gloved hands tight on the steering wheel as the car lunged forward. It was embarrassing what this rush of speed did to him. The surge magnified his senses and sent an erotic euphoria through his entire body. Only in fighter jets and fast cars did he feel this. Never with a woman, never to this point of pure ecstasy.

Goose Creek Road dropped out of the Bull Run Mountains and converged with Interstate 66. The Porsche dipped as the driver climbed onto the brakes. A flick of the wrist brought fifth gear and a pleasant scream from the exhaust.

The tight right-hander came fast. Brake hard, drift, accelerate, double-clutch down to fourth, more acceleration. A quick glance in the mirror. Clear. More acceleration, shift to fifth, then to sixth.

The European coupe and its driver rocketed past 150 miles an hour as they danced into the left lane of the interstate. Easing back, the driver switched on his headlights and settled the car down to a comfortable 95.

"I'll have her fuck'n ass," Sampson said to the leather interior as the Virginia countryside passed. "Goddammit!"

With his left hand on the steering wheel, Jake Sampson bit at the leather knuckle of his right glove. He was mad, red-hot mad. I don't need this shit, he thought. Fifty-three is time to retire. Two days, just two fucking days for a little fishing and hiking. Was that asking too much?

It must have been, for the call had come at four A.M. over the satellite phone. And since it had come over trackable airwaves, the message had been scrambled and coded.

Sampson's one-room cabin retreat near Goose Creek was, by design, built without electricity or running water. He had hoped it would be just that, a retreat. But as the Rogue's senior director of operations, Jake Sampson could never truly retreat from his responsibilities.

Two briefcases traveled with him constantly. The first was filled with paperwork, while the second was his electronic office equipped with a laptop and fax, the satellite phone, and a digital decoder with a lithium battery pack. He even carried a fist-size camera that attached to the computer for video conferencing.

At 4:09 A.M., while the coffee was beginning to brew at the edge of the fireplace, the lithium batteries had decided to die. It was a quiet death, a simple fading away that left Sampson in front of his smoking fireplace with a pad and pencil trying to decipher the gibberish that had come over the phone.

He had gotten only halfway through by a quarter past six and found he had interpreted enough information to make him insane. The last four words he had transcribed onto the notebook jumped into his throat as if choking him.

Four words, one sentence. "Chase in Hong Kong."

He had stopped after that. AnnMarie was involved, he

was certain. Though the report didn't mention her, he remembered her two agents. She had come to him screaming about the Brits and the brush-off treatment she was getting. Sampson's decision had been to let the MI5 handle it, and now he knew she hadn't listened. She had gone behind his back. He was also troubled by the CIC picking Lindsay up in Bardsdale. His visit should have been reported directly and not by the damn satellites. Too bad, he thought, but that would also have to be dealt with.

By six-thirty A.M. Sampson had faxed out his own coded orders, had the cabin door locked and the coupe rolling down the dirt road toward the highway.

Traffic thickened through Arlington. Sampson slowed to the commuters' pace of seventy-five miles per hour.

"Fuck her!" Sampson said, emphasizing the "her." Leaning forward, he turned the Carrera's air conditioner to full. He ran his gloved hand over his short-cropped military haircut. "Goddamn bitch."

The rest of the trip into Washington, D.C., was made in the silence of a pressure cooker. Sampson never made a decision without knowing all the facts, and now would be no different. But time was a menacing factor. He wondered how long Lindsay had been in Hong Kong, how the Brits had found him, and how the hell he had gotten away. God, he hoped Lindsay hadn't killed any of them.

The morning commute of young lawyers and would-be politicians over the Roosevelt Bridge was beginning to coagulate as Sampson dropped onto 23rd Street. He turned left, circled his way around onto Hampshire and then onto Massachusetts Avenue and up toward the U.S. Naval Observatory.

It was within the secured grounds of the observatory that Sampson and his special section had their offices. He wondered if the Iraqis knew they were there, or the Chinese or the French or the Israelis or anyone else who photographed and logged every automobile in the city.

Sampson approached the side gate and stopped. A uniformed Marine stepped out from the tiny guardhouse that blocked a direct path onto the grounds. In one hand he carried a large clipboard. Under the board, Sampson knew, was a feather-triggered .44 magnum automatic.

The officer recognized the car and smiled as he moved around to the driver's side. "Thought you were going fishing, sir," the guard said.

"So did I," Sampson said, trying to laugh it off for appearance's sake.

"Isn't that always the way," the officer said with an understanding shrug. "Well, have a good one anyway," he said, stepping back from the car.

Sampson forced a smile. He looked toward the hidden camera that had been watching them. Actually, it watched the guard and the way he stood, how he gestured with his hands, how he shifted his waist. They were each specific signals so that the men on the other side of the cameras knew exactly what was going on at the gate. It was much like a catcher telling his pitcher what throw to give. Except the odds in this game were always stacked.

Sampson eased out the clutch and rolled forward. On the other side of the guardhouse, just out of sight of the street, were two giant steel wedge-shaped barriers perched in the center of the road. With a sharp hiss, they slowly descended flat into the pavement.

Modern moats of a modern castle, Sampson thought as he drove over them and deeper into the lush wooded grounds. He parked in an undesignated spot and climbed from the Carrera. As he crossed the lot with his briefcases in hand, Sampson noted AnnMarie's Toyota wasn't there yet.

The white two-story Georgian-style house at the edge of the parking lot was another deception. It was mostly empty except for upstairs, where there were a half dozen tables for eating and a Ping-Pong table for a quick match during lunch or after work. The Rogue's offices were actually three stories below ground.

Sampson descended the long flight of stairs, opened the reinforced steel door, and stepped into the security capsule, a tiny cylindrical room that was the only way in and out of the Rogue's headquarters. It was similar to a revolving door, except the entire room rotated.

With Sampson standing in the center, the steel capsule turned ninety degrees and paused. The doorway was now blocked by a ten-inch carbon fiber and steel barrier. The fast-CAT scanning machine was reading his body, matching his skeletal makeup with that of the Jake Sampson on file. It checked for his once-broken arm and the scar tissue in his chest cavity where an East German soldier had placed a rifle bullet. It looked for weapons and explosives and recently had been updated to scan for bio-weapons.

Luckily, it didn't scan for hot tempers. Sampson would have never passed. Especially today. The capsule turned another ninety degrees and the doorway opened to the front offices.

Although it was manned by only a staff of five, the office was already bustling with commotion. Operations was only an hour into the latest shift and each Handler, as the staff were called, was checking on the seventeen Chiefs Of Station located throughout the world. They reviewed the most recent developments in the COS's region, recorded and noted active and passive communications between informants and agents, and paid special attention to whether a Prowler was under sanction or if it was all quiet. And absolutely, without fail, the Handlers reported everything to Sampson.

Grabbing a handful of messages from his secretary's desk, Sampson headed to his office and closed the door. It was the same every day, fifteen minutes of uninterrupted time to look over the night's phone calls, check his electronic mail and the latest reports.

His secretary would bring in coffee—no cream, no sugar—take notes on what he wanted done before noon, remind him of appointments, and then disappear until he needed her again.

Next there would be the forty-five-minute Handler meeting for more updates and more instructions. If there was an emergency, that took precedence and the routine shifted until it was solved.

Today, with the spymaster's unexpected return from the mountains, the staff knew the routine would be shifting.

Joan came back from the ladies room and saw Jake's

messages gone from under her brass whale paperweight and the door to his office closed. Well, he's in, she thought as she headed for the coffeemaker. At forty-seven years old, Joan had been Jake Sampson's secretary for most of her government career. She knew he didn't like failed assignments, fouled plans, or interruptions. He had all three this morning. She had been the one to send the coded message to Goose Creek. Now she could only sit and wait for the storm.

Seated behind his large pressboard desk, Sampson tapped on the enter button of his computer keyboard and toggled through his E-mail. He found nothing pressing. One was from the Air Force liaison stating that his request for a jet ride out of Edwards Air Force base had been okayed. Funny, Sampson thought, it never crossed his mind that it wouldn't be.

As he expected, the reports on his desk showed no changes in any regional assignment. Thankfully, no one had been activated in the last twenty-four hours. His agents were quiet.

He pressed the intercom button on the keyboard. "Joan?"

His secretary's cheery voice came back. "Morning, Jake."

"She here?"

"Not yet, but your guest just passed the front gate. You want coffee?" she asked.

"Bring two cups and those files I wanted."

"You got 'em, boss," she said.

Sampson sat back, tapping the fingers on the phony grain of his desk. He was deciding on how to handle his guest when Joan walked in.

"Coffee, hot and black," she said, setting one cup in front of him and the other on the opposite edge. She slipped a stack of files from under her arm. "Here's Chase's file, the counterintelligence photographs, and that one there is AnnMarie's report on Hong Kong."

"When he gets here, show him right in," he told her.

Joan nodded as she backed out.

Rubbing his hand over the top of his head, Sampson lifted Lindsay's file and stared at the cover. Stamped in bold red letters it said: SENSITIVE MATERIAL: TOP PRIORITY ACCESS ONLY. He changed his mind and didn't open it.

Instead he picked up the CIC folder and pulled out the high-resolution pictures of Lindsay walking across the empty street in Bardsdale toward his truck. Sampson was amused he still drove the old thing.

There was the light tap of Joan's knuckles on the door. She entered and showed the unshaven man into the office.

"Jake," the man said with a half smile, the edges of his mouth twitching nervously.

"Truby." Sampson shook his hand. "Sorry to have you pulled out of bed."

"That plane ride was enough to wake the dead." Truby had dressed hastily, unpressed pants and shirt, a mismatched tie.

"Yeah, they're a kick, aren't they?" Sampson agreed. He returned to his seat. "Sit down," he said, motioning to the single chair behind the retired agent. "That coffee is for you."

Truby looked from the chair to the coffee and then to Sampson. He stiffened. "No niceties, Jake. I've been in the business too long. I know when I'm going to get my ass chewed."

This is going to be a fucked day, Sampson thought. He handed Truby the photographs. "They're from the counter-intelligence center."

The old man stared blankly at the images. The shock he felt didn't show. So the eyes in the sky were watching him. He shouldn't have been surprised. Trust was never in the Agency's vocabulary. But, Jesus, he had given them thirty unquestionable years and still they watched.

He set the photos on the desk. "What do you want to know?" he asked.

"Why didn't you report him?" Sampson asked flatly. His face was expressionless. He just wanted facts from Truby, nothing more.

Truby seemed to sense it, too. He didn't want a confrontation. He just wanted to go back to his desert town and fill orders for guns and missiles. "It didn't seem that important."

"What did he want?"

"A gun," Truby admitted. "I gave him a gun. I was over-stocked." He made the decision not to mention the cane.

Sampson stared at him. "Do you know what he wanted it for?"

"He didn't say."

"You didn't question him?" Sampson was beginning to lose hold of the anger he was wrestling with.

"He's a good man, Jake. I wouldn't question him any more than I would question you."

"There's a difference, Truby. I wouldn't have gone to you unless I was told to. Those are the rules."

Truby didn't say anything to that. He stared at Sampson and waited for more questions.

Sampson thought about pressing Truby to admit that Lindsay had told him he was heading for Hong Kong. If Lindsay had and Truby didn't report it, then the old agent would be in a lot of trouble. Sampson let out a sigh.

"Unless you want to see him bury himself, you'll tell me what you know."

"Nothing more to tell."

Sampson eased himself out of his chair. "That's all, then," he said, dismissing him. "But get yourself a hotel room in D.C. At least for the next few days."

As Truby reached for the door, he turned back to Sampson. "I do remember one thing."

Sampson looked up. "What?"

"When I was active, the Agency was always bogged down by bureaucratic bullshit. That's why we created this section. We wanted a black hole where no one could walk in and screw things up. By design, Jake, you're supposed to look after your own," the old man said, and then shut the door hard behind him.

Jake Sampson sat with that echoing through his head for the next fifteen minutes. What a fucked day, he thought again. Joan came into the office twice, asked him a few questions, brought him fresh coffee, and informed him of someone's birthday lunch the following Friday. Otherwise he sat in the sparse office and listened to the muffled phone calls and the buzz of the fax machines.

Finally AnnMarie arrived. She rushed in short of breath from her dash across the parking lot and down the stairs. She apologized for being late but gave no explanation.

"I got a phone call yesterday," Sampson began as he lifted himself out of his chair and moved around to the front of his desk. He sat on one corner and looked down at her.

AnnMarie felt the wrath coming. She unconsciously pulled the coat of her kelly green business suit tighter over her chest and crossed her legs. "I thought you were taking a few days off."

"So did I," Sampson said in a monotone. "But this phone call came all the way from across the Pacific."

AnnMarie looked at him with innocent eyes.

"You were in California?"

"For a couple of days." She had guessed why she had been called in so suddenly. Now she was sure.

"Why the hell did you go to him?"

"I came to you first, Jake," she defended. "You told me to let MI5 handle it. Well, they didn't. The Limeys jerked me around." AnnMarie's face was turning red. She pointed a manicured nail at him. "So did you."

Sampson rubbed his hand over his hair.

"What do you care? We didn't go in. Chase did." she cocked a smile. "He's a discharge," AnnMarie said, turning her voice to a pleasant tone, trying to dissolve the tension that was building to a flash point. "We've got no control over him. He's a loose cannon who's trying to find who killed his buddy."

"You know there's more to it."

"So? He can still find out what happened."

Sampson returned to the other side of the desk. He was thinking it through. He picked up AnnMarie's report about the Hong Kong affair, saw his notes stapled to the front sheet, remembered them, closed the file, and dropped it back on the desk.

"Three days, Jake. Give Lindsay that," she urged.

Sampson shook his head. "We have people to answer to, AnnMarie. You, me, all of us."

"Goddammit, Jake. Teresa and Kent were good agents. Now they're statistics on a hard drive."

"You shouldn't have gone to Chase."

"You never believed he was a mole. Why start now?"

A voice leaped from the computer screen. "Because now, Miss Gandel, a loose cannon in Hong Kong is far more dangerous than just an intelligence problem."

Sampson watched AnnMarie's eyes widened. He mouthed the words, *You shouldn't have gone to Chase.* The door opened and Sampson rose to his feet.

Crawford MacDoren, a middle-aged politician with thinning silver hair and closely cropped goatee, entered with dignified confidence. Although slight of build, at six-foot-six he was physically imposing. That, and the fact that MacDoren was the National Security Adviser to the President, made his appearance in the underground offices significantly startling.

AnnMarie felt her throat go dry and her palms sweat. She hoped he wasn't going to shake her hand.

He wasn't. He stepped past her, unbuttoning his double-breasted coat, and sat down in the adjacent chair. He set his calfskin portfolio on the desk and leaned back. Sampson returned to his seat.

"No, Miss Gandel," MacDoren said flatly. "No one here would have contacted a dismissed agent. Let alone put him back into the field."

AnnMarie gathered herself. "I consider Lindsay Chase one of the best agents we ever had."

"A moot point, wouldn't you say? You want three days? I'll give you two. After that, the British have informed me they are more than eager to remedy the situation."

"Jake?" AnnMarie looked across the desk. "We're not under his direction," she shot. "We're not under anyone's."

"That's not exactly true," MacDoren said. "There's one person we're all accountable to."

"Who?"

"The President."

AnnMarie looked at him, her mouth slightly open.

"And," the Adviser stressed, "I'm here on his authority."

Sampson tapped his keyboard.

"Yes," Joan's voice came through loudly.

"Reserve a seat on the next flight to Hong Kong."

AnnMarie sprung forward in her chair. "I don't know where he is."

"By the time you arrive, Miss Gandel," MacDoren said confidently, "I will."

She wanted to argue but knew it was useless. She stood, fixed her skirt, and turned toward the door.

"AnnMarie," Sampson called to her. "Remember, you have a career. Chase doesn't."

The redheaded woman with the green eyes looked at the two men with disdain. "Go to hell, Jake," she said, and slammed the office door behind her.

"Well." The Adviser ran his finger along the inside of his collar. "Spirited."

"She's a good Station Chief."

"I don't doubt that."

"Were you serious?

"About what?"

"The President knowing?"

"What else could I do? I had to tell him R-50 existed."

"He'll close us down."

"After this fiasco? Maybe. . . ." MacDoren moved to the door. "Keep me posted, will you?" the Adviser asked as he left.

Chapter Fourteen

Sheung Shui, 1900

Nathan Harrington felt Miss Lockburn squeeze his wrist tightly. She did that every time the filthy Chinese men with their heavy loads of rice or dried fish pushed past her, battling for a better position in line. Normally, the Chinese would give a foreign woman wide berth, but space on the train was scarce and going to only those who would fill it first. No one wanted to ride standing or be left behind.

They were beginning to frustrate Nathan—both the crowd and Miss Lockburn's holding of his wrist. He wasn't a child. He was eight years old and his height was approaching hers. But still she pulled him around like some mindless lamb. Plus, he smoldered, if she allowed one more person to push in front of them, they'd never get back to Hong Kong.

Miss Lockburn also felt the frustration of the dozens of bodies pressing against her, pushing and pulling in endless waves. She tried to be understanding. As a woman of the church, she always tried to be understanding. This was, she reminded herself, the evening train and the last out of the New Territories. Clutching two tickets in her bony hand, she stood firmly until the twin doors of the dark green passenger car slid open.

Mary Lockburn, a gaunt woman in her late thirties with a narrow hatchet face and thin colorless lips, had only been in China for three months. She had come halfway around the world to prove her devotion to God and to the Church of England. Yet she hadn't so much as stepped from the befouled clipper that brought her to this forsaken land when the Anglican priest put her in charge of this young speechless child.

"You have no idea what the boy has gone through," Father Clooney said as he stepped to the window. He ran his fingers over the leatherbound Bible in his hand and looked out at the courtyard below. "An innocent child, and look at the atrocities God has put upon him."

Mary sat properly in the curved chair twisting the white ribbon of her bonnet she held over her lap. She didn't want to be put upon either. She had come to teach the ways of the Lord and to help the peasants understand Him. She felt badly for this boy who had seen his family murdered, but the boy's father, the rumors said, had brought it on himself. He had used the Church to accomplish underhanded doings for the government, and that was clear heresy.

"I've never heard him speak a word of English," Father Clooney continued. "Not in two years. He speaks to our Chinese helpers, but only to a few of them." He glanced at her. "I know this is not what you envisioned as your first duty."

"No," Mary spoke up for the first time. "I came here to spread the word of God, Father."

In his dark clothes, the Father's deep blue eyes seemed to hover beyond his translucent skin as he stared at her. Hiding his dismay, he moved behind his desk and sat down. "Let me ask you this: Do you not think this boy needs the reassurance of God's presence? He surely knows the devil's presence, Miss Lockburn."

That afternoon Mary Lockburn found Nathan sitting in the farthest corner of his room, leaning against the bare stone wall reading a book—an old book on Confucian philosophy, its cloth cover worn thin by numerous hands. It would have alarmed her had she known its content, but the title and the text were printed in the scribbled characters of the intangible Chinese language.

She stepped into the room and sat on the foot of his bed. Nathan glanced at her, then continued to read. At first Mary stared at him in silence, watching him as he turned the pages of the foreign text. Because he turned them so quickly, she thought he wasn't reading at all, but flipping the pages and only pretending to understand the words.

Yet as she continued to watch him, watch his eyes, she knew she was wrong. This young boy could read Chinese quicker than she had seen anyone read the Queen's English. The sisters had told her that Nathan read a lot, mostly at night or in the afternoon when his chores were finished.

"Good day, Nathan," she said finally. "I'm Miss Lockburn. Father Clooney would like us to be friends."

Nathan continued to read.

"I came in this morning from England on the HMS *Farrlon*. She's a beautiful ship." Miss Lockburn moved to the bookshelf. "Do you remember England?" She looked at him. "Father told me you were only three when your family came here."

The mention of his family sparked a reaction from the boy. He glared at her, and for a fraction of a second, Mary saw something in his sharp green eyes. The boy was filled with hatred—deep, piercing hatred. She felt as though he had lashed out and struck her, or had wanted to.

That was Nathan's only response to Miss Lockburn's attempt at kindness and as the weeks passed her frustration with him grew to an unbearable torment. God was testing her, she decided, and she was failing Him.

But it was not just the boy. She could not grasp this unworldly place. Even the language left her deaf and dumb ten paces from the church door. In this small crowded colony where she wanted so much to prove herself, she was lost and useless.

It wasn't long before Nathan became her scapegoat. He persisted in refusing to speak anything but Cantonese and, as Miss Lockburn discovered, Father Clooney was of no help. The priest was even harming the boy by letting this defiance continue.

Nathan would speak to the Chinese cook, to the girl who washed the floors, and to some of the old men who raked the churchyard. To the rest of the staff, he was deaf and dumb.

No, Nathan's violent past wasn't holding his tongue. He was doing it for some ungodly reason and, as Miss Lockburn soon convinced herself, the longer he remained in Hong Kong, the worse he would become.

After three months of trial and failure, Mary Lockburn decided to take Nathan to meet with the visiting Bishop who was stopping in Tai Po on his way into the mainland. She had not discussed her plans with Father Clooney, knowing full well he would try to dissuade her.

This had to be done on her own and when she met the Bishop, she stated her position with a strong argument. Her reasons for taking the boy back to England were, of course, for his own good. It could only be guessed at what would happen to him as he grew older. One thing was undeniable, he would lose his bond to the church as sure as he had lost his tongue.

So now, as they stood in line waiting to return to Hong Kong, Miss Lockburn was grinning her lipless smile. Soon she would be in England again. The weeks on the clipper would be bearable with home at the end of the journey. And once in London, a fine, firm boys' school would quickly be found for Nathan. Yes, she had decided, this was best.

From the rear of the train, the conductor rang his small hand bell and the passenger car doors were pulled open. In one giant surge, a wall of people rushed forward. Miss Lockburn and Nathan were almost lifted off their feet as they were carried with the mass of bodies.

Miss Lockburn stepped quickly, aware of the wide gap between the wooden platform and the train. Miraculously, she got inside without losing the boy. She stepped toward an empty wooden bench as three people dashed around her and filled it. She moved to the center of the car. To the side, one last fraction of a seat between two women showed itself. As she darted for the bench, Nathan sat in the space.

"Nathan." She tempered her voice, although no one near was paying attention to the out-of-place foreigners. "You stand up this instant and give me that seat."

Nathan looked at her blankly. He turned and watched the final wave of people finding secondary places on the floor and against the vertical support poles.

Miss Lockburn's anger flared. She reached down and pinched the top of his ear between her thumb and second knuckle of her first finger. She twisted and lifted as had been done to her so often as a child. She knew the pain it could inflict.

But Nathan remained seated. Only the tightening of his jaw showed his pain. He cocked his head and looked at her with the biting stare she had come to expect. And as always, it frightened her.

Miss Lockburn pressed her lips together and let go of him. She dropped the canvas bag in his lap. "You are a rude little boy," she said spitefully. She hooked her arm around one of the vertical poles.

With his jaw still tight, he spoke to her in Cantonese. "And you have the face of a vulture."

Two men sitting on the floor nearby heard him and burst into laughter. For the first time, Mary was glad she didn't understand him.

Outside, the conductor yelled to the engineer and rang his bell. As the last passenger jumped inside, the car doors slid closed with a clatter. All at once the train lurched forward, stopped, lurched again until finally its motion smoothed into the clack-clack rhythm of the train wheels as they headed south.

"She does not understand you?" one of the men on the floor asked Nathan. He was dark and leathery and laughed with broken teeth. The other man was the same and they both wore thick clothes of bright knitted blues and purples and boots made of soft hides.

"She understands nothing," Nathan said. "Where are you from?"

The second man crouched forward and for the first time

Nathan smelled the pungent odor of their bodies. "From the Valley of Warriors in the Altai Mountains of Mongolia." The man turned and slapped the other man on the shoulder and they both smiled widely. "We are brothers of the same village."

"Mongolia?" Nathan was astonished. "The land of Kublai Khan."

"You know of the Great Khan?" the first one asked, his voice low, respectful.

"I've have read about him and about Genghis Khan and the Mongol Empire."

"It is good to know of great things," the second man said. "Not many speak of the Khans with respect."

"What is it like where you come from?"

"It is not like this place at all. The land is much different. We feel the sun's moods. When he is angry, the desert can be very hot, and when he is sad, the mountain air can freeze your words."

"When the thaw comes," the second man interjected with a crooked finger, "you can hear what you said during winter."

"In the mountains above our village there are forests, but not as thick as those in the south. It is much drier on the plains. The land is covered with strong grasses."

"What about the people? What are they like?"

"The women are gentle," the first said. "Gentle and sturdy, and soft and loving."

"Soft once you find them within their clothes," the second said with a laugh. They both laughed again and so did Nathan, though he wasn't sure what he was laughing at.

"Why are you going to Hong Kong?"

"To sell the skin of a great animal," the first Mongol said as he fiddled with his satchel beneath his leg. "We took him four weeks ago coming through the bamboo forest," he said excitedly as he shook the heavy black and white fur from the bag. "It is the fur of a *beishung.*"

Nathan's eyes widened as he reached out and ran his fingers through the thick hair. The longer hairs were coarse, but those nearer the hide were as fine as silk. He had heard tales about the great bearlike animal from the Szechwan region, but no one in Hong Kong believed such a creature existed.

"Nathan, don't touch that," Miss Lockburn scolded. He ignored her.

"It's a rare fur," the first said. "It will bring us much money."

"It's worth more if you make it into something," Nathan said. "Like a coat or a shawl. The European women wear them."

The two men looked puzzled. "It is not cold enough here for such a coat," the second said.

"They wear furs to the theater," Nathan tried to explain, but still the Mongols were confused.

"Will these women not buy just the fur?" the first asked as if his hopes of riches were suddenly dashed.

"There is a man named Ki Chow who has a shop on Hankow Road. He comes to the church where I live. He knows how to make European coats."

"Ki Chow on Hankow Road," the Mongol repeated to himself.

Nathan looked at the ragged, unkept Mongols and remembered Chow was not a trusting man. "Tell him Nathan Harrington sent you."

The first Mongol nodded. He would do that.

Under them, the train pitched and wallowed as it slowed to a stop. Everyone grabbed something to keep from falling or sliding forward. This was the station at Tai Wai and the train was still an hour from Kowloon. It was past seven and Nathan wondered if they would find a rickshaw to take them home.

The wooden doors opened and a new rush of passengers changed places with the jostling outflow. An old man was helped through the doorway by the conductor. He must be a hundred years old, Nathan thought as he watched him. Wisps of white hair clung to his chin and the naked skin on his head was loose and baggy over his sparse eyebrows. His clothes were tattered and worn thin, their color gone from a century of washings. He moved in small delicate steps and in one arthritic hand carried a long walking stick that barely touched the floor.

Using a shoulder here, an elbow there, he managed his
way through the passenger car. Many turned to snap at him,
but thought better of it. He was an elder and the Chinese
respected such elders. But as many years as he had collected,
it still did not lessen the number of people in the car, where
now even standing room was at a minimum. Those who
occupied the benches dropped their eyes to miss his glance,
which would force them to give up their seats.

The two Mongols were now in conversation between
themselves and did not notice the man as he stepped past
them. Nathan watched as he glanced at Miss Lockburn and
then to him. Their eyes met.

The train surged forward, causing everyone to hold fast.
The man grabbed the rail just below Miss Lockburn's hand.
She moved hers away.

The steam locomotive gained speed as it began the final
leg to the tip of Kowloon. The dense cigarette smoke that
had built up in the car as it sat in the station now cleared with
the cool evening wind that came in through the windows.

Nathan could see the tensing of the man's limbs as he
tried to keep his balance with the rocking train. His unsure
feet were crowded by the packages of the Mongols and bags
of other passengers.

Nathan touched the old man's shoulder. "Please," he
said, motioning to the seat. The man grinned, bowed his
head thankfully, and sat down on the bench.

"Nathan!" Miss Lockburn snapped. "You don't let me
sit, but you give your seat to a Chinaman?"

The man looked up at the screaming woman. "She is
upset you give your place?"

Nathan shrugged. "She is British," he said simply.

The old man was amused. "And what are you?"

Nathan thought. "I'm from Hong Kong," he said as he
set the canvas bag of bread on the floor and took hold of
the pole.

"But you are still British, are you not, young Harrington?"
he asked.

Nathan looked surprise. "Do I know you?"

"I would see you play in the garden when visiting with
your father," he said. "Too bad he died shamelessly."

"Don't say that." Nathan grabbed the old man's walking stick from his hands. "You know nothing of my father."

"But I do."

"Like what?"

The old Chinese heard the anger in the young voice and felt a fierceness when he snatched the stick from his hands. "I know it was not the Manchurians who killed your father, but the British. They used him and his position in the colony."

"No," Nathan snapped. "The scar-faced man killed my family."

"Because your father was working for England."

Nathan looked hard at the man. He knew the lies. "My father taught the word of God. We lived in the church on the peak and Elisa and I played in the garden. She was afraid of the snails," he said, remembering. "I'd chase her with them."

All at once, cold needles pricked at the back of Nathan's neck and thoughts of his family came flooding back to him. He saw his father inside the vestry and the blood and heard the thunder of the guns. "They killed for no reason," he said as tears began to form. "Hong Kong belongs to the Chinese," he whispered, handing the old man his walking stick.

"Yes," the man agreed. "Hong Kong belongs to the Chinese," he agreed as he studied the boy's face. A wave of sympathy washed over him and the old man was embarrassed for his trickery.

The train shrieked as it pulled into Kowloon. Miss Lockburn had not noticed the conversation between Nathan and the Chinese man. Watching the station slide into view, she grabbed the bag of bread and Nathan's wrist and yanked him toward the car doors. The woman of God was bent on leaving the train before being trampled to death.

Nathan struggled to get free. He wanted to know more of his father and what the old man was talking about, but as the crowd pushed for the door Nathan was enveloped and the Chinese man disappeared behind the dark wall of pressing bodies. Nathan felt his feet hit the hard cement of the station as Miss Lockburn pulled him along.

The man remained on the train until everyone else had departed and the car was empty. He really had no idea who this boy was, who his father had been, or what they had talked about.

He had only said what he had been instructed to say. His questions had been practiced inside a small office at the police station for the past two days. And now, as he stood with the help of his walking stick and moved toward the door, he hoped he could remember everything the boy had said and that Chief Inspector Forbath would be pleased with his performance.

Mary Lockburn stood defiantly across from the Father. She had kindly refused the chair and waited nervously for the priest as he read over the letter she had attained from the Bishop.

"You can't be serious," Father Clooney said as he finished.

"Indeed, Father. The boy needs what you cannot offer him here. He needs to be with his own kind."

"He is with his own—"

"Beyond the church, Father," Miss Lockburn cut him off. "He has to know that he cannot have a proper life without speaking his native tongue. In London, he will have to use English or he will be helpless."

"As you are here, Miss Lockburn," the Father snapped, "is this really for Nathan's good or for your own?"

"Father!" Miss Lockburn caught her breath, one hand going to her breast in shock, the other to her mouth. "How can you say that?"

"From the day you arrived, you've hated Hong Kong." Father Clooney marched around the desk. "You thought coming here and placing yourself in trying conditions would prove your love of God. I've seen it before, many times."

Mary Lockburn had never been spoken to in such a way. "You've been here too long, Father. You've lost your manners."

"What I've lost is my patience," Clooney said. He yanked

open his office door and called out, "Sister Agnes, will you bring Nathan here, please?"

"There's nothing more to discuss, Father," Mary said to his back. "The Bishop's letter states that the boy will return to London with me on the next ship."

"You don't think Nathan should be asked what he wants?" the Father asked, moving back to his desk.

"I don't think an eight-year-old boy can possibly know what is best for him," she said firmly. "I've already told him to begin packing."

"You did what?"

"I told him to gather his things," she said firmly. "Why not? The next clipper is in two days and I want to be ready."

The Father shook his head in disbelief.

The door opened and Sister Agnes, a fragile young woman, stepped hurriedly into the room. "He's gone, Father," she said softly. He could see the panic in her face. In her hand, she grasped a small scrap of paper. "I found only this."

Clooney looked at it and sighed heavily. "Well, Miss Lockburn," he said as if all his strength had been swept from his soul, "congratulations. You've gotten the boy to converse in the Queen's English. In writing, at least." He handed the note to her.

As Mary read it, her face slackened with dread.

I will never leave Hong Kong!

The piece of paper slipped from her trembling fingers and drifted to the floor.

Chapter Fifteen

Kowloon Peninsula

From within the soft, tranquil depths of sleep, Lindsay's mind began to register pain. Not the dull, droning aches that had accompanied him into repose. Those his brain had accepted, overcome, and set aside. This pain was new and growing.

At first it tugged gently at his nerve fibers, like a lethargic halibut gnawing on a fisherman's lure—a nibble, a nip—so light that the signal barely registered. But the annoyance at his left forearm continued, growing more bothersome until the piercing affliction finally demanded his full attention.

Lindsay opened his eyes and became immediately aware of Suzette's body stretched out beside his. Her face was buried into his shoulder and she clutched his left arm so tightly that her fingernails were digging into his flesh.

Gently, Lindsay pried her fingers away one at a time. She stirred, but continued to sleep, cuddled warmly in the womb of her dream.

The young Chinese student pulled her hand away. "You don't understand, Suzette," he said, his eyes afire. "You've always had these freedoms. You can't understand."

"I do." Suzette tried to sound forceful, resolved like the others in the square. But the firmness of her voice was diluted by the tears streaming down her face. *"You've done enough, Yang. Please."*

"No! We're just starting," he said. The broad white bandanna tied about his forehead was stained from sweat. It kept his black-framed glasses from fitting correctly and he continuously pushed them back on his nose. *"You just came to study. When you're finished, you'll go back to Hong Kong. I have to stay. Beijing's my home."*

"I'm afraid."

"So am I," he said honestly, and for the first time she saw emotion in his heroic eyes. *"But you heard what they said. The soldiers have been stopped at Hujialou. We are going to win."*

Suzette looked across the surreal scene of campfires and floodlights and saw a forest of protest banners made from bedsheets and red paint. The crowd within Tiananmen Square had grown to unbelievable numbers in the past two weeks. The outrage of ideological students had sparked the population into motion.

And holding court over this sea of Chinese faces was the bizarre image of an alien idea. The thirty-seven-foot sculpture of the Goddess of Democracy, inspired by the Statute of Liberty, stood purposely across from the huge portrait of Mao Zedong. This iron and plaster woman was by far the loudest and clearest cry from desperate souls.

Maybe, Suzette thought. Maybe he was right. How could the government do anything else but listen to its people? The students' hunger strike was being broadcast around the world to an audience that had seen the dissolution of the Soviet Union and the crumbling of the Berlin wall.

Yang had to be right. They were on the threshold of history and the people filling Tiananmen Square were pounding at its door. Suzette suddenly wanted to be a part of it. Her pride of her Chinese heritage swelled within her. *"I'll stay,"* she said.

Yang smiled. *"You'll see. The soldiers might come, but they won't shoot."*

"How do you know?"

"They can't. They're the people's army."

When he leaned to kiss her, she opened her eyes.

Lindsay was staring at her curiously. "You okay?"

Suzette rolled to the far edge of the bed and dropped her feet to the floor. The carpet was warmed by a wedge of sun coming through the torn curtain. She cupped her face in her hands. "Yeah," she said.

He slid close and touched her. "You sure? You were crying."

She forced a smile. "Sorry I woke you."

"Only after you drew blood." He revealed her fingernail marks in his arm.

"Oh, my God," she rubbed his forearm with her palm. "I'm sorry."

"I'll survive."

"I can't believe I did that."

"I don't care what you say, next time we're getting separate beds."

She laughed. "I'm really sorry."

"What was in the nightmare?"

She looked into his eyes and had the sensation of falling in.

"I've had plenty," Lindsay admitted as he unzipped his leather carry-on and pulled out a dark blue polo shirt. "I've even had doctors tell me what they meant."

"I know what mine mean," Suzette said, moving to the bathroom. "That's the problem." Suzette closed the door and found that in the sunlight the bathroom was worse than she had feared. She looked into the dirty mirror and ran her fingers through her hair. Splashing water into her face, she thought of Yang and the moment she had lost sight of him in the chaos as he rushed forward against the fleeing crowd. And how she had found him the next day in the basement of the Fuxing Hospital, his body piled grotesquely atop the bodies of six other idealistic young students, all drenched in their own blood.

"Suzette." Lindsay knocked on the door.

"Yes?"

"I'm going to the office to make a phone call. Keep the door locked."

"Okay," she said, staring into her tearing eyes.

A few minutes later, when Lindsay returned, Suzette was refreshed, with her makeup reapplied and her hair combed.

"Who'd you call?"

"You ready?" Lindsay asked, ignoring her question.

"You don't trust me?"

"It's nothing personal. I don't trust a lot of people."

"If I was going to kill you, I would've done it last night."

"Not while I have the pendant," he said.

Suzette pursed her lips in frustration.

"I called a friend," Lindsay relented. "We're going to swap cars." He slipped Truby's automatic into the bottom of his carry-on and tucked the small Walther into the back of his pants.

Fifteen minutes later, Lindsay peeked through the curtains and saw Mun's delivery van pull around the corner and out of sight of the hotel. It took Mun only a few minutes to cross the harbor and follow Lindsay's directions to the dilapidated little motel. But Lindsay had said nothing over the phone about the woman Mun recognized from the photograph. He grinned as they approached. "You stayed here?"

"We didn't have a lot of choices," Lindsay said.

"Sure . . ." Mun continued to grin.

"It's not like that."

"Okay. If you say so."

"Shut up, Mun. And say hello to Suzette."

"Hi." He grinned wider.

"Nice to meet you."

"You could have stayed at my folks' house."

"That's where we're headed," Lindsay said, tossing him Suzette's car key. "It's the silver convertible in the back."

"A convertible? Cool."

"Don't go racing around. I don't want you noticed."

"All right," he said, disappointed. "What do you want me to do with it?"

"Tuck it into one of those big parking structures downtown. And here." Lindsay handed him four thousand Hong Kong dollars. "Buy what I told you."

"What size?"

Lindsay turned to Suzette. "What size do you wear?"

"I have clothes."

"Not with you."

Suzette sighed. "A size three."

Lindsay and Mun stared at her.

"Size four."

"Anything else?"

"Don't get brown or anything with flowers."

Lindsay and Mun exchanged a glance. "Take this, too." Lindsay handed him the small automatic.

"Wow." His eyes widened.

"Dump it in the harbor. It was Tommy's. You don't want to get caught with it."

"No kidding."

"And do like I told you: Watch your back."

Mun nodded. "Watch my back and nothing with flowers. Got it." He pocketed the money and headed around the corner.

Lindsay and Suzette climbed into the tiny cab of the microvan. With a few grinding complaints, the truck accepted first gear and they pulled slowly away from the curb.

Lindsay maneuvered through the chaotic traffic as he headed down the tip of Kowloon. "Tommy and Mun's father grew up together."

"He studied in the States?"

"You can tell?"

"Cool," she mimicked the young man, and both Lindsay and she laughed.

Buses and cars filled with midday commuters rumbled through the harbor tunnel at a decelerated pace. Inside the darkness, with the eerie glares of headlights dancing around them, Lindsay thought about the two young agents who had come through here and lost their lives.

There were a multitude of scrapes and scratches across the tunnel wall and hundreds of skid marks on the road. Each one attested to the fact that accidents often happen in the most inopportune places. And in Lindsay's mind, Hong Kong was a very inopportune place.

As the tunnel rose back into the sunlight and the ranks and files of vehicles began to open up, Lindsay weaved his way across two intersections, through a one-way alley, and back onto a westbound street.

They reached the spice shop at half past one o'clock. Mrs. Zhang, dressed in a white smock like that of a chemist, was at the cash register finishing a sale. Seeing Lindsay, she grinned widely.

"There you are," she said, stepping between the counters.

"I hope you don't mind," Lindsay said.

She looked closely at him and saw the bruises. "You don't look good."

"Rough night," he admitted. He introduced Suzette.

"Nice to meet you," Mrs. Zhang said pleasantly, but was silently making a different assessment.

"I'm sorry we're imposing," Suzette said, shaking her hand.

"No, no trouble," Mrs. Zhang said as she led them through the door and into her home. "Come, I have dim sum."

"We couldn't . . ."

"Sounds great. And we each could use a shower."

"Linds," Suzette scolded.

"Aiya." Mrs. Zhang glanced at Lindsay. She patted Suzette's hand. "He is like a son to me, but he'll always be a *gweilo.*"

Suzette laughed.

"Ladies shower first, *gweilo,*" she said, then pointed Suzette down the hall.

"Yeah, *gweilo,*" Suzette repeated as she headed toward the bathroom.

Mrs. Zhang put her hand on Lindsay's forearm. "She's the girl in the picture?" she whispered.

"Yes," Lindsay said, knowing the Chinese woman was formulating shrewd opinions.

"She said she was working for him. Doing research."

"Research? Looking like that?"

Looking like that, Lindsay thought, and remembered what the assistant at the museum had said about her.

Lindsay found Jing sitting in the yard. Anson was standing at his shoulder reading the morning paper with him.

"Ni hao," Lindsay said to them as he stepped outside.

"Good morning," Jing said. He prodded Anson toward the kitchen. "Bring us tea."

Lindsay sat at the rickety table.

"Have you heard about the troops?"

"In Guangzhou?"

"Yes."

"They're military exercises."

"That's what the newspapers are saying. But they're enough to make the stock market nervous and everyone else."

"Anything official?"

"If a communist tank rolled over the Governor's foot tomorrow, he would say it was part of the reunification."

"He's a politician."

"He used to be *our* politician. More than any other Governor, he worked the hardest to give us elections," Jing said. "But with the deadline so close, he's become a realist like the rest of us."

"That's because he can always get on a plane and fly home."

"I tell you, Linds," Jing said, lifting his weak hand to the table, "if the British Parliament hadn't outlawed Hongkongers from immigrating, we would have a better deal with Beijing. And they'd be concerned with keeping us happy and keeping the foreign investors here. Instead, they send us tanks."

"Why would Beijing march into Hong Kong when they're getting the place anyway?" Lindsay asked. As soon as he had, he began to think about what Suzette had told him.

"Who understands communists?" Jing spat. "Find anything about Tommy?"

"I found the girl. She's here with me."

"Oh?"

"The name Lauhu sound familiar?"

"No, but Mun told me the name before. I've asked around. Someone will know her."

Along with the tea, Anson brought her father a small rosewood box. "Want to try again, Ba-ba?" she asked with a playful smirk.

"You are like your mother; you enjoy tormenting me. Give it to Lindsay."

Anson offered the box.

Lindsay finished filling his teacup and took it from her. The finely constructed wooden case with its delicate herringbone pattern seemed to have no opening. He flipped it over several times. "What is this?" Lindsay asked, mystified.

Anson giggled. "You have to open it."

"How?"

"You push a corner or pull the bottom," Jing said. "I've tried. I can't do it."

"Show me," Lindsay said.

Taking the small box, she pressed the center pattern of the herringbone. A small block suddenly protruded from the opposite side, unlocking a sliding corner, which allowed the box to pull apart and magically open. She revealed the long center cavity hidden within. Then, reversing the process, she closed the box and presented it again to Lindsay.

"It looks simple, doesn't it?"

"Only after you know how it works," Jing said. "Take your torture into the house," he told his daughter.

"Tommy's death is like the box. It makes no sense."

"Not yet."

"Why do you think she is with you?"

"She's scared. The Sun Yee are after her because she helped Tommy."

"And what did they want with Tommy?"

"I'm not sure," Lindsay said, deciding not to bring up her unbelievable story. It was easy for him to lie and probably safer for Jing.

"Well, it's time for mah-jongg," Jing said, and as he stood, he patted Lindsay on the shoulder. *"Ts'o Muk Kaai Ping,"* he said.

Lindsay chuckled. He knew the Chinese saying: "Behind every tree and thicket, a soldier."

Jing had hit on the very nerve that was pinching at the back of Lindsay's brain. Why did she remain with him? Especially when she knew the British were after him as well. There was something more she wanted. Something she needed from him, and it was neither the pendant nor Tommy's killers.

At the same moment, down the hall and sitting in front of the bathroom mirror, Suzette was asking herself the same question. Why did she have to stay with this American? Why didn't they give up and get out? They could. They could easily live anywhere in the world; Tokyo, New York, Paris . . . even London if they wanted.

She felt Mrs. Zhang pull her wet hair through the large-toothed comb. "You must have been growing this since you were a teenager," Mrs. Zhang said. The comb was drawn through the black silk again and again.

"My mother had long hair," Suzette said.

"She was Chinese?"

"Half. Her father was English." Suzette reached back and grabbed a length of her thick moist hair. "Could you cut it?"

"Cut it?"

"Would you, please?"

Three hours later, Mun arrived at the house. He came in through the back door, his arms filled with shopping bags. As Lindsay had instructed, Mun bought both of them a wardrobe of blue jeans, T-shirts, tennis shoes, walking shorts, and an assortment of sweatshirts with colorful advertisements. He was also able to find a matching pair of nylon traveling bags that converted into backpacks with hidden shoulder straps.

"Perfect," Lindsay said as he rifled through the bags.

"I got these, too," Mun said, handing Lindsay two mid-priced cameras. "No tourist would be without them."

"You figured it out."

"Sure," Mun said. "The dudes after you are looking for a *GQ* American and a Chinese woman. You're going to fool them."

"Let's hope so," Lindsay said. "What about the dress?"

"Oh, here." He handed Lindsay a long white box from Mayleelok's.

He glanced inside. "And my suit?"

Mun handed him a hanging bag from Alfred Dunhill. "They still had you on file."

"Doesn't everyone?" Lindsay said under his breath. He took the dress box and walked to the back of the house.

The soft knock at the door woke Suzette from her nap. She slipped off the bed.

"Suzette?" Lindsay called.

"Just a sec."

"I brought you some clothes."

Suzette pulled Mrs. Zhang's gold rayon robe tight around her and opened the door.

Lindsay was shocked. "Your hair?"

"You don't like it?"

Mrs. Zhang had cut off eighteen inches, yet her hair still reached the top of her shoulders. She had also added a curl that put in a fullness it hadn't had before. Mrs. Zhang's lack of knowledge in hairstyling gave Suzette a completely different look, a reckless, untamed beauty.

Lindsay caught himself staring. "No, it's ... it's fine. Here." He pushed the box into her hands. "You've got a date."

She stared at him wide-eyed as he disappeared into the bathroom with his suit bag.

Lindsay showered, shaved, and slipped into a wastefully expensive black Egyptian wool suit, a black turtleneck sweater, and black Gabino oxfords. The concierge at Alfred Dunhill had come through. He no longer looked like a man on the run. He was a gambler who was reshuffling the deck and storing the ace of spades into his sleeve.

Lindsay and Mun were in the kitchen packing the rest of their new clothes when Suzette stepped from the hallway.

"Wow ..." Mun gasped.

Lindsay looked up. "Oh, boy," he added.

The aqua-blue *cheongsam* shimmered in the fluorescence of the kitchen lights. The classical Chinese dress hugged her willowy body like a silk sheath. The slit along her right leg revealed Suzette's dark stockings and high-heeled shoes.

Her hair, brushed forward, swept wildly across her cheek and with makeup borrowed from Mrs. Zhang she had darkened her eyebrows and reddened her lips.

"Do I pass?"

"I'd say so."

She eyed Lindsay's suit. "So do you," she said.

"Wow," Mun repeated himself.

Suzette smiled at the young man. "You have very good taste in clothes, Mun."

"Linds told me what to buy."

"Did he," she said, moving to the table. She looked inside the backpacks and saw the jeans and sweatshirts. "Are we going somewhere?"

"Tomorrow we're going to Macau."

"Why?"

Mun closed the pack. "That's where they found the pieces."

"What pieces?"

"Of Tommy."

Suzette stared at him.

"Good goin'," Lindsay said.

Mun cringed. "Sorry."

Chapter Sixteen

Ap Lei Chau Island

Danny Wei sipped dark Colombian coffee from a tiny porcelain cup exquisitely decorated with hand-painted blue flowers. He set it in the saucer he held with his left hand and stared out the nineteen-foot tinted window that lined the second floor of the main house. Beyond the trimmed hedges, the stone patio and the kidney-shaped swimming pool of his three-acre estate lay the calm waters of the Aberdeen Channel.

Turning from the window, Danny crossed the room's plush mint-green carpet. Decorated with rosewood furniture, priceless artifacts from mainland China, and a variety of European expressionist art, the large study was a mixture of past and present.

Danny glanced at his watch as he stepped behind his desk. He set his cup and saucer beside the towering model of the Transworld Shipping Service Building. The display stood three feet over the desktop. Now under construction in Sydney, Australia, the seventy-seven-story black mirrored monolith, trimmed in deep green, would stand at the leading edge of Port Jackson and directly across from the billowing white concrete arches of the famed Opera House.

It was already being called the Jade Palace and would be to international shipping what the Opera House was to Australia. Instant recognition. And in that, Danny Wei found immense satisfaction.

As the thirty-two-year-old president of the multibillion-dollar company, Danny understood the misgivings of nervous stockholders who thought he was possibly too young for such a position. But his decisions and actions in T.S.S.'s investments during the first part of his tenure had been correct to the last decimal point. That alone should have dispersed any doubts.

It hadn't, and that ate at Danny from the inside out. All those docile old men with their powerful votes saw one thing, and one thing only: that he was little more than the Chairman's son.

It was true that Kenneth Wei had removed himself from the top position and then used his reigning leverage to elect his only son to the presidency. But there were other factors explaining why the senior Wei felt Danny was the proper heir to the shipping throne.

It was an indisputable fact that the young Wei was a business wizard, a master of finance and accounting, and had proven himself a foreseer into the world's corporate trends. In short, Danny was a genius when it came to international business.

And Danny had proven it over the last year. Although it was his father's idea to move T.S.S. out of Hong Kong and to Australia, it was Danny who figured out the logistics and how to divert six hundred million dollars for relocation without compromising T.S.S's shipping schedules, international commitments, or other interests. Danny knew the continent country would be welcoming hundreds of businesses from the doomed colony. And he knew T.S.S. would be the largest.

The initial investment in Sydney came with the promise that three times that amount would be generated and invested into Australia over the next decade. Six months after T.S.S. was firmly in place, Danny promised to construct new dry docks and storage facilities in Brisbane and Melbourne.

The Minister of Industry and Trade had welcomed the company with open arms, not to mention an extensive series of tax breaks and shelters. The Minister had pressed hard for these special favors, constantly reminding the Australian Parliament that the Hong Kong–based company was fast becoming the world's largest shipper. With one hundred and twenty-seven freighters, forty-nine tankers, and a new cruise line, it would soon control a major portion of the sea transport industry. Its move to Australia would create at least five thousand jobs in Sydney alone. Its economical effects over time were limitless.

Danny looked up from the building model as he heard a knock at the door. His father stepped in.

At fifty-four years old, Kenneth Wei was still a broad, powerful-looking man with dark hair and a round face and large fleshy cheeks. He was short, five-foot-four, which was a trait of his generation. His son was four inches taller, and he was happy for that. Height, Kenneth felt, induced success.

"Do you have time to finish?" Kenneth asked, moving to the single chair in front of Danny's huge desk.

Danny nodded. He sat down in his high-backed leather chair and opened the thick file that rested in the center of the blotter. "What time's your flight?" he asked as he flipped through several papers.

"After the dinner."

It was curious how events had changed them. Once his father had moved to the less demanding position of chairman, they were both amazed at the silent shift of power.

"You are coming to dinner, aren't you?" Kenneth asked.

"No," Danny said. "I have other business."

"Such as?" Kenneth liked to know everything that was going on in the company, though it was an impossibility. T.S.S. was far too large and too complex, but he asked just the same.

Danny glanced at his father with suspicious eyes. "You worry about the Greeks, I will take care of the rest."

"I simply asked," his father defended. An argument was coming, Kenneth sensed. He had tasted the odor of verbal battle when he entered the room. Or maybe he had just expected it because their bouts were so frequent.

"You don't think I can handle it?" His son's voice jumped three decibels.

"Of course I do." Kenneth suddenly felt tired. He could say nothing without Danny descending upon him. "I know you're capable."

"Then why do you ask?" Danny turned back to the file.

With a sigh, Kenneth settled into his chair and folded his arms across his chest. The barrier was erected: their discussion from this point would be formal at best. Kenneth had to admit it, more and more he was taking a backseat to his son. It bothered him a little, wore against his ego. A silly thing, ego, especially in an old man. But still, it couldn't be denied.

"Tomorrow you meet with Mr. Keramidas," Danny said, finding the notes he was looking for.

Kenneth was thankful to move on.

"He doesn't have the final say in the sale, but he has a lot of pull over the shareholders," Danny continued.

Kenneth saw the beverage cart and moved to it. He poured himself hot tea from the second silver pot.

"The Odysseus Cruise Line has five ships. We're only interested in three. The two latest and the one that still hasn't been commissioned," Danny said as he looked over the papers. "Be temperate in dealing with the Greeks. They still think we work in laundromats. They're slow in all matters, especially business."

Kenneth listened as Danny prepared him for the trip to Athens. He didn't particularly like the idea of a cruise line under the family's banner. Too much of an insurance risk. But Danny was right in trying to build a line that would fill the potential of the South Pacific islands. Besides, the Greek ships were a good bargain.

He watched as Danny skimmed the report and picked out the details. Danny's business intuition was quick and sound. He was becoming a formidable opponent, if not a shrewd one, when dealing with competitors. That, perhaps more than anything else, made Kenneth Wei proud of his son. In his eyes, Danny was a reined-in lion waiting to stake his claim in the corporate world.

The company had begun as a family business and was meant to be run as such. Kenneth's father had been a smuggler before the Second World War, then he and his partner had turned their skills of illegal trade to legitimate shipping and founded T.S.S. From then on, the business had been handed down from father to son and Danny was third in the unbroken chain.

Kenneth had seen to that. Danny had been educated at the finest schools in America and England. He held a doctorate degree in international business and finance and another in Western philosophy. There was heritage at stake and Kenneth knew how to hedge his bets.

But one thing bothered him. Rumors of Danny's Triad connections still lingered in the hallways of their corporate headquarters. And there were the peculiar corporate holdings he uncovered when a secretary mistakenly passed the younger Wei's private files to Kenneth's office.

At first, curiosity opened the file. Then, as Kenneth realized what he had found, he made several quiet inquiries. The investments were in a small hotel and several waterfront buildings and docks now leased to smaller shipping companies who couldn't afford to move before the transition. They were of no consequence other than they had no explanation.

He knew Danny didn't like the idea of cutting ties with Hong Kong. Neither did he. But he remembered the war and he remembered the establishment of the People's Republic of China, the Cultural Revolution—Tiananmen Square. It all made him uneasy. At the moment, he thought better of raising the matter with his son. There was still time.

"I've estimated it'll cost about twelve million dollars to refurbish each ship," Danny was saying. "The line could be in operation by the summer."

Kenneth finished his tea and set the cup back on the tray. "Have your secretary make copies and I will read them on the plane," he said, moving toward the door.

"But you think it is a good investment?" Danny asked.

Kenneth stopped and looked at his son. There was still uncertainty in his voice. The lion wasn't quite ready. "Yes," he said. "We'll arrange the year-end meeting aboard one of your luxury liners." He grinned. As he stepped through the door, he stopped. "It is a good idea, Daniel. But I expect that," he said matter-of-factly, and left.

Danny closed the file and let out a low whistle. The investment was a long shot and they both knew it. They also knew that unless the company was striving forward, taking chances, it would become stagnant, a shadow, a paper tiger. It was the same in life as in business.

The modern phone with no receiver handle on his desk buzzed. Danny simply spoke and it switched on. "Yes?"

His secretary from his Kowloon office spoke pleasantly. "It's five-fifteen, Mr. Wei. You wanted me to remind you."

"Thank you, Olivia," a shiver of excitement ran through him as he verified the time on his jeweled Cartier. "Would you make a copy of the Odysseus file and deliver it to my father's office before he leaves?"

"Yes, sir," she said.

Danny descended the wide stairs to the polished floor of the entry hall. Exiting his island home, he was met by the cool breeze of dusk. The loose gravel driveway crackled beneath the soles of his shoes as he approached his black Mercedes 600SL. He slipped into the convertible and fired up the sedate V12 engine. Against the leather steering wheel, he felt his hands cold and clammy. He smiled. He was certain everything would fall into place. There was still time to find Tommy Fong. He had earned tonight and he was going to enjoy it.

With the steady hand of a surgeon, Danny formed a long line of white powder with a razor blade. He scraped it back, pulled it forward, piled it higher on top of itself until a miniature snow-covered mountain range ran along the glass table. When he had a perfect line eight inches long, he cut it in half and started the procedure over again until he had two perfectly parallel lines.

Then he cut one of those in half and worked the amount

with the razor until, once again, he had two smaller but identical doses of the potent drug.

The lobster in eggplant was from Bentley's, the champagne from Gaddi's, delivered in Styrofoam chests filled with ice. But when the food and wine could spur them no longer, he broke into his coveted powder.

It was, after all, the highest-quality *sabu* out of the Philippines and was part of a gracious gift from a Manila druglord for Danny's help in obtaining a new pipeline into Canada and the States. With Danny's family connections in shipping, it was a surprisingly simple matter.

Danny looked up from his work, across his penthouse bedroom, and at the two young women laying on the waterbed. The one with the short-cropped red hair lay on her stomach at the edge of the bed facing him, her head propped up on her hands, watching him with anticipation. Her companion, the sandy-blonde with the long, sharp fingernails, was playfully trying to push the redhead over onto her back to get at her breasts. She was like a kitten who had lost its ball of yarn under a chair and was intent on capturing it.

Across the floor, tossed thoughtlessly about, were two expensive velvet dresses, one black, one bistro blue, four high-heeled shoes, and two sets of lingerie, one in black and one in white. The sheets and the bedcover were also on the floor, crumpled and thrown there in hurried lustful moments.

Danny, however, had taken the time to hang his clothes properly in one of the closets hidden behind the mirrored walls that surrounded the bed. Only then did he join the women in their erotic tussle. They explored him during the night, toyed with him, brought him to the edges of ecstasy, only to hold him off so they could bring him back time and time again.

Just before dawn, he left them and moved to watch from the couch. He was surprised that the sight of such beauty engaged with the sole aim of pleasure could bring him so much enjoyment.

Danny took a tightly rolled one-hundred-dollar-bill and held it against his left nostril. Leaning over, he laid it at the beginning of the longest rail, and with a deep breath he inhaled the bitter powder.

Instantly the skin on his face felt as if it were being pulled tight over his skull. He pinched his nose, sniffled, and blinked his eyes. For a second the bedroom seemed to turn surreal, the brightness of the lamps and the sunlight creeping from beneath the curtains flared with sharp clarity. It slowly subsided, leaving Danny in a state of heightened awareness.

He leaned in his soft leather couch, feeling its coolness against his skin. "Ladies," he called.

The redhead rolled away from the blonde and raced giggling to the table. Folding her long, tanned legs beneath her, she nestled beside Danny on the floor between the table and the couch.

By the time the blonde got to the opposite side, the redhead had taken the rolled bill. She leaned over, her pert breasts pressing against the cold glass table, and easily consumed the thin line. Wiping her nose with the back of her hand, she sighed deeply. "Lovely," she said. Resting her arm on Danny's thigh, she turned and kissed the outside of his knee.

"My turn," the blonde said, snapping the bill from her girlfriend's hand. She, too, made the powder vanish. "God, Danny, that's the best."

"For you." He smiled as he ran his fingers through her silky hair.

"And for you," the redhead teased as she looked at him with dark eyes. She wetted her thumb with the tip of her tongue and dabbed it to the remaining powder. Shifting to her knees, she leaned over him, her nipples brushing the tops of his thighs. She wrapped her fingers about him, his body reacting immediately to her touch.

The blonde giggled as she climbed the couch. She kissed him, her mouth open, her darting tongue playing with his. Danny felt the warmth of the redhead's mouth between his legs. He slipped his left hand down the smooth thigh of the blonde. She moaned deeply and parted her legs as his searching fingers found her.

The high-pitched ring of the cellular phone cracked the room like a siren. All three of them jumped.

"Fuck." Danny slapped the seat of the couch in aggravation.

"That scared the shit out of me," the blonde yapped.

"Watch out," he said, untangling himself from them.

"Let it ring," the redhead said.

"Yeah, don't bother with it." The blonde tried to hold his arm.

He pulled away from her and leaped across the room, hoping to catch it before it rang again. He didn't quite make it. The pitch cut into his brain a second time. "What?" he yelled into the phone.

There was hesitation on the other end of the line. Finally the caller spoke. "He's here."

Danny recognized Zigao's voice. "Who?"

"Lee. He just entered the lift," the big man said hurriedly.

"Fuck."

"You want me to come up?"

"Who's with him?"

"No one."

"Good," Danny said with relief. "Did you find the girl?"

Another hesitation. "No. But I got a line on the *gweilo.*"

Danny sat down on the bed. He cupped his hand over the receiver. "Out," he said to the girls. They were entangled on the couch.

"But we're not finished," the redhead said, not wanting to leave the remaining powder on the table.

"We'll be quiet," the blonde promised.

"I can't promise that." The redhead snickered at her partner.

"Now," he said, feeling his impatience grow. He held it, knowing these women could be stubborn at times and might not come back. He enjoyed them too much for that. He lessened his tone. "Please. Go into the kitchen and tell the cook to make you breakfast," he said. "There are robes in the closet." He pointed to one of the mirrored doors and turned back to the phone.

"Okay," the redhead said, wrinkling her nose. "But we're coming back." As she yanked the robes from the closet, she saw the blonde smile and wet her finger. She ran it through the remaining powder, then she placed it seductively on her tongue. Giggling, she leaped for the robe and ran out of the room. The redhead pranced after her.

Danny brought the phone back to his mouth. "Give me something good."

"He was a reporter at the *Tribune.*"

"That's it?"

"He must have known Tommy."

Danny sighed. "Find them. Find them all." He hung up the phone. He laid back on his bed and stared up at himself in the ceiling mirror. All plans had mishaps, even the best. It would turn. He trusted Zigao.

The knock at the door was neither light nor heavy. It was solid. Confident. Danny quickly pulled on a pair of slacks and a white shirt. He buttoned it as he hurried across the living room. "Coming," he called to the door.

The stocky, middle-aged Chinese man in the tight jeans and Polo shirt standing on the other side of the door greeted Danny cheerfully. "Don't you ask who it is?" he joked as he stepped in. The Triad elder knew very well he had been seen entering Danny's apartment complex. He expected it.

"I didn't have to."

"Of course not."

"A drink?" Danny offered as they eased into the living room.

"*Aiya* . . . at eight-thirty in the morning?"

"I'm sorry, Mr. Lee. How about tea?"

"Nothing, Daniel. Nothing at all."

The kitchen door suddenly burst open and the redhead stepped through with a piece of toast in her hand. "Danny? Do you want . . . Oh." She smiled shyly at Lee. "Good morning," she said.

"Good morning."

"I'll be there in a minute," Danny said firmly. His tone ushering her away.

"Okay," she said. "Bye-bye." she waved to Lee as she disappeared.

"Good-bye." Lee smiled.

"Sorry about that, Mr. Lee."

"I was young, too," Lee said understandingly. Then, with the back of his hand, he hit Danny across the face.

The young Chinese reeled backward.

"You stupid fool," Lee spat. "You wanted into our world, so I let you in. But to do so, I had to give my word you'd help us."

"I know."

"Do you have this deed? Can you show it to me?"

"Not yet."

"You promised us Hong Kong, Danny. I hope you can deliver."

"I will."

"There'll be plenty of time to slip your pecker in these pleasures. So don't give me a reason to shear it off," Lee said. He marched to the front door. Then, as he stepped through, he mocked the prostitute and waved. "Bye-bye."

Chapter Seventeen

Macau, 1901

In the dark chasm between the bulkhead of the Lingsyou's cabin and the outer hull of the Chinese junk, Nathan inched along the raw wood on his elbows and knees. He moved to the pillow and blanket he had put there weeks before. As he slid over the woolen blanket, the strong smell of mildew choked him. He swallowed back a cough that would give him away.

Young Nathan had found this tiny gap that ran the length of the junk when the ship's cat had born kittens here. She had slipped inside through a loose board beside his bunk in the storage locker.

Crawling along the inner hull to bring mother and kittens milk, Nathan discovered the space was adjacent to the captain's cabin. From where he lay, he could hear and see everything through the cracks between the wooden beams. The hollow soon became Nathan's secret place. A place for hiding when he did something wrong and was sure he was going to get the back of the Lingsyou's hand. Or when he just needed a place to disappear. With its entrance next to his bunk, it was easy to slip in and out without being seen.

When the Lingsyou and Fu-laing met late at night in the cabin, Nathan was already in his hiding place. He knew they were not fooled easily and he had to be careful. He was afraid of what they would do to him if they found him eavesdropping on their conversations.

But Nathan enjoyed listening to their plans for their next raids and how they would avoid the Chinese patrols along the various routes. And sometimes, after a good run, the two pirates would drink together and talk about long-ago days: their adventures smuggling, the fights they had partaken in, the storms they had survived and the women they hadn't.

Nathan understood about the storms and the boasting of battles, but the talk of women bored him. He wished they would talk more about their narrow escapes.

Over the ten months since Nathan had been taken aboard as cabin boy, he had learned many things about the Chinese, about ships and running the coastal waters throughout the South China Sea. Fu-laing had taken a liking to the young *gweilo* and was teaching him the language of the Manchurians.

Nathan learned quickly to both respect and fear the Lingsyou. Many times Yak-san had beaten Nathan for doing his duties poorly or for hesitating to carry out an order. Once, after Nathan had only been aboard for a few weeks, he was told to relay a compass course from Fu-laing to the helmsman. But Nathan mistakenly had told the crewman 215 instead of 251, and as punishment the captain threw Nathan overboard.

Barely able to tread water, Nathan watched as the junk disappeared from sight. For three terrifying hours he bobbed in the cold choppy seas, but he refused to give in to the liquid void. Finally the ship returned and they plucked him out of the water.

"Now do you understand the sea, little devil?" the Lingsyou asked, his voice loud and crisp, his eyes dark and hard.

Shivering, Nathan stood in front of him with his head bowed.

"It is not forgiving," the Lingsyou continued. "Make a mistake and it will open up and swallow you whole."

"Yes, Lingsyou," Nathan said.

"Good," the Lingsyou said. He took off his great winter coat and wrapped it over the boy's shoulders. "Never forget what you learned. Now go below and get warm."

Nathan never did forget about Yak-san tossing him over the side, nor did he forget about the time the priests came to take him away and Yak-san threatened to slit their throats if they stepped aboard his ship.

"The boy is mine," the Lingsyou told them, saying he had purchased him in Wan Chai. The priests promised to send the authorities, but they never did.

Through the hull, Nathan could hear the wooden beams of the junk rub against the stiff pylons of the Macau dock. They had been moored there since noon and with the approaching night the ship was deserted. The Lingsyou had let all but three of his crew go ashore. Fu-laing also went, promising Yak-san that he would send Rosie back.

Nathan remembered the fat woman from the last time they were in the Portuguese port. Her face looked like one of the junk's block and tackle, oblong and flat. Her hair was short and oily and she covered her cheeks with heavy white powder.

And Nathan remembered how she teased him about knowing just the right girl when he was ready to become a man. Nathan's face flushed red from embarrassment when the nearby crewmen laughed.

Now, with everyone gone, it was easy for Nathan to sneak into his secret place, set the old pillow under his head, and wait for the Lingsyou and the fat woman to enter the cabin and close the door.

Closing his eyes, Nathan listened as the waves slapped gently against the hull. The spring evening in Macau was warm and the sea entered the harbor as small rolling swells. Straining against the iron cleats, the dock lines grumbled and muttered as they held the junk in place.

A woman's giggling and Yak-san's rough whisper woke Nathan. All at once he realized that he had fallen asleep and the Lingsyou and the woman were already in the cabin. Easing himself onto his elbows, Nathan looked into the cabin through the gap. Only one paper lantern hung in the far corner was lit, its tiny flame flickering with a weak, diffused glow.

Nathan stared intensely across the room. Tossed over Yak-san's small chart table and his chair were Rosie's silk dress and coat. The captain's pants and shirt were scattered across the floor.

Nathan saw movement. He sat up higher to see them in the Lingsyou's wide bunk, the shiny orange silk sheets covering their nakedness. Yak-san was on top of the woman but seemed to be trying, over and over, to climb off her. Yet, as hard as he tried, he could not.

In their low voices, Nathan could only make out a few words. He heard the captain groan and say something about a softness and warmth. The oval-faced woman giggled as she wrapped her arms around his neck, keeping him from moving away from her.

Suddenly from outside the cabin door Nathan heard hastened footsteps. Someone knocked quickly at the door. "Lingsyou," the voice called, and Nathan recognized it as one of the crew.

Yak-san stopped his struggle with the woman. "Curse you, man, what do you want?"

"Forgive me, Lingsyou. Chief Inspector Forbath has come aboard and wants to see you."

Nathan felt his heart stop. The darkness of his small hidden place seemed to suddenly close around him.

Yak-san pushed himself away from the woman. As he grabbed his trousers and pulled them on, Nathan could see what had been holding the captain to the woman. How funny, Nathan thought, that he would do that to himself. The young boy looked at the naked woman as she swung her legs off the edge of the bunk.

"Tell him to go away, Yak-san," she pleaded as she pulled the sheet around her.

Yak-san laced his trousers. "I can't. Not Forbath."

As Yak-san moved to the door, Nathan heard shouts and scuffling on the other side. Suddenly someone pounded a fist against it.

"Open up, Yak-san," Forbath called.

Nathan swallowed hard. He remembered that voice, that voice screaming at him.

"One moment," Yak-san hollered. "Allow the woman the decency to dress." He moved back to the bunk, reached around the woman, and pulled out his revolver.

"Open the door, you dung-eating swine!"

Yak-san held the gun behind his back as he moved to the door. "All right! Hold your tongue," Yak-san said, unlocking the latch.

The door burst open and in two steps Forbath's assistant was inside. He grabbed Yak-san by the throat and pressed the barrel of his own gun against his forehead. "Drop it," Bradley ordered.

"Your English manners seem to have dissipated, Mr. Dean," Yak-san gasped through his restricted throat. His eyes were crossed as he stared at the gun barrel.

"They have at that," Bradley agreed. "Now drop the gun."

Reluctantly, Yak-san tossed his revolver onto the table.

From behind Bradley, the Chief Inspector stepped into the cabin. "Good evening, Lingsyou."

"Tell her to get out." Bradley motioned to the woman. *"Chu-huoi,"* Yak-san said.

Without hesitation, the fat woman gathered her clothes in one hand and rushed past Forbath.

The Chief Inspector moved to the chart table and pulled out the chair. "Have a seat, my friend."

Bradley released his grip. He leveled the gun at Yak-san's chest and stepped back.

Yak-san sat down. "Had I known you were going to call, Chief Inspector, I would have kept the cook aboard."

"Shut up," Forbath snapped. Placing both hands on the tabletop, he looked down at Yak-san. "We made a deal and you crossed me."

"I would never."

"I've kept this pathetic ship from being boarded a dozen times over."

"And I've kept the boy as I promised. He's worthless, but I've kept him."

"You gave me one dead Manchurian and said the other

had been shot and fell overboard." Forbath's eyes narrowed on the Lingsyou.

"He was, three times in the back," Yak-san argued.

"He was shot, all right, but you left out one minor detail," Forbath said. "He's still alive."

"Impossible."

"Boat people in Aberdeen nursed him back to health," Forbath said. "We almost had him there, but he got away."

"He fits your description, Yak-san," Bradley added.

"It was only by chance he was caught hiring a boat to Canton."

"It can't be him," Yak-san said. "He would have fled into China before now."

"No." Bradley stepped forward. "The Boxer Rebellion has turned from chasing out foreigners to threatening the Manchurian throne. The Dowager Empress herself couldn't return to Peking until a few weeks ago."

"Had he entered Canton before now, he would have ended up dead," Forbath said.

"What do you want from me?" Yak-san asked.

"I closed the case on the Harrington murders because of your information," Forbath said, slamming his fist into the table. "I'm not going to do it again until I'm sure."

With the mention of his family name, Nathan pressed his face closer to the opening.

"The man that fell from my ship was dead," Yak-san told him. He suddenly realized Forbath wasn't sure about the man he had in custody.

"You better hope so," Forbath said, his voice low like that of a growling animal. "If the boy recognizes him, I'll have your skin."

"Where's Nathan now?" Bradley asked. "He has to identify the Manchurian before the Portuguese will turn him over to us."

"He's asleep."

"Get him," Forbath ordered. "Any tricks, Yak-san, and with God as my witness, I'll see you dead before the night is over." Yak-san didn't look at either of them. He moved to the cabin door and stepped through. Forbath closed it behind him. "After we get the boy, kill the Lingsyou."

"Why?" Bradley protested.

"Because I said."

Nathan shimmied backward from his hiding space, as it was too narrow to turn around. He slipped through the opening and into his bunk as Yak-san turned the latch of the cabin door.

"Nathan," Yak-san said as he struck a match and started the lantern. "Wake up, little devil."

Nathan sat up in his bunk, trying to act as if he had just been woken.

Yak-san held the lantern high. "Get dressed," he said. Yak-san didn't notice the boy's eyes were wide with terror or that he was still wearing his clothes from the day. The Chinese pirate was thinking about his own safety, and thinking fast.

What if it is the Manchurian and the boy recognizes him? Yak-san thought. He won't be able to hide that even if I told him to. And Forbath, the captain knew, would already have placed men on the docks so he couldn't escape. He'd wait until they took the boy. Then, Yak-san decided, he'd slip over the side and make his way into town and find Fulaing. The two of them could easily get back to Hong Kong.

"Come on," Yak-san said as he put his hand on Nathan's shoulder and they headed back to his cabin.

"Nathan." Forbath smiled at him as he stepped inside the cabin. "How are you, son?"

But Nathan remained next to Yak-san and looked coldly at the Chief Inspector. Then he looked at Bradley. The man's gun was gone now, hidden somewhere in his clothes.

"Good evening, Master Harrington," Bradley greeted him. He was surprised at how the boy had changed in the months since he had seen him last. His hair was long and disheveled and he looked more like a bilge rat than a boy. But his shoulders had broadened and his body had thickened with the first hints of muscle.

Nathan's stare turned back to Forbath.

"I need a favor of you, Nathan. I need you to come with us. Just for an hour," Forbath said.

"Mum-dug," Nathan snapped, telling them no.

Remembering the boy would only speak Cantonese, Forbath knelt down in front of him. "You have to come," he said in the Chinese tongue.

"No, I don't," Nathan said.

Forbath looked at Yak-san. "Tell him."

"How can I?" Yak-san shrugged.

"Tell him," Forbath said through a stiff jaw.

"Go with them, little devil. You'll be back soon enough."

Nathan turned and looked up at the Lingsyou, and for the first time saw fear in his eyes. "I won't go."

"You must."

"Not without you," Nathan said. He looked back at Forbath and for the first time in four years, he spoke the Queen's English. "I won't go unless Captain Yak-san comes with me."

The increasing folds in Forbath's forehead revealed his growing anger. He could make the boy go, but then the little beggar might hold his tongue and not identify the Manchurian. "Okay," he relented.

"There's no need for me," Yak-san said hurriedly. He was sure they'd kill him if Nathan identified the man.

"Perhaps it would be better," Forbath said.

"I must stay with my ship."

"And I must insist. Your vessel is in fine hands," Forbath said. He nodded to Bradley to take the lead out of the cabin.

As the assistant moved around Forbath and past the smuggler, he grinned at Nathan. He realized the boy had gotten the best of both men.

On deck, Yak-san saw his three crewmen sitting near the helm at the gunpoint of two Portuguese soldiers. And on the dock along the junk were five more soldiers of the Governor's private forces.

"You see, Captain," Forbath said as they descended the gangway to the awaiting carriage, "the Portuguese and the British are learning to work together. The Governor of Macau has been most helpful."

Yak-san said nothing as they walked.

Leaving the port exterior, the carriage took them up a dark winding road filled with potholes and ruts cut deep by autumn rains. The road followed the slope until it inter-

sected with Rau de Monte and climbed toward the hilltop
fortress overlooking the peninsula and bay.

Nathan felt sick to his stomach as the carriage rolled
along the road. He was trying to think of a way out, but
couldn't. What if it was the Manchurian who had murdered
his family? He had to pay for shooting Elisa. But if he
identified him, they would kill the Lingsyou and Nathan
would have no one again.

Finally the driver reined in his two horses and edged
them through the open gate of Monte Fortress. Inside the
thick steep walls, the military headquarters was small and
simple, as were most of the government buildings in Macau.
For hundreds of years the tiny colony had been a center of
export throughout Asia, but its buildings had never been
flamboyant, just efficient.

They walked through the rose garden courtyard and
climbed the wide stone steps to the large doors that hung
on thick black hinges.

Bradley stepped up and knocked. "It's Chief Inspector
Forbath," he announced.

The door creaked as it opened. A Portuguese soldier
ushered them into the brightly lit entry hall. "The General
is waiting in the library, Chief Inspector. If you'll follow
me." The soldier turned on his heels and led the odd group
down a long hallway. On the walls hung heavy gold frames
with paintings of famous Macau Governors and Portuguese
sea captains.

Just behind Forbath and the solider, Yak-san walked next
to Nathan as they moved down the hall. Bradley was a step
back.

The soldier tapped on the double doors. He opened them
and Forbath and the others entered a lavish library with a
huge blazing fireplace.

"Good evening, Chief Inspector." General Sauceda stood
up from the couch. He was a thin man who moved straight-
backed as if his spine had jelled solid from a lifetime of
standing at attention. Even his jet-black hair laid stiff on his
head and, although he had been sitting, his dark uniform
was without a wrinkle. His dark mustache curled above his
fleshy lips as he smiled.

Forbath could tell, as could everyone else, that the General's pleasantries were forced. He was a dignified man of the Portuguese army and did not care to deal with the British.

"Cognac?" the General offered.

"No, thank you," Forbath said. "If we could see the prisoner."

The General looked at Yak-san and then to Nathan. Forbath had told him about the boy and about the murders. He looked in the youth's eyes and saw an unsettling coolness. Sauceda had three sons of his own, one near Nathan's age, and he wondered if they would have as much fortitude with such a burden before them.

"My Lieutenant, the one who speaks Mandarin, has not arrived."

"It doesn't matter. We just need Nathan to identify the prisoner. He'll be given an interpreter at the courthouse," Forbath said. He was becoming impatient with the General. "It's getting late, General. The sooner we get this over, the sooner the Captain can return to his ship."

"Of course," Sauceda agreed. He called out and the soldier on the other side of the door stepped into the room. "Bring him."

The soldier saluted and disappeared.

It was quiet in the library. A quiet Nathan found screaming in his ears. He looked up at Yak-san and wanted to cry out to warn him, but he couldn't. The Chinese smuggler's face was expressionless as he looked into the flames of the fireplace. He knows he is about to die, Nathan realized. Oh, God, Nathan prayed, let it not be the clubfooted man.

As the sounds of men walking along the marble floor of the hallway echoed into the room, Nathan felt his heart twist in his chest. He became lightheaded and the room faded from around him. The footsteps grew in his brain and one, distinct from the rest, intensified. Scrape, slide, clomp, scrape, slide, clomp.

Nathan was in the *wan,* the pain in his side unbearable. He saw Elisa lifeless on the ground. He felt the warm gun barrel against his head and once again saw the clubfoot beside him in the alley.

Without turning around, Nathan heard them enter the

library. Yak-san looked at the prisoner. Nathan felt the Ling-syou's body stiffen, but the smuggler's face remained staunch and expressionless. It did not show what his body said.

Nathan turned to Forbath's prisoner. The man was shoul-dered between two Portuguese soldiers with his hands bound in chains. He held his head low against his chest.

"Lift his face," Forbath ordered.

One of the soldiers pushed the man's head up.

Nathan's eyes locked onto the Manchurian's. The two black holes in his badly scarred face did not waver. They stared fiercely at Nathan, stabbing into his soul and cursing him to death. The young boy did not falter. He returned the man's glare with added hatred.

"Well?" the General asked.

"This is the man that murdered your family," Forbath said.

"Please, Inspector, do not put words in the boy's mouth. You have brought serious charges against this man. And on very little evidence," General Sauceda reminded him.

"Tell him, Nathan," Forbath said. "Tell him this is the man."

Nathan looked at Forbath. He looked at Yak-san. He stepped closer to the chained man, so close that their bodies were almost touching. He stared directly into the man's dark eyes and in a low voice, so that only the clubfooted man could hear, Nathan said in Mandarin, *"Xiatsz."*

"What?" Forbath snapped. He grabbed Nathan by the arm. "What did you say?"

Nathan looked up at the Chief Inspector. "It is not him," he said in English.

"You're lying." Forbath's eyes darted around the room. "He's lying." He moved in front of the General. "This is the man, this is the one I've been looking for."

"No," Nathan said as he moved back to Yak-san's side. "He's not the one."

"Are you sure, young man?" the General asked.

"Yes."

Sauceda waved to his men. "Let him go."

"You can't!" Forbath hollered.

"What will you have me hold him on, Chief Inspector? For being crippled?" the General asked. He turned to the officer. "Release him and give him money for a meal."

"Yes, sir," the soldier said, and then led the clubfooted man away.

It took almost three hours for Nathan and Yak-san to walk back to the docks. The night was pleasant and quiet. Above, stars filled the sky like sparklers in a New Year's parade. They passed no one on the dark road as they traveled.

During the entire time neither spoke. Yak-san didn't know what to say. He was sure Nathan would have recognized the man. He carried a face not easily forgotten. Maybe that night, when the Manchurian warriors came to his father's church for the deed, the boy never really saw them. Maybe they had been shadows, demons in the darkness.

The Chinese smuggler stared down the twisted road. He realized Forbath didn't know why the Manchurian was trying to get back to China. The Chief Inspector knew nothing about the deed. If the police hadn't found it with the warrior, then it was still in Hong Kong. Aberdeen, he remembered. That's where he had been nursed back to health. The Lingsyou quickly made up his mind. They would set sail on the tide.

When they finally reached the docks, the Portuguese soldiers were gone and Fu-laing and the rest of his crew were aboard, waiting for them.

"Lingsyou!" Fu-laing rushed down the gangplank. "They told me Forbath came for you."

Yak-san nodded. He patted Nathan warmly on the back. "Tell the cook to fix us something to eat, little devil," he said cheerfully. "We'll eat together in my cabin."

"Yes, Lingsyou," Nathan said with a smile. He darted around Fu-laing and up the gangplank.

"What happened?"

"You've been teaching the boy the Manchurian tongue?"

Fu-laing looked questioningly at him and nodded.

"Tell me, my friend, what does 'xiatsz' mean?"

The half-Chinese, half-Manchurian man looked at his captain, his eyebrows raised. "It means only, 'Next time.' "

Chapter Eighteen

The New Territories

The green Chinese-made sedan, with its sole headlight giving a cyclops' view of the road ahead, raced south along Lung Cheung Road, through Lion Rock Tunnel, and toward the airport. In the misty morning of the peninsula, the battered automobile could only manage one windshield wiper.

The middle-aged man behind the wheel was running late. He always ran late. He had taken a little too much time to find his jacket, brush his teeth, and piss away the last six-pack of beer.

Shifting into the car's highest gear, he pressed his foot hard on the gas pedal. Through his half-drunken haze, he fought to keep the vehicle between the road lines.

He had to be there by 2 A.M. That's what his brother-in-law told him. 2 A.M. Not 2:05, not 2:03. The flight he was to meet landed at 2:15, but the man in the Chinese sedan had to be in position by 2 A.M. His brother-in-law had stressed that.

If all went well, the man thought as he drove, this meeting would allow him to repay half his debts. Before leaving his hillside shanty, he decided that he could not concern himself with the money his brother-in-law was making for this. He could only be sure it was more than he.

The man struggling with the wheel of the car knew he would never have found this job by himself. He didn't know the right people, the ones who were willing to pay for such simple, heartless tasks. His brother-in-law knew them. He knew lots of them. So, whatever he was paid, the man thought, his brother-in-law was due his cut.

But then the man countered his own argument. The least his brother-in-law could have done was offer to come with him. He never did. He didn't have the stomach for such things. Why the hell did his sister marry such a spineless man, the driver wondered.

But neither did he have the stomach for this. In all honesty. Not really. Thus the reason he put himself in this pleasant state of drunkenness. Just enough beer to raise his courage but not hinder his driving.

By the time he arrived at the airport, the man in the green sedan had forgotten what he was arguing about with himself. He decided to concentrate on the business at hand.

He hid his sedan against the curb and fifty feet behind the line of taxis. Without shutting off the engine, he closed the lone headlight, sat back, and watched the exit gate for the overseas flights.

The gentle mist coming off the harbor that had wetted his windshield created small rainbow halos in the airport's street lamps. The line of red and white taxis awaiting incoming flights was fifteen cars deep and continuously inching forward to nab the next fare.

Within minutes, the driver had fallen asleep in his idling sedan. He woke in a panic, checked his cheap plastic watch, and was relieved to find he had only slept a few minutes. That was going to be the first purchase, he told himself. Not an expensive watch, but a nice one. One with a sweeping second hand and the date. Maybe he'd get a Swatch or a nice Citizen.

At the double glass doors of the terminal, a few passengers trickled out. All were Chinese businessmen in expensive suits and they walked to Mercedes limousines rolling to the curb.

Near two-thirty A.M. the driver became antsy. He rolled the sedan several feet forward without turning on its headlight. Concentrating through the fogging window, he watched the exit doors intently. Over and over again he repeated the description of the woman he was supposed to find. Then, as if he had willed her from the building, she appeared. Carrying a thin leather briefcase and an overnight bag slung from her shoulder, she approached the curb. She was a tall American with short reddish-brown hair and she was looking up and down the roadway as if expecting someone.

The man behind the wheel watched her closely as he rolled the sedan forward a few inches more.

The American didn't seem to see who she was looking for. She turned toward the taxis. Lifting her briefcase, she motioned to the first cab. Its driver saw her and motored out from the line. As the woman stepped from the curb to meet her taxi, the man in the green sedan punched the accelerator. The car lunged forward. Picking up speed, he shifted into second gear.

The woman heard the scream of the engine behind her. She looked and froze in disbelief as she saw the oncoming car aim at her with determination. For a fraction of a second, their eyes met, the American woman's and the Chinese driver's. Then the green, unmarked sedan, one of thousands in the colony, hit the woman doing at least sixty kilometers an hour. The blunt force of impact threw her body fifteen feet in the air and ten yards down the road.

The sedan's driver, now frantic to get away, clipped the front fender of a taxi, veered past a bus, and accelerated down the three-lane expressway. The impact shattered his remaining headlight and now he managed his escape by streetlight alone.

The woman landed on the edge of the curb, her body twisted unnaturally above the waist. Her head had fractured like a fine Chinese vase against the cement curb, yet there was only a trickle of blood from her right ear. And though her lips were pursed together in an expression of unwant, her face had come through the violent ordeal unscarred. It was a face that would make the front page of every Hong Kong newspaper by morning.

Chapter Nineteen

Hong Kong Island

Suzette's *cheongsam* shimmered under the flashing yellow lights over the dance club entrance. Sauntering through the doors, she immediately caught the young hostess's attention. The young girl, dressed in a revealing red leather miniskirt and halter, with black combat boots, black fingernail polish, and a sterling nose ring, moved directly to her.

"Hi." She smiled, her eyes sweeping slowly over Suzette.

Suzette played along. "Hello," she handed her a small folded piece of paper.

The hostess opened it, found a five-hundred-dollar bill and a table number.

"You sure?"

"He made the call."

"From here?"

Suzette shrugged indifferently.

"We don't allow cell phones," the hostess said.

Suzette ignored her by scanning the fashionably dressed crowd that flowed through the smoky club.

"He's never entertained anyone . . ." she calculated her words, "like you before."

Suzette smiled seductively. "It's a special occasion."

"Oh." The hostess was surprised. "The manager should send champagne."

"No, you know how he is. Secretive."

"He's one of the best customers. But you're right. He doesn't like attention." The hostess called to a flamboyantly dressed Chinese man to watch the door. "This way," she said to Suzette.

The Propaganda, one of Hong Kong's latest dance clubs, was designed with minimal decor. A maze of corridors led from the center dance floor and the thundering Canto-pop music to dozens of small and very private booths. As the colony's most popular gay nightspot, it was designed with purpose.

Suzette and the hostess arrived at the private alcove to find only a lone martini standing guard on the table.

"I know he's here," the hostess said. "Maybe he's dancing."

Suzette slipped into the booth. "Thank you."

The hostess pushed Suzette's money across the table. "Consider it a favor. And if your plans don't work out . . ." she ran her fingers down Suzette's forearm, "I'm off at midnight." She disappeared around the edge of the secluded booth.

Suzette rolled her eyes. She checked her ruby lipstick in the mirror of her compact. I do look like a whore, she decided, uncomfortable that the illusion was so simple to apply.

"Excuse me," said a middle-aged Chinese man in an Alex Sebastian double-breasted suit. His heavyset body filled the narrow opening of the alcove. Looking over his right shoulder was a Caucasian teenager with one side of his head shaved clean, the other side sporting tight blond curls. A large gold cross dangled from one ear.

"A friend sent me," Suzette said seductively. "For your birthday."

"Wow, your birthday. That makes you a Pisces," the boy said. He was drunk.

The Chinese man looked nervous. "Go," the man told him. "I'll find you later."

"Hey, I may not be around."

"Then I'll find someone else."

"Whatever," the boy said as he bumped the wall leaving.

The Chinese man looked harshly at Suzette. "It's not my birthday."

"No, it's not," Lindsay said, slapping the man on the shoulder. "Nor is she exactly your style." He pushed him into the booth. Lindsay hung his cane on the edge of the table and slid in beside Suzette.

"I heard you were dead," the man quipped.

"Don't you wish."

"Not really. But I know others who do." The Chinese chuckled, but his laugh was lost to the pounding music radiating throughout the club. "Who is your lovely diversion?"

"Suzette Lauhu, Comrade Ying Mingyu, Chief Editor of the *Wen Wei Po*," Lindsay said in a formal introduction.

Suzette suddenly felt claustrophobic in the small cubicle as she shook hands with the editor of the powerful communist newspaper.

Ying sipped his martini. "Would you like a drink?" he asked Suzette.

"No, thank you."

"Are you sure?"

Lindsay nodded.

"All you have to do is ask. The waiters seem to come out of the walls."

Lindsay's eyes met the deadpan stare of the Chinese's.

"They make a wonderful drink here. I think it's called the Peak."

"No, thanks," Lindsay said as he suddenly stood up. He grabbed Suzette's hand and pulled her from the booth. Taking his cane, Lindsay nodded to the Chief Editor. "Sorry, wrong table."

Lindsay pulled Suzette quickly through the fashionable crowd of same-sex couples, across the densely packed dance floor, past the bathrooms, and out the back door.

"What was that all about?" she asked as they stepped into the narrow alley.

"The booth was bugged."

"You sure?"

"He was." Lindsay looked up and down the alleyway, made his best guess, and headed into the darkness.

"Maybe he lied to get rid of you."

"He can't. He's an asset."

"A what?"

"A soft asset for the CIA."

"The Chief Editor of the communist paper is a spy?"

"No, a soft asset is only an informant. He passes on information handed him. If he dug for information, then he'd be a spy."

To Suzette, the thought of the Chief Editor passing information to the West was staggering. "Jeeze, you can't trust anybody."

"You're catching on," he said as he led her down Wyndham Street toward Garden Road and the Victoria Peak tramway. Nearing midnight, the century old cable tram was carrying only young couples to the top of Victoria Peak. Here, walking hand in hand, young lovers could disappear along the jungle paths to find their own romantic views of the glittering city below and escape the bounds of public etiquette and delve into the wanton ways of nature and the night.

Suzette sat at the rear of the cable car as it rolled smoothly along the rail. "I remember the time my father brought me here," she said. "I was ten. We had ice-cream cones together and spent all day on the peak." She smiled. "I was supposed to be in school. My mother was madder than hell at him." Suzette unconsciously touched her hair. "That was the year she died."

"I've got a feeling the ice-cream parlor is going to be closed. Take a rain check?"

She smiled slightly. "Sure," she said as they watched the city retreat below.

At the top, the Peak Galleria, a three-story shopping plaza of restaurants and gift shops, the Häagen-Dazs ice cream parlor, was indeed closed. A cluster of tourists and a handful of snuggling couples stood at the green rail of the outdoor terrace and viewed the opulent jumble of high-rises that glittered on the harbor waters.

They strolled the terrace in silence, Suzette's arm laced in his, their eyes not meeting anyone else's. There was no mistaking them as a *gweilo* and his high-priced escort. They moved differently. Their bodies touched differently. Steps not as comfortable as husband and wife, nor as precious as lovers.

"It's nice here at night," Suzette said.

"Yeah." Lindsay felt her hair brush across his neck. He hooked his cane over his right arm as they descended the plaza steps and walked toward the Peak Café restaurant that was on the opposite side of the parking lot.

"What do we do now?"

"Wait for Ying."

"What makes you think he's coming here?"

"There's no drink called the Peak."

Suzette shot him a sidelong glance.

In front of the café, a red and white double-decker bus pulled up. The destination sign was flipped to OUT OF SERVICE. The entrance door opened and the expressionless Chinese behind the wheel stared at them and waited.

Lindsay scanned the bus's lower level and saw it deserted. In a second-level window, he saw Ying's silhouette. "Wait here," he instructed Suzette.

"Not on your life."

They climbed the spiraling stairway to the upper deck and found Ying in the rear bench, alone and annoyed by this inconvenience.

"What do you want, Mr. Chase?" he asked sternly.

"My associates think I'm a double agent. You know otherwise."

"Do I? In Beijing, I'm of minor importance. They tell me very little."

"But you know I've been retired."

"So I thought. But we both know better than to believe what we see and believe nothing of what we are told."

"Just the same, I want you to understand I'm here with no alliances," Lindsay said as he casually toyed with his cane.

"I'm listening."

"I need to get into Tommy Fong's computer files."

"The dead reporter from the *Post?*" Ying looked aghast. "Why do you come to me?"

Lindsay glanced out the window.

Suzette noticed the communist's dead eyes had changed, as though fear had given them life. "I don't know what you're talking about. I've never met this Tommy Fong." He turned to Suzette for sympathy.

"Don't look at me." Suzette shrugged. "I'm just along for the ride."

"Mr. Chase, I—"

Lindsay raised his hand, silencing him. "You front Beijing's intelligence. I know you've got a tap on every phone and computer line that goes through this place. Files were sent to Tommy through a modem. That means you have them."

Ying stared at the steel floor of the bus. "I can't—"

"What would your comrades think about all your deposits at Merrill Lynch? Big numbers there."

"You wouldn't. I'm too important."

Lindsay laughed coldly. "Not to me. I'd compromise you in a heartbeat, Comrade."

Ying looked into the American's face, trying to decipher him. He could usually guess the intent of an Englishman's face, given his knowledge of their staunch, gentlemen rules. But Americans? Who knew Americans? Ying relented. He stepped to the stairwell and called down to the driver. "Go to the store," he instructed.

The British-made Leyland bus rumbled away from the curb, swung wide, and headed down Peak Road.

"If you think I'm going to escort you inside, you might as well shoot me here."

Lindsay seemed to consider it. "No," he said finally. "I can always find you later."

The cool night air blew through the bus as it ambled into the Central district. Suzette slouched in the padded bench seat and looked out at Victoria Harbor, at the twinkling lights along the shore, and at those of ships slipping through the narrow passage as so many had for the past hundred and fifty years.

The bus, its air brakes screeching through the early morning, stopped at the curbside along Queen's Road. Ying walked them to the bottom of the stairs.

"The store is midway up the block, on the right. There's a scissor gate in front. The morning operator will be there in a few minutes. Please don't hurt him. He's my wife's nephew."

"Thank you, Comrade," Lindsay said as he stepped to the street.

"Good luck, Mr. Chase. I hope not to see you again."

Lindsay took Suzette's hand and hurried across the boulevard. They followed Ying's directions east and through a grimy black alley. From there, they hurried along New Street until they found the avenue entrance.

"Possession Street," she said, noting the name on the street sign. "How ironic. This is where the British annexed the colony in 1841."

"Who says communists don't have a sense of humor?"

The short, steeply ascending avenue was deserted, its line of adjoining shops locked and sealed for the night. They found the porcelain store dark, its rusting scissor gate still stretched across its facade. With his arm about her waist, Lindsay and Suzette walked farther along, browsing the windows as if they were late-night shoppers.

Four doors down, they looked into the bakery shop plateglass window. Suzette eyed a bin of glazed almond cookies. "I'm getting hungry."

"Later," Lindsay whispered.

Suzette noticed him staring at something in the reflection. She glanced over his shoulder and saw a Chinese man walking quickly down the street.

The young man brushed his long oily hair from his face as he reached into the deep pocket of his puffy coat. He fished out the tangle of keys. Sorting through them, he found the one that unlocked the padlock of the gate. It was only then that he sensed someone standing behind him.

"Don't turn around," Lindsay warned.

"I have no money. I'm only the cleaning man."

"Open the door."

The man muscled the fence aside, used two more keys,

and opened the front door to the innocent-looking store. Lindsay and Suzette slid in behind him.

As he reached for the light switch, Lindsay cracked him across the knuckles with the tip of his cane. "*Aii* . . ." he cried out.

"No lights," Lindsay said quickly. He handed Suzette his cane, grabbed the Chinese man by the back of the neck, and pressed the barrel of Truby's automatic to his temple. The man shivered fearfully.

"I tell you, there's nothing to steal—"

"I beg to differ," Lindsay said, pushing him deeper inside.

The narrow store was crammed with every imaginable size and shape of ceramic vase, jar, or bowl. They were garnished with ornate flowers or carps or dragons and colored in blues, reds, and golds and all were cheap contemporary pieces. This was a tourists' paradise.

The man selected two more keys and gave entrance to the back room. It was a simple office: one desk, one chair, and myriad of shipping crates.

"You see . . . Nothing."

"I see. But I don't believe it," Lindsay said, pushing him into the chair. "The computers?"

Terror gripped his soul. He had been told this moment might come and that he must prepare himself for it. He had said he was. "What computers?" he blurted.

"Wrong answer." Lindsay adjusted his stance and turned to Suzette. "Don't watch," he said to her. "It's always messy." He aimed the 9mm at the Chinese.

The man gasped. "No, no." He jumped from the chair and scrambled through a stack of cardboard boxes, revealing a hidden door.

Lindsay looked over his shoulder and winked at Suzette.

One more key, a single key from his breast pocket, and they were shown the heart of the electronic intelligence and acquisition center of the People's Republic of China.

The secret room, not more than ten by ten feet square, was chilled to sixty degrees by a Westinghouse air conditioner built into the back wall. Resting on two long tables were five outdated 486 IBM personal computers interconnected by a twisting vine of cables and buzzing contently to themselves. At one table was a single keyboard, monitor, and a cellular modem.

"This is it?" Lindsay asked. "You've got to be kidding."

"This is all of them. I swear," the man said, and Lindsay realized he was crying.

"Don't worry I believe you."

Suzette quickly summed up the operation. "They're not storing data here. These are network terminals. It's a relay station."

"See what you can find."

She sat down and pulled herself to the keyboard. "Password?"

The man hesitated. Lindsay showed him the gun. "Indiana," he said.

"The state?"

"The movie character," he said, a bit embarrassed.

Suzette chuckled as she typed in the password. Like the computers themselves, the communist's filing system was plain and simple and stolen from the West. Suzette was familiar with it and she easily found the log of transferred files.

"You in?" Lindsay asked.

"Wait . . ." she said as she entered Tommy's newspaper name. A long list of reporters scrolled down the screen. "Now I am."

"Good," Lindsay said, and slammed the butt of his gun into the young man's temple. He collapsed to the floor.

"You weren't supposed to hurt him."

"He'll need the excuse."

"Oh," she said. Clicking through the list, Suzette found Tommy and his directory. "The files are gone," she said, disappointed.

"Everything?"

She delved further. "There's one."

"Open it."

Suzette highlighted the file with the screen pointer, then double-clicked the mouse. The monochrome screen flashed as it launched a word-processing program and revealed the file's text. There was only two words, at the top of the page: Hu Men.

"Hu Men?" The name was familiar to Lindsay. He tried to place it.

"Hu Men is the Tiger Gate," Suzette said. "It's on the Pearl River. Part of the old route to Canton."

Lindsay stared at the computer screen. "North of Macau," he remembered.

Chapter Twenty

Hong Kong Island

From Possession Street and the discovery at the porcelain store, Lindsay and Suzette went directly to Jing Zhang's house. The sun was just breaking the binds of the eastern horizon when they slipped into the yard through the creaking gate that hung on one hinge. They knocked at the back door.

Mrs. Zhang answered with a face of concern. "You have not eaten?"

"We just need to change and get our things," Lindsay explained as he limped into the house. He hadn't had a chance to rest his leg and it was beginning to take its toll. Suzette, too, was feeling worn out and tired.

Mrs. Zhang took Suzette's face in her hands. "*Aiya*, Lindsay. She has circles under her eyes. What are you doing to her?"

"I'm fine, really," Suzette said, but felt exhausted. She plopped down at the kitchen table across from Lindsay.

"We've got to catch the eight o'clock ferry for Macau."

Mun came into the kitchen wearing Batman boxer shorts and a baggy sleeveless undershirt. "Why? They leave every half hour," he said, half asleep. He reached for a box of breakfast cereal from the cabinet.

Mrs. Zhang set the brass tea kettle on the electric stove. "Take a nap now. You can catch a later boat. Go. I'll wake you in an hour for pancakes."

Lindsay looked across the table at Suzette. She did have dark circles under her eyes. Such captivating eyes and he was ruining them.

"Would an hour hurt?" she asked.

"I guess not."

"Good." Mrs. Zhang already had the pancake mix in her hand.

As Lindsay followed Suzette from the kitchen, he asked Mun, "Is your father still asleep?"

The boy glanced nervously at his mother. "He didn't come home," he whispered quickly. If Mrs. Zhang had heard, she didn't show it as she rifled through the pantry cupboards.

In the last year, she had gotten accustomed to her husband's late nights and long disappearances. She excused them as bouts with his demons, the ones who taunted him for being only half a man with a sick heart and an arm that was as stricken as his manhood. She understood his torment, but silently wished it was alcohol or gambling or another woman that kept him away. At least she could bear terrestrial monsters.

Lindsay slid onto the low bed next to Suzette. After a moment, he felt her breath slow and deepen and her body ease against his. She was asleep.

Lindsay never reached slumber and, although his mind drifted in and out, something nagged at him. A burr that stood out from a glossy surface, a shadow that fell wrong from the light. Something. Something grappling with his subconscious and vying for immediate attention. His inner animal was stirring, mulling over what it knew, wondering what it didn't. It was tasting the air again, watching for movement.

Finally, after forty-five minutes of staring at the ceiling, Lindsay left Suzette to sleep alone. He showered, changed into a pair of jeans and a sweatshirt, and returned to the kitchen. He helped Mrs. Zhang with breakfast.

"Is he gone often?" Lindsay asked.

"Now and then."

"You don't worry?"

"I worry," she said, spreading a perfect puddle of batter into the hot frying pan. "He'll be home for lunch. He always is."

Soon Suzette walked down the hall with a lighter step. "I sure needed that," she said as she entered the kitchen. She, too, had showered and changed into her new clothes. Her transformation was remarkable. The light blue jeans and yellow cotton blouse Mun had purchased took her beauty in a different direction than the silk *cheongsam* had. The denim was tight around her long thin legs and above her narrow waist; the shirt billowed fully about her.

If Lindsay had not known better, he would have sworn she was one of those exercise-minded California girls in love with the freedom to do what they pleased, untethered by the latest fashion. He was beginning to wonder if Suzette's transformation was going to bring them less attention or more. At least she didn't look like the same girl, he decided.

After a breakfast of American-style pancakes, Chinese salted eggs, and rice porridge, they thanked Mrs. Zhang and hoisted their packs to their shoulders.

"Do I really have to carry a backpack?" Suzette asked.

"It adds to the disguise."

"Do we have to add that much?"

Lindsay hired a cab at the corner and had the driver drop them off near the Wharney Hotel on Lockart Road. It was just the place an American couple on a budget might stay. From there, they caught the bus to the three-story Macau terminal.

Lindsay purchased two round-trip tickets aboard the Far East jetfoils from an unconcerned woman with thick tortoise-shell-framed glasses. She barely glanced at Lindsay as she tore off two small stubs, stamped them with the sailing time, and pushed them back across the counter with Lindsay's change. Numerous people, both Hongkongers and foreigners, took the luxurious high-speed ferries for a daily jaunt to the Portuguese colony. Lindsay and Suzette were faceless travelers amongst so many others.

Lindsay set their luggage on the black steel bench near gate number five. "You want something?" he asked, pointing to the small lunch counter on the opposite side of the building.

"No."

Using his cane, Lindsay made his way across the crowded terminal. *"Wo xiang yibei kaishui,"* he said, ordering a cup of hot water from the teenage girl behind the counter. Holding a cellular phone to her ear with her shoulder, the girl continued her giggling conversation as she poured steaming water into a paper cup and took Lindsay's money.

Lindsay dropped in a pinch of Mrs. Zhang's black powder and mixed it thoroughly with a red plastic swizzle stick.

Near the counter was a small newsstand. Lindsay wandered past a group of teenage boys flipping through car magazines. They looked at the advertisements of racing equipment with an intense interest.

Lindsay sipped at his bitter concoction as he scanned the news rack. Then, from a stack of newspapers on the ground, a headline photo leaped out at him.

Suzette watched with amusement as a toddler, bundled tightly in a thick sweater, clopped after his older sister. The sister stayed just beyond his outstretched hands and led the child in a myriad of circles.

Lindsay dropped the newspaper on her lap.

"What?" Suzette recoiled.

"She was coming for me."

Suzette read the caption. "Who was she?"

"My Station Chief." He dropped into the bench. "Their double agent is still active," he said. He looked at the crowd merging toward the boarding gate. It was three minutes to the hour. "Come on," he said, and stoically helped her with the pack. They crossed the terminal and entered the swelling tide of travelers at the gateway.

As they moved through the gate, Lindsay was suddenly swept by a cold chill. He looked around, but in the mass of multiethnic faces, no one caught his attention. He took Suzette by the elbow and they boarded the jetfoil to Macau.

* * *

As the sleek ferry blared its horn twice and relinquished its dock lines, the Triad member with the dragon tattoo on his throat sitting in the terminal building lowered his copy of *BusinessWeek*. He watched from the window as the husky blue and white vessel reached mid-harbor. Then, he tucked the magazine under his left arm and withdrew his Motorola flip-phone. He dialed.

"He was telling the truth. They just left," he told the person on the other end of the microwave signal. Then, he slipped the phone into his pocket and headed for the exit.

Chapter Twenty-One

Victoria Harbor

Suzette walked from the main cabin through a companionway and outside onto the ferry's aft deck. It was a working part of the ship, black and oily. Hopscotching over the heavy ropes that crisscrossed the steel decking, she moved to the rail. Fifteen feet below, the silt-brown water of Victoria whirled and eddied as the ship motored away from the docks.

Lindsay had gotten them two seats near a large window that was sealed closed for safety. He piled their bags up against the bulkhead as the other passengers continued to board en masse, building mountains of packages across the cabin floor. It was then Suzette had the sudden need to escape.

The midmorning sun washed Suzette's face. She closed her eyes and tilted her chin toward its pleasant warmth. It was nice to be on the water even if she was still within earshot of the bustling city. She had spent most of her life shuttling between Victoria Harbor and Stanley Bay on the decks of ferry ships.

She wasn't the only student in the affluent middle school

who had lived aboard a yacht, but her family's was by far the most luxurious. Now, with the harbor breeze on her skin, she was returning to those times.

"Excuse," the Chinese crewman said in his best English. "Nowhere out here. You back inside."

Suzette turned to the small man. "I needed the air," she said.

He shook his head and pointed to the thick dock lines at her feet. "When we take off, it not safe."

"We'll be inside by then," Lindsay said as he stepped through the hatch.

"No." The man shook his head. "You'll get me in trouble with the captain."

Lindsay slipped the crewman twenty Hong Kong dollars. "We didn't see you."

The man continued to shake his head but took the money. "I didn't see you, either," he said. "But go inside before we lift," he warned, referring to the ship rising onto its waterfoils. Once above the waves, the ferry would turn and bank steeply like an airplane. The man grabbed two lines, hoisted them over his shoulder, and pulled them farther astern.

"You still don't trust me," she said pointedly.

"Can you blame me? So far you've tried to split my head open with a lamp, run me down with your car, and you shoved a gun into my gut."

"That was before."

"How rude of me. You've been good for at least twelve hours."

"The woman in the photo. She was a friend, wasn't she?"

"We knew each other a long time," Lindsay admitted. "Which usually doesn't happen. Most people don't last as long as we did. They get burnt out on it."

"But not you?"

"I didn't get the chance."

"I don't think you would've."

Lindsay didn't answer her. He didn't have an answer. He looked at the harbor trailing behind them. "Nice out here, isn't it?"

"There's no place in the world like this," she agreed.

"Manhattan, maybe." He moved beside her. "At dusk."

"From the tour boat off Seaport Village." She grinned, then her face turned somber. "Orson must know you're not the double agent. Not after your friend was killed."

Lindsay stared at her. "Who's to say I wasn't part of a team? That would be my guess."

"They're using you to flush out the real agent."

"Possibly."

"That's just wonderful," she said as her eyes met his. They held. Paused. She felt her body move toward his and her arm wove itself around his neck and she leaned to him. His lips were softer and more gentle than she had expected. And their kiss lingered less than she had hoped.

"Why are you here?" Lindsay asked softly.

"I thought I'd be safe with you. Now I'm not so sure." She extended herself, wanting more of this newfound tenderness.

"I mean in Hong Kong. Everyone is scrambling to get out, but you're not." He had broken the mood. He hadn't meant to, but he had.

"Why should I leave?" She stiffened and pulled away. "This is my home."

"You have a passport." He said it as if it were an accusation.

"My grandfather's English," she said, her eyes faltering, embarrassed.

"Then you're lucky."

"I don't feel lucky. I feel ashamed. Why should it matter where my grandfather's from? I was born here. Just like the people on Gibraltar or the Falklands, I should have the right to emigrate to Great Britain. But I wouldn't, not without my grandfather. And it's because I'm Chinese. That's the reason my government is turning its backs on three million people and handing them over to the communists," she said, grasping the rail with both hands, strangling it. "We've been British subjects for a hundred years and now, the first time we need our countrymen, they shun us like illegitimate children."

Lindsay leaned on his cane as the ship rolled beneath him. "This deed isn't going to stop it."

"Yes, it is. It was signed by the Empress and stamped with the Imperial Seals."

"A hundred years ago."

"You don't think it matters?"

"I wish I did."

"Why do you think the tanks are at the border? Beijing knows if the deed's found, Britain is going to have a new claim on Hong Kong."

Lindsay let out a slow breath. She was right. For the last fifteen years, Beijing and London had been haggling over the transition of the most influential piece of property in the world. The hint of such a document could threaten the entire political and economical stability of Asia.

"Even if you find it, nobody's going to believe it's authentic."

Suzette's eyes narrowed. "Yes, they are, because I'm going to shove it down their throats," she said. She pushed away from the rail and left him on the deck alone.

Lindsay leaned on the railing and stared back across the sea. He felt the wind change. The ship's captain had altered course and aimed the ferry's bow away from the crowded archipelago. Six million people in barely four hundred square miles, the most concentrated population on earth. A pressure pot heated by British apathy and simmering under Chinese arrogance. How could it survive the Red Chinese, he wondered, and suspected it couldn't.

They passed the shelter of the inner islands and continued beyond the southernmost tip of Lamma Island and out to the South China Sea. The smell the diesel exhaust swept across Lindsay's face as the twin turbine diesel engines roared deep within the hull. Lindsay felt the steel deck shudder beneath him as the huge machines powered up and began to lift the craft onto its underwater wings.

Although Lindsay was watching the horizon, he didn't notice the black and gray yacht shadowing the ferry. It blended in with the many other large and luxurious craft traveling the route. The yacht's skipper would have been happier to set a more direct course, but the owner had other plans and wanted to keep the ferry in sight.

There was nothing more for Lindsay to stare at, nothing

more to think. He slipped through the hatch and walked surefooted across the carpeted cabin to his seat.

With her tennis shoes kicked off and her knees to her chest, Suzette sat sideways, curled like a kitten in the ship's airline-type seat. Her head rested on crossed arms over the tops of her knees. She had left the seat next to the window for him. Lindsay set his cane across their packs. He bundled his sweatshirt into a makeshift pillow, pressed it between the seat and the window.

Around the cabin everyone was trying to make themselves comfortable in any way they could. There were at least another fifty minutes left to their voyage. One could either try to read on the rolling ship or sleep under its bright fluorescent lights. There were few other choices.

In the far corner, two men played checkers on a piece of worn cardboard, the game's ranks and files drawn in pencil. Three seats from Suzette, a young woman rocked her infant in her arms. She was singing quietly to the child. The melody was vaguely familiar. Lindsay finally recognized it and smiled. He closed his eyes and listened to her Chinese version of "London Bridge Is Falling Down." And under the song, he heard the faint drone of the engines. Thump, thump, THump, thump. THump, thump. THUMp, thump.

Turning his head, the animal tried to locate the direction from which the pounding originated. Rising to his feet, he moved cautiously through the tall grass. It was dry and brittle and cracked as he pushed through it.

The beating began to grow louder and louder. It seemed to be everywhere. He moved left, but that only sent him closer. He veered right, but still it neared. His ears picked a gap in the wall of sound and he dashed toward it.

All of a sudden, the pounding intensified as the wall closed behind him and collapsed in front of him. A hundred open hands beating a hundred skin drums marched through the tall grass to chase him out.

The animal stopped and crouched low. Death was here. Death was upon him. He lifted his head, looking for somewhere to run. His nostrils flared as his lungs filled with air. Deep in his massive chest, his heart thundered.

*No fear, he thought. He blinked slowly. No reason for fear.
Concentrate. Control it. Turn it around to an advantage.*

*His pulse slowed with his breathing. Under the hot sun, the
panic he had just felt subsided. Now, with his mind clear, he flexed
his muscles in defiance and waited for the first to try to take him.
No fear, he told himself over and over and over. To his right, the
high grass parted as a hunter rushed at him. He lunged.*

Lindsay's eyes opened suddenly as he heard his name.

"Lindsay!" Suzette screamed at him. "Lindsay." She had
hold of his shoulders and was shaking him roughly. "Are
you okay?" she asked. She brushed his hair off his forehead
and cupped his face in her hands. Her almond-shaped eyes
looked, caring, into his.

Behind her, Lindsay saw the ship's steward standing in
the aisle. "Is he sick?" the steward asked Suzette.

"Lindsay?" her voice was soft. "Are you all right?"

Other people in the cabin were also staring. Some stood
to see what the fuss was about. The woman with the infant
had moved away.

"It was just a nightmare," Lindsay said, trying to calm
her.

"A nightmare? Look at your hand."

Lindsay stared at his right fist. The skin on the first two
knuckles was cut and slightly bleeding. He looked at the
cabin window beside his seat and saw a spider-web crack in
the corner and a two-inch hole where a piece had been
knocked out.

"Dui-bu-qi," Lindsay apologized to the steward. "Bad
dreams," he said.

The steward, his forehead furrowed deep with dismay,
turned from the American to the woman. "We are coming
into Macau, but if you want I will bring the first-aid kit,"
he said.

"No," Lindsay said, flexing his hand. "I don't need it."

"Are you sure?" Suzette asked.

"We'll get a doctor at the hotel," he said as he continued
to flex his hand. There was no pain in his knuckles, no hint
of damage except for the blood. "Thank you," he said to
the steward.

With a curt nod, the man stepped away. As he moved through the cabin, he coaxed everyone back to their seats.

Suzette sat down. "What in the world were you dreaming about?"

"Nothing," he said. "Nothing."

She stared at him.

With his left hand, he touched her cheek. "I'm okay," he promised.

Chapter Twenty-Two

South China Sea, 1909

It was dawn. Cold and misty on the waves. The sharp edge between night and day was still hidden by angry clouds on the far horizon. For six days the monsoon had raged like a demon. It had come up from the south unexpectedly and turned the skies black and loud with thunder. The seas had become mountains; their crests, tumbling avalanches of water.

The low-slung junk had pulled and strained all night against her two forward anchor lines as she lay within the shallow cove of the obscure island that had been the nearest shelter. In surges, the ocean lifted her on its race toward shore, and each time she moaned as if trying to break free and give herself up to the rocky beach only a hundred yards away.

But with the morning the storm had passed and now Yaksan stood on the bridge barking orders to weigh anchor and hoist the sails. Men scurried to their places at the bow. Hard callused hands gripped the damp ropes and pulled in unison until the iron anchors broke free of the muddy bottom. Hurriedly, the crew set the junk's three batwinged sails to the wind.

By the time her canvas filled and the ancient vessel made headway beyond the outer rocks, bright rays of sun were seeping through thinning clouds. The day was looking to be gentle.

"We were lucky you knew this island," Fu-laing said as he pressed his weight to the tiller and held course.

"Luck was to make landfall," the Lingsyou said. "Not in knowing the island."

"True," Fu-laing agreed. He remembered that Yak-san knew all the islands and waterways of the South China Sea. It was the Lingsyou's advantage over the other captains who competed for their share in the illicit trades.

It was well known that since Yak-san first sailed these waters he had kept secret detailed records of all his voyages. Not just a log of tides and weather, nor simply of island locations and soundings, but of which islands offered fresh water and food; which were inhabited; and of those that were, which were hostile and which were friendly.

When Yak-san finally commanded his own ship and crew, he had begun to make routine visits to the islands, befriending the local people with offerings of gifts and supplies. The Lingsyou had known early on that in the business of smuggling, a man could not have enough friends.

But the world was changing, and both Yak-san and Fu-laing knew it. The repercussions of the ill-fated Boxer uprising was strangling his trade. The rebellion had tried to oust the power base in China but instead had incurred the wrath of the European armies as they marched on the capital.

Now, with the radicals crushed and the feeble government forced to sign concessions, what was illegal trade yesterday was legal and filling the holds of foreign sailing ships.

And to make matters worse, Peking was redirecting its frustration by tightening controls on the commerce coming into the empire that didn't conform exactly to the new treaties.

No, Yak-san thought, being a smuggler and a pirate was not as gratifying as it had once been. He watched four of his crew, two on each amidships rail, passing large wooden buckets to men below as they bailed water from the hold. It was a race that only after the rain stopped they could win.

"A course, Lingsyou?" Fu-laing asked.

Yak-san stared out at the horizon, watched the direction of the wind waves and the flight of sea birds as they skimmed over the water. Studying the ancient signs, he was satisfied there was no second storm beyond the horizon.

"Aberdeen," he said. "Let's make for Aberdeen. We'll make repairs there and stay a few extra days."

"A rest will be good for everyone," Fu-laing agreed. Then he shouted a series of orders and three men pulled in on the sail sheets. The Chinese junk, whose design had sailed these waters for over two hundred years, turned east and headed toward the rising sun.

The Lingsyou descended to the main deck and entered the ship's galley. He hung his heavy canvas coat on a wooden peg inside the hatchway to dry. It was still cold in the cabin as the fresh morning air had yet to break the dampness.

The cook, a hairless old man with a knowledge of both medicine and foods, sat with his back against the bulkhead. With a cutting board on his lap, he was busy slicing white pasty blocks of curd into thin strips with a large knife.

"What are you making?"

"Curd cakes and bean noodles," he said, looking up.

"Cold?"

"I can't use the stove, Lingsyou. Still too dangerous. Maybe we'll have hot food by nightfall."

That had been Yak-san's orders. No cooking or lanterns during the storm. Fire was a rolling ship's worst enemy. But a week of cold bean curd was trying on his men.

Nodding his approval, the Lingsyou made his way to his cabin. Suddenly a large wave slapped the bow of the junk and kicked the deck from beneath him. He hit the bulkhead with his shoulder, but caught himself before he fell. Cursing under his breath and rubbing his arm and elbow, he continued down the passage. He pushed open the door and stepped into his salon.

Nathan was there, on his hands and knees cleaning up what appeared to be several shattered glasses. "Sorry, Lingsyou," he said, looking up. His long ponytail of sandy blond hair fell along his back. "The last wave."

"Leave it. Bring me the brandy." He moved to the chart table and sat down. In the center of the table was his large leatherbound logbook. He ran his fingers affectionately over the cover.

"How are your studies?"

Nathan set a full bottle of brandy and a glass in front of Yak-san. "There's so much to read."

"You read word for word?"

"Everything," Nathan said. "I trace the sketchings with my finger to help me remember."

"Good," Yak-san said. "This is more than a ledger, little devil. What is in my head is on these pages."

Nathan already had a deep respect for the book and understood what it meant for Yak-san to hand it to him so freely.

Pouring the gold liquid into his glass, Yak-san leaned forward. "You must know it completely."

"That'll take forever."

"Then stop wasting time." Yak-san pushed the book to him.

Nathan sat down and opened the logbook again.

There was a knock at the door and Fu-laing stepped in. "We are on course. The winds are steady, but the seas are still high. It will be a rough sail," he reported.

"It was good we were returning from Canton and not crossing with a full ship," Yak-san said. "The rains and the waves might have swamped us."

"Not your ship." Fu-laing grinned. He found a glass and sat in the chair beside Nathan. When he saw what the boy was reading, he looked to Yak-san. "You let the boy read that?"

"What boy? Do you see a boy, Fu-laing?"

"I see a mischievous green-eyed devil," Fu-laing said, but realized Yak-san was right. The feeble English child they had taken aboard as part of an agreement with the Chief Inspector was now stronger than most of the crew and the blue *shamfu* he wore had been lengthened many times. The sea had broadened Nathan's shoulders and strengthened his arms until he was unrecognizable as the runaway boy. But the fierceness behind the eyes, that was always there.

"Is he still teaching you the Manchu tongue?" Yak-san asked Nathan.

"There's no more to teach," Fu-laing said. "He speaks as well as I."

"What do you think, Fu-laing? Isn't he a bit old to be a cabin boy?"

Nathan perked up. His future was being discussed.

"Though he will always be a foreign devil, the crew are not hateful of him."

"He'd be wasted on deck lines."

Fu-laing looked at Yak-san questioningly. "What do you mean?"

"I've been thinking. We have what no other ship has. A young Englishman who speaks Cantonese and Mandarin as well as his own tongue."

Fu-laing leaned on one elbow and unconsciously ran his index finger along his lower lip. "But can we trust him?"

"You know you can!" Nathan snapped.

The two men laughed at his outburst. They were teasing him.

"Yes," Yak-san said, remembering. "He proved his loyalty a long time ago."

"What are you thinking, Lingsyou?"

"Give him Englishman's clothes, cut his hair, and he can go anywhere in Hong Kong or Canton. He could walk into the Governor's House if we stole the proper papers."

"He could uncover a wealth of information about shipping routes and cargo," Fu-laing agreed.

"He remembers everything. Here." The Lingsyou tapped Nathan on the side of his head with his finger. "He reads the charts and the ledger and remembers."

Fu-laing was skeptical. "Still, he is only a boy."

Nathan's eyes narrowed.

Yak-san smiled. "If you were at the tiller and heading into Macau, what course would you keep?"

"Bearing two eighty-nine for the south-facing harbor, two thirteen for the north," Nathan answered.

"Simple," Fu-laing said dismissingly.

"Then you ask," Yak-san challenged.

Fu-laing turned to the boy. "Along the Pearl River, passing Yu-wei Sha. What can you do there?" Yak-san's second-in-command remembered a discovery they had made about the river. He had seen the Lingsyou enter it into his logbook.

The question instantly brought the pages of the ledger into Nathan's mind's eye. He read what he saw. "There are sandbars, but it is still deep enough to sail if the ship's not overloaded. Close to shore, the tide swirls. Stay toward the center of the river as long as possible, then head directly at the leeward shore. As you come about, the wind running over the marsh will push you past the white waters. The authorities are too spineless to follow."

"*Aiya . . .*" Fu-laing said in surprise. He knew the boy had repeated the Lingsyou's entry word for word.

"I told you," Yak-san said proudly.

"Maybe there are demons in his head?" Fu-laing grunted, displeased.

"No, Fu-laing. I just remember. That's all," Nathan told him.

"I smell a profit," Yak-san said.

"Lingsyou!" a voice called from outside the cabin. There was quick rapping on the door. "Schooner off the port bow," the crewman yelled.

Nathan followed Fu-laing and the Lingsyou aft. They stood on the port rail. A thousand yards off, an American sailing ship sat low in the water. Her rigging was badly damaged. Only her jib remained, but it luffed loosely in the wind.

"Nathan," the Lingsyou snapped. "Fetch my spyglass."

As the boy pushed away from the rail, Fu-laing stepped closer to Yak-san. "She must have been caught in the storm." Yak-san nodded as he stared suspiciously at the black-hulled ship.

Nathan returned with the collapsible brass scope, extended it, and handed it to the captain.

Yak-san brought the scope to his eye and surveyed the vessel. For several minutes he scanned her decks. "She looks deserted," he said finally.

"Abandoned?" Fu-laing asked.

"Her lifeboats are gone." Yak-san handed the scope to Fu-laing. "Looks to have taken on a lot of water," he said.

Fu-laing looked through the eyepiece as Yak-san turned to his helmsman. "Bring us alongside," he ordered. Then he called down to his men gathered along the port side. "Break out the arms."

The men moved quickly to their captain's orders. Two of them took their position at the bow where the small Dahlgren deck cannon was mounted. It had been a handsome prize from another ship that had fallen prey to Yak-san's men. They wiped it down and loaded it with shrapnel.

"A trap?" Fu-laing asked Yak-san as he returned to the port rail.

The Lingsyou shook his head. "I think her captain was surprised by the monsoon and abandoned her prematurely."

"I wonder what she carries," Nathan said excitedly.

"We'll soon know."

It was quiet during the moments the junk approached the schooner. The sea cooperated fully, the waves flattening to gently rolling swells as they pulled alongside the drifting vessel and made fast with three lines.

Yak-san's crew had never boarded an American schooner before. The Americans' presence in the South China Sea was not nearly as frequent as the Europeans'.

With their guns ready, Fu-laing and eight crewmen crossed quickly to the schooner's slanted deck. Two men raced toward the stern, two forward. Fu-laing and the remaining party moved cautiously into her main cabin.

Yak-san stood by the gangplank with pistol in hand. Nathan paced the deck of the junk, where he had been told to wait.

From an aft hatch, Fu-laing appeared with his rifle slung over his back. He cupped his hands about his mouth and called out. "No one, Lingsyou. She's deserted!"

Yak-san pushed his pistol into his thick belt and moved onto the gangplank.

"Lingsyou!" Nathan called after him.

Yak-san turned and looked at the eager boy. "Come on."

Nathan leaped from the upper deck to the lower. Weaving

around the men remaining aboard the junk, Nathan crossed the gangplank that connected the two ships.

He stopped suddenly as his bare feet hit the smooth teakwood. Looking up, Nathan saw the upper portion of the mizzen dangling above him in a jumble of lines and tackle. On the bow, two of the Chinese crewmen lowered the tattered jib and pushed it into the shrouds. Sliding his hand along the polished mahogany rail, Nathan slowly walked the length of the long curving deck. He tried to imagine her cutting the seas as she crossed the Pacific in high winds. He had seen such ships on the horizon and was amazed by their speed.

For so many years he had known only the slow wallowing junks of China. The schooner could run from them in even the lightest of weather. It was only closer to shore or in the shallow rivers that the junks proved more useful for carrying cargo and passengers. Two different designs based on two different uses.

Moving to one of the hatchways, Nathan found his way into the captain's quarters. Unlike Yak-san, the American captain had surrounded himself with luxuries. Everywhere, the brass fittings were polished to a mirror shine. There were thick velvety curtains over the portholes and a hand-woven rug under the legs of mahogany chairs whose cushions were covered with smooth leather.

The storm had taken its toll on the cabin. The oak table was toppled, the drawers thrown open, and their contents scattered everywhere. Walking across the rug, Nathan could feel the salt water squish through his toes.

Wedged under the companionway ladder, Nathan found a leatherbound book not unlike Yak-san's. As he pulled it free, he discovered it was just that, the captain's log left behind in a hastened escape.

In the cargo hold, Yak-san and Fu-laing stood knee-deep in water. A crowbar cracked open the last of several crates. Like the rest, it was filled with bolts of Chinese silk soaked in salt water.

"Perhaps it can be saved," Fu-laing said.

"A waste of time. It's worthless," Yak-san said in disgust. He let the lid drop hard on the crate.

"Lingsyou," Nathan called down. "Look what I've found."

The Lingsyou glanced at Fu-laing. "I hope he's had better luck."

The clouds were breaking into soft balls of cotton and the sun was beginning to warm the air. Already the decks of both ships were drying in patches.

"What do you have?" Yak-san asked, his tone low and tired. He leaned against the rail next to Nathan. Fu-laing stood in front of them.

"The captain's log," the boy said grinning widely as though the book were made of gold. "She's the *Blue Star* and her captain was Douglas Wiltern."

"Very nice," Yak-san said.

"He kept records like yours, Lingsyou," Nathan said. He pointed to an entry in the book. " 'The British cutter, H.M.S. *Bath*, rounding the headlands for Macau. February seventeenth. We display colors.' And here." Nathan read the next entry. " 'March tenth, the *Stallworth* crosses aft as she heads toward Hong Kong. Captain Neeson waves as we pass.' "

"I congratulate Captain Wiltern on his pleasantries," the Lingsyou said. "Too bad he wasn't a better seaman. Perhaps he would still have a command."

Fu-laing laughed.

"Don't you see?" Nathan flipped back several pages and read, " 'The *Stallworth* on the horizon, January fifteen.' And here on March second, Captain Wiltern records the *Stallworth* again." Nathan looked at Yak-san. "It is the same for all the others."

"What does it do for us? Nothing," Yak-san said, still aggravated about the schooner's worthless cargo.

"Could we determine their routes from this?" Fu-laing asked, thinking he understood Nathan.

"*Aiya* . . ."Nathan hissed in frustration. "It's not the book that matters, it's the ship."

"What are you talking about?"

"Whenever we have attacked a British ship she was either at anchor or her rigging was damaged. With a schooner, Lingsyou, every British merchant on the wind would be ours."

"You see." Fu-laing pointed. "Demons."

Yak-san looked at the boy with interest. "Go on, little devil."

"We tow her to one of the islands and repair her rigging."

"We don't have men to sail her," Fu-laing argued.

Yak-san looked along the length of the wallowing vessel, her washed decks and broken topmast. Rubbing his chin, he stared across the water in thought. "Imagine what we could do with a ship like this," he said, placing his hand on Fu-laing's shoulder.

"You are listening to foolishness."

"No. He's right. With a good crew, we could smuggle whatever we wanted and thieve whoever we found."

"She runs too deep for upriver."

"We use the junk for that," Nathan said. "Two crews, one Lingsyou."

Yak-san chuckled at Nathan's resolve. "And who's to say we couldn't take her north?" Yak-san said, dangling possibilities in front of his second. "To Shanton or Shanghai?"

"Shanghai . . ." Fu-laing sneered.

"Think of her under full sail with her holds overflowing with silk and opium."

"*Sin faat tsai yan,*" Nathan said to the half-Manchurian. The old saying was clear to both men. "Whoever makes the first move, wins."

A reluctant grin formed on Fu-laing's face.

"Demons or not," the Lingsyou said, "our young *gweilo* is going to make us wealthy."

On the deck of the wallowing schooner, the two pirates and their apprentice laughed with glee at their newfound fortune.

Chapter Twenty-Three

The New Territories

"Bitch of a road, huh?" the American teenager yelled over the clattering of the truck's decaying engine as it strained against the incline.

The Chinese driver, an elderly man with a pair of gold teeth and gray stubble on his chin, nodded to the broad-shouldered boy. He swung the limp steering wheel back and forth as they sped along the narrow road that was fenced by thick walls of bamboo.

Barry, the teenager's companion, was stuffed against the frail passenger door. He pulled the toothpick dangling from his lips and glared at his buddy. "He didn't understand a shitt'n thing you said, Moose."

"I should talk louder, then?"

"Don't be an asshole."

"It's my job," Moose said. "Isn't it, Pop?" he said loudly to the old man.

The driver nodded and grinned. He looked around the young *gweilo* and at the Chinese-American with the toothpick. *"Ni cong nar lai?"* he asked.

"California," Barry said in awkward Cantonese. "We're students. You know, on vacation."

The teenager's words grated on the old man's ear. His diction was clearly book-learned and his accent oddly perverse. It was a shame, the man thought, that the Chinese that migrated to foreign countries let their children grow up uncultured.

But seeing him at the Fanling station with his *gweilo* friends made the old man feel sorry. They had been standing around their heavy-framed hiking packs arguing over a tourist map and trying to decide which bus to take.

The old man needed help unloading a dozen tubs of honey for the train and the teenagers needed a ride to Ma Tseuk Leng, where the hiking trail began. He and Barry had struck an instant deal. Working in unison, as if they unloaded trucks for a living, the teenagers moved the honey from the pickup to the freight room, where it was weighed, tagged, and loaded onto the returning train.

"How long are you staying on the mountain?" the man asked.

"A day or two," Barry told him as he stared out the open window. He hoped the old man would leave it at that. Questions made him nervous.

"Don't go too far beyond the peak. The boundary is there," he warned. "And the fence."

"Yeah, we know," he said, remembering the photographs of the prickly barbed-wire barrier. They also knew about the series of infrared sensors and minute seismographs placed along the fifty-kilometer fence by the Hong Kong Field Patrol.

He reached into his vest pocket and fished out a Ziploc bag. As he opened it with his teeth, the tart bite of beef jerky filled the cab. He offered some to the driver.

"No, no." The old man waved the black peppered strips away. "Can't eat that."

"Why not?"

With his right hand, the Chinese man pulled his front teeth out of his mouth and held them in front of the teenagers.

"Jesus." Moose recoiled. He didn't know what they were talking about and now he didn't care to know.

The man slipped his teeth back in and laughed with the Chinese-American.

At a bend in the road, the man pulled over. Barry and Moose slid from the cab as their two other companions climbed from the truck bed. Bobby and Franklin transferred their four brightly colored backpacks to the roadside as Barry thanked the man.

"The trail starts over there," the Chinese man said, hooking a finger in that direction.

"We'll find it." Barry nodded and bowed slightly. He wasn't sure why his body did that. His father did the same when bidding his grandfather good-bye. It was automatic, Barry figured. Somehow genetic.

"That was easy," Barry said to Moose as they watched the old man in his old truck pull back onto the highway. He waved. They waved. And the truck disappeared around the next curve.

"Better than the bus," Bobby agreed as he lifted one of the packs. Barry slipped his arms through the straps, then helped Bobby with his.

"These people are too fuck'n nice," Moose commented as he muscled into his gear. The straps dug into shoulders from the excessive weight.

Barry glanced one last time down the road to be sure the old man hadn't doubled back. Satisfied, he and the others crossed the highway and headed up the rarely used footpath that lead to the top of Hung Fa Leng, the highest and most northern mountain of the New Territories.

For an hour, the four teenage-looking men marched silently along the wooded trail. Finally, as they entered a dense thicket of giant bamboo and big-leafed Moraceae trees that created a cathedral ceiling over them, Barry signaled with his left hand. They stopped in unison.

They stood in silence for thirty seconds. Barry looked up the trail. No one. Bobby, at the rear, gave him the all-clear sign.

"Okay, time for work," Barry said as he slipped his pack from his shoulders and pushed his way into the trees. The others did the same, each making his own way through the thicket. Although the forest fought against them, the four slipped delicately through without disturbing a single branch of the ancient plants, and simply disappeared from the trail.

Fifty yards inside the bamboo, Barry found a natural clearing. "Here," he said, his voice now a whisper. He peeled off his USC sweatshirt and faded jeans. The others did the same and in under two minutes they had stripped off their civilian clothes, stuffed them into the side pockets of their packs, and donned camouflage body suits.

Moose took a swipe of olive and black oil-based paint from a tin and wiped it generously over his forehead and cheeks. Except for his ice-blue eyes, his face disappeared under his jungle hat. He turned to his pack and began to double-check his equipment.

"Bobby," Barry whispered as he took the tin from Moose and concealed his own face. "Position?"

Capping the night-vision scope of his R.A. sniper rifle, Bobby withdrew the palm-size NAVSAT positioning computer from his vest pocket. He punched his private code into the small triangular device and cupped his hand over its L.E.D. screen. Instantly the navigation satellite system downloaded their longitude and latitude. "Edge of sector two-three, Captain. First post is four clicks bearing two-eight-four."

Barry checked his watch. He looked to Franklin and Moose. "Well, gentlemen? Are we happy?"

Franklin nodded as he zipped and sealed his bag. "I'm good," the soldier confirmed.

Moose sat cross-legged on the ground with his stubby riflelike targeting laser upside down on his lap. He had the bottom of the designator open and was poking at it with a sharp stick.

"Don't do this to me, Moose," Barry warned as he knelt beside him.

"Nothing I can't fix."

"You didn't drop it again, did you, Moosehead?" Franklin joked.

"Hey, fuck you."

"Moose . . ." Barry was taking on his authoritative voice. "We have to be in position and hot in two hours. Otherwise we're going to scrub."

"Just give me a second. I can fix it."

"Frankie and I can still set up, Cap," Bobby offered. The young Italian from Myrtle Beach was dying for action. He was the youngest of the foursome and had missed out on Desert Storm.

"The Birds won't come unless they can both light their way," Barry said. This wasn't Iraq. In the desert, the elite forces of the U.S. Marines Corps knew exactly where the enemy had dug in and had plenty of time to highlight the Iraqis' weapons with their lasers. They could do it from three miles away and sit back and watch the F-16 Falcons follow the invisible red beacons and deliver their deadly payloads.

This wasn't even Bosnia. There they had been in the war zone for twelve months recording the Serb troop movements, noting fuel depots, ammunition sites, and vulnerable supply links.

When NATO finally realized the Bosnian Serbs had no intentions of recognizing safe zones or bargaining tables, the Marines were in place and warming targeters. A day after the Falcons thundered over the skies of Sarajevo, the warring parties were making plans for peace talks in Geneva.

But here, it had only been fifteen hours since these four baby-faced soldiers had been sitting in a strip bar outside Kadena Air Force Base watching a brunette dance over Moose for his twenty-second birthday.

Two sergeants found them, handed Barry their orders, and drove them directly to the base. Their en route briefing was short and simple. Get into the northern forest and set up two targeting points.

With the communists threatening to roll into the territory and Hong Kong patrols on alert, the Americans couldn't be there. Not officially and definitely not with their weapons and high technology. To be discovered would be a diplomatic nightmare and could, in and of itself, give Beijing the excuse to invade the colony.

And, as always, time was of the essence when there wasn't

any. There would be no time for a buildup, no beach assaults or counterstrikes. These men *were* the front line. If the Chinese tanks crossed, their primary mission was to light up as many as they could and hope the Falcons would blacken them and force the communists to reconsider their course of action. To make matters worse, the serpentine line that had long divided the Red and British Empires was an electronic hot zone drenched in passive and active radars denying a parachute insertion. Thus, the Marines entered Hong Kong via the reclining seats of a civilian jetliner instead of the belly of a Stallion transport.

Captain Barry Chung knew they were pitting technology against brute force and sheer numbers. He didn't care for the gamble, especially now when his first problem was electrical. "Well?" he asked Moose again as the birthday boy poked at his delicate piece of equipment with a dirty stick.

The tiny cooling fan whistled as it came on. "There," Moose said proudly. "Told ya!" He slapped the cover closed.

"Jesus." Barry shook his head. "Are we all ready, then?" The Captain got a nod from everyone. "Thank you." He looked to Bobby, who was already unfolding his radio dish. "Let 'em know."

Bobby typed the coded message into the weatherproof laptop and high-frequency communicator. The powerful signal leaped invisibly from the wooded mountainside and into space.

Two hundred and seventy kilometers above the equator, a tiny black box in the corner of a Japanese telecommunications satellite snatched the encrypted message, held it for several seconds, then sent it at the precise nanosecond to the CIA's receiving station in Okinawa. From there, it flowed freely to the basement of the Pentagon and into the planning room of the Defense Intelligence Agency.

MacDoren sat alone in the glass booth that overlooked the planning room. He sat in one of twelve thick leather chairs aligned in three rows on a richly carpeted slanting floor. The National Security Adviser pulled thoughtlessly at the tip of his goatee as he watched the men and women in the brightly lit room below.

The horseshoe-shaped chamber with its semicircles of control panels reminded him of the Houston control center and the scenes of busy men during the early Apollo missions. Staunch tacticians in front of long flashing computer screens.

It was the same here. Except these people were a different breed of tactician. The men and women in this room didn't launch astronauts, they launched wars.

His gaze crossed the three wall-size screens in front of the room. The right screen gave constant updates on the CIA's Defense and Space Groups: the satellite systems, AWACS aircraft, and the newly incorporated reconnaissance drones that were on station around the world.

The left, superimposed over a world map, delivered precise data on each arm of the military: battle group location, Army force and readiness, and the status of the ever-patient nuclear missile systems scattered along the U.S. border and those beneath the sea.

The center screen—the Feature Show, as they called it— was thankfully dark. The American war machine was currently not at a crisis level. Had it been, the Feature Show would be bright with 3-D geographic maps of the conflict arena and real-time information and statistics.

With battlefield data downloaded into the Centurion mainframe computer, the screen could create any number of expectation scenarios for the Commanders and Generals who would gather in this luxurious booth.

It was an interesting tool, MacDoren thought. No more pushing plastic battleships across a tabletop with a long stick. That was done now with a cursor and a ball mouse.

Along each side of the wall screens were two columns of monitors. Earlier this morning a boldfaced label had been fixed with adhesive beneath the top right-hand monitor. HONG KONG.

That's all the label said. That's all it needed to say. The eleven people below had already been briefed on what was taking place at that pinpoint of land. Staring at the world map, MacDoren imagined the entire mass of China sliding down onto the little settlement.

The Hong Kong monitor flashed red, signaling the room of an incoming message. Then it displayed three bold words: DRAGON'S PAW—ONE. That's what MacDoren was waiting to see. The first team was in place. In eight hours, four more teams would take their positions in the wooded hillsides, ready to ambush a Chinese blitzkrieg.

A Marine Gunnery Sergeant in civilian clothes stepped to where the Director was seated. The man stood rigidly silent, waiting for acknowledgment.

MacDoren continued to watch the screens, then, after the proper time, glanced at the man. "Yes?"

"He's here, sir."

MacDoren paused again. "Send him in," he said.

The Sergeant returned to the door.

Jake Sampson replaced the Sergeant at the end of the row of chairs. In his hand was a thin manila envelope with no label.

"Sit down, Jake," MacDoren said, motioning to the chair on his right. He noticed the spymaster was unusually quiet. He knew why.

Jake sat down and stared blankly at the planning room. He handed the envelope to MacDoren.

"Gandel?"

"Yeah." Sampson nodded.

"I've seen it," MacDoren said, tossing it into his open briefcase on the chair to his left.

"I'm going to M15 about this."

"No, you're not," MacDoren said flatly.

"Goddammit, Crawford. They know what's going on."

The big man with the goatee crossed his right leg over his left and shifted his position to look more squarely at Sampson. "I'm going to break our own rules and let you in on information that's beyond your clearance."

Sampson shot him a sidelong glare.

"Believe it or not, there are levels beyond you, beyond me, beyond everyone. And I mean everyone. Intelligence isn't a pyramid. No one sits on top knowing it all," Mac-

Doren said. "See the seventh monitor? Marked Hong Kong?"

Sampson nodded.

"Dragon's Paw means stage one is in place," MacDoren said. He reached into his briefcase and withdrew three computer-enhanced aerial photographs and handed them to the Rogue's director. "Latest recon," he said.

Sampson was taken completely by surprise. The images were clear and unmistakable. More than a hundred dark silhouettes of T-80 battle tanks and various armored personnel vehicles lined a wide ribbon of road. "Where is this?"

"Guangzhou, forty miles north of the border. And we have reports of another brigade moving in from Fugian."

"They can't be serious."

"One would hope not. But we're dealing with arrogant communists and stubborn Englishmen." MacDoren sighed. "Let me paint you an ugly picture. As procedure calls for, our people in Imagery passed those photos to the Brits. They take a look and the Prime Minister pretty much soils his Oxford breeches."

Sampson listened intently, wondering about his place in all this.

"Last Friday," MacDoren said, "the crew of a Lynx chopper stationed in Hong Kong dipped its ears into the drink for a little practice. Instead of picking up a passing motor yacht, their sonar snagged a diesel-powered submarine. They tried to identify her, but as soon as she knew she was tagged, she bottomed. By the time the Brits got a surface ship in the area, she was gone."

"A Russian India?"

MacDoren was impressed. "That's what they're guessing. The Russians sold Beijing two India-class subs, one in 1994 and one in 1996. One of them carried two small submersibles on her deck."

"I remember when the Swedes discovered the Soviets using them to infiltrate their coastline," Sampson said, realizing where MacDoren's logic was leading. "But if they've got this much iron forty minutes from the border, why sabotage the harbor?"

The Adviser sat back in his chair. "Because a British

aircraft carrier is currently steaming north from Sydney. She'll rendezvous with her Task Group by midnight and then continue into the South China Sea."

"Jesus . . ." Sampson suddenly felt sick to his stomach.

"If the People's Liberation Army crosses the border, they'll be in clear violation of British sovereignty."

"That's ludicrous. The Chinese aren't the Argentineans."

"Let's pray someone's mentioned that to the Prime Minister."

Sampson looked at the Hong Kong monitor and the three words that were suddenly taking on deadly connotations. "Honestly, Crawford. How serious is this?"

"The Hill is nervous. The President hopes this is nothing more than a dick-waving ceremony. But he's made it very clear, if the PLA crosses the border, Dragon's Paw becomes Dragon's Claw and we're committed to immediate battle-field air strikes from our bases on Okinawa." MacDoren stared out at the electronic map of the eastern Pacific. "There's still one way to make them reconsider, if the President is willing to use it."

"You're leaving out the obvious. Why all this when the bastards are getting out of the fucking place at the end of June?"

"I'm glad you asked, Jake," the Adviser said. "The Brits are blaming us . . . and your man Chase."

Chapter Twenty-Four

Macau

The jetfoil crew leaped like ballet dancers from the deck to the dock and quickly looped the hemp lines around four iron cleats. With powerful arms, they muscled the ship into place and secured her to the landing.

Moments later, Lindsay and Suzette moved with the disembarking crowd down the wide gangplank. They were herded onto the cement and steel pier and through a long series of tunnels to the terminal building. Colorful welcoming posters adorned the high walls boasting the Portuguese colony's gambling clubs and nightlife.

The officer, in a crisp white uniform, glanced at their passports in a weak attempt at protocol. This was, after all, Portuguese territory and not British. But Macau was not in the business of turning away visitors, it was thriving off them. Thriving once again, as it had in the 1500s when the Portuguese laid claim to this tiny spot of land at the underbelly of the China beast.

Collectively made up of the Macau peninsula and Coloane and Taipa islands, the colony barely covered six square miles, yet within its first century, Macau grew into the most important trading center in all of Asia and with the Portuguese monopoly on world commerce. It was soon the richest city in the Far East.

With ginseng and silk from China filling their holds, Portuguese merchants ventured to Malacca to barter for spices, then to Nagasaki for swords and silver. Across the decks of English Indiamen, American clippers, and Chinese junks, the Portuguese procured the exchange of tea for German clocks, European crystal for Japanese lacquerware, Indian ivory for incense and gold. For three hundred years before Hong Kong existed, tall-masted ships brought travelers and merchants to this tiny outpost from the four corners of the world.

But the arteries of trade were not to flow forever to Macau. In the mid-1800s British merchants, backed by the guns of the mighty English navy, founded their own colony and pressed their station in Asia. Macau would have drifted into the backwaters of history had the Asian underworld and the dark temptations of men not found sanctuary in the tiny colony. Ironically, the very reason for Hong Kong's existence, the trade of opium, the "foreign mud" that washed across and polluted China's population, quickly ran through the clearer passages of Macau.

And now, in its latest reincarnation, Macau had discovered a new trade. Tourism. If its harbor was no longer filled with great trading ships of canvas sails, it was now burgeoning with the lumbering ferries and powerful hydrofoils bringing weekend vacationers.

They came to see a sliver of the Old World luster, where flamboyant Portuguese architecture blended oddly with the particularities of Chinese merchants. And they came for the casinos, where they could gamble their life savings on blackjack or fan tu.

Macau's reversion to Red China would not take place until the end of 1999, and with a new boom of resort hotels and office buildings, perhaps after a hundred and fifty years, Macau would ultimately outlast Hong Kong.

*   *   *

Lindsay and Suzette stepped from the terminal and moved to the chain of black and white taxis that awaited incoming visitors. As the first car was hired, the next shimmied forward to replace it.

"If Valdez isn't at the hotel, Jing said he'd be in there," Lindsay said, pointing at the huge cream-colored building across from the terminal. A green sign on the roof flashed, in both English and Chinese characters, CASINO JAI ALAI.

"What makes you think this guy's going to help?"

"Call it a hunch," Lindsay said as he held the taxi door.

The boyish driver, wearing a New York Yankee cap backward, hit the flap arm of the meter, then looked at Lindsay in the mirror. "Where to?"

"The Lisboa."

The taxi screeched on bald tires and into traffic. The driver found a spot behind a slow-moving truck. The meter ticked away as they crept along Avenida da Amizade. The busy boulevard that once ran along the inner arch of the harbor and used to remind Lindsay of a small Mediterranean town was now landlocked by the latest reclamation project that filled in a thousand feet of shoreline with dirt and stone from Coloane and created a foundation for dozens of new high-rise buildings.

Suzette stared between the buildings, looking for a familiar shape among the gathering of yachts and sailing ships. She didn't see it.

"Where'd they find him?" she asked hesitantly, not sure she wanted to know.

"In a suite at the Lisboa."

Suzette reacted as if she had been pricked by a pin. She hugged herself and looked out at the harbor.

Lindsay couldn't help but wonder if she could make her eyes tear on command or if she really felt for Tommy. He thought about the details, about what AnnMarie had told him. Then he thought about AnnMarie.

The traffic, comprised of mostly taxis and buses, moved slowly toward the center of town. Alongside the blacktop snaked a path of dirt trotted flat by skinny men pulling large wooden carts laden high with bags of rice bound for Hong Kong.

A quarter mile down the road and at the edge of the circular plaza appeared the tall cylindrical Hotel Lisboa. With its elaborate custard-yellow facade and white window trim, it looked like a wedding cake in the bright sunlight.

"Pull over."

"What?" the driver looked at him in the mirror.

"Stop here." Lindsay pointed to an empty curb. He had an idea.

"What's the matter?" Suzette asked.

"Get out."

"What?"

"Go up to the desk and ask for Tommy," Lindsay said. "Room seven-oh-six. When they say he's not there, tell them you want to see Mr. Valdez or you'll go to the police."

"I'm getting tired of being your decoy."

"It worked before," Lindsay said, putting his hand on her hip and pushing her from the car. "I'll be near the desk."

Before she could argue further, Lindsay pulled the door closed and waved the driver on.

Furious, she tucked her blouse tails further into her jeans, ran her fingers through her hair, and began walking down the dusty street toward the hotel.

Beneath the hotel's arcade, a doorman in a stiff double-breasted black uniform moved quickly to the taxi. He opened the door and greeted Lindsay; then, having completed the minimum of his job, he moved to the next taxi and did the same.

Paying the driver with loose change, Lindsay looked out at the activity of the traffic circle that looped the statue of Vasco da Gama, a bold-looking man with broad shoulders and a high, upheld chin. Could the first Portuguese navigator to sail the Cape of Good Hope in search of India have ever envisioned what his descendants would create here? Lindsay doubted it.

He shouldered their two bags and entered the twin glass doors of the hotel. He crossed the oval floor and stepped up to the Lisboa's check-in counter.

"Good evening," the olive-skinned man said from behind the high counter.

"A room for the night," Lindsay said. He looked around the lobby, noted the four elevators to the left and the fine jewelry store on the opposite side of the entry.

"Your reservations are under . . ."

"No, no reservations. Whatever you have will do."

The man's fingers tapped across the keyboard as he stared into the computer screen. "I'm afraid all I have are suites, sir."

Lindsay wasn't surprised. "That'll be fine," he said. He made up a name for the register and paid in cash. "Could you have my bags taken up to the room? I think I'll try the casino."

"Very good, sir. And good luck."

Hooking his cane over his forearm, Lindsay walked past several expensive shops and the hotel bakery as he made his way to the casino entrance. The noise inside hit Lindsay like a punch to the chest. It was quickly followed by the choking smell of handmade cigarettes and cheap cigars.

The huge room was filled with Chinese businessmen, fishermen, and a vast mixture of foreigners. Some were dressed in the drab simple clothes of the working class, and others wore Western styles at least five years out of date. He continued nonchalantly around the room.

The casino pulsed with the beat of fast money. Banks of slot machines stood at attention, their left arms high in salute as they were assaulted by men and women intent on recouping what they had already lost. To the right, separated by velvet ropes, were the baccarat tables. Well-dressed patrons played intently while surrounded by an envious crowd of watchers. The game meant status in Macau as it did in Monte Carlo and Vegas.

Beyond these, two lone craps tables stood empty. It was a dice game that had never taken hold here. In stark contrast, several dozen blackjack tables filled the rest of the floor and were packed with players. Twenty-one had by far become the most popular modern game, as the tables' worn vinyl rails showed.

Lindsay moved past a row of slot machines. A short fragile Chinese woman took her purse, and with all her strength pelted the one she had been feeding. She pummeled the uncooperative machine twice more before stepping away, mumbling profanities under her breath.

Amused, he continued through the tables, watching the blackjack dealers as if he were looking for the right one to invest his cash.

Lindsay knew the cameras behind the one-way mirrors in the ceiling had already picked him up. Though he didn't think himself particularly suspicious, he knew the men watching the monitors would take a certain interest in an American entering the casino.

Lindsay found a newly vacant chair at a blackjack table and sat down. "Good evening," the female dealer said with a thick Cantonese accent. She was dressed in a one-piece red velvet uniform with black trim.

"Chips, please." Lindsay pushed a Hong Kong hundred into the center of the table. The potbellied, middle-aged Texan with a Japanese camera slung over his shoulder in the next chair clapped his short stack of chips together. He waited patiently with three other players for the exchange.

"It's a hard table tonight, friend," the Texan said to Lindsay. He grinned at the woman. "Just like every night."

"Then why do you keep coming to my table?" the woman retorted.

"I like the company."

Lindsay sensed the fishing game. The Texan thought, given enough time and effort, he could cajole the dealer to a more private setting, and she was nibbling enough on his compliments and innuendos to keep him coming to her watering hole to spend his money.

"You like to lose," she said.

"Sometimes you have to give a little to get what you want," he parried.

She pushed Lindsay his stack of five-dollar chips.

"Isn't that right, friend?"

Lindsay set two chips on the table. "Sometimes."

The game began as the dealer slid the cards from the shoe to the players.

The Texan looked at his hand. "Yup," he said. "Gotta give to get."

Lindsay glanced at his cards. A nine and a six. The dealer

showed a king of hearts. He signaled for a hit. A four of clubs. He stayed.

She moved around the table. The Texan stayed right off. Two Chinese women each drew and broke. The Chinese businessman at the end with the silk shirt stayed after a two of diamonds.

The dealer opened her hand and revealed the queen of spades. Twenty. She took everyone's money.

Lindsay glanced at his watch.

"Yup," the Texan mumbled as the next hand was dealt. He looked directly at Lindsay. "Cards can be like governments. The power hands are usually well hidden."

Lindsay's and the Texan's eyes locked together for a moment. Lindsay set twenty dollars in front of him. He glanced at his watch again as the cards were dealt. Twenty minutes had passed since he had pushed Suzette from the taxi. Plenty of time, he figured.

"Insurance?" the woman dealer asked, bringing Lindsay's concentration back to the blackjack table.

"No," Lindsay said. "I'm done." He took his cane from the edge of the table. The dealer nodded as she pulled in his money. Flipping over his cards, she saw he had blackjack. She looked at the potbellied tourist and shrugged.

Exiting the casino, Lindsay reentered the lobby. He moved casually to the jewelry store as Suzette stepped through the glass doors. She walked directly to the check-in desk and began speaking to the clerk. The man looked into his files and shook his head.

Suzette leaned further over the counter. Good, Lindsay thought, she was insisting. He pretended to look into a case of Rolex watches as he kept her in view.

The scene played over again. The clerk looked into his computer screen. Suzette slapped her hand on the countertop.

From the office, a Chinese man wearing an impeccable blue suit with a pure white shirt and black polka-dot silk tie moved to her. His face was wide, with a broad flat nose and thinning hair. The manager listened to Suzette, then shook his head. She said something and all of a sudden he stopped and stared at her. He called to the office and another man stepped from the doorway.

Wearing a classical Chinese coat with large white turned-back sleeves, a small, delicate-looking Chinese with a long, whisper-thin mustache stepped around to the counter and took Suzette by the arm. They walked directly to the elevators.

The man's grip was like a vice. "You're hurting me," she said through clenched teeth.

"You wanted to see Mr. Valdez."

"I'll scream," Suzette threatened.

"Be my guest," he said as he reached into his pocket and produced a single key. He inserted it in the panel next to one of the elevators. Immediately the steel doors slid open and the man forced her in.

As the elevator closed, Lindsay jabbed his cane between the doors. He smiled casually as he stepped in. "Almost missed the lift," he said, trying his best British accent. "Sixth floor if you will, ol' boy."

Suzette let out a sigh.

"This is a private elevator," the Chinese man said.

"A private lift? You don't say?"

The doors slid together. The Chinese reached to stop the doors, but before his finger found the button, Lindsay snapped the cane hard across his wrist. Cringing with pain, the man instinctively pivoted on his right foot and positioned himself sideways in one corner. With the speed of a viper, his left foot lashed up and caught Lindsay across the right cheek. The sting teared his eyes.

The man reversed himself. A side kick caught Lindsay in the rib cage and sent him backward into the wall. Lindsay deflected the next with his cane. He rapped the tip across the man's forehead, drawing blood.

Stunned, the Chinese launched another well-practiced kung fu kick. It found Lindsay's right leg just above his knee. A cold spear of pain shot through him. Lindsay screamed. The cane slipped from his hand as he dropped to the floor.

Grinning confidently, the Chinese shuffled for a better position over his downed assailant. As he took aim at Lindsay's favored leg, Suzette lashed out from behind, raking her fingernails across his face and neck. He screamed and turned on her.

It gave Lindsay time to recover. Rolling to his feet, he lunged at the Chinese. Lindsay grabbed a handful of the man's hair, yanked him back, and caught him with an upper-cut. Blood splattered across the elevator's mirrored walls as the man's nose split open. Lindsay clamped his thumb and index finger around the his throat and squeezed.

The man tried to break Lindsay's grip. But his blows had sparked a keg of black powder within Lindsay and the ex-agent of the United States' most elite and covert force now reacted without forethought. Using the weight of his entire body, Lindsay brought an elbow crashing down across the man's forehead. The Chinese's arms dropped. Lindsay hit him again. His eyes rolled up into his head and his body went limp. Lindsay hit him again. And then hit him again, before releasing his body and letting the man fall to the elevator floor.

Suzette stared at the unconscious man. "I didn't think he was going to stop."

"Thanks for the confidence," he said. He leaned down and picked up his cane. Looking at him, Lindsay had to admit, for an instant neither had he.

Truby's words came to mind. *There's always someone better, Linds. Always somebody who's trained one more hour on how to kill you.*

"Not this guy," Lindsay said to himself.

"What?" Suzette looked at him.

"Nothing," he said.

They felt the elevator stop. As the doors parted, a hot blaze of light blinded them both, but only Lindsay recognized the sharp metallic clack of someone racking the bolt of a Spectre submachine gun.

Chapter Twenty-Five

Macau

"Please. No unnecessary movement." The voice was heavy with a Latin accent. "Step forward please, slowly."

"Do what they say," Lindsay told Suzette. As they stepped into the room, the elevator swallowed the unconscious man. Lindsay squinted into the lights. He could only make out partial silhouettes of two men.

"Turn and face the wall. That's it. Hands high."

As she placed her hands against the elevator doors, Suzette sneered at Lindsay. "Great plan."

"No speaking," the Portuguese said as he moved behind Suzette. He was a chubby man with a fleshy face of coarse charcoal skin and long oily hair. He ran his hands roughly down her right leg and up her left. As he slid his hands between her thighs, she instinctively struggled to get away.

"Don't," she snapped.

Chubby grabbed her by the neck and pushed her against the steel door.

Lindsay's body surged to protect her, but he stopped as the cold barrel of the black submachine gun touched his neck.

"No, no," the armed man said, his forehead wrinkled over his gaunt face. "He searches her, then you."

Lindsay put his hands back on the elevator doors. Suzette held Lindsay's stare as she parted her legs. She bit her bottom lip as Chubby continued to run his fingers around her waist, under her arms, and methodically across her breasts. He found her passport and removed it.

The search proceeded the same way with him, but when Truby's 9mm was discovered, Chubby became more precise in his hunt.

The unarmed man took Lindsay's cane and, after a quick inspection, leaned it against the elevator in front of him. Lindsay silently thanked Truby.

Then the machine gun was withdrawn and the bright lights clicked off. "Mr. Chase, Miss Lauhu, please . . ."

They turned to see four halogen lamps rise automatically into the ceiling. The man with the submachine gun had moved to the far side of the luxurious penthouse.

Chubby motioned to a long, white leather couch positioned in front of huge, floor-to-ceiling windows. The glass arched with the cannular room and overlooked the traffic circle and Macau's harbor. The penthouse was decorated with expensive Western furnishings from Lorin Marsh, Niermann Weeks, and Avanti.

"The Patrón will be with you soon," Chubby said, eyeing Lindsay. "Is there something I can get you?"

"My gun."

"I meant a refreshment."

"Oh." Lindsay feigned disappointment. "In that case, I'll just have a rum and orange juice."

The man stepped behind the marble bar. He placed Truby's automatic on the edge near the ice bucket.

"Miss Lauhu?"

"No, nothing." She stared hard at Lindsay, not knowing what she expected but expecting something.

"What?" he asked. "We came to talk to Valdez. He said he's coming."

She folded her arms across her chest and moved to the window.

Half an hour and two drinks passed before they heard

the arrival chime of the private elevator. The doors slid quietly open and the Patrón emerged. Dressed in a midnight-blue pinstriped suit, Valdez was an imposing man. He was at least six-foot-five, with broad muscular shoulders and a narrow waist. Had forty years magically shed from his sixty, he could easily have been an NFL draft choice. Under thick dark eyebrows, two passive black eyes scanned the room. They locked on Suzette.

The Chinese man from their earlier ride in the elevator was with Valdez, only now he wore a row of black stitches in his lower lip. He glared at Lindsay.

"Trust me, it's an improvement," Lindsay commented.

Fury boiled in the man's eyes as he stepped forward. Valdez seized his shoulder. "You enjoy living dangerously, Mr. Chase," Valdez said as he sauntered into the penthouse.

Lindsay leaned on his cane. "It's a bad habit."

Valdez stepped to Suzette. "Rolando Valdez," he said, extending his hand. "Have we met before, Miss Lauhu?"

"I don't think so."

"You look familiar." Valdez tilted his head. Chubby hurried across the room with a glass of merlot. "Nothing for you, my dear?"

"No . . ."

Chubby passed Truby's automatic to his boss. "Interesting," Valdez said, inspecting it. "It's very light. Aluminum?"

"Aerated ceramics."

"Undetectable to airport security?"

"That's the idea."

"Is it accurate?"

"You want a demonstration?"

Valdez grinned. "I'll take your word for it. So what is it I can do for you?"

"Zhang asked us to drop in and say hello."

The Patrón's dark eyes rose slowly from the gun to Lindsay. He turned to Chubby. "Wait for me downstairs."

"But Patrón . . ." he began, his face wrinkling with worry. He had seen what Lindsay had done to the other man.

"Go on," Valdez said, waving the gun at him.

"Yes, Patrón." He knew better than to argue. Valdez's

three men stepped into the elevator and disappeared to the lower floors.

Valdez continued to stare at the American. Then, to Suzette's surprise, he tossed Lindsay the automatic.

"When did the *Tribune* start issuing guns?"

"Macau's a tough town," Lindsay said sarcastically as he slipped the gun into its holster.

"You've placed me in a very uncomfortable position."

"Jing said you wouldn't mind."

"He thinks saving my life grants him limitless favors." Valdez grunted. "But," he relented, "I guess it should."

"He saved your life?" Suzette asked.

"So did Tommy," Lindsay added.

"My family lived in Hong Kong in '41," he said, referring to the Japanese takeover of the colony. "Tommy was another one who never let me forget about his help."

"So he did come to you?"

Valdez sat on the bulbous arm of the couch. "I couldn't believe his audacity. You'd think his bosses would have helped him."

"The *Post?*" Suzette questioned.

"He meant Beijing intelligence," Lindsay said flatly.

Suzette stared at Lindsay. "Tommy?"

Lindsay looked at her with calm eyes. He sipped his drink.

"The newspaper was a charade." Valdez laughed. "What a perfect place to put a spy."

"Amazing no one else has thought of it," Suzette said pointedly.

"What did he want from you?" Lindsay asked.

"A room. A suite, actually. And a boat to take him upriver."

"Do you know where?"

"No, but a lot of people are interested. After the maid found his body, you'd never guess who showed up with the police."

"The British," Suzette said.

Valdez was impressed. He grinned. "You better be careful, Mr. Chase. She is a step ahead of you."

"I've noticed," Lindsay said. "The Brits? Was there a short dumpy guy with a big nose?"

"You know him?"

"We're the best of friends," Lindsay said. "What did you say?"

"As little as possible."

"Anything about Beijing?"

"Are you kidding? Hong Kong's new landlords will be mine soon enough. It's not the time to make enemies."

"At least Portugal gave their citizens passports," Suzette said.

"My government has been very gracious with our travel documents. But I don't want to leave. Macau is my home. I've spent a lot of time and effort building my business and my reputation."

"What about the boat? Did you tell Babbitt about it?"

"That slipped my mind, too."

"Can you find us the same one?"

"To go into China?"

"Exactly," Suzette agreed.

Valdez looked at them, surprised. "Tommy came out of there dead. Dead in a very bad way," Valdez reminded her as he refilled his glass.

"Whatever he was after and whoever killed him are upriver," Lindsay said.

The Patrón shook his head with dismay. "I'll have the boat found by morning. In the meantime, can I at least offer you my hospitality?"

Lindsay lifted his cane from the edge of the couch. "Thank you."

"You're welcome to stay, my dear, while Mr. Chase is off on his crusade," Valdez said, taking Suzette's hand.

"Then who'd keep him out of trouble?"

Valdez kissed her hand. "If it's you, I won't worry about him."

Stepping into the elevator, Suzette waited for the steel doors to close before she asked, "Do you trust him?"

Lindsay brought his finger to his lips. Valdez's private elevator wasn't the best place to discuss the Patrón.

They stepped out into the bustling lobby of the Lisboa. It wasn't surprising that they could hear the casino still in full swing. Smoky and loud with the crackling sounds of gambling chips being shuffled and stacked and tossed and bet. The Chinese, it seemed, loved to gamble as much as the rest of the world.

Lindsay and Suzette caught another elevator to the eleventh floor, walked the hall to their suite, unlatched the door, and entered.

The suite's entryway was decorated with large high-backed chairs covered in maroon velvet and polished end tables. There was a sitting room with a wet bar, and to one side a small couch and coffee table in front of the curved window. The broad view revealed the Baia da Praia Grande, the natural bay that welcomed the first explorers onto Chinese soil.

Behind a set of louvered doors was a spacious bedroom. The bellboy had deposited their two bags on the end of the king-size bed. The thick pastel bedspread was turned back and the pillows fluffed up.

"Not quite as charming as the Blue Hotel, but I guess it'll do," Suzette joked.

"You can have the bath first, if you like," Lindsay said.

"You go ahead. I'll order some hot water and make Mrs. Zhang's tea for you."

"Really?"

"Don't look so damned shocked."

"Sorry." Lindsay shrugged as he opened his backpack.

"Do you trust Valdez?" she asked suddenly.

Lindsay thought. "To a point."

"He wasn't telling us everything, was he?"

"I doubt it." Lindsay said as he retreated to the bathroom.

Suzette unzipped her bag and inspected the clothes Mun had bought. There was an ivory pleated skirt and blouse that weren't too badly matched with off-white dress shoes. Two pairs of jeans, three button-down shirts, two sweatshirts, and another pair of tennis shoes. They were, after all, trying to be an American couple traveling the Orient on a fixed budget.

Suzette heard the bathtub water and unconsciously she smiled as she remembered how she had walked in on him before. "I'm going to call room service. Do you want anything besides the tea?"

"No," Lindsay called out. He added a touch of cold to the hot water spewing from the faucet. This tub was going to be a nice change from what he was used to. Made from rich-colored marble, it was twice the normal size and molded with steep-sloped sides. He pulled off his sweatshirt and jeans and hooked them to the back of the door. He set the 9mm across on the vanity that ran the length of the wall mirror. Waiting for the bathtub to fill, he sat on the edge and arched his back. His spine crackled as the vertebrae recentered themselves. He rubbed the spot below his ribs where Valdez's bodyguard had landed his blows.

With his fingers, he massaged his knee and was pleased it wasn't as tender as he had expected. He slipped into the tub and allowed the steaming water to engulf him. Closing his eyes, he stretched out fully along the bottom. The heat absorbed his stiffness and withdrew the aches of the last few days. It was calming, quiet, and peaceful, and the perfect time to think and evaluate.

"Lindsay?" Suzette was at the door again. "You decent?"

"Just a second," Lindsay said, grabbing the edge of the shower curtain. He pulled it closed. "Okay," he called.

She entered. "How's the water?"

Lindsay sighed. "Wonderful. The knee is becoming an excuse to do this."

To his pleasant surprise, he noticed the vanity lights behind Suzette projected her curved silhouette against the thin curtain. As he watched her, he suddenly realized she was shedding her clothes.

She reached up and pulled the curtain back. Holding the teacup in one hand, she smiled down at him. "What, no gun?" She had removed her jeans and wore only her blouse, its tails riding high on her thighs.

Lindsay began to sit up.

"Don't," she said as she knelt down beside the tub. She handed him the teacup.

"I hope you're seducing me, Miss Lauhu, and not poisoning me with tea."

"It must be poisoned, Mr. Chase," she said softly.

"Because I'd never think of seducing you." Suzette's eyes darted from his face to his shoulders, then to his chest, and back to his face again.

"Okay," Lindsay said heavily. He took the teacup, but his eyes never left her delicate face.

Their eyes held each other for a moment, a long silent moment. There was nothing to say. Nothing to whisper, nothing to promise. She wanted this as he did. She moved forward and kissed his lips. She leaned back ever so slightly, then kissed him again, longer this time, more intense.

When she finally released him, Lindsay watched her mouth and hoped for a smile. There wasn't one. Not a happy smile, anyway. It was more of a shy glance, the unsure grin of whether to proceed or stop. When she reached down and unfastened the last button, Lindsay knew she had made up her mind.

Slowly, thoughtfully, she slipped the blouse from her narrow shoulders. As she stepped into the tub, the hot water stung Suzette's skin. Her stare did not leave his face as she watched his eyes devour her. Careful of his knee, she lowered herself into the bath.

Lindsay's body reacted quickly to the sight of her, the touch of her, the sensuous feel of her silken skin against his. His heart pounded in his chest as he slid his hands along her legs. They trailed the outside of her thighs up to her slender hips and to her waist. His thumbs touched the edges of her taut stomach as his hands glided higher still until his fingertips reached the gentle curves of her breasts.

He leaned forward and kissed her stomach as she sank into him. His lips drifted to the peak of her right breast and he felt it harden against his tongue. He tilted his head back, and his mouth met hers.

She held his shoulders for balance as she continued. Her legs parted over his as she opened herself for him. Then, in the hot water of the marble bathtub, she felt him. There was pressure. She arched her back and rolled her hips forward and the pressure eased. Gasping lightly, she enveloped him and looked into his hazel-blue eyes and finally smiled as she felt his hands grasp her body firmly.

They kissed again, her wet mouth over his as she began to move back and forth. His head fell back and his eyes closed, and she grinned with satisfaction. Soon the water cooled and they withdrew to the king-size bed and continued their lovemaking into the afternoon.

Chapter Twenty-Six

Lau Fau Shan, 1921

In the dim light of a lone candle, Nathan watched the slow, painful breathing of the man laying in the bed before him. His every rasping breath echoed off the room's brick walls.

In the distant village a rooster crowed from a rooftop, prematurely welcoming the dawn. Sunrise was still hours away, but the fowl had been awakened by the fishermen pulling their tiny boats across the pebbly beaches and out onto the sea. So the rooster was repaying the rest of the town for his sudden startle.

Nathan struggled to fend off the sleep his body wanted. His eyelids were as heavy as his head on his shoulders, and his shoulders on his back. He had been here for two days, making sure the old man was safe and comfortable.

Nathan had never been to this temple before, nor to this fishing village. But this is where Yak-san wanted to come. The monks welcomed him without hesitation. They took in all the crew, fed them, and offered them sleeping quarters while the captain rested.

But of Nathan, the holy men were wary. It was understand-

able. Many of their brethren had died at the hands of igno-
rant foreigners. To the Europeans, the monks were idolaters
with satanic rituals.

"Can I get you something?"

The voice from behind caused Nathan to reach for his
American-made revolver under his coat.

It was a young monk and he grinned at Nathan's jumpi-
ness. "This is a temple," he said. "There is no need to
worry here."

"Death walks where he pleases."

"I've heard that the foreign devil that commands beside
the Lingsyou is an outcast among his own."

"I wouldn't know," Nathan said.

An elder monk with a thick gut entered the room, sending
the younger one to do his duties. The elder moved to the
bed. Like the captain, he was old and weathered. Nathan
moved from his chair. He watched as the monk set his hand
on the captain's chest.

"He grows weaker."

"What can you do for him?"

The monk looked on with a heavy brow. "This is the way
of things. We are born, we grow strong, we grow old. You
cannot change the order of the universe."

Nathan looked to his captain. He could see the coarse
gray hairs of his unshaven face in the light. When did he
become so fragile, he wondered. The powerful man who
used to beat him with his thick belt now seemed so feeble
and helpless. Nathan could still see him at the helm of the
schooner screaming out orders, and hear his laughter as
he jumped up and down on the poop deck waving to the
British as the schooner left them in her wake.

"Why did you let us come?"

The monk tenderly brushed the Lingsyou's hair from his
face. "A temple is the only place for his sickness."

"But you know who we are."

"I know Yak-san Kung. We shared the sleeping chamber
beyond the kitchen."

"He lived here?"

"As a young man he studied to be a monk." The man

smiled at the sleeping pirate. "He brought me in off the street. Now I do the same," he said, his voice low, thoughtful.

"Why did he leave?"

"Why does any man pick up his belongings and move on? It is something in the heart."

Yak-san moaned and his eyes flickered. "Nathan?" he said.

"Here, Lingsyou. I am here."

"The schooner? Where is my *Dragonfly*?"

"In the ponds, away from the sea and well hidden."

"Safe?"

"Yes."

The captain grinned crookedly. He looked at the monk beside him. "Ah, my friend," he said, and the effort of speech suddenly brought on a coughing siege.

Nathan helped him to sit up while the monk brought an extra pillow for his head.

"He needs water," Nathan said as he held the Lingsyou in his arms.

The monk grabbed the pitcher from the table. It was empty. "I'll get some more," he said, and rushed out the door.

Yak-san's coughing subsided. From under heavy eyelids, he looked up at Nathan. "I will follow Fu-laing into the next world today," he said calmly.

"Don't talk like that."

"I am not afraid."

"Of course not," Nathan agreed. "The spirits are the ones who should worry. If there is anything to own in the beyond, you'll find a way to cheat them out of it."

Yak-san laughed, but it brought back the coughing.

"The monk has gone for water." Nathan patted him on the back as gently as if the old captain had been a newborn child.

"There are things to tell you, little devil."

"Rest now. You can tell me later."

"There is no time," the Lingsyou said, shaking his head. "Years ago when you were just a boy, you saved my life. Now I return the favor."

"Please, Lingsyou." Nathan felt his own throat going dry.

"No!" Yak-san squeezed Nathan's hand. "Listen to me. You must know these things before I die."

"Okay, I'll listen. But you're not dying."

The Chinese smuggler eased his grip. He closed his eyes and gathered his strength. "Do you know why the Manchurians came to your father's church?"

It was a moment of time, an instant of his life Nathan had tried to forget. He never could. Though he had never spoken of it, the question of who and the question of why had always haunted him. "No, Lingsyou."

"Hong Kong, Nathan," he said. "They came for Hong Kong."

Nathan didn't understand.

"There was a deed that gave the British the lands of Hong Kong and the New Territories. Not a treaty, but clear title. Signed by the Dowager Empress herself."

"Why would there be such a thing?"

Yak-san smiled as he remembered the handwritten note. "She made a pact with your countrymen to save her own cursed life."

The Lingsyou stared into Nathan's green eyes. "It is still here, Nathan. Somewhere in Hong Kong." He sighed. "I have looked. I have had an army look, but every time I have gotten close to that clubfooted demon, he has escaped me. As he will today."

Nathan's mind flashed on the hideous face of the Manchurian assassin.

Yak-san coughed, choked it back, and continued. "In the bilge of the *Dragonfly* there is silver. Thirty thousand pounds worth. It's yours."

"Thirty thousand?" Nathan stammered. "From where?"

Yak-san smiled wryly, his sleepy eyes twinkling under their thick lids. "Over the years, when Fu-laing and I divided our takings, he was far too trusting. And I couldn't help myself."

Nathan couldn't believe what he was hearing.

"Use it, little devil." Yak-san's voice weakened. "Use it to find the deed. It will bring you wealth and power. And what good is life without that?" The old pirate smiled at Nathan. "I'm sorry I never had the chance to thank Forbath," he said, then closed his eyes for the last time.

Nathan felt the Lingsyou's body slouch against him and he knew his captain was gone.

Suddenly he was in another church and another body was over him, pressing the wind out of his chest. Nathan could smell the jasmine of his mother's hair and feel her nightgown on his skin.

He could hear his father again. *Don't feel, Nathan, not now.* But Nathan did feel. Deep inside of him, he did feel. With one hand, he pulled the extra pillow out from behind Yak-san and then laid him back onto the bed.

The monk stepped into the doorway, the water pitcher in his hand. He said nothing as he watched the foreign devil pull the bedcover over the Lingsyou's face.

Nathan stood and looked at the lifeless figure.

"We will take care of him now," the monk said.

Nathan nodded as he stepped past the man and into the cool air of the early dawn.

"You are the Lingsyou now." The words echoed across the sandy beach. Nathan walked along the path that ran adjacent to the shore north of the fishing village. "You are the leader, Nathan," the young man with the stringbean build said as he matched Nathan's quick pace.

Nathan stopped suddenly and grabbed Peng by the collar of his coat. With one muscular arm, he practically lifted him off his feet. "Stop saying that," he warned, and threw the teenager to the ground.

Gasping for his breath, Peng got to his feet. Undaunted, he ran after Nathan.

"It's what Yak-san wanted," Peng said. He spoke English, learned from working in the British's Hong Kong garrison as a cook's helper. When he had turned sixteen they had tried to enlist him, but Peng had managed to sneak away.

He had joined Yak-san with the romantic hopes of pirating, only to become the Lingsyou's cook.

Nathan turned on him again.

This time, Peng kept his distance.

"You're lying," Nathan said.

"Am I?" Peng questioned. "Who cared for him when

you were on the junk? Who talked with him late into the night?"

Nathan stared defiantly.

"The crew is split between you and Tuen. If you don't act now, Nathan, Tuen will."

Nathan knew he was right. "Where are they?"

"Waiting aboard the junk."

"Tuen thinks he's to be the Lingsyou? We'll see about that," Nathan said as he spun on his heels and headed toward the harbor.

The junk of the smuggler Yak-san Kung was anchored two hundred yards off the beach. As Peng rowed the small boat toward the three-masted ship, Nathan made sure his revolver was cocked and ready.

Nathan climbed the rope ladder to the deck. The crewmen stepped back. In Nathan's face they could see that their fears were true. Their captain was dead.

Nathan focused on no one as he moved across the oily deck to the main cabin. Without knocking, he pushed open the door and entered. Peng slipped in behind him.

A dozen crewmen from both the junk and the *Dragonfly* sat at the galley table. At the head, an empty chair awaited Nathan.

"Are you in such a hurry that you need to pick a new captain before giving respects to the old one?" Nathan demanded as he stepped around the table. His firey green eyes fell on every man in the room.

"We are all sorry that Yak-san has passed to the next world, but there will be time for mourning," Tuen said from his chair beside the empty one. He was thirty-five, six years senior to Nathan. A strong, broad-shouldered sailor from Singapore, he had an untamed tongue and said what he wanted. And it was long known that Tuen wanted Nathan's place at the helm of the junk.

Nathan moved behind Yak-san's heavy chair. "Out of respect for the dead, Tuen, this can wait."

"The men need to know what is going to happen."

Nathan could not deny that. There had been many rumors when the Lingsyou's health had begun to deteriorate. Some thought Nathan and Tuen would simply continue in the footsteps of Yak-san and the late Fu-laing. But others knew there were hostile differences between the two men and the finely orchestrated operation of the two crews would soon end.

The strategy Nathan and Yak-san had devised for the adrift schooner and their shallow-drafted junk had turned them into the most menacing and profitable pirates in the South China Sea. The authorities had hunted them for years but without success.

And a large portion of that profit, Nathan now knew, still remained in the bowels of the *Dragonfly*.

"We must decide," Tuen said.

"I will save you the trouble," Nathan said as he reached into his coat. He saw Tuen's eyes lock on him, anticipating his next move. Nathan pulled Yak-san's swallowtailed banner from his pocket. He spread the red flag across the table.

Nathan had brought the one from the top of the mizzen-mast of the schooner. Another flew from the mainmast of the junk.

"I have stolen and cheated and killed a lot of men under this flag," Nathan said. "No more." From his sleeve, he drew a small dagger. He placed the razor-sharp blade at the top edge of the flag and looked at Tuen.

The sailor's brow furled with uncertainty.

"Let each man decide for himself. Those who wish to continue as smugglers go with you. But those who want a new life come with me aboard the *Dragonfly*." Nathan looked around the room.

"Why should you take the schooner?" Tuen questioned.

"It's the cost of getting rid of me. Agreed?"

The room was dumbfounded. No one was sure of what he was hearing. The foreign devil with the Chinese heart had surely been taken over by demons on his way from the temple. They controlled his mind.

Tuen, however, was not about to let such a chance slip through his fingers, demons or no demons. "Agreed," Tuen said quickly. "You take the *Dragonfly*. This ship is mine. The men will decide who they sail under."

Leaning into the hilt of his dagger, Nathan drew the blade across the flag, cutting the insignia of a cat's black paw print symmetrically in half. He handed one part to Tuen. "We are still brothers under the banner of Yak-san. Any ship that flies this half-flag will not be interfered with."

Tuen reached out for the flag, but Nathan held on to it. "Understood?"

"You have my word," Tuen promised as he took the cut flag from Nathan's hand. He could not believe his joss. The schooner would be a loss, but to be rid of the foreign devil so simply . . . He had come ready to kill Nathan, but now he smiled broadly and slapped him on the shoulder. "You have decided well, my friend."

Like the rest of the men in the galley, Peng was stunned. Then he heard Nathan call his name.

"Tell the crew what's been decided and let them choose. We set sail on the tide," Nathan said.

As Peng climbed to the upper deck, he heard the galley in an uproar over what they had just witnessed, but as he glanced back at Nathan, he saw him grinning smugly.

The jib and mainsail of the *Dragonfly* filled with the morning wind. Peng stood at the wheel, his instructions clear. "Keep her bow into the wind until the anchor is free, then fall to port to let her sails fill," Nathan had told him. Peng watched his heading carefully. He had never before been at the helm.

On the bow, Nathan grabbed the anchor line in unison with three other crewmen, the muscles in their backs bulging under the strain. Normally six men would weigh anchor, but from a crew of twenty, only seven remained with Nathan. The rest had decided to join Tuen. That left three men to hoist the sails and Peng to steer.

Finally, after the iron anchor broke the surface and was lifted over the bow rail and secured, Nathan walked back to the stern. Automatically, Peng relinquished the helm to Nathan.

"Where are you going?" Nathan asked.

"I thought . . ."

"You're doing fine," he said. "Just stay on this course until we round Black Point." He looked to the mainsail, making sure the trim was right and the foresail was set to complement it.

Slipping his hands into the pockets of his coat, Nathan found his half of Yak-san's banner. He had crammed it there as his former crew bade him farewell. Not surprisingly, Tuen was at the forefront with best wishes. Nathan, however, knew very well he would have as easily wished him to the devil had events not turned in his favor.

But Nathan had managed to get the Chinese to give his word in front of a full audience. To go back on it, the new captain of the pirate junk would lose too much face. It was an unspoken custom that dealt with the importance of respect and honor. And Nathan knew it bound Tuen to his promise.

Nathan reeled in the halyard clasps of the mizzenmast, hooked the half-flag onto it, and ran the banner to the top. In the brisk wind coming from the south, the odd flag stood straight out.

Pleased with himself, Nathan walked back and stood next to Peng. "You make a better helmsman than you do a cook."

Peng grinned but concentrated on his task. "What will we do now?"

"Head for Sha Chau."

"Are you really giving up the smuggling?" Peng asked. He was beginning to wonder if white men went crazy at a certain age. Then he began to wonder about his decision to stay with Nathan.

"Yes," Nathan said. "No more opium, no more killing, no more Chinese or British navy men firing at our stern. I'm tired of it."

"Then what will you do?"

Nathan did not answer him. He stood there, his feet shoulder's-width apart, his arms crossed over his chest. The schooner heeled firmly in the slow broad swells. The sun was crawling up the sky into a beautiful cloudless day.

As they rounded the headlands, Nathan called another crewman to the helm. He gave the man the ship's heading and instructed Peng to follow him below.

They moved through the main cabin and galley and headed for the captain's quarters. Nathan tapped lightly on the door. It was habit, and though he knew Yak-san would not be on the other side, it seemed odd not to knock.

"Lock the door," Nathan said as they entered. Bending down, he grabbed one edge of the large wicker mat that covered the floor. With Peng's help, he rolled it to the side of the cabin.

On his hands and knees, Nathan inspected the long wide deck boards. They were cut and trimmed and set into place by the master woodworkers of a New York shipyard. Between two of the planks, Nathan saw where the chalking tar was cracked. Drawing his dagger, he pressed the blade into the grain of the wood and lifted. Creating a gap, he slipped his fingers underneath and pulled it up. The plank groaned in protest.

"Grab the other end," Nathan said.

Together they lifted the ten-foot length and set it to the side. Nathan pounded upward until the next board was freed. Peng helped him remove four sections.

Reaching deep into the black void of the bilge, Nathan felt along the moist beams of the ship's ribs. Then he found them. Cool, smooth and half again the size of his open hand. They were stacked two high against the hull.

Nathan lifted the first. It was caked black with a grime of the algae and oil that accumulates in the bowels of ships. He wiped it on his pants.

As the ingot of pure silver caught the sunlight coming through the cabin's open porthole, Peng's eyes widened in disbelief.

"There will be a share for you and everyone aboard," Nathan said, handing it to him.

"Tuen didn't know?"

"You think he would have given up the ship if he had?"

Peng caressed the silver brick. "He'll be madder than a cat when he finds out."

"Most likely," Nathan said with a chuckle.

"What do you plan to do?"

Nathan stretched out his legs and sat back on his elbows. He thought for a minute. "I'm going to build something, Peng. I'm going to take everything Yak-san taught me and

I'm going to build an empire." Yes, Nathan thought, that's exactly what he was going to do.

"I know what I'm going to do," Peng said happily.

"What?"

He leaned forward and handed the ingot back to Nathan. "I'm going to invest in you, Lingsyou, in your empire."

Nathan laughed aloud. Peng's face widened in a tooth-filled smile and he joined in his jubilation. Their laughter drifted out the porthole and, like the odd banner overhead, caught the wind of the South China Sea.

Chapter Twenty-Seven

Washington, D.C.

Sampson used his thumbnail to scrape a dried spot of toothpaste from his tie. Luckily it was camouflaged in the tie's dark paisley and low enough to hide under his coat as long as he kept it buttoned. Of course he'd keep his coat buttoned. As he kept scratching at the tie, he realized how nervous he was. He had no idea why MacDoren had insisted he come, nor could he decide what he could say. How much information did the Adviser expect from him before it infringed on R-50's secrecy? Was MacDoren willing to compromise the division in order to stop someone else's war? Or was that his plan?

The Rogue had been the creation of another administration. Perhaps the current one had decided it was finally time to clean house and this was the perfect opportunity.

Sampson made up his mind to hold to his bottom line. No compromise of R-50, no matter what. Just as it had been all day at Langley. That's where MacDoren had found him. At CIA headquarters in the middle of his seventh briefing of the Far East Station Chiefs on the situation and the importance of finding Chase. It was a delicate dance through a minefield as he tried to tell them about Lindsay while not telling them too much. The men were unaware of his shadow agency, and so far there was no reason for them to know.

But they had to know what to expect. Did Chase know he was being sought? If he discovered he had been tagged, would he retaliate or simply try to shake their agents? And they wanted to know why Sampson was in charge of this operation. Several of the chiefs knew him, but thought he had retired years ago. They were surprised to see he was active. And, of course, they wanted to know who in the Agency had actually authorized this. What resources could they expend and was this going to cut into the budgets of their current operations?

Sampson chewed on his pen in frustration. The phone call that had pulled him out of the meeting was a relief until he heard MacDoren's insistent voice on the other end.

Sampson scratched at the tie stain as his driver pulled the dark blue Lincoln Town Car up to the South Gate. The Marine recognized the car and driver and, with a chest salute, allowed him in.

"Fresh coffee for you, gentlemen?" the secretary asked as she held the door for Sampson.

MacDoren smiled from one of the two matching cream-colored couches in the President's Oval office. "I think we're okay, Maggie. Thank you."

She smiled and retreated behind the reinforced door leaving the two men alone.

"So as an adviser, you get to borrow his office?"

MacDoren chuckled. "On occasion."

Sampson stopped at the edge of the blue rug that featured the presidential coat of arms woven into its center. Beyond it was the President's walnut desk. The spymaster stepped farther into the room, taking in every detail of what represented the very center of world power.

"You've been in here before, haven't you?"

"Once," Sampson admitted. "Bush gave a few of us a quick tour." He looked up at the presidential seal in low relief in the center of the ceiling.

"The mantel's the only original thing in the room. Every president has to change the place one way or another. The layout always seems to be the same."

"Not much you can do with an oval room."

"I guess not. Did you want coffee?" MacDoren asked as he moved to the coffee tray. He poured himself a cup and added three cubes of sugar.

"Is he here?"

"The President?" MacDoren returned to the couch. "He's leaving for Camp David in about thirty minutes."

"So tell me, Crawford. What are we doing in here?"

"Making a point. He wants us to play open-handed with this one."

Sampson felt his nerves tighten. "How open?"

"Don't worry, Jake. I don't plan on giving the Chinese anything they couldn't find out with a little effort on their side. I just don't think we have the time to wait for them."

Relieved, Sampson moved to the tray. "I think I'll have that coffee."

"Help yourself," the Adviser said. He sipped his. "We made a mistake not replacing Chase with another Prowler. Now we're groping for answers."

"Not to sound smug, but I tried to tell you that."

"I thought we could rely on MI5."

"Don't kill yourself over it, Crawford. So did I."

"What do you make of him?"

"Chase?" Sampson sat in the couch opposite MacDoren. "I never believed he was a double, but every breach we had pointed his way. I thought of just withdrawing him. Then I remembered the Ames case and how it tore the guts out of the Agency. I couldn't let that happen to R-50. When the Brits offered to sideline him, it seemed the best way."

"And now?"

"It plugged the holes . . . for a while."

"Until Gandel?"

"And the two agents she lost."

"So maybe he wasn't the only mole."

Sampson looked into his coffee cup, wondering about the question.

The intercom chimed gently from the desk.

"Yes?" MacDoren spoke up.

"Ambassador Kwong is here, sir," Maggie stated.

"Show him in."

"Yes, sir."

"And the games begin." MacDoren smiled at Sampson.

The Chinese Ambassador was a very small man with fine black hair, a narrow face, and frameless glasses. He entered the office stiffly, his hands clutched into fists at his side. As his eyes darted from the empty desk to the rest of the room, Sampson realized he was anticipating an audience with the President. His brow eased when he saw only MacDoren and Sampson.

"Thank you for coming on such short notice, Ambassador," MacDoren said, shaking his hand. "I don't think you've met my new assistant, Mr. Smith."

"How do you do," Kwong said, shaking Sampson's hand firmly. From the Ambassador's gaze, Sampson knew he didn't believe he was anyone's assistant.

"Please, sit down." MacDoren turned on the charm of a gracious host. "Coffee, Ambassador? Perhaps tea?"

"Coffee, thank you. No sugar."

Sampson poured.

"I hope you don't mind my dispensing with the usual formalities," the Adviser said. "But I think we can sort this matter out quickly."

Kwong accepted the coffee and sat down at the end of the couch. "What matter is that, Mr. MacDoren?"

"The military activity in the Guangzhou Province." MacDoren handed his cup to Sampson for refilling. He sat in the other couch opposite the Ambassador. Sampson served him the coffee and sat at the far end.

"Activity?" the Ambassador looked perplexed. "Oh, you're referring to our military exercises?"

"I'm not a military man, Ambassador." MacDoren smiled. "But I have associates who are. From what they tell me, a hundred T80 battle tanks, two hundred and ten armored personnel carriers, and a hundred and sixty thousand troops resembles more of a buildup than an exercise."

If the Ambassador was surprised by MacDoren's information, he didn't show it. "As you know, China has a long border. For the People's Liberation Army to defend it effectively, it often trains in large numbers," he said confidently. "But that is an internal matter and of no concern."

"It's a concern to us, Ambassador. Intentions are difficult to judge. It can be dangerous if people don't talk frankly with each other. It's easy to assume the worst."

Kwong looked over his coffee cup. "You must forgive me for being so naive, Mr. MacDoren. What sort of dangers are you referring to?"

MacDoren set his cup and saucer on the table. He leaned forward on his knees. "These forces are near the border of Hong Kong and constitute a direct threat to the sovereignty of the British colony. And that, Mr. Ambassador, is a threat to the region."

Sampson sat up. This was getting interesting.

"If there are concerns about our repossession of the colony"—the Ambassador's voice deepened—"I suggest you take it up with the British Prime Minister. If he is in fact having second thoughts, well, rest assured, Mr. MacDoren, we view Hong Kong as an inalienable part of China. Our military has both the determination and the ability to reunite the motherland." He took off his glasses and cleaned them with his handkerchief. "You speak of the region as if your country were part of it. Let me remind you, it is not. The People's Republic of China is its prominent resident."

"Yes, but—"

The Ambassador pressed on coolly. "Your implications undermine the relationship of our governments, Mr. Adviser. Am I to return to my office with suspicions?"

The secondary door to the office suddenly opened and the President of the United States stepped in. "I'm sorry, Crawford. I forgot you were in here," he said, and smiled to everyone in the room.

Sampson jumped to his feet. The Ambassador quickly set his coffee down and stood.

"Ah, Ambassador Kwong." The President put out his hand as he crossed the room. "How nice to see you."

"Mr. President." He bowed cordially.

"I don't think you know Mr. Smith," MacDoren said, introducing Sampson.

"Mr. Smith, is it?" The President grinned, holding Sampson's gaze. "Nice to meet you, Mr. Smith." Sampson realized the President's entrance had been arranged.

"Congratulations, sir."

The President cocked his head questioningly.

"On the new term."

"Oh, yeah. Four more years. I just hope it's a quiet four years."

They all chuckled respectfully as the President rounded his desk. He opened the deep drawer of the credenza behind his chair and withdrew a richly polished wooden box. He lifted the lid and took out a half dozen cigars. "Thought I'd sneak a few of these into my bags. The First Lady doesn't care for the habit. But hell, while I'm fishing, what can she say? Can I offer you gentlemen one? Ambassador?"

Kwong declined politely.

"I know you don't smoke, Crawford. Perhaps you, Mr. Smith. You look like you enjoy a cigar from time to time."

"Actually, sir, I do."

"Then please ..." the President turned the humidor toward him. "Sorry they're not Cubans. I love a good Cuban cigar. But we can't always have what we want, can we?"

"No, sir," Sampson said, taking a dark Royal Jamaica maduro.

"It's a shame. But sometimes there's too much at stake to be greedy," he said, his eyes holding on the Ambassador's for a time. He closed the humidor and returned it to the drawer. He shook their hands again. "It was nice to see you again, Mr. Ambassador. Mr. Smith, good to meet you finally. We'll have to talk cigars one day." He moved back to the secondary door with a confident stride. "Crawford, call me tonight if you get the chance?"

"I'll be sure to, sir," MacDoren promised.

The door closed and the Ambassador turned back to MacDoren and the mysterious man called Smith. He had lost his edge.

"There are people on the Hill," MacDoren said pointedly, "that want to contain Beijing. The President isn't one of them."

"If you treat China as an enemy, China will be an enemy."

MacDoren stared at the Chinese Ambassador for a long time. "I assure you, making enemies is the last thing the President wants. But there are grave consequences in underestimating his resolve. As a precaution, we have deployed the *Independence* and the *Nimitz* and their battle groups into the area."

Kwong frowned. "We've been down this road before, Mr. MacDoren. Last year, I believe, we were under similar circumstances. Your military made a grandiose and wasteful appearance, and for what reason? To sail around Taiwan a few times and then to go home. Your tactics didn't intimidate us then, they won't now."

"The difference, Mr. Ambassador, is that last year was an election year. This year isn't. And outside the Pentagon and this office, no one knows they're on station." MacDoren grinned. "We all know the importance of retaining honor, or, as you call it, saving face in these matters. However, Ambassador, we also need to keep our promises to our British allies."

The desk phone buzzed sharply. MacDoren excused himself and lifted the receiver. "Yes? Wait a sec." He scrambled for a piece of paper, slid the presidential writing pad under his hand, and grabbed a pen from its stand. "Go ahead . . ." He scribbled. "What time?" the Adviser asked. "Okay. Thanks." He hung up the phone and tore the paper from the pad. He folded it in half. "If you would, please," he said, handing the paper to Kwong. "Pass this along to your intelligence service."

The Ambassador took the note from the Adviser's hand. He glanced at what was written. "What is this?"

"Coordinates."

"I have complete trust in you, Mr. MacDoren. If you say the *Nimitz* is in the area, I believe you."

"Those coordinates, sir, are for your three attack submarines now stationed in the Taiwan Straits. The *Red Bridge,* the *Great March,* and your newest boat—I believe it's called the *Great Wall.*"

"How could you know . . ." Kwong fumbled.

"Trust me, Ambassador, we can."

Kwong's eyes narrowed behind his frameless glasses. "Reunification of the mainland is an internal matter," he stressed.

Sampson watched MacDoren's face and for the first time understood why the man who looked like a college professor held such a powerful position. His eyes went cold, stonedead like those of an attacking shark. "Hong Kong is anything but internal, Mr. Ambassador. And we are definitely not going to stand by and watch it turn into another Tiananmen Square.

"If your soldiers cross the border a second before the transition," MacDoren stated, "we are prepared to offer any assistance the British government asks for. And let me be very clear, Ambassador, military action in Hong Kong will greatly change our position on the Taiwan issue."

"There is no discussion on Taiwan. It is a renegade province of China." Kwong's voice rose.

MacDoren matched it. "That's Beijing's opinion, sir. We believe Taiwan has made a successful transformation from an authoritarian regime to an honest-to-goodness democracy. As you know, there's a majority in Congress who'd like to recognize the island as an independent state."

Kwong gasped and his face reddened. "You can't . . ."

"We're not charging into this situation. We're reacting to it. America's Taiwan Relations Act is very clear; any threat toward Taiwan's future is a threat to the security of the Western Pacific Area. Your troops now constitute just such a threat. And, sir, I've been authorized by the President of the United States of America to inform you that as a precaution to your government's military buildup, two battalions of the Patriot missile defense system are currently on their way to Taipei."

In Kwong's eyes, Sampson could see his temper flaring, his guts boiling over. But he was an ambassador, a diplomat. He fingered the piece of paper handed him. He wiped the moisture from his lip. "I will let Beijing know of your intentions," he said stoically.

"Thank you. I'm sure we can find a solution to satisfying everyone."

The Ambassador bowed courteously, spun on his heels, and marched from the room. For a time, MacDoren and Sampson stared at the closed door.

"Well," MacDoren said calmly, "we just played our best hand."

"It was a good hand. It should make the bastards think twice."

MacDoren stroked his goatee. "I wouldn't count on it."

Chapter Twenty-Eight

Macau

The thirty-foot *kaido* Lindsay and Suzette had been pointed toward by the taxi driver was laced to a makeshift dock by tattered lines. The fishing trawler's flat wide forward deck was overrun with tumbles of gill nets and drag cables. Old car tires dangled along the hull. A smoking cooking fire in a small iron barbecue behind the square pilothouse was the only indication of life aboard.

Lindsay swung his daypack over his shoulder and stepped like a tightrope walker down the dock's warped planks. He reached for Suzette. "Here," he said, taking her hand.

The boat rocked sharply as they stepped aboard. Weather beaten and deteriorating from neglect, her tiny pilothouse was missing its door. Inside, a narrow hatchway led into the hollow ship. Over the stern and draped from aluminum poles was a canvas tarpaulin that shaded more tangled nets and lines.

Lindsay sided the pilothouse. "Hello?"

"Ni zao," the captain said as he came out of the companionway. He was in his forties but looked to be sixty. The sea

was a hard life anywhere in the world, but the Chinese seemed to show it the most.

"*Ni zao,*" Lindsay said. "Are you for hire?"

"Yes, always," he said, his lower lip drooping comically as he grinned.

"How much for the day?"

"What do you want to do? Sightsee or fish? Thirty dollar to sightsee. Fifty dollar to fish."

"Sightsee," Suzette spoke up.

"Okay." He disappeared into the pilothouse. A sudden belch and a startling backfire, and the *kaido*'s engine came to life. "You"—he pointed a scarred finger at Lindsay— "cast off."

Moving to the bow, Lindsay glanced at Suzette and saw her amusement. "Go ahead, laugh," Lindsay warned. "You'll be swabbing the decks before lunch."

"Wanna bet?"

The morning was cool under wide blue skies, and a gentle breeze rippled the coffee-brown waters off Macau. The captain spun the boat's wheel under his palm and headed away from shore. Suzette grasped the rail that circled the pilothouse and looked forward. As Lindsay moved to her, he recognized her devilish grin.

"What's that for?"

"Just thinking about last night."

"Well, don't."

"No mixing business with pleasure?"

"Not in this business," he said seriously.

She grimaced. "How much cash do you think he's going to want?"

"To take us to where he dropped off Tommy? A lot, if he knows what happened to him."

"What are you going to do?"

"Convince him."

"I don't like the sound of that."

"You want to get there, don't you?"

Suzette nodded. They were in a race; whether Lindsay realized it or not, she did. At the finish line would be Tommy's killer and perhaps Lindsay's double agent. But for her, there was more. Much more, and she couldn't let anything stop her. Not now, not when she was so close.

"Beer?" the captain called as he leaned out the side window.

"Sure." Lindsay nodded.

"Two dollar extra," the captain said.

"Of course."

"You come take the wheel, then." He pointed at Suzette. "I go below for the drinks."

"Me?" Suzette said, surprised.

"What? You no drive car?" he asked angrily.

"I can drive."

"Then you drive boat," he ordered her.

"Swabbing is next," Lindsay joked as he followed her inside. It was a cramped fit.

"Here." The fisherman relinquished the wheel. She stepped in front of the podium control panel. It was filled with an array of pressure and temperature gauges and a chrome gooseneck throttle handle stuck up from one side, with the shifter on the other. The old wheel vibrated under her hand.

"Where you want to sightsee?" the captain asked Lindsay.

Lindsay's eyes met Suzette's briefly. He looked at the captain. "Upriver. Hu Men."

"Hu Men? No, no. That's in China. We don't go to China."

"Last week you took a man there. We want you to take us to the same place."

"No go into China," the captain said without batting an eye. "You head out that way." He pointed Suzette toward the peninsula. "We go around to west side and see the fort. Good place for pictures." Then he turned toward the hatchway. "I get the beer."

"That went well."

Lindsay leaned on the podium. "He needs a little persuading."

Suzette maneuvered the *kaido* through a line of slow-moving sampans then brought the bow in line with the green hilly finger of the main peninsula.

Neither Lindsay nor Suzette heard the captain reenter

the pilothouse. Suzette caught his reflection in the dusty window and saw the long dark object jutting from his hands.

Instantly she spun the wheel starboard and shoved the engine throttle to full. The heavy wooden boat lurched and heeled drastically, sending the deck out from beneath the captain's feet. As he fell back against the wall, the shotgun fired, blasting a basketball-size hole through the roof.

Lindsay, too, had been taken by surprise. He fell against the control console but managed to keep his footing. He sidestepped Suzette and dove at the captain as he swung the shortened barrel around.

Lindsay parried the shotgun with his forearm and dropped his knee hard into the man's crotch. The captain shrieked in agony and the gun fell from his hands.

"Such a nasty toy for a fisherman," Lindsay said as he kicked away the cut-down Ithaca pump. Lindsay drew Truby's automatic and shoved it into the man's eye socket.

"Any last words?"

"I take you," the captain choked. "I take you where you want to go."

"How considerate." Lindsay yanked him to his feet.

Suzette had the boat back under control and was heading them out away from land.

"See?" Lindsay said over his shoulder. "I knew he'd come around."

"And I had my doubts." She rolled her eyes.

"Well?" Lindsay said to the Chinese.

"I take many people into China. Two, three times a week."

"To Hu Men?"

"Not many, but some."

"He was about this tall," Suzette said, holding her hand five and a half feet over the deck.

"And heavyset," Lindsay added.

The captain stared at them, his eyes darting from Suzette to Lindsay and up to the gun now pressed against his forehead.

"He smile a lot?" the captain asked.

"Yeah," Lindsay said. "Usually for no reason."

The captain nodded. "I took him past Hu Men to a small

outlet that comes in from the east. It flows around Dani Zhou. He pay me good but it was dangerous."

"We're not going to pay you anything until we get there. Understand?"

The captain nodded.

"What's on Dani Zhou?" Suzette asked.

"A village full of *taubouhs*," the captain said fearfully.

"Poachers?" she looked at Lindsay.

"It used to be opium they smuggled. Now rhino horns fetch thirty thousand Hong Kong dollars and if they're caught they barely get a slap on the wrist."

"Live animals, too," the captain said. "Worth more than the pieces."

"Did he say who he was meeting?" Suzette asked.

"No."

Lindsay slid the 9mm from the man's forehead to his temple. "You're sure?"

"Yes. He spoke of nothing during the trip."

"What happened after you dropped him off?"

"The gunboat came. I drifted into the reeds to escape."

"Where are your charts?

"Below."

"Show me."

The captain moved quickly.

"You've got the helm, skipper," Lindsay said as he disappeared belowdecks.

"Wonderful," she said sarcastically. Suzette slowed the *kaido* until it was making just enough headway to keep them pointed into the wind. Standing at the controls reminded her of when she was a little girl and of her grandfather kneeling beside her as she grasped the giant polished wheel of his yacht. She wondered if they had ever been in these waters off Macau. But those slivers of memory were too faint and too distant. What she really remembered was the man, the powerful man who used to tickle her into laughing fits and who could lift her off the ground with one arm.

"This shouldn't be too difficult." Lindsay's voice brought her back to the present. He unrolled a chart. The Chinese captain wasn't with him.

"Where's the old man?" she asked.

"I tied him up," he said. "We may still need him." He hung the chart on the back wall with the four pushpins he had seen sticking out of the wood. The large square chart of the Pearl River was colored in shades of gray and blue. The gray represented land, while the blue showed the flow of water, the different hues distinguishing the depths. The river was a maze of channels, tributaries, deltas, and shoals.

Lindsay didn't tell her, but there was a chance the captain would have to be persuaded further if they were going to reach Dani Zhou. The chart showed the marshy islet was surrounded by an infantry of sandbars. Lindsay knew it would be tricky to reach it without the captain's full cooperation.

Drawing on a thousand such streams, the Pearl River flowed from deep within China to the southern sea. But the main waterway was wide and the sounding showed it deep and clear. Lindsay gave Suzette a heading and she brought the *kaido*'s bow to the compass course leading toward the river's gaping mouth. The banks had changed many times over the eons, widening and narrowing, shifting to the north and then to the south. Long before there was stitched clothing, marriage, prepared foods, and other such inventions that defined Chinese civilization. Before there was an Emperor sitting on the Dragon Throne, and even before the land itself was called China, the waters poured from the great mountains to the sea.

By midday, the forest of dingy buildings and crowded townships were left behind and the Pearl began to collapse around them. They motored now along the restrictive banks of a river edged more by rice paddies and marshlands than by concrete and steel.

Suzette entered the pilothouse with a bowl of steaming broth and three small salted fish. "It's not the Palace," she said, handing Lindsay his lunch. "But we won't starve." She had pulled her shirt out of her pants and bound the tails in a knot over her stomach.

"How's our host?"

"Nervous but quiet. He keeps asking me what I'm doing with a man like you."

Lindsay laughed as he looked out over the bow. They were passing Wanqingsha, a low peninsula at the western edge of the delta.

Suzette stepped close to him. "How much further?"

"A couple of hours. When it's dark, we'll put our captain back at the helm."

"You think he'll take us to the same place?"

"As long as he thinks I'll kill him if he doesn't," Lindsay said, leaning into the wheel to hold their course. It freed his hands to eat the sardinelike fish that was caked white with salt crystals. It was dry and brittle like overdone jerky. Suzette had made fresh rice on the stern barbecue.

As they continued up along the coastline, Lindsay kept a sharp watch for the dark green gunboats of the Chinese border guards. Though the small junks and slow-moving fishing boats that came upriver from Hong Kong were blatantly breaking international law, Lindsay knew there were far too many for the patrols to check them all. Even the junks suspected of smuggling were left mostly undisturbed. It wasn't so much tolerance as indifference.

It was late afternoon when they passed the southern end of Dajiaotou Dao. Two miles farther and they slipped through Hu Men, the Tiger Gate that was once the main route from the world to Canton. Here, Lindsay found that the river traffic became noticeably heavy. Dozens of fishing boats were returning from the delta with their catches of grass carp and eel. Many of the larger ships were steaming back from Shanghai.

Off the starboard bow, the white multidecked ferry of the Pearl River Shipping Company passed on its voyage to Hong Kong. Its upper deck was filled with tourists, their cameras flashing to capture the last images of the river before the night.

Lindsay maneuvered around it, trying to keep himself in the shadows of the pilothouse and out of sight. They continued along the western bank, where clumps of houses with rusty tin roofs crowded the shore. Beyond them lay flat farmland, rich and green. Everywhere fragile piers reached out into the channel, giving the resident fishermen a place to land without burying their hull into the soft mud.

These were the deceptive waters, where the tide came in and went out quickly and the opaque river cleverly hid its hazards just inches below the surface. With dusk turning to night, the shoreline became less and less distinct. Lindsay decided it was time to reinstate the captain. The last thing they needed was to run aground.

"Here," he said to Suzette, who was watching the unattractive little houses drift by. "Take the wheel." He grabbed the shotgun and went below.

The captain was sitting quietly in his chair, his chin to his chest, his hands bound securely behind his back. As Lindsay entered, he looked up.

"You cut me loose?" he asked.

"On two conditions," Lindsay said, moving behind him. He set the gun down and began to untie his hands. "You take us to where you dropped that man and you don't try anything."

"No monkey business," he promised.

"Good." Lindsay released him. "Otherwise, you'll be floating downriver without your boat."

Rubbing his wrists, the captain nodded. "Where we at now?"

"From what I can make of your chart, we just passed the Tiger Gate."

"We head to the east inlet that skirts Dani Zhou."

"Whatever you say." Lindsay motioned toward the cabin stairs.

The captain hurried into the pilothouse and looked past Suzette's shoulder. "Good," he said happily. "You haven't missed it."

"Then she's all yours."

The captain took the wheel and adjusted their course.

Lindsay stepped outside to the starboard rail. The twilight had darkened enough that he wouldn't be seen from the beach and recognized as a foreigner. The weather was changing on them. A cold wind had picked up across the marsh and a fist of black clouds was peering over the horizon.

Suzette moved next to him. "It's going to rain," she said. She had put on her sweatshirt.

"How much, Suzy?" Lindsay asked casually.

She looked into his hazel-blue eyes. "My father used to call me that."

"Sorry . . ."

"No, it's nice to hear it again," she said, reaching for his hand.

"So how much did you offer him?"

Suzette bit her lower lip like a schoolgirl caught in a lie. "A thousand dollars."

"I hope that's Hong Kong dollars." Lindsay pulled her close, lifted her chin gently and kissed her.

"What happened to business first?"

"Did I say that?"

Suddenly the captain kicked the pilothouse wall to get their attention. Lindsay saw him waving through the window.

"We go here," the captain said as he swung the wheel to port and slowed the engine. The three of them were again crammed inside the tiny control room. "I have to keep in middle of channel or we will scrape bottom."

With an expert hand, he guided his craft up the slow-moving stream. They motored past a small pier that stretched from the shore. With the encroachment of night, a teak lantern illuminated by a flickering wax candle was hung from its end, a street sign on a dark and watery avenue.

A moment later, the captain swung the boat toward the bank and shut down the engine. Forward momentum nudged them into a thicket of shore weeds.

"This is where you brought him?" Suzette asked.

"Yes."

"You're sure?"

"Yes. There is a path that runs along the marsh to a village. He went into the third house near the water."

"I thought you stayed aboard," Lindsay said, his voice deepening.

The captain's face lost its pigment as he realized his slip.

"If this isn't the village," Suzette said pointedly, "I'm going to kill you myself."

"It is," the Chinese said, frightened. "I walk with him to the clearing. Then returned to my boat."

"Did soldiers scare you off or did you leave him?"

"The gunboat came, I swear."

"You're going to wait this time, aren't you?" Lindsay pressed.

"Yes," the captain promised. "I tie her off and wait for you." He scrambled to the front deck, grabbed the bow line, and jumped into the soft marsh grass below. He secured the line to a large piece of driftwood buried in the weeds.

Lindsay went downstairs and took out his dark blue sweater from the bottom of their daypack. Taking the shotgun, he ejected the remaining shells out the bottom and counted them. Three left. He replaced the cartridges, locked in the safety, and returned to the main deck.

"Ever use one of these?" Lindsay asked Suzette.

"No."

"Simple," he said, handing her the Ithaca. He showed her the safety button behind the trigger. "Release this and hold the gun against your hip. Spread your feet to brace yourself, square your shoulders, and pull the trigger. You'll kill anything in front of you."

"Do I need this?"

"I hope not," he said. Moving out onto the bow, he swung his leg over the rail, took the shotgun from her, and helped her climb over. The moist grass cushioned her fall but trapped her feet and sent her to her knees. After brushing herself off, she looked to Lindsay, but the railing was empty. A moment later, he reappeared.

"What happened to you?"

"I forgot something," he said. "Here." Lindsay handed her the shotgun and jumped ever so carefully to the ground. Although he tried to land with most of his weight on his left leg, the uneven ground sent a jolt of pain through his right knee.

"You okay?"

"Wonderful," Lindsay said in a gasp for air.

"I no leave," the captain promised.

"You won't this time," Lindsay agreed.

''That way to the village.'' The captain pointed to a narrow footpath that ran through the tall grass.

Taking Suzette's hand, Lindsay headed inland along the same track of mud Tommy Fong had crossed only a week before.

Chapter Twenty-Nine

Dani Zhou Islet, China

The evening breeze chilled Suzette as they crossed the marsh. The looming clouds thickened and eclipsed the moon, casting dull shadows over the uneven trail. Though her eyes had grown accustomed to the darkness, Lindsay was but a silhouette in front of her. The path widened where the unclaimed wetlands were replaced by the shallow waters of checkerboard rice fields. Fifty yards farther, a row of seven rickety houses lined the edge of the worked parcels.

As they crept silently along, Lindsay began to feel his metamorphosis. First in his chest as his breathing deepened and slowed. Then his body began to thirst for its natural rush of adrenaline. But Lindsay's subconscious knew the surge the chemical would give his muscles would also constrict his mind.

It held itself in check. Right now, Lindsay needed his finer senses. With long measured breaths, Lindsay held his state of calm. By the time they eased to the edge of the village, he could see and hear everything. His thoughts were clear and focused on his intent. An unwilling smile crossed his lips. The sensations ran through him with a euphoric vitality.

Beyond the houses, a dog barked. No, it was two dogs. Big, heavy-chested dogs. There were other animals, too. He could see odd pens and rows of sheds between the houses. Pulling Suzette with him, he dashed across a spread of dirt and made for a shadow near the first house. He brought his finger to his lips, signaling for silence. Then he listened. Nothing. He stepped to a single window and looked through a gap under the bamboo shade. The interior was dark and deserted.

Between the first and the second houses, and under thick canvas tarpaulins, they discovered aisles of wire cages. Suzette wrinkled her nose as the cages were packed with hundreds of lizards and snakes. "The cash crop," Lindsay whispered.

Finding the second house also empty, Lindsay and Suzette headed around back, only to be stopped by a high chain-link fence surrounding a fifty-foot pen. In the center was a large hollow log, probably driftwood from the river. A black shape lying next to it moved. Then something nearby hissed loudly and shifted to its feet.

Suzette saw it. "What is it?" she clutched his arm.

"Shhh," he warned as they watched the long ebony body lumber oddly toward a steel trough of water. In the drifting moonlight, Lindsay recognized the huge, ten-foot creature. "It's a Komodo dragon," he whispered, his eyes transfixed to the low-slung reptile as it moved defiantly across the ground. He had seen them on a *National Geographic* special and remembered the discomforting scenes of them devouring a large island deer. Another one hissed from within the enclosure.

"Ah, there's more of them," Suzette said with disgust.

Lindsay realized the blackness around the log was not a shadow but a group of the sleeping monsters. "A lot more," he confirmed, and his stomach turned as he thought of Tommy and how he had been found. His friend had made it to Dani Zhou, all right. Right to here.

"Come on," Lindsay said. They moved away from the dragon pen and toward the third dwelling. Unlike the rest of the tiny hamlet, the steel corrugate-sided house was alive with lights and music. From the open windows, men's laughter floated on the night air along with the aroma of fish and vegetables cooking in sweet sesame oil.

Lindsay and Suzette knelt behind a two-wheeled wagon that was near the rear door. He handed her the shotgun. "Wait here," he whispered.

"Let me go."

"Wait until I get a closer look." He slipped his automatic from beneath his sweatshirt and dashed to the house.

The wind rustled the bushes behind her and she turned quickly and stared into the unyielding darkness. The changing moonlight played games with her, sending ghosts and demons from shrub to shrub. She ran her index finger along the trigger of the shotgun and released the safety.

Lindsay made his way to the angular porch. He moved to the window and peered in. The house was filled to capacity, as if the entire village had been crammed into the main room. A long low table in the center of the room was covered with dishes of steamed bamboo shoots, spicy eggplant, steamed rock cod and haddock and rice. The delicacies were being served in banquet proportions. The men were all dressed in fresh cotton shirts and the women wore their best silk coats and finest jewelry.

An elderly broad-faced man seated at the head of the table was the focus of conversation and was clearly the guest of honor. His sixtieth birthday, Lindsay guessed. It was a milestone the Chinese held in high regard and always required a large celebration of family and friends.

Amongs the dishes and teacups, Lindsay was pleased to see a large amount of contraband Japanese beer in tall bottles. He moved away to wait in the shadows.

A seventeen-year-old boy grinned from ear to ear. He couldn't remember a party like this during which he had eaten so well and drank so much. The music rang in his ears. He hated to leave, even for a moment, but he felt the growing need to relieve his bladder. He had consumed more beer than he ever had and now his body was telling him it was time to leave the table and go outside. Standing, he bowed respectfully, if unsteadily, to the head of the table and then sidestepped his way out the door.

At the edge of the yard, he found a familiar bush and

untied the front of his baggy blue pants. With a deep belch, he began.

From out of nowhere, someone cupped a hand over his mouth and yanked him backward. His pants fell around his ankles, causing both of them to tumble to the ground.

The young man rolled to his hands and knees and found a gun barrel in his face.

"Scream and you'll never hear it."

"Don't hurt me."

"Don't give me a reason."

"No . . ."

"Get up."

The young man did.

"Tie your pants," Lindsay told him.

He did. "I have nothing to give you."

"Shut up." Lindsay glanced at the house, making sure no one else was coming. "Who lives there?"

"Tang Shiu," the young man said quickly.

"It's his party?"

"Yes."

"Good," Lindsay said. "We're going to crash it."

When the foreigner with the gun stepped into the crowded room, the laughter and conversation ended. All eyes went to Lindsay as he held the teenager in front of him.

"Dui-bu-qi," Lindsay said, apologizing for his intrusion.

No one moved. They stared at him, the women frightened, the men surprised and startled. That would soon abate, Lindsay knew, and anger would follow.

"What do you want, *gweilo?*" the broad-faced man at the head of the table asked.

"Mr. Tang?"

"I am Tang Shiu," he said as he began to stand.

"Don't," Lindsay warned.

Tang stopped. "If you've come to rob us, you have picked the poorest village on the river," he said.

"I'm not interested in lizards or bear bladders. I've come about Tommy Fong."

Tang's face never changed, it remained stone cold. "Who?"

On the opposite side of the table, Lindsay didn't notice the middle-aged man with the weathered face reach under his coat.

"Tommy Fong was here for a reason," Lindsay said pointedly. "And I know you know what it was."

"You have made a mistake," Tang said. "There are many villages and a lot of old houses like this. You have chosen the wrong one."

From the porch, the shotgun blast rocked the entire room and sent everyone scrambling for cover. The buckshot ripped a tattered hole in the wall directly over the head of the middle-aged man. Lindsay dropped to a knee, double-gripped the 9mm, and aimed at the door.

Suzette marched in with the shotgun leveled on the terrified man. "Take it out slowly," she commanded.

Wide-eyed, the man looked at the fierce Chinese woman standing before him and drew an old revolver from beneath his coat. He set it on the table.

Lindsay stood up. She was a never-ending surprise. This one had taken a year off his life. Turning to Tang, he cleared his throat. "You were saying, Mr. Tang?"

The honored guest regained his composure. "No one has come here," he said.

"You're lying," Suzette said. She swung the Ithaca toward Tang and pumped a fresh cartridge into its chamber.

Of all the sounds in the world, Lindsay thought, the racking of a shotgun was the most international. It was unmistakable. Everyone inched away from Tang's end of the table.

"You're the nephew of Ming Zi. Tommy needed to know what happened to him," Suzette stated.

"Ming Zi?" Tang cracked smile. "That wretch is dead. He died when I was a boy."

Suzette took a step closer and pressed the serious end of the Ithaca against Tang's right ear. The Chinese lost his smile.

Lindsay cleared his throat. "Let me give you some advice, Mr. Tang," he said in a monotone. "Don't make the mistake of underestimating the lady."

He looked from Lindsay to Suzette. "No one has come to me about my uncle."

Lindsay saw Suzette's eyes narrow. He was suddenly worried she was going to kill Tang. He gently pushed the barrel of the shotgun aside. "The pen with the dragons? Any accidents lately?"

"Last week. There was . . ." Tang began, then his eyes locked onto Lindsay's. "There was a man who was trying to hide from the patrol. We didn't get to him in time."

Suzette cringed.

"What happened to the body?"

"The soldiers took it," the teenager said. "They wrapped it in canvas and took it with them."

Suzette found her stomach again. "What about Ming Zi?"

Tang shrugged. "He was a worthless man. Nothing but a poor craftsman who lived on the charity of monks."

"What monks?" she asked.

The man looked at her as if not understanding the question.

"I said, what monks?"

"At the temple in Sha Tin. The temple of the Buddhas."

Suzette's reaction caught Lindsay by surprise. She laughed. "Thank you," she said, and turned to Lindsay. "Let's go."

"That's it?"

"You found out what you wanted. So have I," she said, backing out of the room. Once Suzette was outside, Lindsay turned to Tang. "Again, my apologies. Please continue." With that, he stepped through the door and into the night. Suzette was waiting for him near the corner of the building.

"Never used a shotgun before," he quipped. "You've got a lot of explaining to do," he said, stepping past her.

"Can we get out of China first?"

"No. Researcher, my ass. You know too much and you're pushing too hard."

"We have to find the deed."

"This wild-goose chase is exactly what killed Tommy," Lindsay snapped.

"I guess there must be something to it, then."

He stared into her beautiful nutmeg eyes and sighed. "Let's get out of here," he said.

As they hurried toward the river, the sky decided it was

time to release the rain it had been hoarding. It pelted them with large drops. Lindsay let Suzette lead as he stayed a few yards back listening for Tang and the villagers. He couldn't understand it. No one was following them. They continued into the marsh and through the thickening rain-soaked mud.

"Shit," Suzette said. "He's gone."

"He can't be," Lindsay said. But the only thing waiting for them in the deep pool was the slow-moving river.

"Why'd you trust him?"

"I didn't," Lindsay said, reaching into his pocket. He revealed a handful of rubber-coated wires. "I disconnected the distributor. He couldn't have gone on his own." As soon as the words left his mouth, a chill of realization raced up Lindsay's back.

"Come on," he yanked her toward the path. They barely took three steps when the men in black fatigues appeared like phantoms from the tall grass. The first man dove at Lindsay, trying to tackle him. He missed the American's legs. Lindsay struck him hard across the back of the neck with the edge of his hand.

Suzette screamed, but as Lindsay moved to her, another assailant grabbed him. The man slid his arm around Lindsay's neck and locked him into an unbreakable choke hold. Instinctively, Lindsay grabbed the man's groin and squeezed as hard as he could. Tender flesh tore through the man's pants. He screamed and released his grip. Lindsay spun around, catching him in the temple with his elbow. The man crumbled to the mud.

Two more men rushed Lindsay, hitting him together, their moves precise. One managed to pin Lindsay's legs as they fell into the reeds. The other landed heavy on Lindsay's chest knocking the wind from his lungs. The big man dug his fingers into Lindsay's eyes. "Not so tough now, *gweilo,*" said the familiar voice of the Buddha-sized man, Zigao. Lindsay whipped his head back and forth, allowing Zigao no more than shallow scratches across his face.

What was happening in front of Suzette in the grays of rain and night was unreal. By the time she reacted, hands were grabbing her. Her attacker came from behind, trying to slip his arm around her neck. But when the man's forearm landed across her mouth instead of her throat, Suzette bit into his flesh through to the bone. He cried out as he pulled free.

A second man rushed headlong at her. Lifting the shotgun with one hand, she managed to level it with his chest. Her finger found the trigger. The blast tore out his stomach and left lung and sent him backward into the marsh. Using the gun's steel barrel, she clubbed the man with the bleeding arm across the forehead.

Suddenly, a thunderous roar rumbled above. The ground shivered and a blanket of wind swept across the wetlands. Light exploded around them, illuminating the flattened grass.

In the powerful searchlight of the helicopter, Suzette saw Lindsay wrestling with two men. One of them stood up and drew an ugly black pistol from his hip. Suzette swung the shotgun around and fired its last cartridge. It took off the man's arm at his shoulder and sent him screaming into the night.

"Run," Lindsay yelled as he tried to get away from the Buddha. Zigao grabbed Lindsay by the throat and pressed his weight onto his windpipe.

Amid the roar of the helicopter and the screaming of the men, Suzette did what Lindsay said. She ran. She ran as fast as she could without caring where she was going. She had to get away, away from it all. With the rain blurring her vision, she bolted through the marsh and into the rice field.

Lindsay grabbed the big man by the belt and pulled him higher on his chest, then kicked his feet up and hooked them over Zigao's shoulders. Arching, Lindsay pulled the man backward and off him. As large as he was, the Chinese Triad moved with the agility of a cat. He was quickly on his feet with a dagger appearing in his hand.

In the whirling wind of the helicopter, the rain sprayed into their faces as if under the pressure of a fire hose. Lindsay tried to use the onslaught of water to his advantage by keeping it coming from over his shoulder and into Zigao's direction.

Buddha stabbed at Lindsay, tearing open his sweatshirt.

He thrust forward—Lindsay ducked. He lunged—Lindsay blocked it with his forearm; the knife drew blood.

Truby's words came from the recesses of his mind. *It is not the blade that will kill you, Linds, it's the man.*

Zigao dove at him, the dagger extended. Lindsay slid to the left, ignored the weapon, and attacked his assassin. A knee to the ribs and an elbow to the jaw sent Zigao staggering. But he was only stunned. Lindsay sidestepped behind him, grabbed the Chinese by his chin and his oily hair, and with all his strength snapped the Triad's neck. Zigao collapsed to the ground, his body shaking in uncontrollable spasms.

Lindsay saw Suzette running. He started after her, but the earth exploded at his feet. Triple-tap bursts from a .50-caliber machine gun mounted outside the helicopter ripped fist-sized chunks out of the mud. He dove into the high grass, drew Truby's 9mm, and fired into the belly of the chopper. It lifted away, pivoted on its nose, and headed after the fleeing girl. Lindsay continued to fire until the huge steel bird was out of range.

Lindsay raced after it as fast as he could. But the syrupy mud clung to his feet as if it were thickening cement. "No," he screamed as he watched the helicopter swoop down. He brought the 9mm to bear, but the pilot landed on the opposite side of Suzette. He couldn't risk the shot. He watched helplessly as Danny pulled her inside.

Then the chopper rose from the rice field, banked right and came at him. The cyclops eye of its searchlight blinded Lindsay with sudden daylight. The machine gun barked again as the gunner leaned out of the doorway and lined up his target.

Lindsay fought his instincts to fire back and dove into the shallow water. Burrowing his hand into the thick mud, he held himself to the bottom, listening for the undulating helicopter blades and the popping of the heavy gun. Any moment it would spit hot lead into him and tear open his back. For as long as he could, he waited for the onslaught. Finally he had to breathe.

The night was quiet. Unearthly quiet, as though every living thing within a hundred miles had been squelched out of existence. Even the rain had stopped.

Finally a frog croaked a few feet away. And then another and another in their attempts to find a mate. In the village, the dogs began to bark again. Lindsay sat up and looked across the empty sky. The helicopter was gone.

Defeat hit him hard in the form of pain. It was strange, but as he walked back to the river where the men had attacked them, he was thankful for it. Thankful because at least the pain drew him from his fear for Suzette and his anger at himself.

Lindsay rolled the Buddha over. He rifled through the pockets of the dead man's vest, hoping to find something, anything that would lead him to the Triads.

From the riverbank, Lindsay heard the water lap softly against something. He looked up to see the dark outline of a boat gliding silently toward shore. As his mind recognized the distinct military silhouette, the forward floodlight clicked on.

"Oh, wonderful," Lindsay said, looking away from the light.

"Drop weapons and put hands up," a voice ordered in broken English over a crackling loudspeaker.

Lindsay set his automatic on the dead man's chest and placed his hands on his head. From behind the light, Lindsay heard someone approach.

"You are a very skillful man," the stranger said as he stepped over the bodies. The Chinese soldier held an old Soviet- made automatic in his hand and wore the red shoulder badges of a captain.

"There's been a mistake. My tour guide must have given me bad directions."

The Captain laughed. "I like Americans. You're so witty when you're about to die."

"If you wanted me dead, Captain, you would've kept your boots clean and shot me from the boat."

"True, Mr. Chase. He wants you alive," Captain Huang said as he stepped around behind Lindsay.

Surprised, Lindsay looked up at the Captain, but all he saw was the butt of the Soviet pistol as it came across the side of his head.

Chapter Thirty

Lantau Island, 1943

The makeshift lean-to thundered like a warrior's drum from the onslaught of the torrential rain. The weather had not lessened in six days and had turned the forested island into a mountain swamp. The soil runoff was so heavy that Lantau seemed to be bleeding into the sea.

From under the broad palm frond, Sergeant McEwan scanned Victoria Harbor with his binoculars. From his vantage point, he could see far into the shipping lane. There was no movement. The docks were empty and the channel between the peninsula and Hong Kong Island was filled with only whitecapped waves.

At least the storm was delivering the same difficulties to the Japs as it was to his jungleers, his contingent of soldiers specially trained for jungle warfare. They had been dropped on Lantau two months ago by submarine with simple orders: Report on all shipping and military movement from the Crown colony. The Japs had occupied Hong Kong for two years now and it was time to disrupt their overly efficient post.

Within a few weeks' time, McEwan's operation was already

chipping away at the enemy. The American submarines patrolling the coast used the jungleers' communiques to attack several Jap freighters sailing from the port and had sent forty thousand tons to the ocean bottom.

The Sergeant had little doubt that his enemy would soon figure out they were there. But for now, as the storm raged across the islands of southern China, the war in their region was on hold. The only ship to dare the seas was an old ferry that had gone out the day before. It was filled with another shipment of Chinese refugees bound for Macau. The Japanese were having trouble feeding the local population and they were solving the problem by systematically deporting them.

"Sergeant?" Private Clifford Leeland moved up beside McEwan. He raised his voice over the rain. "Kendall is worse, sir. The wound is going to fester if we don't get him out of the weather."

McEwan pulled his gold watch from his uniform pocket. He popped open the case and wiped the dirt from its crystal with his thumb. Noon. He'd give Harrington another hour before entering the temple and simply taking the shelter they needed.

The British Sergeant had no affection for the Chinese, nor did he care if the monks welcomed them or not. If the bloody priests hadn't noticed, they were in a war zone and a Japanese booby trap had wounded one of his men. He needed shelter. Dry shelter. But McEwan had told Harrington he would wait to see if he could convince the monks to take them in.

"We'll move out at 1300," McEwan said as he wiped the rain from his face.

"Yes, sir." Leeland tucked low and ran back to the lean-to.

Nathan Harrington totally mystified McEwan. Why the man stayed to help the military was beyond him. When most of the British citizenship were escaping the colony by any means possible, he volunteered as a guide for the Royal Army. And the man was no newborn, McEwan mused; he had to be near fifty. But with his knowledge of the region and his fluency in the local dialects, Nathan proved to be indispensable. Whether he liked him or not, McEwan had to admit that.

McEwan wiped his field glasses and slipped them into their leather case. As he returned to the lean-to, he saw movement on the steep hillside below. Two dark figures moved quickly from one tree to the next as they ascended the slope. McEwan eased himself into the thick bush and slipped his short carbine from his back. He stared into the rain-soaked forest. He saw nothing for a moment; then from behind a thicket of bamboo, not fifty yards away, a man stepped forward. He walked several more paces, stopped, and looked ahead.

McEwan pressed himself farther into his background, hoping to dissolve into the leaves. He couldn't make out the man's face, nor any details of his uniform, but he could see some type of long rifle in his hands.

Hesitantly, the man took a few more steps. He looked in McEwan's direction but apparently could not see him. Closer now, the Sergeant could make out his round face and slanted eyes.

McEwan brought the carbine slowly to his shoulder. He snaked his finger over the trigger and carefully brought the sights in line with the man's chest. As the soldier was about to kill his enemy, someone stepped up behind him.

"I knew you'd shoot at the first thing that moved," Nathan said.

McEwan jumped. "You?"

"Expecting the Queen?"

"You bloody idiot!" McEwan grabbed Nathan by his jacket lapel. Both men were about the same size, just over six feet. And although Nathan was twenty years older, he had an easy thirty pounds on the soldier. A solid thirty pounds.

"Save it, Sergeant," Nathan said through his matted blond beard. He pushed him away and waved down the hill. The Chinese monk, wearing a long mud-stained silk robe and carrying a walking stick, ran to them.

"This is Woo Sang. He's from the monastery."

The monk bowed low to McEwan, then spoke in a seemingly endless run of Chinese.

"He says he's sorry for not being able to climb the peak as quickly as when he was younger," Nathan translated for McEwan. "Should I tell him you were going to put a bullet through him?"

"How the hell was I to know he was with you? Jap or Chinaman, the bastards look the same."

Nathan glared at McEwan. For an instant, he would have liked to slip his bayonet into the Sergeant's ribs and be done with him. But it was useless. The army would just send another one like him to take his place. "He'll lead us down the back of the peak," Nathan said. "There's an old trail there and he's sure it hasn't been trapped."

"Can we trust him?" McEwan asked.

"Can he trust us?"

"What the hell is that supposed to mean?"

"They're letting us stay until the storm passes. Then we have to leave. That's the bargain."

McEwan wiped his mouth with the back of his hand. "What if Kendall isn't any better?"

"That's our problem. If the Japanese discover they've helped us, they'll slaughter everyone in the monastery and burn it to the ground."

Reluctantly, McEwan agreed. "Okay, you've got my word."

"Don't think I won't hold you to it, Sergeant."

The lean-to Nathan had built the day before was wedged between two thick-trunked palm trees. Covered with broad fronds, it was almost invisible from a distance of ten paces.

"Clifford!"

The private pushed the leaves from the entrance and made room for them. "Glad to see you, Mr. Harrington," Leeland said with a smile. Knowing Nathan had grown up in the colony gave the young soldier an unqualified sense of comfort.

"How's he holding up?" Nathan asked.

"Not so good, sir."

Nathan pulled back the canvas blanket and looked at Kendall's legs. The gash in the left leg had stopped bleeding. Leeland's stitches were uneven and clumsy, but they were working. The right leg, however, was another matter. The sharp wooden spikes at the bottom of the pit in which Kendall had fallen had practically torn his calf muscle from the bone. And now, as Nathan looked at the gangrenous wound, he suspected the spikes had been coated with some kind of poison.

Woo Sang looked over Nathan's shoulder and whispered to him. Nathan nodded.

"What did he say?" McEwan asked harshly.

"He doesn't think he's going to make it."

"I'm not going to leave him."

"No," Nathan said. "Neither would I."

Disassembling the lean-to and using two heavy sticks cut from nearby trees, they managed a makeshift stretcher. Leeland covered Kendall completely with the canvas blanket to protect his face from the heavy rain.

"Watch our flank," McEwan ordered Leeland as he slung his carbine over his shoulder and grabbed the end of the stretcher. Nathan took the front and the two men lifted their wounded together. Nathan spoke to the monk in Cantonese and the man took the lead.

The trail on which the Chinese led them was longer than Nathan had hoped and much steeper. They had to duck under and push through low branches and traverse twisting roots that grabbed at their boots. And the rain worsened, hitting them as if it were buckshot.

Sheets of water ran off Nathan's wide Gurkha hat and into his face, making it difficult to follow the monk. His shoulders ached from the weight of the soaked stretcher and the dying man. They walked for over two hours before the narrow trail eased into a wider one. A little farther, the ground leveled and the forest gave way to a flat meadow.

Finally Nathan saw the glow of candles within the dark silhouette of the multilevel temple. It stood a sentinel against a black sky. Off to the side of the sacred compound were two smaller temples and a line of stone buildings that made up the monastery's living quarters.

"This way, this way," Woo Sang said as he directed Nathan and McEwan to one of the sleeping rooms. Carrying Kendall onto a covered walkway, the two men stepped out of the rain for the first time in almost a week. They entered the first open door. It was a tiny room with one entrance and a narrow window in the opposite wall. As Woo Sang lit a tin lantern, they set the stretcher next to a single bed and gently lifted the unconscious man onto dry woolen blankets.

A moment later, Leeland entered. "I made a quick run of the grounds, sir. All seems in order."

"Good," McEwan said. He stepped outside and pointed to one of the secondary temples at the edge of the compound. "Take up a position there, Private. I'll relieve you in an hour."

"Yes, sir," Leeland said, and hustled out.

Nathan knelt beside Woo Sang as the monk unbuckled Kendall's belt and holster and lay it at the foot of the bed. He cut away the soldier's trousers with a knife. "If this were a hospital, I would take this leg away," the monk said. "It is going to kill the body."

"That's up to the Sergeant," Nathan said, but he knew McEwan would never let the monks operate on Kendall.

"I would not want my life depending on such a man. He thinks we are uncivilized and butchers like the Japanese. He doesn't understand us like you do, Lingsyou," Woo Sang said.

"He is a soldier. He knows nothing but orders and war."

Another monk entered the room carrying a clean robe for Woo Sang. This monk, too, was elderly and looked upon the wounds with concerned eyes. He and Woo Sang consulted briefly and agreed on a treatment. Oddly, the second monk used the Mandarin tongue to call for boiling water.

A third man appeared just outside the doorway. Dressed in shoddy rags, he was not a monk but a helper. Nathan caught only a fleeting glimpse of him before he hurried to fetch the water.

There was something about him, something unsettling that swept over the onetime pirate. Nathan moved to the door and listened to the sound of the helper retreating down the wooden floor of the monastery. The clumsy gait rang in Nathan's ear as he recognized the awkward steps of a clubfooted man.

"Tell the Sergeant," Woo Sang was saying, "the leg will kill his man."

"Yes." Nathan had to bring himself back. "I'll tell him."

McEwan had crouched against the far wall, where he could watch both the door and the monks. At the other monk's suggestion, he had removed his wet jacket and shirt and was wrapped in one of their blankets. Still, he held the carbine across his lap.

"They want to amputate the leg," Nathan said in a low voice as he bent down beside him. Nathan, too, watched the door. He casually moved his revolver from its holster to his coat pocket.

He expected McEwan to react in outrage, but instead the Sergeant simply shook his head. "Let him go with honor."

"What honor?"

"If he can't recover fully, Harrington, then he can't recover. We've got four more months on this bloody island," McEwan said, glancing at the bed. "At least he won't die in that godforsaken jungle."

At that moment, Nathan understood McEwan a little better. To the Sergeant, dying was okay, as long as it was with some thread of dignity.

The man with the clubfoot shuffled into the room carrying the steaming pot of water. His hair was thin and gray and the deep scars that crossed his left cheek and ended at the nub of an ear had softened with age, but they were the scars of only one man. A clubfooted man who spoke Mandarin.

As Nathan stared at him, anger and rage surged from deep within. There was no doubt. This was the man who had lifted him off the ground in an alley in a Hong Kong *wan* and pressed a gun barrel to his head that was still warm from killing his sister. The man he had to set free to save Yak-san Kung. For years Nathan had searched for the murderer of his family. Now fate brought them together again in another house of God.

The clubfooted man set the steaming pot beside Woo Sang, stood back, and watched as the second monk dipped a stiff-haired brush into the water and scrubbed the infectious wound.

"What has been decided, Harrington?" Woo Sang asked. Perhaps he recognized the name, or maybe it was the hatred in Nathan's glare that caused the clubfooted man to slowly look across the room and into Nathan's eyes.

Realization was immediate. His face went white with horror. He dove for Kendall's gun, but he had no chance to draw it. Nathan fired twice from inside his coat. The first bullet shattered the man's forearm, causing him to drop the holster to the bed. The second entered the upper thigh of his left leg. He fell backward against the stone wall, clutching his arm.

Nathan drew his gun from his pocket. McEwan was suddenly beside him, his carbine aimed at the two monks, who had scrambled to the opposite side of the room.

"What the hell?" McEwan's nerves were taut, his voice high.

Nathan grabbed the scarred man by the shirt and lifted him to his feet. The man cried out in pain.

"Sergeant?" Leeland called from the darkness outside.

"It's all right, Private."

Leeland, his carbine ready, stepped quickly into the room. Following McEwan's lead, he aimed his rifle at the monks.

"Cover them," McEwan ordered. He moved to Nathan. "Is he a Jap?"

Nathan's face was only inches from the scarred man's, his jaw forward, his teeth clenched. "No," Nathan said in a voice that sent a chill through McEwan. "This is personal." Then he spoke in Mandarin. "You remember."

Sweat beaded on the man's forehead. "It was another life."

"Yes," Nathan agreed. "And I gave you an extra one once."

"I have already paid for my sins, Harrington. Now I serve the monks."

Nathan pushed his revolver into the fleshy skin under the man's chin. He felt McEwan tugging at his arm and heard him yelling something, but he could see only one thing: the image of his sister's limp body on the ground in the darkened alley. "You killed my family."

"It was the other, not me. I was only there to recover the deed. That was all."

"You lie." Nathan pressed the gun hard into the man's

throat. "You killed all of them." He cocked the gun's hammer with his thumb.

"The deed, Harrington," the man pleaded. "The deed to Hong Kong. It's here. In the territories." He reached into his shirt and yanked something from around his neck. "The craftsman Ming Zi has hidden it in Sha Tin." The Manchurian opened his clenched fist, revealing a small green jade pendant inset with a flat of gold. "This will lead you to it, Harrington," he said.

Nathan uncocked the hammer and lowered his gun. He took the pendant and let go of the man's coat. The elite Bannerman of the Guard slid slowly to the temple floor. With tears rising in his eyes, he was a tragic picture of the once-mighty Manchu Empire.

Leeland continued to cover the monks with his carbine as the Sergeant checked Kendall's pulse. "He's dead," McEwan announced. He pointed to the clubfooted man. "Mind explaining what the hell this is about?"

Without a word, Nathan snatched McEwan's carbine from his hands. He aimed the weapon from his hip and fired. The .30-caliber round thundered through the temple as the bullet exploded into the cripple's skull. Blood and bone splattered across the room as Nathan continued to fire again and again. The body slouched lifeless, jumping as the rounds were emptied into it.

Then, with a deep sigh, Nathan handed the gun back to McEwan.

"He was a gentle man," the monk said from a daze.

"He was an assassin."

"And what are you, Nathan Harrington, now that you have taken a life on sacred ground?"

Nathan looked at the corpse. "I'm what he made me," he said. He moved to Kendall and lifted the soldier's body in his arms and walked out the door.

McEwan glanced at the ravaged body as blood puddled beneath it. "Let's go, Private," the Sergeant said as he followed Nathan out into the storm.

Chapter Thirty-One

Stonecutters Island

Lindsay woke slowly and found his body stiff and sore. He waited for the pounding in the back of his brain to stop. It didn't. He replayed the night before: the men from the shadows, the contorted face of the Buddha, the sounds of gunfire, the smells of pungent mud, the wet, sticky marsh. It all increased his headache. The only clear detail was the sight of Suzette disappearing into the helicopter.

With a concerted effort, Lindsay peered from his darkness one eye at a time. Above him was a low pure-white ceiling inlaid with sculpted planks of rich Honduran mahogany. This wasn't the prison cell he had expected. He rose to his elbows and found himself in the center of a large bed in a spacious cabin. From the polished wood walls, fine rosewood furnishings, and heavy brass fixtures, Lindsay knew this wasn't the patrol boat, either. This ship was large and expensive. He was immediately grateful the swaying wasn't in his head.

Moving from under the cotton sheets that covered his naked body, Lindsay felt an unusual tingle in his knee. He reached down to touch it and was stabbed by a needle.

Flipping back the covers, he discovered a half dozen fine steel pins protruding from the white gauze wrapped tightly around his knee.

"Don't touch," the Chinese man coming through the doorway said. He was a fragile-looking man and he shuffled to the bed without lifting his feet off the carpet. From behind old-time pince-nez glasses, the acupuncturist inspected his work. He wiggled one of the needles and Lindsay felt a prick of pain.

"Hey!"

"Shhh." The man lifted his hand as he proceeded to manipulate another needle. Then, slowly and in a precise order, he withdrew them one at a time.

"This is supposed to help?" Lindsay asked cringing.

"It'll be stiff for a few hours, but after, no more pain."

"Ever?"

"I'm not a magician," the doctor said as he wiped the tiny droplets of blood that were spreading over the gauze. "You treat it poorly, it will hurt."

"Like walking on it?"

"So cynical, the Western mind," he commented as he pushed Lindsay back into the pillows. "Your head hurts?"

"No, it's fine."

"Quiet." he pressed his bony thumbs onto Lindsay's forehead and rubbed Lindsay's temples with strong, determined fingers. Immediately, the headache subsided. Seeing the relief in his face, the Chinese sat back. "You are as strong as a horse, *gweilo,*" he said, patting him hard on his naked chest. "And as lucky as a cat." Finished, he headed for the cabin door.

"Mind telling me where I am?"

The doctor waved as he shuffled out the door. Before it closed, another man entered. He, too, was Chinese, but dressed flawlessly in the traditional morning coat and striped trousers of a British butler. "Good morning, sir. I trust you slept well. I am Po, the chief steward," he said, opening the curtains to the bright morning. "Your host has asked if you'd join him for breakfast on the fantail. I hope that's agreeable?"

"That depends on who he is."

"You won't be disappointed, Mr. Chase."

Lindsay knew he would get nothing out of this man. "Do I have time to clean up?"

"Breakfast won't be for another thirty minutes. Your things have been retrieved from the hotel. They've been cleaned and put into the drawers for your convenience."

"Everything?"

"Of course. But if you'd prefer more appropriate attire . . ." He opened the wall closet revealing a full rack of coats and slacks from Alfred Dunhill and suits from Gieves & Hawkes. "I hope you don't mind, I guessed you a forty-four regular."

"Good guess." Lindsay swung his legs over the edge of the bed.

"Thank you, sir. The shower and bath are through there. If there's anything you need, ring number seven on the phone and it'll be brought to you."

"One more thing, Po?"

"Yes, sir?"

"Where the hell am I?"

"You are aboard the *Lona*, Mr. Chase."

"A captive?

The Chinese steward smiled. "Not at all. There is a runabout off the port side. It's at your disposal if you wish to leave."

"I wouldn't dream of being so rude."

"Very good, sir. Would you like me to collect you at the proper time?"

"No, I'll find my way."

Po bowed and closed the door silently behind him.

After a shave and a hot shower, Lindsay chose white linen slacks, a Navy blazer, and a striped tie. Very British and very maritime. He felt in place as he stepped onto the deck of the yacht and into the bright sun. The rain from the night before had either dissipated or been limited to the Pearl River delta. The air was fresh and clean and the sky blue for as far as he could see. He recognized their anchorage as the calm bay of Stonecutters Island. The channel that separated the island with the western edge of Kowloon seemed forever narrowing as Hong Kong visionaries and construction companies continued their nonstop reclamation of Victoria Harbor.

Looking from bow to stern, Lindsay saw that he wasn't aboard a true yacht but a refurbished research ship. A hundred and seventy feet of British design retrofitted to a life of luxury. Painted in a high-gloss black and gray trim, her high bridge and a long low stern created a beautiful vessel with the advantage of seaworthiness.

Walking along the long chrome rail, Lindsay noticed a red banner flying from one of three radar masts. He couldn't quite place its odd black insignia. At the port accommodation ladder, he saw the sleek runabout exactly where Po said it would be. A crewman in a crisp white uniform with gold stripes on his shoulder stood at the top of the ladder as if waiting for inspection.

"Good morning, sir."

"Morning," Lindsay said as he leaned over the rail. "Has she got gas?"

"The petrol tanks are full, sir," he said. "Would you like to take her out?"

"Maybe later," Lindsay said, continuing along the main deck. Amidships, a large flat expansion of steel grading stood over the deck and stretched aft for twenty feet. Lashed to it was a shinny black Bell Jet Ranger helicopter.

"Mr. Chase . . ." Po appeared. "Breakfast is served."

"After you." Lindsay gestured.

Descending two flights of stairs, they followed the sweeping turn of the deck to the spacious fantail that once held an assemblage of sea-bottom dredges, nets, Nansen bottles, and other types of equipment. That was all gone now. Mahogany tables and chairs and a wet bar had taken their places atop a bleached Burmese teak deck. The ship was fulfilling a new objective. Pleasure and comfort.

An upper deck stretched halfway over the stern, lending shade to a circular table that was set with fine china and silver. Lindsay could smell the aroma of Chinese delicacies from the ship's galley hidden somewhere below.

Po stopped in the center of the fantail. "Mr. Chase, sir," he announced.

Leaning heavily on the rail, a tall but frail man stood watching the life of the harbor. The breeze disheveled his fine white hair and rustled the edge of his red silk robe. The emblem on the robe was the same as on the banner and Lindsay tried to remember where he had seen it before. A short green oxygen tank in a wheeled dolly stood next to him and from its silver valve a clear hose snaked under his robe.

"Hong Kong is a wonder, Mr. Chase," the man said in a gravelly voice. "Here, East truly meets West and they collide like freight trains running at full steam on an open stretch of track."

Holding the rail for balance, he turned to his guest. He was old, ancient. His translucent skin was tight over his skeleton face. The oxygen hose reappeared over his ears, draped across his cheek, and ran under his nose. Sunken deep into his skull were dark green eyes that were surprisingly sharp and bright. They dissected Lindsay. "It shouldn't work, but it does." Po moved to his employer's side as he took unsure steps to the table.

Lindsay suddenly remembered where he had seen the odd insignia on the banner and on the old man's robe. It was the icon of a huge telecommunications company that dominated the western Pacific region with satellite and cellular technologies.

"Sorry, economics has never kept my interest," Lindsay stated.

"But you'd be amazed how much your forte has in common with the business world. Corporate men are more warriors than anyone understands." Once settled, Po offered him a napkin on a silver tray. Then the attentive steward circled the table and offered a chair to Lindsay. "You were busy last night," the old man said.

"And there are a few loose ends I need to tie up. So if you'll excuse me . . ."

"Sit down, Mr. Chase."

Lindsay stood firm.

"Please sit down," the skeleton said. "The girl is safe. At least for now."

"You know where she is?"

"I know who has her and I know what he wants."

Lindsay sat, took the napkin from Po, and nodded to an offer of coffee.

"How is your knee?" the man asked. "I was told they used a teflon bullet. Nasty bit of work. Forced you from the Rogue, didn't it?"

"Is this about the time I should be impressed?"

"Not really," the man said. "I want you to realize I'm neither an eccentric nor a senile old man." He waved at Po.

The steward knew what his employer wanted. He offered Lindsay a covered tray, removed the silver dome, and revealed Truby's 9mm automatic.

"And the other, Po." The steward retrieved Lindsay's black cane from inside the saloon. "Clever weapons," the man said. "Check them if you like; they're in working order."

Lindsay would check, but not at the moment. He hooked the cane on the edge of the table and set the gun next to his plate. He added two spoons of sugar to the coffee and stared at his host.

"Have you figured me out?" the man asked.

"You're the money behind Tommy's treasure hunt."

"Oh, Mr. Chase. I'm disappointed in you."

"Sorry. It's been a rough week."

The man grinned, his bluish lips stretched thin over his broad row of false teeth. "My name is Harrington. Nathan Harrington. Don't be embarrassed if it's not familiar. I'd be surprised if it was." He took a sip of the steaming tea Po had poured. "I have been many things in my life. Taking whatever guise I needed. For almost ninety years I've been the invisible monarch of this tiny corner of the world. Yes, young man, ninety years. You'll not find my name on a board members' roster or stock certificate. Yet there is nothing you can lay your eyes on, from Victoria Peak to Victoria Harbor, that I don't have a financial interest in."

"Plus the telecommunications."

"That was a little company I bought on a whim. Amazing how important it has become."

A second steward wheeled a dim sum cart to the table. Po unshuffled the bamboo containers and offered their contents to Nathan.

"The deed. Is it real?"

"Oh, yes, Mr. Chase. It's real," Nathan said. "And if the wrong people should get hold of it, it will be used to tear Hong Kong apart. They are shortsighted monsters who will end up, how do you say, changing the deck chairs on the Titanic?"

"The wrong people? You mean the Triads?"

"Among others."

"Better that you get it first, right? After all, you have wealth and power—you must know what Hong Kong wants as long as your companies continue to make their profits. Let's sell Pepsi-Cola and McDonald's hamburgers and forget about the Chinese dissidents making Christmas lights in prison."

Nathan laid down his chopsticks and slowly applauded Lindsay. "Very good. Very, very good. And you're absolutely correct," he said, returning to his dumplings. "The British government is a paper tiger that has continuously kowtowed to Beijing. They ignored the protests of the entire population, even their own Governor. But then, why is it so surprising to find an apathetic ear at Ten Downing Street? Can you imagine the backlash the Prime Minister would receive if he entertained the idea of allowing Hongkongers to emigrate to Britain? After all, these royal subjects are first and foremost Chinese."

"You don't believe they'd push to keep the colony?"

"If the deed is found and made public, it would be a catastrophic nightmare for the British government. At the moment, they're obligated by a treaty to hand six million people over to the communists. It's the perfect excuse," Nathan said firmly. "But let's not absolve your government. The United States never hesitated to grant China its Most Favored Nation status even after Tiananmen Square. No, politicians and businessmen are whores. They feed on opportunity, and China is the newest."

"But you're different . . ." Lindsay said sarcastically.

"There's a Chinese saying, Mr. Chase: 'Outside the motherland, the Chinese are dragons—inside, they are worms.' I believe it's time for the dragons to return home."

Lindsay sat back in amazement. "You want the transfer to take place."

"I welcome it with open arms."

"You're not worried the communists will take everything you've built."

"What I've done is insignificant. And I'm not concerned about the communists. History bears witness that rulers come and go. Beijing is no different." Lindsay caught the gleam in Nathan's eye. "I'm going to start a revolution, Mr. Chase. Not with guns, mind you. And hopefully with little bloodshed."

Nathan pushed his plate to the side and lifted his wine glass. Po was there immediately with a chilled bottle of chardonnay. Lindsay declined a glass from the steward.

"Beijing relies on Hong Kong more than anyone realizes. The world banking community estimates forty-five percent of China's income is from the colony. I know it is closer to sixty percent and increasing every year. The market economy developing inside her borders is incompatible with its dictatorship. They are oil and water. The fall of the puppeteers is inevitable."

"They've promised to run two separate systems."

"*Aiya . . .*" Nathan dismissed. "One country, two systems, they say. It is like one body with two souls."

"And you plan to topple it?"

Nathan leaned on the table. "Do you know what most governments are concerned about?"

"Nuclear proliferation?"

"That, too." Nathan shrugged. "But also the Internet. Your country worries about the flow of pornography. China worries about ideas." He grinned again with his blue lips. "Information, Mr. Chase. Information broadcast to the village television set or to the growing number of fax machines in the town center. Don't get me wrong. I don't mean information about free speech and democracy. The daily lives of nine hundred million peasants in the center of this sleeping dragon care little about such romantic endeavors.

"No, what they need to see is Hong Kong. The stores of new clothes and showrooms of big cars. It's the computers and the electronic games and the Home Shopping Network. It is strong Buddha tea on the palate with a taste that lingers heavily. That's what will start this revolution, Mr. Chase. Nike tennis shoes and Gucci wallets."

"They already have their special economic zones."

"But they are nothing compared to Hong Kong." Nathan pointed a finger in the air and grinned. "And that's what the Chinese will discover when there is no more border to keep them from their new Crown Jewel."

"And if Wei gets the deed?"

Nathan frowned. "If the Sun Yees try to stop the transition, Beijing will unleash its tanks. I have no doubt of that. Deng Xiaoping once said he would rather recover a barren piece of rock than leave Hong Kong to the British."

"You knew Tommy was an agent."

"Of course," Nathan admitted.

"But you couldn't possibly tell him what you were planning," Lindsay said. Then suddenly Lindsay looked across the table, dumbfounded. "I can't believe I didn't see it."

Nathan smiled mischievously.

"Suzette didn't work for Tommy. He was working for her."

"She is doing this for love, Mr. Chase. And because I am an old man and too damn feeble to search myself."

"You're the family money," Lindsay said, remembering the comment from the assistant at the art museum.

"Suzette is my granddaughter. But she didn't know Tommy was a communist agent until he disappeared on Dani Zhou."

"He never contacted the nephew."

Nathan's brow furrowed deeply. "He didn't?"

"No, but we did. The uncle died in a Buddhist temple in Sha Tin."

Nathan clutched his jaw, his false teeth clicking hollow. "That much I already knew. Suzette searched them, and so did Tommy. But do you know how many temples there are in Sha Tin? And how many have been torn down to make room for high-rise apartments?''

"He didn't just say a temple. He called it something else." Lindsay tried to remember. "The Temple of the Buddhas.''

"The Temple of the Buddhas?'' Nathan scratched his ear. Then his eyes brightened. "The Temple of the Ten Thousand Buddhas. It's in the hills above the city.'' He clutched his hand in an uneven fist. "That has to be it.''

"Wei will get that out of her.''

"He needs more than just the location,'' Nathan said.

"A poor craftsman . . .'' Lindsay said aloud as the pieces began to fit. "The pendant's a map.''

"And Suzette's ransom,'' Nathan admitted. "Wei phoned this morning.''

"Did he know I was aboard?''

"I don't think so.''

Lindsay lifted the 9mm from the table. With steady eyes, Nathan watched Lindsay drop the magazine from the handle of the gun. One by one, he thumbed the cartridges onto the table. Using a chopstick, he pinned down the magazine follower and spring and removed the plastic base. Then he poured the pendant from inside the magazine and onto a linen napkin. Lindsay read the thrill in the old man's face. "This is not worth her life.''

"No,'' Nathan agreed. "The deed to Hong Kong has already cost me more than you can imagine. I'm not willing to pay that price again,'' he said. "But it's worth everything to Wei and the Sun Yee.''

"You know he's going to kill her.''

"Given the opportunity, he'll kill all of us.''

Stepping quickly from the main cabin, the second steward handed Po a slip of paper. Po read the message and passed it to his employer.

Holding it at arm's length, Nathan squinted over the paper. He laid it in front of Lindsay. "The police found a body in the harbor. It's your friend Zhang.''

Lindsay stared at the facsimile sheet from the Hong Kong Police Department.

"Take the skiff,'' Nathan told him. "I'll have a car for you at the docks.''

Chapter Thirty-Two

Hong Kong Island

The helmsman maneuvered the runabout up to the oil-soaked, barnacle-encrusted pylon of Queen's Pier. Lindsay leaped onto the low wooden ramp that hung just over the waves. He scrambled to the top of the dock and hurried to Harrington's white Rolls-Royce Silver Wraith that was waiting at the curb.

The morning traffic was still thick, but the driver knew the urgency and skirted the knotted ribbon of cars and buses along Connaught Road and east into Sheung Wan district.

Lindsay was out of the car before the massive Rolls had come to a complete stop. The door to Jing's spice shop was locked. Lindsay cupped his hands to the glass and peered in. It was dark and deserted. He pounded on the aluminum frame with his fist. The door shook violently. He continued until, finally, from the rear of the shop, Lindsay saw a light.

Anson opened the door.

"Where's your mother?" Lindsay asked, stepping inside.

Tears filled the little girl's eyes as she tried to speak. She couldn't. She pointed to the back.

In the living room of the house, the television had been removed from the low bookshelf and replaced with a large color photograph. It was not of Jing as Lindsay had expected, but of Mun. It was his graduation picture and the young Chinese was smiling for the camera from under a mortar-board cap and tassel. Next to the photo, incense sticks burned with pungent offerings to the gods.

Mrs. Zhang, dressed in a linen robe of pure white, the Chinese color for mourning, knelt with her two young sons in front of the improvised alter. Hearing footsteps, she looked at Lindsay with a dead expression. "Why this, Linds?" she said in disbelief.

Lindsay had no answer.

"Jing thinks it is his fault."

Lindsay swallowed hard. "Where is he?"

"In the back."

Jing sat alone at the wobbling table staring at nothing. He, too, wore white. Lindsay sat down beside him. "I've lost my eldest, Lindsay," he said weakly.

"What did the police say?"

"That he was robbed."

"I'm sorry."

"It's not so?" Jing asked. "Someone called with information about the girl. I wasn't home," he said painfully. "Mun went in my place."

"It's not your fault."

"The ones who killed Tommy killed my son."

Lindsay could say nothing.

"They shot him in the face. My son . . . they executed him like the Japanese."

"I shouldn't have—"

"No. It was me. I wanted him to learn the world is vicious, Lindsay. You and I know. But college didn't teach that. I wanted him to know if he was going to live with the communists . . . I thought he needed to know . . ." Jing's head sank as tears streamed from his face.

Lindsay took Jing's weak hand and placed it in his. This was not supposed to happen, he thought. The violence that hung on Lindsay like a comfortable well-worn coat shouldn't have taken a young man's life. Not this one.

"I'm a helpless old man," Jing said. "I can do nothing to avenge his death. But you . . ." He stared hard at Lindsay. *'Ying Yan I Kaai,"* he spat.

Lindsay nodded solemnly. He knew the ancient saying— 'Once the problem is found, the solution follows easily'— and he knew what Jing meant.

"I'll find them," Lindsay promised. He squeezed his friend's shoulder as he left him at the wobbly table in the quiet garden.

Lindsay exited the spice shop and stepped to the Rolls. His mind was filled with frustration and anger and it kept him from noticing the driver's frown. It wasn't until he hesitated to retrieve the rear door that Lindsay saw his apprehension. Then it was too late. Another man was in the front seat holding a gun to the driver's back.

"Chase . . . !"

Lindsay instantly slipped the safety trigger on his cane and spun around. But three heavy bodies rushed him, smashing him hard against the car.

"Nice to see you again, Chase," the Scot with the dense red beard said as he limped forward. " 'Member me?" he glared with two blackened eyes over a thick white bandage that covered his swollen nose.

"The face is familiar," Lindsay said. His arms were twisted behind his back and locked together with police handcuffs.

"Babbitt's going to be sorry he missed you," the Scot said as he pulled Lindsay's 9mm from his holster. "Get him inside."

The street-clothed soldiers hustled Lindsay into the vacant store next to Jing's shop. With the windows boarded up, the narrow store was a ghostly cavern with only a single row of fluorescent lights flickering overhead. The back door to the alley was locked with a dead bolt, several broken packing crates lined the walls, and the floor was covered with a carpet of dust. Lindsay discovered the dust as his legs were kicked out from under him.

One of the men slammed his boot into Lindsay's rib cage. Lindsay curled in pain. Another man joined in the kicking spree—a blow to the back, another to the ribs, across the face.

"Enough," the Scot said. "Don't you boys know anything? I'll show you how to do this without making him messy." The Scot placed his foot on Lindsay's bad knee and stomped it into the floor. Lindsay screamed. He felt a wash of unconsciousness sweep over him as his mind tried to pry itself from the unmentionable anguish. Lindsay fought it back. If he fainted, he knew he'd never be waking up.

The shop door burst open. A quick dull thud resounded through the room as the overhead lamp exploded in a spray of sparks and shower of glass. The men scrambled.

The Scot drew Truby's automatic.

"Try it, fuckhead," Sampson challenged.

Seeing the silenced automatic trained on him, the Scot lowered his aim.

"Where's Babbitt?"

"He had another engagement."

"Unlock him."

The Scot hesitated, thought better of testing the American, and fished the key to the cuffs from his pocket. He tossed it to Sampson. "You do it."

"Take your prickheads and get out of here," Sampson snapped.

The Scot glared but relented to the gun. "Everyone out," he ordered. As the Scot filed out with his men, Sampson snatched Lindsay's automatic from the Scot's hand.

"Babbitt said you were soft."

"Get out."

The Scot slammed the door behind him, leaving Sampson and Lindsay alone.

"I thought you gave up fieldwork, Jake."

The director of the Rogue aimed the silenced weapon at Lindsay and glared over its sights. "You stupid motherfucker. I should shoot you myself." He lowered the gun instead.

"Just the same, I'm happy to see you," Lindsay said. For a moment, he feared his former boss might do just that. "How'd you find me?"

"We tapped into their network," Sampson said as he rolled Lindsay over and uncuffed him. "I knew you couldn't use the assets. You had to be using your friends. When the kid's name came across the police database, I figured you'd show up here."

Lindsay rubbed his knee. "He was doing me a favor."

"A lot more people are going to get killed unless we sort this thing out," Sampson said as he paced the room, tapping the six-inch silencer against his dark slacks.

"Let me go, Jake."

"You've got no idea what you're into, Linds."

"Wanna bet?" Lindsay got painfully to his feet. "The Chinese army is about to crash the Brits' going-away party and you can't figure out why."

Sampson's eyes narrowed. "Let's have it."

"They're worried about a document that nullifies the original treaties. It's a deed from the Empress. Beijing's afraid Britain is going to use it as an excuse to stay in Hong Kong."

"Empress? What fuck'n Empress?"

"The last one."

"Christ . . ."

"Think of it as the Seventh Army rolling into Manhattan because of a promise from George Washington."

"You've gotta be kidding."

"Your being here shows I'm not," Lindsay said, testing the open gash the Scot had put over his eye.

Sampson paced the dusty room. "Okay. So what do you need?"

"Need?"

"You're ground zero, Linds," Sampson said flatly. "There's no other agent inside."

"Aren't you forgetting something? I'm the mole, remember?" He pointed at the front door. "The Queen's finest put a bullet in me and you sanctioned it."

Sampson stared at the former agent. "I had reports—"

"You had shit."

"Goddammit, you were friends with a communist agent. What'd you expect? An inquiry? Let Congress find out that Central Intelligence has a secret agency?" Sampson ran his hand over his crewcut. "We're a house of assassins. They don't want to know about us. We're undertakers, Lindsay. Nobody wants to look into our faces."

"You should have asked me straight out," Lindsay said as he moved to a wooden crate and sat down.

The director of the Rogue sighed. "Yeah, maybe I should've." Sampson sat beside Lindsay. "But everything pointed to you."

"He was a friend."

"You're not supposed to have friends, Linds."

"Better to slip me into a body bag?"

"There were assassination threats against the Royals. MI5 overreacted to your being there."

"AnnMarie asked me to go, so I went. What's so suspicious about that?"

"Nothing," Sampson admitted. The two men sat in an uncomfortable silence. "The British have parked an aircraft carrier a hundred miles to the south," Sampson said finally. "Day before yesterday, the Prime Minister asked the President for a commitment of forces to secure the colony. He complied and Beijing responded by placing the entire Nanjing Military Command on alert. There's now over three hundred tanks in Guangzhou, all armed and ready to go."

"Welcome to Sarajevo East."

"It doesn't get better. The President has threatened to recognize Taiwan as an independent state if the people's army enters Hong Kong."

"Isn't this how World War II started?" Lindsay asked. "Are the Chinese that stupid?"

Lindsay shrugged his shoulders. "This is their land. To them, the British are invaders. It doesn't matter how many carriers you park out there, they're going to take back Hong Kong one way or another."

"Then let's make it easy for them," Sampson said. He took aim at the back door and blasted the lock open with a single shot. "Find their fuck'n piece of paper," he said as he handed him Truby's 9mm.

"What about you?"

"I'm going to have my hands full keeping Babbitt off your ass."

Lindsay picked up his cane. "Be sure to give him my regards," he said as he hobbled out the door.

* * *

Lindsay caught a taxi back to Queen's Pier and found the skiff waiting for him. He descended the ladder and hopped aboard.

"The *Lona* has weighed anchor, sir. She's sailing for Sai Kung," the helmsman informed him as they headed east through Victoria Harbor.

"How long until we get there?"

"Thirty minutes."

Lindsay stood on the port side of the cockpit and held one of the cold aluminum handrails. The skiff lurched under his feet as it mounted each swell, shot down its crest, and sliced into the next. The reverberations sent lightning bolts of pain through Lindsay's body. They crossed Junk Bay, slipped through the narrow channel of Fat Tong Mun, and headed north past Shelter Island and into Ngau Mei Hoi channel.

A half hour later, the helmsman aimed his bow at Harrington's huge yacht in the farthest position of the fishing harbor. Po was at the top of the accommodation ladder to greet Lindsay. "This way, Mr. Chase," Po said, leading him inside. Lindsay followed the steward down a companionway and into a beautifully decorated salon. It was done in dark red woods with beautiful Persian rugs and Impressionist paintings. Leatherbound books lined one wall and at the far end there was a long crescent bar. It reminded him of an English men's club he had frequented in London.

"Mr. Harrington will join you shortly. Something from the bar?"

"Yeah . . . something strong," Lindsay said, then decided he couldn't wait. "I'll get it."

"As you wish," the steward said, then left Lindsay alone.

Circling behind the bar, Lindsay set his cane on the counter and searched the lower cabinets. He found a bottle of Royal Crown whiskey, cracked the top, and poured himself two fingers.

A moment later, with Po giving his wheelchair momentum, Nathan entered. "I'm sorry to hear about Mr. Zhang's son."

"Did you know he was dead before or after you had the steward bring the fax?"

"Before," he admitted.

"Who killed him?"

Nathan's green eyes locked onto the American's. "Danny Wei."

Lindsay gulped down his drink. He refilled the glass.

"Wei wants to trade. But we trade on my terms," Nathan said. He motioned to the plastic case against the far wall. Po brought it to the bar.

Lindsay opened the lid and immediately recognized the German-made Walther WA2000 sniper rifle. "You're still willing to gamble with Suzette's life?"

"The only time I gamble, Mr. Chase, is when I've stacked the deck. The Triad thinks you're dead. Or at least in the hands of the Red Chinese."

Lindsay lifted the blunt rifle and weighed it in his hands. It was light, not much over fifteen pounds. He wrapped the shoulder strap under his arm and slipped his thumb through the hole-type grip and felt the weapon's balance. It was perfect. He pressed his right eye against the stubby infrared scope that would change night into day.

Nathan watched with satisfaction as Lindsay systematically inspected the Walther.

"Where?"

"Tonight at the temple."

"What time?"

"Midnight."

"Lindsay pulled his sleeve back and checked his watch. "I'll need a duffel bag and some dark clothing."

"Po can get you whatever you need."

"I'll go on my own. You don't show up until one A.M."

Nathan's jaw tightened. "Now you're the one who's gambling?"

Lindsay slapped a magazine into the rifle bottom, yanked the bolt back, and chambered a .300-magnum cartridge into the breech. "That's because the cards have changed hands. I'm dealing."

Chapter Thirty-Three

Sha Tin

Tucked in the steep foothills amid a thick grove of Litsea trees and yellow-leafed camphors, and above the sprawling, sparkling city of Sha Tin, was the sacred Temple of Ten Thousand Buddhas. As Lindsay assaulted the narrow stairs that snaked their way up the hill, he forced himself to concentrate within, to draw forth the animal that haunted his dreams and walked his subconscious.

He needed it now. Needed it to take charge, to help him forget his frailties and weaknesses. To make him the hunter, to make him fearless. To stop the stabs of pain radiating from every nerve in his body. He had tried to defer it by letting Harrington's Chinese doctor work his miracles with his arsenal of fine needles. If it helped at all, it helped little.

At the end of his pilgrimage, Lindsay found the entrance to the temple guarded by two decrepit iron gates held loosely together with a chain and padlock. He rooted a tiny flashlight from his duffel bag, slung the bag back over his shoulder, and slipped through the gap between the gates.

It was ten o'clock and the worshipers and tourists that visited the temple with their joss sticks and throwaway cameras were gone now. Even the monks had retired to more comfortable quarters in the city. Lindsay had picked up a visitors' brochure about the temple at the Kowloon train station and tried to memorize it during the ride into the New Territories.

The monastery's main level was a stone forecourt encircled by three primary buildings. Closest to the entry was the first structure, the Temple of the Gods of Heavens. Inside, and despite the monastery's name, there were more than twelve thousand small statues of Buddha arranged on hundreds of shelves stacked from the floor to the ceiling along forty-five-foot walls. The small bulbous figures looked down upon Lindsay with empty eyes and knowing grins. Lindsay drew Truby's automatic and cautiously backed out of the building.

At the far end of the court was a towering nine-story pagoda. Painted pink with white trim, it was designed in ornate Indian fashion with each floor representing a step toward Nirvana, and in every window there were more statues of the Enlightened One.

To the left of the pagoda was an oversized sculpture of Manjusri, one of the ten disciples of the Sakyamuni Buddha, sitting on the back of a blue glazed lion. To the right, Kwan Tei, the fierce God of Righteousness, was posed on horseback clutching a dragon sword.

And in the center of the courtyard, between the pagoda and the temple, was Kuan Ying, the women's deity. The large, bleached-white statue of the heavyset goddess was protected by a solid roof supported by red pillars adorned with golden Chinese writings. In front of her stood a barrel-size incense pot on two coiled dragons. The black sand inside was still glowing with the crimson embers of the day's offerings.

Lindsay noticed the moon had reached the zenith of its springtime arc. He was disappointed the night wasn't going to be as dark as he had hoped. He circled the rear of the temple and found a small footpath. It was a groundskeeper's trail that cut through the long grass and wound around the back of the complex.

He followed it to where it climbed steeply onto the citadel's upper level. Here the path ended at the edge of the temple's upper terrace, which had been carved out of the steep hillside. Its width was fifty feet at the most. Beyond that, the hill fell steeply away into the lights of Sha Tin.

At the back of the terrace were several more buildings. Crouching low, Lindsay crossed the open span and slid into the night shadows of the first structure. The sanctum was dark and silent. The second building, too, was deserted. In the third, however, Lindsay was expecting someone.

As the brochure had promised, the mummified body of the temple's founder, Yuet Kai, was seated inside a sealed glass cabinet. Lindsay's flashlight illuminated the monk's ghostly figure. His body was gilded with gold leaf and lacquer and set respectfully in the cross-legged pose of the Buddha.

Concerning himself with the living, Lindsay finished his sweep of the terrace. There was still an hour until midnight. Just enough time to settle into his vantage point. Lindsay followed the path down to the main temple, dashed to Kuan Ying, and dissolved into her shadow. For several minutes he stood motionless, letting his eyes search the surroundings, the roofs, the doorways, and the thick jungle that pressed against the courtyard. He had underestimated these men once. It wasn't going to happen again.

He caught an odd smell, lifted his sleeve to his nose, and realized it was merely the grassy smell of the bamboo leaves that had torn with his passing. Then he noted his breathing. Deep, relaxed, comfortable. His heart rate, too, had calmed. The drapes that shrouded his subconscious had been withdrawn. As the Rogue's psychologists had taught him, he was inducing it again, bringing it forth and controlling it. Sampson was right. They were nothing more than government assassins—triggermen on the federal payroll. For the first time in a year, Lindsay was thankful for the psychologists.

Lindsay crossed the court and entered the arched doorway of the pagoda. Inside, the darkness was sliced by slivers of moonlight seeping in through the windows. He moved directly to the bottom of the spiral staircase and listened. Only the rattle of the bamboo in the evening breeze outside. Tucking the pistol away, he removed the Walther from the duffel bag. He shoved the bag into the bottom of a metal waste barrel against the wall. Sliding his finger to the trigger guard, he flipped off the safety. Then, gently, he placed one foot on the first stone step and he began to climb. There was nothing worse than a spiral staircase. It was an unforgiving gauntlet with no protection from either above or below.

Lindsay made his way to the top of the pagoda, checking each floor as he went. He returned to the fourth level and moved to the small alcove overlooking the courtyard. A two-foot statue with its arms extended to the heavens filled the arched window.

Lindsay slid the silenced rifle through the openings beside the venerable deity and leaned into the eyepiece of the infrared scope. Through the lens and aided by light-enhancing circuitry, the courtyard was instantly bathed with a bright amber haze. A few adjustments in density and focus, and Lindsay had the scope tuned to his satisfaction. He could see most of the courtyard, the entrance to the main temple, the area around Kuan Ying, and the wide pathway that led up to the upper terrace.

Ten minutes passed before anything happened. Unexpectedly, it happened just below him. The hard-soled footsteps began at the bottom of the pagoda and slowly ascended the spiral stairway.

The Triad checked each level with a pocket flashlight and a chrome .45. On the fourth floor, he inspected the alcove of the Buddha with the raised hands. The man's flashlight peered though the darkness and discovered only what he had found in the other corners: dust and spiderwebs.

Outside the window, Lindsay hung across the tiled roof clutching the statue's thick leg, with the Walther dangling over his shoulder. In his other hand was Truby's 9mm. He remained on the narrow roof until he heard the man reach the ninth story and then descend the stairs to the ground.

Lindsay squeezed through the window as the man stepped into the courtyard and continued his reconnaissance. As he stopped at the incense pot and tied his shoelace, Lindsay recognized him from the Imperial Suite of the Conrad. It was Dragon Throat. Through the rifle scope, Lindsay watched him speak into a small hand radio.

A moment later, Suzette was escorted roughly into the main temple by two Chinese men. And walking casually behind them was Danny Wei. The Sun Yee Triad wore an expensive silk suit with a collarless shirt and his heavy cowboy boots. Dangling from his right hand was a .44-magnum revolver. Looking repeatedly over his shoulder, he motioned his men to the main building.

As they climbed the wide steps that led to the temple's interior, Lindsay trained the scope's crosshairs at the upper crest of the young Chinese's cranium. A shot from this angle would be decisively lethal. Lindsay, however, eased his finger away from the trigger. Too soon, Lindsay told himself. Too soon. He knew others would surely kill Suzette if he put a bullet through their leader now. No, he had to wait for Harrington.

Fifteen minutes past midnight, Lindsay saw Danny step from the temple and look around. A cigarette burned between his fingers as he looked at his watch. He paced the steps twice and looked at his watch again. Just as Lindsay had hoped, Harrington's tardiness was making the Triad edgy.

"Where the fuck is he?" Danny said as he bit the end of his cigarette. He walked back into the temple to where Suzette was sitting on the floor. "He doesn't show in fifteen minutes, he's going to find you in pieces."

Suzette glared at him but said nothing.

"Maybe he doesn't have it," Dragon Throat said.

"That'd be a shame," Danny snapped. He looked at Suzette. "A painful shame."

Suzette's eyes filled with hatred, but still she said nothing.

Along the top edge of the scope lens, Lindsay saw a flare of light. He tilted the rifle toward the building's flat roof and focused in. There in the corner, the Walther's scope magnified the burning embers of a cigarette and revealed a man with a high-powered rifle. Danny's own sniper. Lindsay made a quick mental note of his location and labeled him as number two.

A few minutes later another figure appeared. This man

was posted in the thicket of young Toog trees. Crouched for the last forty-five minutes, he needed to stretch his legs. Shot number three. Two men outside, three men inside along with Suzette. He looked at the time. 12:54 A. M.

A moment later, the drum of helicopter blades filled the night sky. The black Bell Jet Ranger came from the direction of Sha Tin, flew low over the convoluted hills, and circled the temple. It banked over the pinnacle of the pagoda, dipped sharply, and headed for the second level, where the pilot had located the narrow terrace.

Danny and the tattooed Triad stepped into the courtyard. Inside the shrine, Lindsay could see Suzette still seated on the sacred steps, but the other Triad was hidden from his view.

The helicopter touched down on the second level, and a few minutes later Lindsay saw Po inching Nathan's wheelchair down the stone steps that linked the complex. With great effort, the steward managed Harrington and his oxygen-equipped chair. He rolled the old man in front of the young Chinese. With a thick maroon blanket covering him, Nathan looked archaic and frail.

"Where is she?" Nathan demanded.

"The pendant first."

Nathan shook his head. "You're getting what you want. Why should it matter if I see her first, Danny?"

Danny grinned. "So you know who I am. Congratulations."

"You'd be surprised by what I know."

"I know exactly who you are, Mr. Harrington," Danny said. "You gave my grandfather Wei Peng a schooner to start his export business. Every time he spoke of you it was with the greatest respect. But he always talked about your search. It took me a long time to realize it wasn't just a crazy story." Danny grinned. "Now let's have it."

Nathan removed his hand from beneath the blanket and revealed the gold and jade pendant in his palm. Danny reached for it, but Nathan snapped his hand closed. "My granddaughter."

Danny waved into the temple.

In the amber light of the scope, Lindsay followed the

Chinese who walked Suzette from the building. The man was pressing a gun to her ribs.

"Wai-gung," Suzette called to her grandfather. "Don't."

"The pendant," Danny demanded.

"What do you think? That I'm a senile old man? I know you're going to kill us."

"Do you?" Danny asked, somewhat entertained by the man's resolve. "And why is that?"

"Because that's what I'd do."

The Triad stared at the ancient man. Then the blood drained from his face as he looked into burning green eyes that had seen more death and carnage than he could ever imagine. Danny reached for the big revolver tucked in his waistband.

For as old as he was, Nathan Harrington's reflexes were lightning fast. His aim, however, was less than accurate. He fired three quick rounds from his Beretta hidden under the blanket. The first bullet ripped into Danny's left shoulder, knocking him off his feet. The next two shots missed completely.

Lindsay, on the other hand, was flawless with the sniper rifle. His first shot pierced the forehead of the triad holding Suzette, blasting open the rear of his skull and denying his finger the impulse to work the gun in his hand. Even from his position, Lindsay heard Suzette's scream as the man's head exploded.

Lindsay swung the Walther to the man on the roof. He was gone. A barrel flash revealed him in the opposite corner. Lindsay fired, and a heartbeat later the man lay dead across the top of the temple.

Kill number three was still crouching in the Toog trees and made the mistake of thinking their branches would afford him protection. Four rapid shots, and he was dead before he hit the ground.

Lindsay turned back to the center of the courtyard. Dragon Throat had tried to run, but Nathan's next barrage found him. He laid sprawled across the shrine's steps.

To Lindsay's horror, he saw Danny holding Suzette in front of him, the blunt end of his gun pressed into the soft flesh under her chin. He stared over her shoulder at the fourth-floor window of the pagoda.

Nathan was still in his chair, with Po crouched beside him. The steward was nursing his own arm as the sleeve of his white coat darkened with blood. The Beretta lay a few feet away where Nathan had been ordered to throw it.

Lindsay knew the ballistic shock wave from the high-powered bullet passing so close to Suzette's face would undoubtedly rupture her eardrum. Perhaps it would even tear her skin. But he had no choice. Danny was about to kill her.

Ying Yan I Kaai, Lindsay thought as he brought the fine crosshairs of the scope together on Danny's right eye. It was going to be a very close shot.

Suddenly a cold finger of steel touched his ear. "You keep popping up in the wrong places," Babbitt said from behind him.

Lindsay cringed. "I'm sanctioned, Orson."

"Sure you are. Just like the last time."

"You're making a mistake."

"You know what's sad, Chase? I'm really going to miss Hong Kong. When we leave, this place is going to lose its soul. We gave it a foundation. We gave it a fair field and made everything work. Now our little jewel is going to die a slow, heartless death. It's a shame." He tapped Lindsay's ear again. "But what can you do?"

Lindsay lowered the rifle.

Suzette gasped as she saw Lindsay coming across the courtyard. She was certain he had been killed in the marsh and had blamed herself for it. From the moment the Triads had taken her aboard the helicopter, she had hoped they would simply kill her and be done with it.

"Lindsa—" Suzette tried to speak, but Danny tightened his grip.

"You," Danny screamed. He pointed his gun into Lindsay's face.

"Enough bloodshed, lad," Babbitt said. "Just make the trade and let us be done with our business."

"You're giving the deed to the Brits?" Lindsay looked at Danny and laughed. "You might as well leave it wherever it is."

"Shut up, Linds," Babbitt spat.

"He's right," Nathan said. "You hand them the deed and it'll disappear forever."

"Hardly. It gives them title to everything. It's the only way to keep Beijing out."

"You're assuming London wants Hong Kong," Nathan said calmly. "They don't. They want to lower their flag and retreat with whatever dignity they can patch together."

"They're crazy," Babbitt shot.

"Are we?"

Danny looked into Babbitt's chubby face. The Brit's nervous eyes gave away everything. Danny saw he had been used to find the deed only so it could be destroyed. "Bastard *gweilo,*" he screamed at Babbitt. He aimed the .44 and fired deliberately into Babbitt's chest. The force of the massive caliber lifted him off the ground and blew a fist-size chunk of flesh out of his back.

Lindsay reacted with animalistic reflexes. In three quick steps he scooped up Nathan's discarded Beretta and dove into the wall of bamboo as the .44 barked at his heels.

To Lindsay's surprise, the thicket hid a hillside that fell away. He tumbled end over end through the stiff brush. When he managed to stop himself, he realized the Beretta had been twisted from his grip. He groped through the leaves, but they had digested the weapon without a trace. There was no more time. He scrambled diagonally up the hill.

As he reached the courtyard, he heard Suzette screaming as Danny pulled her up the steps to the second level.

Lindsay ran through the trees to the groundskeeper's path and circled around the back of the main temple, hoping to cut them off. There was no pain now. His mind blocked it, suppressing the signals that would surely have told him he couldn't make it.

Danny forced Suzette toward the awaiting helicopter. With its engine idling, the pilot sat in the cockpit checking his flight systems.

"Let go." She pushed away and fell.

"Get up." The Triad tried to yank her to her feet.

"No!"

He aimed at her.

"Danny!" Lindsay yelled as he broke from the underbrush and raced across the terrace.

Danny saw him. "Chase," he yelled, firing as he ran after the American.

Lindsay opened the cockpit door, seized the pilot by the collar, and yanked him out. As the pilot hit the ground, he saw Danny running toward him with the blazing gun. Desperately, he flattened himself into the dirt and covered his head.

Lindsay dove into the cockpit as Danny's bullets ripped into the aircraft's thin aluminum skin.

"Gweilo!" Danny screamed as he circled the chopper. Just ten feet away, the Chinese aimed the .44 at Lindsay. "You're dead—"

But his scream wasn't heard. The roar of the helicopter's engine drowned him out as Lindsay pulled the throttle arm. With a sudden roar, the Bell leaped off the ground. Lindsay pressed the left control pedal, twirling the chopper on its axis.

Danny managed one round before he realized what was happening. He turned to see the blur of the tail rotor as it swung into him. The steel blades obliterated his head and shoulders and the powerful torque of the machine threw his body thirty feet into the air and forty feet across the terrace. Blood splattered everywhere.

Lindsay pushed the throttle down and the helicopter dropped hard onto the dirt. He flipped off the engine and breathed again.

As he slid out of the cockpit, he saw where the Triad's last bullet had buried itself into the copilot's seat two inches from where his head had been. As Lindsay leaned against the chopper's skid, he saw the pilot look up. The man's face was white. "You okay?" Lindsay asked.

The man stared at him blankly.

"Linds." Suzette ran to him, dropped to the ground, and wrapped her arms around his neck. She kissed him hard on the mouth. "I thought you were dead," she said as tears rolled down her cheeks.

"I thought so, too."

With their arms wrapped about each other, Lindsay and Suzette walked almost casually into the courtyard. But reality returned as they found Nathan doing his best to tie a tourniquet around Po's arm. Seeing his granddaughter, Nathan smiled broadly and lifted his hands.

"I'm sorry," he said weakly.

She kissed his cheek. "Don't be, Wai-gung."

"I could have lost you."

"But you didn't."

Lindsay moved to Babbitt and checked his pulse. The Brit was dead. He pulled the 9mm from beneath him. For Queen and country, he thought. What a waste.

"She didn't show much mercy tonight, did she?" Suzette said, slipping her hand into his.

"What?"

"Kuan Ying." She pointed to the large statue. "The Goddess of Mercy."

A smile crept onto Lindsay's face. "Harrington! Where's the pendant?"

The old man drew it from his breast pocket and handed it to him.

Lindsay returned to the steps in front of Kuan Ying. He placed the pendant flat on his palm and looked around the yard.

"What is it?" Suzette asked.

"Which way's north?"

"What?"

"The Chinese character in the center of the pendant means tenderhearted, or . . ." He pointed at the statue.

"Mercy . . ." Suzette said as she began to understand.

"Tang Shiu said his uncle was a craftsman."

"At this temple."

"Yes." Nathan sat up. "Go on. . . ."

"Four of the gold bands show compass points. The fifth band," Lindsay explained, "the one between the south and east, means fire."

"Fire?" Nathan said with a raised eyebrow.

"Which way is north?" Lindsay asked.

Nathan looked to the sky. A star-studded sky from which he had navigated for a lifetime. "That way," Nathan said, pointing over his shoulder excitedly. His breathing quickened as he sensed Lindsay was on to something.

Suzette watched Lindsay turn the pendant in his hand and aim its northern mark in the direction her grandfather had indicated. The fifth band now pointed directly at Lindsay. Together, they looked over his shoulder. Behind him was the incense pot with the dragons at its feet.

"The pot," Lindsay said, moving to it.

"Yes," Nathan said as he rolled himself to it. "In the sand." He yanked the oxygen tubes from his face and struggled out of the chair. "Underneath the sand," Nathan said. The prayers and wishes of the day were swept aside by a frantic hand. "It all fits." Nathan was beginning to hyperventilate. "You have to be right, Chase, you have to be." He dug through the filthy sand with his bare hands. But the fine gravel filled a deceivingly shallow tray.

"Wai-gung." Suzette put her arms around her grandfather. "Let them, Wai-gung." She tried to pull him back to his wheelchair.

"It's there." Nathan's eyes were wide like a rabid animal. "Under the tray," he said.

Lindsay helped Suzette. "Harrington," he hollered into his ear. "Sit down. We'll get it." Lindsay almost lifted him off the ground as he pulled him to the chair. "Keep him there," he instructed her.

"Let him do it, Lingsyou," Po said as he replaced the tubes under Nathan's nose. Angry, the old pirate swatted him away.

"Po, get the other side," Lindsay said.

The Chinese steward looked nervously at him. "Isn't this sacrilege?"

"Just grab it." The top edge of the vessel was forged with a dozen tiny edges so perfectly matched, Lindsay couldn't tell where the tray began and where the pot ended.

"Go get Babbitt's belt," Lindsay told Suzette.

"What?"

"His belt. Go get his belt."

Suzette returned to the dead agent. She unbuckled his leather belt and, pulling with all her strength, managed to slip it from his waist.

"Here," she said, choking back the urge to vomit.

Pulling the steel clasp from the leather, Lindsay revealed a T-shaped push knife. "Standard equipment," he said.

Using the thin blade, Lindsay dug along the minute tiers. They each seemed solid. Then the third revealed a crack between the pot and sand tray. Lindsay pressed the blade in and twisted until the gap opened further.

With the tips of their fingers, Lindsay and Po grabbed the iron lip and lifted. Suzette moved to help. It took all their strength, but the heavy pan finally gave way with a bitter hiss. The sand and tray flipped up over the edge of the incense pot and crashed to the ground.

"Yes!" Nathan leaped madly from his wheelchair and pushed past Lindsay. He drove both hands into the dark canister, searching it blindly. "This is it," he screamed as he withdrew a deteriorated leather pouch, the same pouch that he had grabbed inadvertently as a little boy as he ran from his father's assassins.

He fell to his knees. "So long," he cried. "So long I've looked, so long. . . ." He opened the flap and, to his horror, there was nothing inside but the staunch smell of dried leather.

"No!" Nathan screamed. He lifted himself to the rim of the pot and reached inside again. "It has to be here!" But it wasn't. Nathan gulped for breath; his face twisted with agony as he searched the hollow bowl. Suddenly life became unbearable. The prize that had driven him endlessly had escaped his grasp, just as it had done to the Empress Tzu Hsi, to Brigham, to Shaftsbury, and to Yak-san Kung. It was too much for this ancient man. Pain shot through him, wrenching his left hand into a fist. He clawed at his chest and gasped.

"Get his oxygen," Lindsay yelled at Po.

The steward grabbed the chair as Lindsay lifted him into it. Nathan reached for Suzette and pulled her close.

"Wai-gung," she cried.

"I was wrong," he said, his voice not more than a whisper. Slowly, as if finally giving in to his fate, the pirate's eyes flickered and his last breath eased from him.

In front of the statue of the Goddess of Mercy, the Lingsyou's body sank awkwardly into his wheelchair. His watery red eyes remained partially open as he continued to clutch the leather pouch. Lindsay gently wiped Nathan's eyes closed, and when he looked to Suzette, he saw she was gone.

Chapter Thirty-Four

Hong Kong Island

On the park bench across from the entrance to the Conrad Hotel, the observer sat patiently sipping coffee from a paper cup and reading the newspaper. After an hour, a taxi pulled under the facade and let Suzette out at the curb. She paid her fare and disappeared into the hotel.

The observer smiled. Everything was coming to a nice conclusion.

Suzette hurried across the lobby and caught the first elevator. As it rose, she leaned against the cool mirrored wall and thought of the night before. She was running. Running away from the temple and down the endless twisting path through the darkness. The bamboo branches grabbing at her, trying to seize her body and draw her back to face her grandfather. She had failed him. And it had killed him.

Reaching Sha Tin, she managed to find a taxicab to take her into Hong Kong. She returned to her ransacked apartment, ignored its shambles, and stood under the hot shower for an hour trying to wash the guilt from her skin.

She imagined Lindsay pacing. Somewhere pacing back and forth wondering why she had run and where she had gone. She'd find him and explain, she decided, but only after she looked one more time.

Inside the Imperial Suite, Suzette tried to guess what Tommy would have done. She knew he hadn't had much time. He had gone to Sha Tin to see if any of the local craftsmen remembered Ming Zi. He had taken the pendant to show them but returned with nothing significant. Or so he had said. She remembered he had returned on the four P.M. train and she had picked him up just before five P.M. to take him to the Macau ferry. That gave him at least forty-five minutes to hide it. But where?

She had already been through the drawers and the closets. The urn. Where was the urn? She saw the white and blue Chinese vase on the rosewood table next to the fireplace. She tried to remove its ceramic lid, but it seemed glued in place. She moved the urn to the center of the marble hearth and grabbed the fireplace poker. Taking steady aim, she lifted the poker over her head.

"I've got this feeling of déjà vu," Lindsay said as he stepped from the bedroom. "How about you?"

"Lindsay? I can explain. . . ."

"Don't bother." He tapped the urn with his cane. "You weren't looking for the pendant when I found you here, were you?"

Suzette's almond eyes held his. She could say nothing.

"You knew Tommy had the deed."

She gave in and nodded.

"And going to Dani Zhou?"

"When my grandfather told me Tommy was a communist, I thought that's how he was getting it to Beijing."

"You were going to double-cross your grandfather, weren't you? And then pass the deed to the British."

She stared at him as if he had slapped her.

"You thought the Brits wanted to stay," Lindsay continued. "Just like Danny did."

"How'd you . . ."

"Figure it out? Tommy's gun. You said you wounded the British agent who took you from the Conrad. But when I checked the gun, it hadn't been fired. And you knew Babbitt's first name. Remember? You called him Orson on the ferry."

Tears swelled and she looked away. "My father was arrested in China looking for Ming Zi," she said weakly. "He was imprisoned and left to die there because my grandfather was afraid to draw attention to his search."

"You didn't know he wanted the communists to go through."

"I didn't know what he was doing. When I told him about Tommy disappearing, he didn't care. That's when he told me Tommy worked for Beijing and what he hoped to do."

"So you knew?"

She nodded.

The door creaked behind them. "Such a sad story," the woman said as she stepped farther into the room.

Suzette gasped. But the shock of the woman's entrance hit Lindsay harder. It deadened his reflexes for a fraction of a second, a fraction that caused him to reach for his gun an instant too late.

"Don't Linds," AnnMarie said, her tone sharp and direct. Her reddish-brown hair was now cut short and bleached to a white-blond. She grinned from behind the sights of a Smith & Wesson automatic. "Draw the gun with your left hand and toss it away."

"You said she was dead," Suzette snapped at Lindsay.

"She's supposed to be."

"The gun, Lindsay, and don't try to be a hero."

Lindsay slowly pulled Truby's automatic and threw it into the lounge. Then, unable to stop himself, he laughed. "Sampson's reports, Babbitt's theories, assassination rumors. They were all you."

"Not bad, huh? People were getting suspicious. I had to sacrifice someone. You were the perfect candidate. I didn't tell you to hang out with a Red."

"And the girl?" he asked as he casually rotated the cane. He slid his index finger under the hook and released the safety mechanism.

"The hit-and-run? A two-bit actress who thought she was going to be in a chop suey movie. A kick how she made the front page after all."

"Who's been picking up your tab, AM?" Lindsay asked, leaning gingerly on the cane.

"Beijing, of course," she said, moving farther into the living room.

The unique weapon in Lindsay's hand suddenly presented its major flaw. He had to strike AnnMarie with the tip of the cane for it to discharge. With the distance between them, he had no doubt she'd squeeze off several rounds before he could reach her.

"I'm disappointed in you. A double agent is one thing. But greedy?"

"Well, spying doesn't do for me what it used to," she said with a shrug. As she sauntered closer, AnnMarie sensed something was wrong. Lindsay was giving up far too easily. Her eyes went to the cane in his hand. "What little tricks do you have, Lindsay? Something of Truby's, perhaps?"

Lindsay feigned innocence.

"Let it fall," she told him.

Lindsay sighed as he lifted his hand from the cane. Truby's weapon fell silently to the carpet.

"Do you think I'm that stupid?"

"I was hoping."

Her eyes narrowed. "Three steps back," she instructed as she kept the gun centered on his chest. She beckoned Suzette with her index finger. "Go on, honey, break it open."

Suzette glanced nervously at Lindsay.

"Do what she says."

Suzette lifted the heavy poker over her head.

"Don't get any ideas," AnnMarie said, taking a cautious step back. "Just the jar."

The force with which Suzette struck the urn pulverized it into a shower of chips and dust. In the middle of the powdery debris was a loose roll of yellowish paper.

"Excellent," AnnMarie gasped.

Suzette reached for the deed, but instead scooped a handful of the ceramic splinters. She threw them as hard as she could into the double agent's face.

The instant AnnMarie dropped the gun, Lindsay dove for it. Snatching it off the carpet, he rolled to his feet. But the woman had grabbed the iron poker from Suzette's hand and was already on top of him. She batted the gun out of his fist and across the room. She whirled the poker around and caught the top of Lindsay's ear with its point.

Diving to the floor, Lindsay managed to evade the next assault. Lindsay kicked upward, landing his heel into her stomach. The blow sent her over the back of the lounge.

She saw Lindsay's automatic was in reach at the same instance as Suzette. Both women dove for it, but Suzette was no match for the former Station Chief. AnnMarie pried the gun from the girl's grasp, pulled her head back, and shoved the gun into Suzette's neck.

Only then did AnnMarie look to see where Lindsay had gone. "I'll kill her," she threatened.

"I'm sure of it," Lindsay said from behind her.

As AnnMarie turned, Lindsay hit her in the face with the tip of Truby's cane. The primer of the 12-gauge shotgun cartridge struck the stationary firing pin as the chamber mechanism collapsed onto itself. Unmuffled by a barrel, the nineteenth century device exploded with a thunderclap as the load of buckshot tore a wedge clean through the woman's skull and sprayed the bloody mess across the room.

Lindsay helped Suzette to the kitchen. He moistened a paper towel and wiped AnnMarie's blood from her face and hair. "You all right?"

She looked at the red-stained towel. "Just wonderful," she said. She cupped her hands under the faucet and splashed cool water on her face. Lindsay moved to the remnants of the urn and picked out the elusive deed to Hong Kong.

Postscript

Hong Kong Island

Dawn poured warm rays of sunshine over the colony as if dispelling the fears of soldiers and war. The rumors that permeated the city were evaporating as the People's Liberation Army had completed their military exercises and were returning to their posts deep within the motherland. The Hong Kong stock market welcomed the news with strong trading and the city trams were again filling with shoppers and not terrified citizens hoarding food and water.

The colony was breathing a collective sigh of relief as the new landlords were not arriving as early as it had seemed. They were still coming, of course, but not until the end of June. Hopefully, there was still time to find a way out.

The old Christian church on the hill above Victoria Harbor had seen a rebirth in the last dozen years. Its flock of Chinese converts was growing among the affluent as it was among the poor.

Suzette had never been here before but knew it from the stories her grandfather had told. It was fitting he should

return to this place and rest in the marble mausoleum beside
Edmund and Lona Harrington and his sister, Elisa.

In his open mahogany casket, Nathan lay peacefully
shrouded beneath the red and black banner that had flown
in the winds of the South China Sea and marked the ships
of the powerful *gweilo*-Lingsyou.

In a long white dress and cartwheel hat, Suzette knelt
solemnly with a burning incense stick in her hands. She
prayed to God and to Buddha and to whomever would grant
her grandfather a safe passage on his last voyage.

A young Chinese priest moved to her. He silently indicated it was time.

"Another moment alone, please," she asked.

The priest understood and stepped away.

From the folds of her dress, Suzette withdrew the rolled
pages on which a royal eunuch had written out a secret
agreement. Although yellowed by time, the Imperial Seals
of the Manchu Empire looked as if they had been pressed
to the paper only yesterday. And with the deed, a note to
the Queen of England from a man named Brigham.

"I found it for you, Wai-gung," Suzette whispered sadly.

Lindsay watched Suzette from outside the mausoleum.
He saw her move closer to the casket and lean in. Her body
concealed the rest of her movements.

At the edge of the cemetery, Lindsay saw Sampson emerge
from a taxi and walk through the headstones. The spymaster
glanced into the tomb. "Too bad. A whole lifetime wasted
for nothing."

"I take it the war's off?" Lindsay asked.

"They've pulled back," Sampson said. "Beijing decided
there was never a deed. And to trust the British to leave on
time."

"And Taiwan?"

"A misunderstanding between the President and his
council. The Patriot missiles were recalled and our maritime
exercises with the Royal Navy were postponed because of
budgetary concerns."

"That sounds honorable enough."

"You did destroy it, right?" Sampson asked. "I mean,
there's no chance of it showing up anytime soon?"

"Let's just say it's been tucked away," Lindsay said whimsically.

Sampson shot him a sidelong glance as they watched the priest seal Harrington's casket and slide it into its stone vault. "It'll be meaningless after the transition."

"Unless the British have a change of heart." Lindsay grinned as he watched Suzette bow respectfully to her grandfather.

"That's not funny," Sampson said. "You did a good job, Linds. Call me when you get back to the States."

"Sorry, Jake. I've got other plans."

Sampson stepped away. "We all have plans," he said over his shoulder. "They just never work out."

Exiting the tomb, Suzette saw Sampson's taxi pull away. "Who was that?"

"A crazy *gweilo.*"

She laughed.

"You're sure about this?"

"My grandfather was right," she said, looking over the forest of high-rises that spread out below them. "Hong Kong belongs to the Chinese. And besides"—she looked into his hazel-blue eyes and smiled mischievously—"where better to start a revolution?"

Lindsay offered his arm and she took it and together they walked through the cemetery to where Po stood holding open the rear door of her Rolls-Royce Silver Wraith.